MW01164742

Night Air

A Novel

To Sandy,

Donna Tytko

all my best,
Donna

ISBN-13: 978-1982055868
ISBN-10: 1982055863

CreateSpace Independent Publishing Platform
Charleston, SC
Available from Amazon.com and other retail outlets

Acknowledgements

I am grateful to the following colleagues, friends, and family members who gave their time, talent, and expertise to the writing of this novel.

Julia Alvarez
Br. Brian Belanger
Dr. Ralph Blasting
Art Carpenter
Mae Carpenter
Laurie Detenbeck
Bill Eichner
Donna Esposito
Lorinda Gandrow
Dr. James Harrison
Dana Kennedy
William Kennedy
Heather Middelkoop
Jennifer Pitts
Amanda Selanikio
Allison Schultz
Mecaila Smith
Dr. Carla Sofka
Dr. Charles Trainor
Mary Jane Tytko
Stephen Michael Tytko
Stephanie White
Dr. Meg Woolbright

Dedicated to everyone who in
the past nine years has asked if
I finished writing this book.
I am grateful to my husband
who never needed to ask.

To Stephen Michael – Forever.

Chapter One

The Howl

Penny Morgan worked really hard to appear normal. If asked, those close to her would have laughed and said, yeah, like the rest of us, normal enough. But having her sleep assaulted, night after night by a man who invaded her dreams wasn't normal.

Penny didn't even like to *think* his name, lest she give him some further foothold into her mind. She left him nearly two decades ago. Well, that wasn't exactly correct. To be precise, he had been taken away eighteen years ago. The circumstances would have cause anyone troubled sleep, but for years, Penny was able to collect enough hours of slumber: four hours here, an hour's nap there, to make it work. But for the past month Penny's sleep had deteriorated to practically nonexistent. He made sure of it.

Penny and Michael Morgan's home, historic enough to have a name, the Van Rensselaer Cottage, was surrounded by fragrant perennial gardens and elegant shag elms in upstate New York. The northeastern autumn breezes alone should have created the ideal sleeping environment. Yet, in the large comfortable bed Penny shared with her beloved husband Michael, Penny was afraid to close her eyes.

Penny's pasty complexion, dark circles, and auburn hair turned lackluster, worried her husband of three years and their "adopted" grown daughters: Annalise, Mayra-Liz, and Eva. The girls were sisters from a family that had fallen apart. They knew how quickly things could go from shaky to shit, and they insisted that Penny see a doctor. Penny hated worrying the members of her little close-knit family, their lives woven together not by genetics, but amity and love; so for them, Penny made an appointment.

Predictably, Dr. Mariani's solution was a prescription. Penny didn't tell him she wouldn't take sleeping pills. Interrupted sleep was one thing, but even the over-the-counter, made from natural ingredients, sleep aid

1

she had once tried, released some sort of safety catch in her brain. When it clicked off, Penny felt certain her thoughts were exposed to him.

In a moment of weakness and sleep deprivation, Penny had the prescription filled. *Maybe prescribed medicine won't have the nasty side effect of exposing me,* Penny thought desperately.

However, that evening fear prevented Penny from turning the protective cap, and she shoved the pills into the back of the bathroom drawer. Michael's heavy breathing tickled her neck as they cuddled, yet she resisted moving away from his comforting arms. For what seemed like the hundredth time, Penny looked at the clock and saw that it was just after three, exactly four minutes and twelve seconds from the last time she had checked. *Come on, Monty,* she silently told her big, tiger-striped cat as he walked up and down her. *Can't you help out here? Purr me to sleep, and then stand guard?*

As the clock clicked to 5:00 a.m., the alarm went off. Michael quickly hit the off button before the quiet *beep, beep, beep* sound increased in volume. He rolled over and looked at Penny's ashen face. "You didn't sleep at all, did you?" he asked, worried marks creasing his brow. Penny was trying to figure out what to say without out-and-out lying. She was biting her lip when Michael asked, "Did you take the medicine?"

"I told you last night I don't like taking sleep pills."

"But you didn't sleep, did you?"

Penny shook her head no.

"Where are the pills?"

"Top drawer in the bathroom." As Michael walked out of the room, Penny called, "But I don't think I should take them." Michael returned with a glass of water and a blue pill to find his wife with her arms crossed defiantly across her chest.

"Of course, it's your choice," Michael said as he set the glass and pill on her bedside table, "but you look like a heartbeat away from a migraine. I hate to see you compound the problem." Michael sat next to Penny and stroked one of her russet colored, long locks. "If it's the shop and café you're worried about – don't. You know the girls can handle it. When was the last time you took the entire day off?"

Michael kissed her forehead and left her to make her own decision. As he walked towards the bathroom, Penny took in his confident, naked stride. He was so comfortable in his own skin, which was taut, muscular, and tanned from the physical work that came with his outside photo shoots. Even in Penny's exhausted state, she felt blessed to have found such a good and caring man.

She leaned back against the pillows and saw the zigzagging, flashing lines of an aura. Yeah, a migraine wasn't far away. *I can't go on like this*, Penny thought as she swallowed the medication. *Please, God. Let it be okay.* When Michael kissed her goodbye, Penny was already sound asleep.

Penny watched herself walk down Jay Street near her shop. She knew she was dreaming and was pleased to have a happy, floating sleep. It was a warm, spring day and Penny wore a new dress, a blue printed cotton shift. No, it wasn't new .... She remembered it from her high school days, a million years ago. But today she felt like an adolescent with no past, anything could happen, something lovely could be just around the corner. A group of folks in professional attire, G.E. people on their lunch break, Penny guessed, were also out walking. They, too, seemed to be happy, enjoying the first spring day of warm breezes. As they started to pass her, one man turned towards Penny. His face is blurry, *she thought like a protected witness during a televised interview.* How weird, *Penny thought,* am I really having my own dreams censored *and, if so, by whom? But as the man's pixilated features settled into place, Penny realized to her horror that the censorship had been for her benefit. The man gave a puzzled, yet narrowed look as he surveyed the area.*

"Jack," Penny gasped. He whipped his head around and looked at her. It was him. His expression changed from surprise to fiendish delight. Penny turned to hide her face while making an escape. But he easily reached out and grabbed her arm before she even took a second step.

"I've looked everywhere for you," he said in that deep, gladiatorial voice that Penny remembered all too well. His expression was neutral, not in any way threatening. But Penny knew he was like the deadly stonefish camouflaged on the ocean floor biding his time.

"Wake up!" Penny silently screamed. "Wake up! For the love of Christ, wake up! He's in your head!" But the sleeping pill wouldn't let her.

"I remember this dress. You wore it at the high school concert," he told her as he loosened his grip.

Penny took the opportunity to jerk her arm away. But he was quick, able to snatch her back, his fingers digging into her arms. "Looks like rain," Jack told her. He was right; the blue skies had vanished, and dark clouds threatened a storm. He dragged her towards an abandoned warehouse. I've signed petitions to have this torn down, *Penny thought hysterically. As if her signature gave her the right of protection. Don't go with him, Penny's mind screamed at her. You know what they say. Make a commotion. Scream! Kick! Bite! Do whatever it takes.*

But kicking and biting meant nothing to Jack; it was if he was made of steel. He held her by her forearms as he walked backwards bringing her along with him as smoothly as a Cajun dance. Jack's long stride meant Penny couldn't keep up and her sandal-clad feet dragged and bounced along the broken sidewalk. One shoe torn off and was left behind. Penny saw to her horror that the lunch crowd was hurrying down the street away from her, looking for their own shelter from the storm. "Hey! Hey! Where are you going? Help me!" Penny screamed. But they didn't even turn, like abduction wasn't occurring just down the street from them. Then Penny realized, for them it wasn't happening. It was only happening inside her head. They can't help me; they can't even hear me. Knowing she was on her own, Penny tore into him, fighting like a wild animal, but he didn't loosen his grip.

Jack easily broke through the rotting door and threw Penny inside. As she fell, her dress ripped. Not taking the time to stand up, Penny tried to crawl away. There had to be another way out. She was vaguely aware that her knees were being scraped raw on the pebbled and chipped concrete and glass from the shot out windows.

He threw himself on top of her, his stubble cheek against hers. "Where are you going? I have something for you," Jack whispered with a warm, whiskey-cigarette breath, a scent that had the power to loosen her guts. The roar of the rain filled Penny's ears; she saw it was coming down in one steady sheet outside the broken windows. When she felt him reach back to unbuckle his jeans, Penny's brain screeched, You must wake up! You must, you must, you must –

"Wake up!" Penny screamed out loud. She awakened to find herself on all fours at the foot of her bed as if she had been dropped there from the sky. Her heart was beating so hard it made her chest hurt, like her rib cage was bruised from the inside. Penny sat back and wrapped her arms and a down comforter around herself. She tried to slow her breathing, lest she hyperventilate. She had sensed him before in her dreams and that had nearly scared the life out of her, but this time it was like Jack had actually … With a trembling hand Penny pulled her damp hair off her face. Out of the corner of her eye, she saw red welts on her forearms. Jerking down the comforter, she discovered her knees were scraped raw and bleeding, a sliver of glass embedded in her shin. With her mouth clamped shut, Penny silently howled in fear and rage.

4

Chapter Two

Chupacabra

Annalise was the eldest of Penny's "adopted daughters." At the ripe old age of 22, Annalise was the "in charge" sister. She had been for a long time through necessity. Just before noon, worry got the best of her. It was so unlike Penny to stay home. Michael had assured Annalise it was simply a situation of Penny needing more sleep. But Annalise had lived a lifetime of situations getting out of hand quickly, never to return to normalcy. Annalise informed Mayra-Liz, her younger sister by two years that she was going to check on Penny; Mayra-Liz would mind the shop.

While Annalise crept up the stairs, she began to question her decision to come unannounced. She had a key and the sisters enjoyed an open door invitation, but Annalise was concerned she could awaken Penny from her much needed sleep. God knows the three hundred-plus year old stairs creaked and groaned as she climbed them. On the other hand, if Penny was awake, she might be concerned an intruder was creeping up the stairs. Annalise was relieved to find Penny sitting at the foot of her bed, facing the window, with a comforter wrapped around her.

"Oh, you're up," Annalise said. "I hope that doesn't mean you haven't slept. We're running out of sugar, yet again. Can you believe it? I tell you, people are drinking sugar coffee. It just isn't healthy. Penny?" When Penny didn't respond, Annalise stepped forward with her heart pounding an unsteady rhythm against her chest. She gasped when she saw Penny's face. For a crazy moment, all Annalise could think was something said to a grimacing adolescent, "You'd better stop or your face could freeze like that!" A hysterical snort burst from Annalise before she could actually formulate syllables. Then, the words spilled over themselves in both English and her native Spanish.

"Are you all right? Penny? *Que pasó?* What happened? What's wrong? Look at me! *Mírame!* I'm getting my purse, with my phone. It's downstairs. I'm calling 911. *Dios mío!* Don't move. Maybe you should move. How long you been like that? No, better not – don't move. Okay, I'll be right back."

"I need an ambulance," Annalise all but screamed into her phone. "I'm at ... *Mierda!* Shit! I can't think! Wait, I got it. 357 Church Street, Schenectady. Her name is Penny Morgan. I don't know. I don't know. I don't know! She's not responsive ... No, she's not my mama. *Dios mío!* She's young. 37. She's just sitting, staring." Annalise took a piece of her long, dark hair and started chewing on it, a habit she had stopped when she was six. Annalise started to sob. *I knew something was wrong, I felt it in my bones.*

"Yes, I'm here," Annalise shouted back into the phone. "I don't know what to do for her. I'm afraid to even touch her. Afraid I'll do something wrong. Tell me what to do! ¿Qué? What? Can she speak? I don't know. *Dime algo, Bebé.* Say something, Baby. Please! Nothing. She's saying nothing. Her breathing is fine, but she's chalk white. How soon can you get here? She looks like she's seen a *chupacabra.* You know, a goat sucker. They're vile things; we have them in Puerto Rico. No, I don't *really* think she saw a *chupacabra.* What I'm trying to explain is she looks terrified, like she's seen a monster. Please hurry!"

Chapter Three

The Referral

Michael was perched high in a maple tree taking photos in the Adirondacks for Greenpeace magazine when his phone rang. Checking the number, he saw it was from Annalise and immediately assumed she wanted him to pick something up for the shop. No matter how well they planned, and the girls were good planners, they always seemed to be running out of something for the café side of the *Ruth and Naomi* business. They could see no rhyme or reason for how things sold. Some days, herbal tea was all the rage. They'd stock up only to have the boxes sit for weeks on end while hot chocolate was in vogue *in May*, not your traditional spring drink. Since they tried to purchase only fair trade supplies directly from poverty-stricken countries, emergency restocking meant a drive to Albany where another Fair Trade store could help out. Michael clicked to take the call, but it was gone. When Annalise called back, Michael was unprepared for the hysterical voice on a phone line that kept breaking up. "Penny ... Not talking ... Not moving ... Staring ... Scared ... Not me, her! Well, I'm scared too. Paramedics ... unsure, maybe a stroke. Huntsby Hospital. Please hurry!"

"I'll be there as soon as I can, but it'll take me at least three hours. I'm north of Saranac Lake –" The connection was broken. One of a dozen things Michael liked about the Adirondacks was the limited building of cell towers. But today, the lack of a reliable phone service seemed downright dangerous. It had taken Michael almost an hour to get up the tree, but it took a quarter of that time for him to get back down. When he hit the ground, Michael's shoulder had already begun to throb from the contortions he made while maneuvering his way down the branches. Then, Michael ran to his car which was parked over a mile away. He was pouring sweat and gasping for breath when he was finally able to collapse against the black Jeep Wrangler. Michael tried his phone again

– nothing. *A stroke? How could that be? Penny doesn't smoke; she's slim and exercises. Family history?* Michael thought. *The only relative I knew of, Margaret, Penny's great-aunt, died of a heart attack in her late sixties which wasn't good, but Penny wasn't even forty.*

Michael alternated between driving 90 miles an hour and backing it down to 70, only to creep it back up to 90 again. He wasn't worried about a speeding ticket, just the delay being pulled over would cause. At the Lake George area, Michael got two bars on this phone and saw texts Annalise had sent over the past hour: Blood drawn. Penny sitting up. Talking, no slurring, good sign Dr said. Waiting for MRI.

Michael was outside of Saratoga Springs when he got a flat tire. "Unfrigginbelievable," Michael said as he pulled over to the narrow shoulder of Route 87. When Triple A told him it would take at least an hour for the truck to arrive, Michael unloaded the back of the car, got out the jack, lug wrench, and spare to change the tire on his own while cars and tractor trailers blew past. It was going fine until Michael came across a lug nut that was stripped. He was still working on it when Triple A arrived. Finally, Michael was able to text Annalise that he was back on the road and would be there within half an hour.

By the time Michael arrived at Huntsby Hospital, Penny was in an examination room signing release forms. Michael pulled her close. He then reached over and took Annalise's hand. He mouthed the words, thank you, finding himself at the moment too choked up to speak.

The nurse flipped through Penny's chart to see if she had signed the HIPAA form allowing the hospital to share information with her husband. She continued with instructions on following up with a cardiologist. The echocardiogram didn't find a clot, but a heart murmur. The murmur was slight and couldn't have caused the episode Penny had experienced.

"Then what caused it?" Michael asked. "It sounded like she was totally unresponsive. Is that right?"

"Mrs. Morgan was listed as catatonic when she arrived. The cause has not been determined. There's also a referral for Mrs. Morgan to see a psychiatrist with a list of qualified doctors. Also, the doctor prescribed – "

"A psychiatrist! Does the doctor think the problem is emotional?" Michael asked.

"I wasn't with your wife when she came in. I'm part of the new shift. I can ask the doctor to speak with you."

"Penny, did the doctor discuss this with you?" Michael asked. "Doesn't it seem like there should be more tests done? We don't want to leave without knowing what's going on."

"The doctor did mention it would be good for me to talk with someone. He's concerned that I haven't been sleeping well."

"I think your insomnia needs to be resolved too, but would not sleeping well cause you to get into such a state?" Michael asked. "You weren't even able to speak, right?"

"It was awful! She wasn't speaking or moving, just staring with *that look* on her face," Annalise said. "Penny, it was like you had left yourself."

"I'll ask the doctor to speak with you," the nurse repeated. "I think he's still here. I'll be back."

"I have such a headache," Penny said as she rubbed her temples.

"Penny, you should lay down. I'll see if I can get you an ice pack," Annalise said. "There's no telling how long it'll take before the doctor returns – Oh! There's Dr. Jamal"

"Mrs. Morgan, you wanted to see me?"

"I know you're busy," Penny said with a hurried voice, "but we're wondering about the instructions to consult a psychiatrist. Does that mean the problem is simply psychological? Although, I'm sure that's better than a stroke."

"As we discussed, catatonia can occur for many reasons," Dr. Jamal said. "We ruled out encephalitis, inflammation of the brain, and stroke. We don't think it's an autoimmune disease such as lupus or multiple sclerosis, but that hasn't been entirely ruled out. The MRI didn't show any abnormalities; but if you have a recurring episode, we'll have you follow up with a neurologist. We haven't ruled out bipolar disorder, post-traumatic stress disorder, or depression. What we do know is that you aren't sleeping well, Mrs. Morgan and that needs to be addressed. Certainly, a sleep study should be conducted. The nurse will give you a number to have it scheduled. Given the level of insomnia you have experienced, it's entirely possible it caused catatonia to occur. Sleep is very important, as vital as food and water."

"I try to sleep. It's not that I don't try."

"Sometimes insomnia becomes a cycle. People don't sleep because they become anxious about not sleeping. I prescribed a mild anti-anxiety medication. I know you feel strongly about not taking sleeping pills, but your primary care physician prescribed the lowest dosage. I think you should give it another try. Of course, medication isn't getting to the root

9

cause which is why I'd like you to see a psychiatrist," Dr. Jamal said as his pager beeped.

"We can go with that plan. It's okay if you need to go. I think we have enough information. Are you good, Michael?"

"I guess so. It would just be nice to have a more definitive reason why Penny is going through all of this."

"I wish I had the answer for you. That's how medicine is most of the time, ruling things out. It's possible with counseling and medication, it'll never happen again."

"Well, wouldn't that be great!" Annalise said. She looked like she had been through the ringer herself.

Chapter Four

The Nightcap

"Good heavens, what are you doing, Michael?" Penny asked when she saw her husband at the kitchen table in the middle of the night, two days after the trip to the hospital. "Oh, I'm sorry. I didn't mean to startle you. I've never seen you play solitaire before. I didn't even know we owned a deck of cards."

"They were a promotional gift from one of the conferences we attended," Michael said.

"Vegas?"

"Wisconsin."

"Why can't you sleep?" Penny asked as she stroked the back of Michael's head.

"My shoulder hurts. I think I pulled something while I was climbing down the tree; you're not sleeping either."

"I know, and I'm so sick of it. I have an appointment with a psychiatrist next Tuesday. It's not easy to be seen and if I need long-term treatment, it'll cost a fortune. We only get three paid visits though our insurance."

"Don't worry about that. Here, have some of my brandy."

"I thought alcohol was supposed to make insomnia worse," Penny said as she took a sip.

"I don't think it can get much worse, do you? Come on, Monty," Michael said as he picked up the heavy cat from the couch. "We're all going back to bed and cuddle. It's your job to get us sleep."

"Listen to him purr," Penny said. "Good boy, Monty. You're trying to soothe us."

"Do you think you can sleep?" Michael asked once they were in bed and under the heavy comforter, the cat curled at Penny's ankles.

"I think I might. I feel pretty relaxed."

Penny drifted down to sleep and nearly startled herself back to wakefulness when she realized she was dreaming. In her dream, Penny was peddling Margaret's old bicycle for all she was worth, but was going no place fast. And Penny desperately needed to get away; Jack was hunting her.

"For the love of Christ – move!" she hoarsely hissed to the fat balloon tires.

Penny approached an elderly Vietnamese woman standing at the side of the dirt road. The woman was clutching a brilliant red printed shawl with one hand and pointing upwards with the other as if to remind Penny that God was listening and did not approve of His name being taken in vain, no matter how dire the situation. As Penny drew closer, the woman also gestured upwards with her eyes. Following her gaze, Penny realized they were under water; she just needed to get to the surface. Penny looked back to thank the woman, for surely she had saved her. But the woman was gone. Only the red shawl remained, as graceful and ominous as a jellyfish adrift in the current.

Penny threw the bicycle aside. She'd swim to the surface. Penny pulled her arms up and out, pushing the water aside with powerful strokes, but her wet clothes dragged her down. She kicked off her shoes and struggled with buttons. Finally, naked and unencumbered, she swam like a sea otter: sleek and fast. Just as a wave of relief started to wash over her, Penny's outstretched hand hit a ceiling of ice. She screamed in frustration, but produced only a muffled burble of air and water. She was so close! Penny clawed and pounded at the ice; her lungs on fire from the lack of oxygen. Finally, a crack formed. Kicking upward with all her remaining strength, she slammed the ice with her head and the frozen ceiling broke open. A hand plunged in, grabbed her arm, and pulled her to the surface.

"Thank God," Penny gasped, as she broke free of the water. "You've got to help me. He's here! I can feel him."

"I know," Jack replied.

Later, Michael tripped over Penny on the bathroom floor when he made his nightly trek to the toilet. To Penny's hyper-sensitive eyes, the snapped on bathroom light seemed as brilliant as the first flash of a nuclear blast. Michael grabbed her by the shoulders, pulling her limp body into a sitting position while his frantic face swam in and out of Penny's vision. She saw Michael's mouth move. Moments later she heard words spread out around her, but they meant nothing. Penny

12

silently asked him to please lay her back down where the smooth floor tiles could cool her face. When Michael did just that, she congratulated herself on her new-found telepathic skills.

Must be something that can be learned in this tranquil zone, Penny mused. *Now perhaps he could turn out the light.* But it must have been beginner's luck because the room remained brilliantly lit, and worse yet, the quiet was broken by Michael shouting into his phone. Their bathroom soon filled with strangers who also wouldn't let her sleep as they poked and prodded her. Penny pried one eye open. Looking across the expanse of the tiles, she saw Michael squatting at the edge of the room, positioned to see her between the paramedics and their equipment.

"Alcohol," said one of the paramedics, and another typed it into a laptop.

"She had a small amount of brandy before we went to bed," Michael told them. "She must have had a seizure or something. The E.R. doctor said they hadn't entirely ruled out a neurological disorder."

"Did you see her have a seizure, sir?"

"No, but you mustn't assume she's simply drunk, even though I know that's how it looks."

The paramedics ignored Michael and continued their examination of Penny while trying to keep her awake.

"Wake up, Penny. Come on, you have to stay awake," the paramedics demanded.

Michael rubbed his hand over his head in frustration, making his dark, bed head hair even messier, giving him a ready-to-rumble '50s tough guy look. It was obvious he thought he knew what was wrong, or at least what *wasn't* wrong, but no one was listening. The woman paramedic shined a penlight into Penny's eyes and pronounced: alcohol *with* drugs. "What did you take? Honey, listen to me. What did you take?"

"What if she has permanent damage because you people aren't *listening*?" Michael said, his voice rising.

"You need to stand back," the scrawny paramedic said, although Michael hadn't tried to approach.

Michael grabbed his cell phone and pawed through his contacts. "We need a neurologist. I must know someone who knows a specialist. My wife does not take *drugs*." Michael snarled out the word. "Penny was given a prescription for sleeping pills, and no matter how exhausted she gets, she rarely takes them."

"Where is the medication? Where does she keep it?" asked the woman, suddenly tuned in to Michael.

13

"Right here in this bathroom drawer." Michael stood up, pulling open the top drawer. He pawed through the contents, flinging items on the counter: a tissue packet, soap bars, a flattened toothpaste tube, Band-Aids, folded hand towels. Michael searched through the second drawer, then the third, but came up empty-handed. With a stricken look on his face, he bolted out of the room, and down the stairs.

Penny knew what he would find in their galley kitchen: the overhead light on, brandy spilled on the counter, down the face of the cherry cabinets, and onto the tile floor where the wayward pill bottle lay, cap off and empty. Penny remembered she had considered cleaning up the mess, but in the moment, it had seemed far too tiresome a task. A paring knife and cutting board with white residue and tiny blue chips would tell the tale. Penny had begun by responsibly cutting a pill in half. When she didn't feel any difference, Penny took the other half. She must have experienced a hallucination that the side effects on the package warned about because Penny could have sworn that Jack was in the room with her. She tried to call for Michael, but found her voice was gone. Why she then decided to consume all the pills with a chug of brandy is anyone's guess. When nausea kicked in, Penny climbed the stairs to the bathroom where she collapsed near the toilet.

Michael climbed back up the stairs, into the bathroom, and handed the pill bottle to the paramedic saying, "I just don't understand." The paramedic examined the label. "Eszopiclone, 1mg." she read to the person manning the laptop. "How many were in the bottle?" she asked Michael.

"I don't know. I'd guess it was nearly full – 28 or so."

"Did she leave a note?"

"There's grocery list: milk, peanut butter, bananas," Michael answered with a dazed voice.

Penny felt as if a stadium full of people were chanting, Stay awake! Stay awake! "Please, please just let me sleep," she begged. *For heaven's sake, was that really asking for so much?*

"What's your birth date? Who's the President?" the paramedics asked.

President ... Penny thought back to an election and the bumper sticker on her previous car: "Hope."

"Ya gotta have hope, miles 'n miles, 'n miles of hope," Penny sang with a soft, slurred voice.

"It's heart," a paramedic said absently as he adjusted the IV port in Penny's arm.

"What's wrong with her heart?" asked Michael with alarm.

14

"Nothing that I know of. It's the song that she's singing: its *heart*, not hope."

The ambulance took off at a sickening rate of speed. "I'm going to throw up," Penny announced. A pink, plastic basin was held in front of her while someone raised the stretcher to an upright position. The siren scream ricocheted inside of Penny's head, while Michael shouted in a continuous loop, "You're fine. You'll be fine. Just hang in there." His voice carried the hard bite of fear.

It seemed in no time the ambulance came to an abrupt stop. The back doors flew open seemingly of their own accord. Fresh, crisp air washed over Penny, helping to purge the combined stench of vomit and antiseptics from the confined space of the ambulance, yet Penny heaved again. She was raced through the hallways on the gurney, rectangular ceiling lights flashing by like a dashed highway centerline, while the medics yelled, "Coming through ... Coming through."

In between gagging heaves, Penny kept trying to explain that all of this was completely unnecessary. "I - uunnhhhh - just need - unnhhh - to sleep," she tried to tell them. But the paramedics didn't answer or even look at her as they concentrated on getting her to the emergency exam area designated for cases such as hers. In fact, they seemed annoyed, as if *she* was the one keeping *them* from their sleep.

When Penny looked around her hospital room, it became all too clear what had happened. Penny winced as she remembered that while she was on the gurney, she had grabbed something metal and smacked her forehead with it. Penny wondered now what she had intended by that impulsive maneuver. Did she think that she could simply brain herself to sleep? Penny recalled hearing over the hospital commotion, someone's command to pay attention to that patient! What on earth is going on?

Penny looked up at the nurse who now stood next to her taking her blood pressure, Liv ... something.

"What time is it?" Penny asked.

"5:37 ... a.m.," Liv answered.

"Why won't he leave me alone?" Penny blurted out, "When will this ever end?"

Chapter Five

A Sinner

Dr. Patrick Allen arrived at the hospital over an hour before the sun rose. His early-rising habit began fifty years ago, when he was ten years old and had a paper route. Back then, he was a fixture with the early morning commuters, his front bicycle basket piled so high with newspapers that only his reddish-brown hair, brown eyes, and freckled nose showed over the top. More than one woman in town, while kissing her husband goodbye, cautioned him to keep an eye out for Patrick.

Nearly everyone in their small town had the paper delivered. Patrick listened to and followed without complaint his customers' varied requests. Some wanted the paper placed between the front and screen doors. Others required their newspaper placed in a bag before leaving it in the mailbox. Most elderly customers wanted a bill, a receipt, and a visit on Saturday afternoon. Often, the visits included work they could no longer do – clean storm windows, change light bulbs. As Patrick rode his bike through town, nodding a polite hello, the town folks would quietly remark to one another what a shame it was about the boy's father; there were few things worse than being brought up by a mean drunk.

Dr. Allen confidently strode down the hospital corridor. He belonged. The hospital was his second home. His hair was still damp from his early morning swim. It was exercise he enjoyed and it kept his tall body toned and trimmed. Dr. Allen's boyish red hair had faded to light brown, but the thickness was nearly the same, except the crown had become thinner. When Joseph Reed, a fellow psychiatrist, teased him about developing a thinning spot, Dr. Allen had frowned in confusion as if he couldn't imagine anyone concerned about something as mundane as thinning hair. It eventually happened to most men. Yet, Dr. Allen unconsciously developed the habit of smoothing his head as part of his thought process, and thus checking the thickness of his hair throughout the day.

Dr. Allen wore dark grey dress slacks, a crisp white shirt, and a grey and black tweed sports jacket. His tie was grey with thin red lines. Dr. Allen looked down at his new Italian leather loafers. His wife Judith had encouraged him to hang the price and buy them. They were remarkably comfortable, but the expense pinched his Irish, Catholic conscience.

Dr. Allen took a corner and stopped when he saw Chloe, a young nurse who was leaning against the mobile computer stand. He couldn't help but frown in sympathy. Chloe's friendly comportment was an asset to the ward and to humanity in general. She was professional and polished. Her dark hair was typically done up in that casual, attractive bun that women have taken to wearing nowadays. But this obviously wasn't a typical day as more of Chloe's hair was down than up. As she read a patient's chart, Chloe held her hand on her forehead looking as if she thought it might explode.

"Good morning, Chloe. Tough night?" Dr. Allen asked as he glanced at the monitor.

"Oh, Dr. Allen!" she said, looking up in surprise. Then she rolled her eyes in exasperation and continued, "It was miserable! No one slept. Everyone was wired. That Mrs. Levy in room 602 cried all night long for her cat. Hear that? She's been at it for over six hours now."

"That's not crying, that's screeching."

"Right! I'd just get Mrs. Levy and the other patients calmed down, and then she'd start back up again."

"It certainly is disruptive. I was on call last night. I wish you had contacted me. I would have come in."

"I know. I hated to bother you. I kept thinking she would stop soon. How is it possible for someone to continue on like that? It was louder; she's gotten hoarse."

"Let's start the rounds with Mrs. Levy and see what we can do. You know, I saw that stray cat this morning, perhaps that would mollify her," Dr. Allen said with a mischievous grin.

Chloe was too frazzled to realize he was joking. "Don't even think about it! We've got enough going on without adding a feral cat to the mix."

Dozens of breakfast trays delivered to the ward created a piquant aroma. Mingled with hospital disinfectant; it gave Dr. Allen a twinge of sadness. The emotion surprised him. He thought he had become immune to hospital smells.

Dr. Allen stopped at his last patient's room and immediately felt more buoyant when he saw Liv Wright. She worked for one of those agencies that hospitals call when they're low on staff, which lately, for Huntsby was fairly often. It was amazing how quickly Liv adapted to the hospital's routine. She was one of the most efficient, empathetic nurses he had come across. Liv was what his mother would have called, *good people*. Dr. Allen had suggested to the head nurse that they find a way to hire Liv full time, but he received the answer back that Liv liked the flexibility of working where and when she wanted. Dr. Allen was reading the notes from the emergency room intake in the doorway when Liv joined him.

"Hi, Liv. How's it going?" he asked quietly as to not awaken the patient.

"Okay. Her pressure has improved. And her pulse is back to normal, but her sleep has been sporadic at best. She had a worrisome nightmare about an hour ago."

"What happened to her forehead?"

"She hit herself with a metal pipe that one of the maintenance workers left on a crash cart."

"Sloppy," he responded shaking his head, "that shouldn't have happened. Has someone spoken to the maintenance crew?"

"Mia Middleton was the supervisor."

"Whew!" Dr. Allen gave a low whistle. "Their ears will still be smarting tomorrow."

The doctor looked across the room at the patient, the white bandage, a stark contrast to her long auburn hair. "Hitting yourself in the head is a tough way to commit suicide."

"There was also the drug overdose beforehand, but I'm not so sure it was a suicide attempt. She's troubled, no doubt about it; but I don't think she was trying to end her life."

"Psychotic?"

"Maybe ... But I don't think ...."""

"Then what?" asked Dr. Allen.

"I don't know. Something ... something else. It's like she's being ... haunted. That nightmare she had. Mercy! She was practically climbing the walls, trying to get away from whoever was in her own mind."

Dr. Allen gave Liv a quizzical look and a nod, giving her the opportunity to further explain. But Liv just waived his concern away and said with a scoff, "Haunted ... not a very professional diagnosis, is it? Don't mind me, I guess I'm just overtired." She walked to the patient's bed, and Dr. Allen followed.

"Mrs. Morgan?" Dr. Allen inquired softly. Penny opened her eyes and Dr. Allen allowed the patient a few moments to collect her thoughts.

"I'm Dr. Allen. I'm a psychiatrist assigned to your case. How are you feeling?"

"My head hurts. My stomach hurts, and I feel like an idiot."

He gently removed the bandage, looking at the cut and said, "It's not deep and should heal fine. However, it's possible there could be a faint scar along your hairline. If that bothers you, I can ask a plastic surgeon to take a look."

"I'm sure it'll be fine," Penny said.

Dr. Allen peered into Penny's eyes with a penlight and was pleased to see the pupils contracted and her eyes diligently following the beam from side to side. He turned off and pocketed the light. While replacing the bandage, Dr. Allen said, "I'm ordering a CT scan, just to be on the safe side. You can't be too careful with a head injury. Liv said you had a nightmare. Do you remember it?"

"It was the standard nightmare. You know, running away from the scary, bad person who jumps out just when you thought you had gotten away," Penny said with a shrug to show the dream was of no consequence.

"Have you had this dream before?" Dr. Allen questioned.

"Well, not exactly this dream, but ones like it. Doesn't everyone? Plus, I'm sure the sleeping pills made me have extra-crazy dreams."

"How often do you take sleeping pills?"

"Rarely. I wait until I get desperate."

"Liv, why don't you get a notepad and a pen for Penny, perhaps she can reconstruct the dream." Dr. Allen smoothed the top of his head, then turned to Penny and said, "I don't put a great deal of stock in dream interpretation, but it might give us a good launching point for when we talk this afternoon. I would also like you to write down anything else you'd like to tell me, anything of significance. I find there's nothing worse than a session where I fire off questions, missing the problem by a mile, while the patient passively waits for me to figure it all out, like I'm a magician. In my counseling sessions, I expect the patient to work just as hard as I do. I need you to communicate with me and *together* we'll figure out how you can face your problems and not land in the emergency room. Sound fair?"

"Of course," Penny said.

"This is a safe room used when there's concern the patient may cause harm to themselves. There's a camera in this room for observation at the nurses' station. You'll be staying here until we feel certain you're not a threat to yourself. Nurses will be checking on you often, so just ask if you need anything. Normally, patients aren't allowed pens in this room. Is it something we can trust you with?"

"A pen? Do you think I'll steal it?"

"I mean can we trust you not to hurt yourself with it?"

"I won't hurt myself."

"There will some forms for you to sign. I'll see you later to discuss the details of what happened last night, probably around three." Dr. Allen was at the door when he remembered a message he had promised to deliver. "I met your husband in the waiting room. Michael, isn't it?"

Penny nodded.

"He asked me to tell you that he's here; he loves you; and that he'll be in as soon as you're allowed visitors."

"He's not a visitor; he's my *husband*. Was he told that he couldn't come in?"

"I wasn't here, but I imagine that he was encouraged to stay out of the way while you were being stabilized."

"Stay out of the way! If it wasn't for Michael I'd be –" Penny's voice had started to rise, almost to the point of sounding shrill when she abruptly stopped.

Dr. Allen waited for her to finish the sentence. When she didn't, he said, "We'll talk more this afternoon. In the meantime, do try to get some rest."

Dr. Allen saw he had a half an hour before he started his counseling sessions. He went to the cafeteria and picked up a coffee pot. Norma, a kitchen worker he had known for years, bustled over. "Put that down," she ordered. "It's been sitting for over an hour. I'm making a fresh pot in the back. I'll bring you a cup, and I set aside one of those apple spice muffins you like, still warm."

"Thanks, Norma. You're too good to me."

"Hush!" she commanded as she bustled back to the kitchen, her large backside swaying.

Every Christmas, Dr. Allen gave Norma and the other kitchen workers gift certificates to a local Italian restaurant. The cafeteria staff worked hard, and Dr. Allen wanted them to enjoy a meal that they didn't have to cook or serve. Their gratitude, for what the doctor believed to be a small gesture, embarrassed him.

Norma returned with the promised cup of hot, fresh coffee and a paper bag. Dr. Allen accepted the bag with a boyish smile. He unfolded the top of it, closed his eyes, and put his face close to the open mouth of the bag to inhale the soul-warming aroma of freshly baked goods. Opening his eyes, he noticed something wrapped in tin foil next to the muffin. He looked questioningly at Norma who answered with a conspiratorial wink.

Dr. Allen folded the bag closed again, took the cup of coffee, and after a nod of thanks to Norma, paid by swiping his tag. He negotiated the maze of tables and chairs, and went out a side door which opened onto a scar of a yard used primarily by the kitchen staff for a quick, illicit nicotine fix. Dr. Allen cautiously lowered himself onto a lawn chair held tentatively together by fraying green plastic webbing. Someday the seat would give up the ghost. But today it held. The doctor closed his eyes and breathed in the java scent, savoring the moment, relaxing his mind, and practicing what he preached: the importance of taking daily, mini-vacations. He sipped the coffee, set it down, and spread an inadequate paper napkin on his lap on which to set the muffin. The doctor said a quick, yet heartfelt prayer of thanks for his many blessings before breaking off a piece of muffin and eating it. Dr. Allen pulled out the foil-wrapped package. He unwrapped it and found a piece of cold fish.

Well, I guess my secret's out, he smiled to himself.

"Here, kitty. Come on, kitty, kitty, kitty," he called out in a falsetto voice. Soon a grey, black, and white tom appeared, hunger overriding his fear. Still, he kept a safe distance.

"It's okay, fella. Look what Norma sent you," Dr. Allen said as he set the food on the ground. The cat ate ravenously, all the while giving warning growls lest anyone mistakenly thought he was in a sharing mood.

"It's okay. It's okay," Dr. Allen soothed. He shivered as a chilly breeze penetrated his sports jacket. It was the first day of November and much colder days would soon be coming to upstate New York. He wondered how the cat would survive. If its thick and matted coat was any indicator, blizzards would soon arrive. The feline would go mad with fright if captured and made to stay inside, yet how could the poor creature make it through the harsh winter nights?

Images of a cold night during his childhood caused Dr. Allen to squeeze his eyes shut against the unbidden memory that hung like a richly painted stage cloth: flat, yet vivid. Each returned visit added another brush stroke, until he knew his memory held more details than the original experience allowed him to consciously register. It was all there, waiting for him: The polished chrome of his father's beloved automobile glinting in the early morning light. The opened car door revealing his father's body slumped in the powder-blue leather seat. The cyanotic hand with dirty, untrimmed nails, resting on the worn, dark blue

22

cotton fabric that covered his father's knee. A gold crucifix fallen to the blue and grey floor mat, the body of Christ polished and worn from constant, nervous rubbings. His father's blue eyes were like those of bloated, floating fish. Standing next to him, his mother was dressed in the same clothes she'd worn the previous day, including a faded apron stained with blueberry juice. She had thrown on her grey winter coat, a garment she had made herself. It had big front pockets, not quite the same size, edged with black piping. Her black, flat-heeled rubber boots zipped up the front and were topped by narrow strips of black fur coated with winter grime. Her Irish face while still hinting at the prettiness of her youth, had lines that mapped out the difficult roads of trouble she had traveled during her marriage. She stood at the open car door and silently sobbed her husband's name until her voice caught. Then her screeches of "Thomas! Thomas!" stopped passing school children in their tracks, lunchboxes held limply at their sides, little mouths agape. One little girl pulled at the hand of her friend and together they ran away down the sidewalk, their white knee socks sagging to their skinny white ankles.

Dr. Allen opened his eyes and saw that his hands were shaking. He folded them and mouthed the words, "Lord Jesus Christ, Son of God, have mercy upon me." He omitted the final words of the prayer: *a sinner*. God knew he was a sinner. No need to remind Him.

Chapter Six

Scary Clown

Michael knew the situation with Penny could have been worse, much worse. His wife was going to pull through. When he received the news that Penny's condition was upgraded to stable, he felt weak with relief. He dropped into the nearest chair, put his head in his hands, and cried. He would not have chosen so public a place to release his emotions, but his body, not his mind was in control and he had no choice. The storm was over almost before it began. Michael pulled a handkerchief from his pocket and wiped his eyes and nose. He was rarely without a handkerchief, a habit formed during his private, grammar school education. He also carried a pen, a small notebook, a pen light, and a jackknife. Penny had teased him when she realized he had even brought these supplies with him in his camera bag to the beach.

"I know it makes me dorky, but it's good to have these things with you when you need them," Michael had said without a trace of defensiveness, being an "I yam what I yam" type of guy.

Penny had stroked his arm and replied, "There is *nothing* dorky about you."

The chair Michael sat in was a hard molded plastic thing, the color of a pumpkin. The left arm had a built-in receptacle with a metal ashtray from the old days, long empty of tobacco, but with the lingering stench of dead cigarettes. *How long has it been since smoking was allowed in hospital waiting rooms: two decades, three?* Michael thought. Other wings of the hospital had been updated many times over while the psych ward seemed to have been forgotten. Out of sight and out of mind.

When will this country smarten up and get universal health care? Michael thought as he absently clicked the spring-loaded lid of the ancient ashtray open and shut. Michael Morgan had enjoyed a comfortably apolitical early adulthood, caring more about the quality of his photographs than the quality of the world. Then, a photographic

25

assignment for National Geographic had taken him to Africa and his comfortable world was turned upside down. Soon, he was involved in all sorts of things that hadn't been on his radar before: orphaned and stolen children, ethnic wars, and with it the mass genocide of innocent people. Like many of those later reformed, Michael worked overtime to make up for his earlier, passive behavior.

I wonder how many more people I could have helped if I had been involved just five years earlier, he often thought. Michael gave generously, more generously than his financial advisor felt he should comfortably do. "This isn't about comfort," Michael had informed him. "It's about life and death. Millions of deaths! We should all do more than what is *comfortable!*" If Michael allowed it, he would feel overwhelmed by the sheer number of those in need.

It's so difficult to make a real difference, Michael thought shaking his head. At first, he tried to help the people of Sierra Leone in the way he knew best, through expressive photographs. Michael thought college students would be receptive to changing the world, so he offered a free symposium. The college auditorium had filled; it had been a long time since Michael Morgan had done an exhibition that wasn't standing room only. However, the students were hardly what would be called *present*. They kept drifting in and out of sleep, doing the lecture doze. They showed all the signs: the jerk of the head, the slackness of the mouth, even an occasional soft snort was heard, the prelude to a snore.

How can they possibly look at this presentation and have such a total lack of empathy? Michael had wondered. Even his colleagues discreetly glanced at their watches. Still, Michael lectured on. "We have a connection to Sierra Leone. A number of former slaves from America settled there. They arrived just after the American Revolution. Sierra Leone is a country rich in resources including diamonds and gold. It had become a major producer of titanium and bauxite but once its civil war began in 1991, manufacturing became difficult, to say the least. Sierra Leone could be a wealthy country, one of opportunity and plenty for its citizens, but because of corruption and brutality, most of its citizens live lives of desperation."

Michael looked at the picture of women holding their dying babies in the makeshift hospital and remembered the day he had photographed it. When they learned he was American, the women surrounded him with pleas to save their children as if his nationality alone could make anything possible. Michael could still hear their desperate chants in his head. "Please, Mister. Please. Save my child. Please Mister."

Michael paused in his talk, steadying his emotions. "In most areas of Sierra Leone, there is no running water, no sanitation. Women have very little to feed their children. They watch them slowly die. In this next photo, you see young boys, not old enough to shave, firing machine guns in the street. The boys were stolen from their families by the Revolutionary United Front, the RUF. The children were forced to fight. Look at their faces. You can see their excitement and horror. Look at this road. It's littered with the bodies of those they killed. This next photo shows children younger than twelve mining for diamonds under deplorable conditions. Diamonds are used by the RUF to finance the war. Reporters have termed them *blood diamonds*. It is a sad and heinous truth that the very gems that could *improve* the lives of the people of Sierra Leone are *destroying* them." Michael turned to look back at his audience. They returned his gaze with dull eyes. "Look at them!" Michael all but shouted, as he gestured towards the picture.

Okay. Easy, Michael, he had told himself. *Raising your voice is not going to raise their awareness. You want them to talk about the photographs, not the photographer.*

"Sorry" Michael had mumbled. "I just want you to understand their plight. Why don't we go over to the gallery and you can look at the photographs I've chosen for display. Take your time with each image; step inside the minds and hearts of these people. I'm going to Congress next week to plead for more aid. You can help by signing a petition supporting a monitoring mechanism for the sale of diamonds. I've also set up a box for donations."

It looked like a fire drill, Michael had thought. Many of his colleagues took a right hand turn and went out the front door. A trail of students followed Michael, took a quick circuit of the exhibit, and then left. Only a dozen or so signed the petition. Michael went to the back of the room and packed up his equipment.

Desperate times had led to desperate choices, Michael remembered with a shudder as he shifted in the uncomfortable chair. *And if what I had done had actually helped those people in Sierra Leone, I wouldn't have cared that it wasn't, strictly speaking, legal within that corrupt government. But none of it went as planned.*

The memory of it caused Michael to pick up the hospital styrofoam cup of coffee and throw it down his throat as if it were a shot of whiskey, used to soothe the nerves. But the coffee had gone cold and bitter, causing Michael to grimace. As he walked to the wastebasket, Michael stretched his arms and back and tugged at his short sleeves. He wore a pair of wrinkled cargo pants and a white tee shirt, clothes he had grabbed out of the laundry basket. The shirt turned out to be one that Penny sometimes slept in. On Penny, the tee shirt was too large, but on Michael the short sleeves cut into his biceps and pulled across his chest. He had stuffed his bare feet into work boots and grabbed his bomber jacket as he raced out the door with the paramedics. Michael knew he smelled ripe, a combination of his own body odor and Penny's vomit that had hit his pant leg. He wanted to wash it off, but hated to leave the waiting room in case the nurse came back with more information.

Michael had thought he would be allowed to see Penny soon after the nurse told him that his wife was stable. But that had been almost two hours ago. Was Penny sleeping? Crying? Was she concerned that he wasn't with her? When would someone bring him to her?

Michael rubbed his eyes. His head was pounding, and with good reason. Michael had grabbed his reading glasses rather than his regular ones. When he remembered an extra set of disposable contact lenses and a bottle of aspirin in his jeep, he thought, *I'll tell a nurse at the station I'll be away for ten minutes tops.* Michael pulled on his jacket. *I'll give her my cell number just in case.* Michael reached into his jacket pocket and discovered that he didn't have his cell and what's more, no keys. *Shit.*

That's right, he reminded himself. *I didn't drive here. When we're ready to leave, I'll need to call a cab from a pay phone. Are there any pay phones around anymore?* Fatigue weighed heavier on Michael as he considered that his wife would certainly not leave the hospital with him today. He didn't know *when* she'd be released.

Walking to the window, Michael looked at the city spread out below him. He simulated a camera's viewfinder by making a square of his index fingers and thumbs. It could make a good image, he decided. The blue-collar city looked like it was having a morning stretch and yawn before putting its shoulder into it. If Michael was actually taking the photo he would have zoomed in on the exhaust of the vehicles. It looked like they were having their first cigarette of the day, smoking and coughing.

"Mr. Morgan?" a young woman asked tentatively.

"Yes?" he said as he turned, dropping his arms.

"Aren't you going to lose the picture?" she laughed self-consciously, gesturing at his hands.

"No problem. I don't have my camera here; I was just ... passing time."

28

"I'm Lucy Levy," she said as she extended her hand. "We met at Union College."

Michael shook her hand while trying to place her. Lucy was kind enough not to make him come up with the right answer. "You were a guest speaker for the gallery opening. I had a photograph on display." She bobbed her head self-consciously. "You said you liked it. It was of my friend, Shatish, who was eating a blue Popsicle – a strand of her hair was blue, and her tongue was blue."

"Yes, I do remember it. I liked the composition. It captured the carefree days of college."

"Thanks, but they aren't so carefree. I only have a few weeks to turn my grade around in calculus; it doesn't look promising."

Michael nodded. Lucy nodded back.

"The hospital asked me to come in," Lucy explained without being asked. "I guess my grandmother was up all night causing a commotion over her cat that died ten years ago. I'm her point of contact when my parents are in Florida, which is where they are now, the lucky ducks. Anyway, I rushed here to find Gram fast asleep. I thought I'd grab a cup of coffee, give it a bit, see if she wakes up. But I have a class at ten."

Michael gave another non-verbal response in the form of a nod. The silence lengthened until Michael realized Lucy was waiting to hear why he was in the hospital in the early morning hours, looking like shit and smelling of B.O. and puke.

"My wife is here. She ... she ... " Michael stopped. There was no way he was going to get into the events of the past few hours.

"Is she okay?"

"Yes, she'll be fine."

"I hope you don't mind me saying so, but you don't look very good. Can I do anything for you? I could get you some coffee or something to eat from the vending machine?" Lucy offered.

"That's kind of you to offer. But I'm fine, thanks."

"My friend, Shatish spent some time in the Psych unit and it didn't take long before she was her old self again. They have great medications now. Sometimes, it's just a chemical imbalance, or something."

"Why do you think my wife has a psychiatric problem?"

"Because this is the waiting area for the psych ward," Lucy answered matter-of-factly. "Look, I'm not trying to pry and I won't say anything. Not that being in a Psych ward is anything to be embarrassed about. It's all medical isn't it, whether it's your appendix or depression?"

"She has a problem sleeping," Michael blurted out. "It's awful. Some nights she hardly sleeps at all."

29

"Don't you hate it when that happens? Everything looks so bleak when it's the middle of the night and you're wide awake, laying there. I think about whether I'll ever understand calculus. I need it to graduate."

"That is a stressor. I still occasionally have dreams that I'm not prepared for class, in fact I've dreamt I've somehow gotten my schedule all messed up; I'd been out shooting photographs, not attended *any* classes all trimester, and now it's finals."

"Yeah, that's a bad one. I can just imagine when I'm done with college I'll probably dream it's my job to solve mathematical equations, and the future of the world depends upon my getting it right or the planet will explode, or something. What does your wife think about when she can't sleep?"

"I imagine the state of world. It's so difficult to sleep soundly when you know there are people out there, homeless and hungry. That's what I think about when I can't sleep, but I don't think Penny has ever really said, and I haven't asked. That's kind of shocking, isn't it," Michael said while shaking his head.

"Mr. Morgan?" asked a nurse, a big bruiser of a woman who looked like she could wrestle the most challenging patient into submission.

"Yes, I'm Mr. Morgan. Michael. I'm Penny's husband."

"You can see her now." The nurse's voice had a hard, raspy sound like a hound dog that had barked and howled herself hoarse while on the hunt.

"Good luck," said Lucy as Michael grabbed his jacket.

"Thanks," Michael said. "You too."

Michael hurried down the hall with the nurse. "How is she?" Michael asked.

"I only know that her condition is stable. I'm not directly involved with her care. I'm sorry we took so long to get you. Halloween is always an extraordinarily busy and demanding night, more nurses ask for it off than New Year's."

Michael nodded as they continued down the corridor. As they came around a corner, Michael gasped. "Oh! Sorry. My nerves must be worse than I thought."

"Not at all. I've known many who have come around that corner and have done the exact same thing."

"Why on earth would they paint a mural of scary looking clowns in the hallway of a psychiatric ward?"

"This was the pediatric center. It's been, oh I guess ten years since the new wing was built. Now pediatrics is down that way. Mrs. Huntsby painted that mural back in the day. Nurses who were here then said it didn't look quite so scary when it was new. Take a look at it when you go back through. You'll see the missing chip of paint next to the mouth of the center clown is what gives him that hostile expression."

"Why doesn't it get painted over?"

"Because Mrs. Huntsby painted it."

"Oh, you mean *the* Mrs. Huntsby!"

"Exactly."

"But she's been dead for some time ... ten years?"

"Yes, shortly after she finished that mural. Well, actually I'm told she wasn't really done. She had plans for a little circus in the background. Mr. Huntsby comes by every so often and looks at it, gets all teary-eyed. The Huntsbys were very attached to each other."

"I remember. You never saw one without the other."

"The nurses say her death changed him. He used to have this booming laugh, chatted with everyone. Now he barely says boo."

Michael found himself getting choked up and he turned his face towards the wall lest the nurse saw his face crumple.

"It's a difficult time," the nurse said softly, showing genuine empathy.

"I'm not normally like this," Michael said with choked embarrassment.

"Here's her room: number 615. Well, good luck to you," the nurse said as she turned on her blue clogs, and strolled down the hall.

She has remarkably small feet, Michael thought absently before he turned and walked into his wife's room. He nodded at the nurse who was standing at a portable table, entering information into a computer. Penny was sitting up in bed, her eyes closed. She looked terribly pale, about the shade of her white bandage. She wore a hospital gown with small blue squares. Her freshly shampooed hair was still damp.

Looking at his wife in a hospital bed, Michael felt not only exhausted, but contrite. *Penny's insomnia had gotten so much worse. Why hadn't I realized the severity? This is my wife! Had I been so involved with the problems of people across the globe, I missed the warning signs from the woman who shares my bed?*

Penny blinked her eyes open and gave him a weak smile.

"I'm sorry –" Michael started to say, but Penny waved his apology away, showing that she certainly didn't blame him.

Michael sat at the edge of her bed, took a lock of her hair and rubbed it against his cheek. "You smell good."

"I just had a shower and brushed my teeth. It felt heavenly."

"Heavenly," Michael murmured and for the first time through this horrific incident, he felt angry. *My God!* he thought. *It had been a close call. I could have awakened to find her cold, dead body on the bathroom floor. Had it been deliberate? There were a lot of pills gone for it to have been an accident.* Michael closed his eyes, not wanting her to see the accusation. But Penny knew him too well.

"It wasn't like that, Michael! I never intended to hurt myself. I ... I don't know what happened." Penny started to cry.

Michael's hardened expression immediately softened as he held her. "I know, I know. It must have been the medication. There have been reports of people eating, vacuuming, driving, having no idea what they were doing"

As she snuggled close to him, her crying slowed.

"You're a brave woman getting that close to me. I really stink," Michael said.

"Doesn't matter," Penny said, her words slurred from fatigue.

"Do you think you could sleep?"

"Uh-huh."

"In that case, I'll go home and get my other glasses, but I'll come right back."

"Stay at home, get some rest. Come back later."

"Are you sure?"

Penny nodded.

"All right," Michael agreed. "How about I come back around dinner time and bring sandwiches so we can eat together." Penny nodded yes again. Michael smoothed Penny's hair back to better study her face and asked, "What do you think about when you can't sleep?"

Penny looked at him thoughtfully for a long moment before sighing. "We should get some rest," she said.

Michael kissed the right side of her forehead, avoiding the cut. "I'll be back at five. I love you," Michael whispered in her ear. He walked to the door, and then on impulse looked back at his wife. Even though it was obvious Penny was exhausted beyond words, her eyes were open, her brow furrowed with concern.

What is it, Penny? What keeps you awake? Whatever the problem is, it's written on your face. If only I knew how to read it, Michael thought as he retraced his steps towards the scary clowns. He stopped in front of the wall painting and stepped closer to examine the center clown with the chipped mouth. When he covered the blemished paint with his finger, it enormously improved the clown's demeanor.

32

Dropping his hand to his side, Michael thought, *that's how it is, not until after you've chipped the façade, can you know how people are underneath their guise.* Michael's eyes narrowed. The clown's threatening expression reminded him of Bogdan Sokolov, that heartless bastard who did so much harm to the people in Sierra Leone. "I hope to God, I never see you again," Michael told the clown through gritted teeth. A couple walking down the hall gave Michael a wide berth as they steered past him.

Chapter Seven

Angry Men

Dr. Allen arrived at Penny's room promptly at three. She was sitting in a corner chair, making some notes when he came in.

Dr. Allen asked Penny if she was ready. Penny stood, bringing the notebook and pen with her. They walked silently through the halls; Penny practically jogging to keep up with Dr. Allen's long stride. "Sorry," he said when he realized she was struggling and slowed his pace. In the counseling room there was a small round table with four mismatched, upholstered chairs placed around it. One had a broken arm. A print of Andrew Wyeth's *Christina's World* hung on the wall.

"Interesting choice for this room, isn't it?" Penny commented as she stood looking at the print.

Dr. Allen glanced at it, "I've never thought about it."

"Is it to remind patients that other people have had it worse? Unless part of the patient's day involves dragging their body through a hay field, then their life could be worse. I was introduced to the painting when I was in high school. My art teacher, Mr. Curly *loved* it. He showed it on an overhead projector. His narrations were accompanied by his white handkerchief that he kept fluttering out of his pants pocket to his eyes and back again. It looked like he was waving surrender to ... I don't know ... nostalgia," Penny scoffed.

"So, I take it you're not a fan of nostalgia."

"That doesn't mean I'm not sensitive to things. I'm probably *too* sensitive. I remember I took a book out of the library on great American artists, so I could spend solitary time looking at *Christina's World*. I thought about the rudimental, earthy details. Did she wear the pink dress just for the painting? Surely, she didn't drag herself around in party attire daily, did she? Were there calluses on her thighs? What was wrong with her family for not buying her a wheelchair? The picture was done in the late 1940's, right? Surely, wheelchairs, manual ones at least were available, like the one used by Heidi's rich benefactor."

"Heidi?" asked Dr. Allen.

"You know, the children's story, *Heidi*. Orphan raised by, then separated from her grandfather, and then reunited. I think it took place in the Alps."

"Oh, yes," replied Dr. Allen as he shifted his weight from one foot to the other, wondering where this discussion was going.

"Perhaps Christina *did* have a wheelchair, and I was being uncharitable to her family. Because what if there *was* a perfectly good piece of equipment, all shiny and new with extra-easy to push wheels that Christina refused to use; preferring to drag her body around instead? But if that was the case, wasn't Christina a little *nuts* and wasn't it insensitive of Andrew Wyeth to paint such a scene and make it look dreamy, with wisps of Christina's hair blowing in the wind?"

"Why don't we have a seat," Dr. Allen said. He put Penny's hospital chart and a pad of paper on the table and withdrew a fountain pen from his jacket breast pocket. Penny also arranged her notepad and pen.

"I feel like I'm on a job interview ... in a cotton bathrobe," Penny said wryly. "I'm not normally so chatty. This is all very strange to me. I've never been admitted to a hospital before. Well once, but not like this."

Dr. Allen unscrewed the cap from the fountain pen and wrote Penny's name on the blank page causing the table to wobble. Without comment, Dr. Allen ripped a piece of paper from the pad, folded it numerous times, and placed it under one leg to steady it. He straightened up, tested the table, and satisfied with its improved stability, turned to Penny and said, "Have you ever had counseling before?"

Penny shook her head no.

Say yes or no, Boy. I can't hear your head rattling, Dr. Allen heard his father's belittling words so clearly in his head that it caused him to shudder. The doctor's stomach turned sour, and for a moment his vision blurred. Dr. Allen shook his head to clear his thoughts as if his mind were an Etch a Sketch. He glanced at his patient concerned she had witnessed his distress, but Penny was staring down at her own page of notes. Grateful for this small favor, he smoothed the top of his head and continued. "Why don't we start with you telling me about your dream?"

"I wrote some things down. Let's see ... okay ... so, the dream started out with me riding my old bike. It had been Margaret's. She had it when she was stationed in England. I wish I had kept it. It was brown with fat balloon tires, and a wicker basket in front."

"Who is Margaret?"

Penny clicked her tongue making a self-scolding sound. "Of course you wouldn't know. She was my aunt. Great-aunt, actually. She raised me. My parents died when I was a baby ... car accident."

"You always called her Margaret?"

"Yes, I'm not sure why. I probably just started out calling her what I heard other people call her, and obviously she didn't mind. She was easy going about most things."

"How old was Margaret when she became your caregiver?"

"I don't know. She was born in 1931 and I was born in 1980. Forty-nine? Yeah, she was forty-nine, more than ten years older than I am now. Hmm." Penny stared off in the distance as she contemplated this newly-thought fact. "It couldn't have been easy for her, such a complete change of lifestyle. Yet, she acted as if raising me was the best thing in the world. She died at sixty-eight. It had been a shock. She had been so full of life."

"Cause of death?"

"Heart failure. She went in her sleep."

Dr. Allen made a note. "Have you ever had an EKG, an electrocardiogram?"

"Two, no three days ago, I had an echocardiogram. They discovered I have a heart murmur. I need to schedule an appointment with a cardiologist."

"Oh yes, I saw that in your chart. Please continue."

"Where was I?"

"You were riding Margaret's bicycle."

"Ah, yes. I was riding the bike as fast as I could, but I wasn't going any place. I was frantic because I was trying to get away from someone. Then, I realized I was underwater. A ceiling of ice kept me under. I broke through and someone pulled me to the surface; but it was the bad man."

"Did you see his face?"

"Not that time. But I didn't need to."

"Is it the same man every time?"

Penny nodded yes.

"Can you describe him?"

"Dark hair, dark eyes. Very angry."

"Why is he angry?"

"I don't –" Penny started to say but stopped. She stared hard at her hands gripping the notepad. "I think he wants someone to save him, but no one has or can. That's why he's so angry."

"Save him from what?"

"From himself," Penny blurted out and then chuckled self-consciously. "I don't know where *that* came from; I'm not normally theatrical."

"Do you try to do that often?"

"What?"

"Save people."

"I try to *help* people. But that's not the same as saving them, is it?"

"How often do you have this dream?"

"I used to have it a few times a year. But recently, I have the dream, or some derivative, every time I fall asleep. It's exhausting. Margaret's bicycle at the beginning is a recent development, but in the dreams, I'm often lost. I wander streets, woods, or shopping malls, calling my own name as if I was a lost pet."

"How do you mean?"

"Come on, girl. Come on, Penny. Time to go home."

"Certainly the dreams indicate a high level of anxiety. Could it be that you're the one who is angry and you want someone to save you? Well, perhaps *save* isn't the right word, but you know what I mean. Maybe you want help in balancing your responsibilities? It's not an unusual phenomenon. It's easy, with the best of intentions to take on too much and end up feeling resentful."

"I really don't feel that's the problem –"

Dr. Allen's cell phone buzzed. He looked at the caller I.D. and said, "I'm sorry, but I need to take this." Dr. Allen walked out of the room and into the hallway, but through the open door Penny could hear the doctor's side of the conversation. After he listened for a bit, he told the caller he was with a patient and since it wasn't an emergency, he would call back. Dr. Allen reminded the caller in a polite, yet firm voice that his office and home telephone numbers were on file, and they should use his cell number for emergency situations only. The doctor slipped the cell into his jacket pocket as he walked back into the room. He sat down again and picked up his pen, only to remember he had forgotten to shut the door. As he started to rise Penny stopped him.

"That's okay. Leave it. It's so warm in here; it feels better with the door open – that is, if you don't mind."

"It's fine." Returning to his notes, Dr. Allen asked, "So, is there some responsibility in your life that makes you feel overwhelmed?

"No."

"How about your work? Liv wrote in her notes that you own a retail business. That sounds like it could be quite demanding."

"It's not just a retail business. We're a non-profit shop and café. It's stressful when sales are slow. *Ruth and Naomi* is a business that supports impoverished women. It's just down the street from the hospital."

"I've heard the nurses talk about how good the coffee is."

"Many families depend upon the shop's success. We buy from women in developing countries, mostly in Kenya, Sierra Leone, and India. Sales have been very good with the approaching holidays. It's very rewarding work. Plus, Annalise, Mayra-Liz, and Eva are a great help. Michael and I affectionately call them "the girls," but we really should stop that. After all, they're grown women."

"Your employees?"

"They're so much more than employees. We consider them our family. They're sisters. Not my sisters, I was an only child. Annalise and Mayra-Liz work full time at the shop. Eva helps out during school holidays."

"Eva? Oh, I think there's a note about her in your chart. She's your foster daughter?"

"Yes. Annalise and Mayra-Liz had been living in a homeless shelter when I met them. They were twenty-one and nineteen, so young and for a couple of years they managed to live without any adult support and were raising their sister, Eva until things financially fell apart. Now, Annalise and Mayra-Liz live in the apartment over the shop. Eva was sixteen and in a group home when Michael and I became her foster parents. She's now in her first year at Siena College."

"It sounds to me like you have a lot on your plate, new parent, and running your own business."

"A lot of women take on a whole lot more."

"But you're not sleeping well. Everyone has their own limit to the amount of stress they can handle. The trick is finding the right balance. Insomnia is something we can try to address in a number of different ways. However, my main concern is that you ingested sleeping pills with alcohol, which can be a deadly combination. Surely, you must have realized the risks involved. Were you trying to end your life?"

"No! Of course not."

"And you hit yourself with a metal pipe."

"I don't know why I did that, I really don't."

Dr. Allen took more notes and then asked, "How were you feeling last week? Any depression, anxiety?"

"I guess ... a little. I don't like this time of the year. It all looks so bleak, doesn't it? But I wasn't feeling so badly that I tried to commit suicide. If I hadn't tried it before, I certainly wouldn't ..." Penny's voice trailed off while the distant clunk-clunk-clunk sound of someone walking down the tiled corridor filtered in through the open door of the conference room.

Dr. Allen waited for Penny to continue.

"I'm just saying that my life is really good. I have a good husband, business, and friends. There was a time when my life was difficult to say the least. I didn't try to end my life then or now. I know better than to take sleeping pills, even half of one, but I was just desperate for some sleep. I certainly didn't intend to take the entire bottle. And with alcohol!" Penny shook her head at her own foolishness.

A long minute of silence ticked by while Dr. Allen waited to see if his patient would add more information. When Penny remained quiet, he turned to her chart saying, "The CAT scan has been scheduled for tomorrow morning at 9:00. I also ordered some blood work."

"More blood work?"

"To rule out conditions that can cause insomnia such as a hormonal imbalance. I'd also like you to participate in a sleep clinic and small group counseling. We'll keep you quite busy while you're here. Do you have any questions?"

After Penny shook her head no, the doctor asked, "You said in your dreams you are trying to get away from someone. Since you feel the stress isn't internal, I need to ask you, is your home environment safe?"

"Michael is a wonderful man," Penny said defensively. "He's so good –" Penny was distracted by hearing a man whistling through his teeth. Jack used to do that. She heard his footsteps coming closer down the hall. Penny looked quickly away, and then braved a peek. Penny was relieved to see he was a stranger, although he did look odd wearing a janitor's uniform and a blue surgical mask, hat, and gloves. He glared defiantly back at Penny with such venom, it caused her to gasp.

Dr. Allen turned in his chair to follow her startled gaze and caught a glimpse of the masked janitor moving quickly away. "Young man!" Dr. Allen called causing the man to quicken his pace. Dr. Allen quickly rose and strode into the hallway.

"Young man!" Dr. Allen called again while asking himself under his breath what *is* his name? When it popped into his head, Dr. Allen called out, "Leonard!"

Leonard stopped, hunched his shoulders, turned, and walked back to Dr. Allen, mask and hat in his gloved hands hidden behind his back. Dr. Allen held out his hand in an unspoken request. Leonard, with his eyes downcast, handed them over.

"We've talked about this, Leonard. I told you not to take hospital supplies. I thought I made that perfectly clear when you took Dr. Chen's stethoscope. I also said you can't wear these, and that you can't say or act like you're a doctor. Do you recall that conversation?" Dr. Allen asked as Leonard struggled to remove the aqua blue, latex gloves.

"Uh huh. Are you going to tell Miss Loretta?" Leonard spoke with the immature voice of an adolescent, although he had graying hair and beard stubble.

"Yes," Dr. Allen replied.

"She said that she'd fire me if I did it again. They'll make me work at the grocery."

"Those were the choices you made, Leonard."

"If it was my choice, I'd stay at the hospital. I like it here."

"What I'm saying, Leonard, is since you chose to disobey the rules, and since you understood the consequences, you made the choice to not remain at the hospital. I'm with a patient now, so we'll talk about this later."

"It's *her* fault. If she hadn't seen me, it wouldn't be a problem," Leonard's voice rose as he glared at Penny.

"Go to the break room now. I'll meet you there when I'm done with this session."

Dr. Allen returned to find Penny shivering like a lost puppy.

"Are you all right?" he asked.

"Yes, I'm just terribly tired. I'd like to go back to my room now."

"Leonard isn't dangerous," Dr. Allen said. "He's just angry."

Penny nodded. She knew just how dangerous angry men can be.

41

Chapter Eight

What's Done is Done

Dr. Allen's cell phone buzzed again as he walked to his car. A different nurse from his mother's nursing home called to ask the same question he had been asked an hour ago. As he talked, he wandered around the parking lot looking for his car.

Well, this is embarrassing, Dr. Allen thought as he tried to look less like a lost soul and more like a purposeful physician. *Where on earth did I park it? Perhaps it was on the upper lot?* Dr. Allen thought back to the morning hours and remembered walking in with Cody McEneny that nice young man in Admissions who talked about the upcoming hockey game between Union and R.P.I. Dr. Allen shook his head. It made no sense, he was certain he had entered through the south entrance.

Perhaps I'm looking for the wrong car, Dr. Allen thought. *Did I drive Judith's Lexus in this morning?* He stopped to envision the car he arrived to work in and saw a blue 1941 Lincoln Continental. The image stopped him cold. The '41 Lincoln had been his father's. Dr. Allen stroked the top of his head and gripped his car key with his other hand. Three cars over to his right, his silver BMW tweeted and its headlights flashed, startling him.

That's it, decided Dr. Allen. *I'm calling Price today.* Dr. Allen had been talking himself in and out of making an appointment with his primary care physician for several months when memories and current events sometimes swirled together, tossing him into another dimension like an old Twilight Zone episode. The possible diagnosis of schizophrenia, brain tumor, or Alzheimer's caused Dr. Allen to delay the phone call.

I'm as bad as my patients, he thought as he opened his car door. *I leap to the worst possible conclusion, and then do nothing about it.* As he settled into the driver's seat a cold rain mixed with sleet started to fall. *No wonder people get depressed this time of year,* the doctor thought.

The nursing home was just up the road from the hospital which made it convenient for Dr. Allen to visit most afternoons on his way home. The nursing facility was only a few years old, yet it had the façade of a European manor. He parked in a lot at the side of the building and reached into the back seat to retrieve a tin of chocolate wafers. Entering the spacious day room, he saw his mother in a wheelchair looking out the window towards the bird feeders. He had chosen this facility over an equally recommended one because of the birds that visited the courtyard. Both establishments were well furnished, professionally staffed, and reasonably fresh-smelling. But the birds were the deciding factor. He had optimistically imagined his mother actively engaged in observing them. However, he wasn't sure she realized the birds were there, even though he often pointed them out.

When he was a child his mother hung bags of suet and filled bird feeders with sunflower seeds. Their backyard had been alive with the vibrant colors and songs of goldfinches, chickadees, blue jays, and cardinals. His mother had loved watching the birds and made up stories about their lives. "Oh look, Paddy! Ain't he a proud fella with all them shiny red and black feathers! See how hard he's working on his nest. He's really trying to impress his lady friend, he is." Outside her window, his mother watched bird families who lived more harmoniously than her own, for no one, not even his saintly mother could appease her miserable husband. Why on earth had she married him in the first place?

Dr. Allen's present view faded and the past sharpened where he saw his much younger mother, Mrs. Elemona McGinley Allen darning socks, a basket of mending on the floor at her feet. She was chatting in her kitchen with the neighborhood women, cups of tea on the table. Three of the seven women had babies in their arms. While the other women fussed and fumed about their husbands, his mother never complained. She had been raised to believe ladies shouldn't say anything if they couldn't find something nice to say.

"Anyone wanting more tea?" Dr. Allen could hear his mother's voice with the soft Irish lilt that never left her. It was the one thing his father couldn't squash.

"Why can't you talk like a normal person?" he would snarl.

"Me is?" She was so unsure of herself when speaking to her husband that she made every sentence sound like a question. Early in their marriage she had learned that nothing she said was ever right in his view, and she tried not to upset him. Yet, Elemona Allen had braved her

44

husband's fists when he went after their children. She had done everything she could to keep her children safe including talking to the local priest whose advice was to pray to be a better wife so her husband wasn't driven to drink and rage. *Thank God, priests have changed since that oppressive time,* Dr. Allen thought.

"Hello, Dr. Allen," a nurse greeted him as she hurried past, jarring him fully back into the present. He looked at his mother in the atrium, no longer young and darning socks, and was taken aback by her appearance. It wasn't just that she had moved in his mind from being young to being old. It was how Alexandra, his mother's favorite aide, had transformed his mother. Gone were the cotton dresses paired with darned cardigan sweaters. Now, the only clothes she wore were pastel-colored sweat suits. Alexandra had talked him into buying them.

"Elemona needs ... " the aide had started to say.

Dr. Allen raised an annoyed eyebrow.

"Sorry, I mean Mrs. Allen. You know, she really doesn't mind me calling her Elemona."

"But I mind," Dr. Allen informed her. "Now, what does my mother need?"

"Pants."

"Pants? You mean slacks? My mother doesn't wear slacks."

"But she's chilly in those cotton dresses and nylon stockings. And really, no one wears garter belts anymore. Well, not unless –"

"Yes, I catch your drift," Dr. Allen had interrupted her. "I'll ask my mother if she wants different clothes."

"She doesn't *know* that she wants different clothes. Has she ever worn anything but dresses?"

"Certainly not."

"Well, there you go."

Dr. Allen's mother was enthralled with her new wardrobe. "I haven't been this warm and comfortable since me was a girl in pigtails. I have the most thoughtful son in the world."

His mother's auburn hair had long ago turned to dishwater-gray. Alexandra talked his mother into having a light auburn/blonde rinse added at the nursing home's beauty shop. *It does look nice,* Dr. Allen silently admitted, although he could have done without the big purple bow worn jauntily next to her curled bangs. Dr. Allen had considered informing the beauty shop that he didn't want pink strands added to his mother's hair in case Alexandra decided *that* would be a good look for his mother, too. But he didn't, because what did it matter? Perhaps his mother would like pink hair. She was certainly over the moon about her purple, glittery nail polish. He had to hand it to Alexandra; she certainly paid his mother a great deal of attention. Even on the days when his mother's mind was vacant, Alexandra still sang to his mother while brushing her hair or rubbing her arms with lotion.

Dr. Allen realized his mother was smiling at him from across the room, but that didn't mean she was in the here and now. As he approached, the doctor evaluated his mother, looking for signs of engaged, rational behavior. Dr. Allen considered the day a gift when she said, "Oh Paddy, look at that cardinal. Ain't he handsome?"

"Yes, Mother! He's beautiful." He leaned down and brushed her cheek with a kiss while placing the cookie tin on her lap.

"Me favorites!" she exclaimed. "How thoughtful of ya."

Dr. Allen gave a silent prayer of thanks for his mother's clarity. Then he thought, *do you really think it's God that turns your mother's delusions off and on?*

They watched the birds in silence for a while until Dr. Allen tried to make conversation by asking, "What did you do today?"

Instead of a shrug of the shoulders he sometimes received, she animatedly recalled her morning. "One of the young lasses got engaged and there was a big hullabaloo about that, I tell ya. Have you *seen* the things that they give at bridal showers now a day? In my day, we gave gifts of hand-embroidered dish towels and tea cozies. Today, the bride-to-be opened presents of giant rubber ..."

His mother whispered the word so softly with her hand over her mouth that Patrick couldn't hear her, but he understood she was talking about gifts in phallus shapes.

"They had them *everywhere*. They even had a mobile of them hanging from the ceiling. They even served *you know what* shaped cupcakes! They offered me one and I said, 'Oh, no thank you, dear. I didn't care to have *that* anywheres near me mouth when I was married, and I certainly don't plan on starting up today.' God love us. We were roaring with laughter, we were."

Patrick smiled warmly at his mother. It was lovely to see her animated. A man seated in an armchair across the room next to the gas fireplace started to softly snore. Patrick and his mother turned their attention to the elderly gentleman. In contrast to the sweat suit attire so much in vogue at the home, he wore a three piece worsted suit complete with a pocket watch and fob, with a gold chain nattily draped across his vest. The man's wavy, steel-colored hair looked freshly cut. Patrick thought the man's hair was thicker than his own. Patrick was admiring the gentleman's freshly polished wingtips resting on the upholstered footstool when his mother said, "That's Mr. Westley. He's deaf as a door knob, but he *is* handsome, ain't he? I received a marriage proposal from him last week."

Patrick looked alarmed.

"Ah, you needn't worry. I don't care to be trying' that again."

They both grimaced in the same inherited facial expression as painful memories flitted past. Remembering the battles they survived with his father, Patrick reached down like a soldier in solidarity, and rested his hand very lightly on her shoulder. Ever since she began slowly sliding down into Alzheimer's, his mother didn't care to be touched. But today, she reached up and patted his hand. The day room was quiet, but in the distance they heard dinner for hundreds being prepared.

"That butterscotch pudding smells like home, don't it?" Mrs. Allen said. "Remember how I used to make it for ya when you were little?"

"I remember."

His mother became quiet; her hand went limp and slid down to her lap. Patrick assumed his mother had fallen asleep, but when he kneeled down next to her as he always did to say goodbye his mother looked back with open eyes, huge with emotion.

"I remember," anxiety edging his mother's voice. "I remember *everything*."

He knew where this was going. "Some things are best left forgotten," Patrick implored, as he nervously smoothed his head.

"Sha," she said, a Gaelic response for the affirmative. "What's done is done. Can never be undone."

"Shhh," he said as he tried to simultaneously soothe and hush her. It always amazed him how Alzheimer's patients could be in the present one moment and then gone in a heartbeat, whisked away by their own tortured mind. All one could do was watch them go.

"Filleann an feall ar an bhfeallaire!" His mother spat the Gaelic words at him.

"What does that mean?" Patrick asked, and then not sure he wanted the translation announced to the room at large, even if it meant the only audience was a sleeping, deaf man. Patrick returned to hushing her.

She glared at her son. "The bad deed returns on the bad deed doer!" his mother shrieked as shrill as a short-changed gypsy.

"We weren't bad!" he said sounding like an unjustly-accused twelve year old. His own lapsed adolescent whine startled the doctor almost as much as his mother's chilling pronouncement. He quickly recovered, smoothed his head, and stated with professional authority, "You mustn't upset yourself, Mother. What you need to do is –"

"When I die, he'll get me. He'll get me! And he'll get you too!" Her eyes darted around the room as if evil could spring out from any corner. She drew in a breath so deep that it caused her body to quiver. Like a child with skinned knees, she used the deeply inhaled breath as momentum for the exhaled wail.

"Mother, calm down! You must consider your blood pressure."

But his mother had gone around the emotional bend and kept on running. Her toddler's wail escalated into a howl of pain and fury.

"It's all right, Mrs. Allen. No one's going to hurt you," the nurse spoke up over the racket as she hurried into the room. "If you promise not tell anyone, I'll dish you up some warm butterscotch pudding, and you can have it *before* dinner."

Mrs. Allen held her face between her hands as she sobbed.

She looks like Munch's painting, The Scream, Patrick thought. *I wonder if Edvard had worried someone would get him when he died.* Patrick rubbed his hand over his own face, checking to see if he held the same expression. He certainly felt like screaming. Screaming and screaming and screaming, until his voice gave out.

Chapter Nine

Harriett Tubman

Eva, the youngest of Michael and Penny's "adopted daughters," answered her cell phone on the second ring and whispered "Hello?"

"E," Michael said.

"Hang on," Eva continued to whisper, "My roommate's sleeping. Give me a minute."

Eva had been getting ready for her eight a.m. philosophy class. She set the phone down on her green and gold bedspread with the big Saint Bernard paw designed in the center, and quickly finished packing her book bag. Eva kicked her sneakers under her bed. Emily, her roommate, hated clutter, and Eva was trying to accommodate.

Eva smiled as she thought of Michael. He was the one who had given her the nickname E. The only nickname she ever had. Michael was technically her foster father, but she loved him like a big brother. Eva has a father, but he was nothing like Michael. Michael was fun. He made up little songs about her and her sisters and sang them off-key. The walls of their home were lined with photographs Michael had taken of them. Before Eva met Penny and Michael there had never been a portrait of Eva framed, not that there had been many photographs of her or her sisters.

There hadn't been enough money to buy school pictures, so Eva suffered the embarrassment of returning her school photo packet unopened while her classmates exchanged mini photos with each other with cutesy lines written on the back like: "2 cute 2 be 4 gotten." Eva's father had no time or money for fun or frills. He had been too busy trying to keep food on the table and a roof over their heads. Her father loved her and her sisters. Now, he was in prison, but that didn't mean he was a bad person. Try explaining that! She didn't even try.

People thought of Eva as a quiet girl. What they didn't know was that Eva thought once, twice, often three times before contributing to the conversation. By the time she was ready to talk, oftentimes the subject had veered into other areas, and Eva would need to start the process all over again. Eva needed to think through what she said because she believed there was so much that she couldn't say.

Like her first overnight visit to Siena College, when she had been a senior in high school. Eva walked with her host, Amy, to the cafeteria. The two of them had had a great evening. They had gone to a magic show, a couple of boys had shown some interest, and Eva had won at Bingo. Even after they got to the dorm, they stayed up chatting. Well, Amy chatted and Eva enjoyed listening to her. They didn't fall asleep until two in the morning. They arrived at the cafeteria at seven, still groggy with sleep.

"Okay," began Amy as she handed Eva a tray, "if you're a big breakfast person, you can have the chef fix you an omelet. Just let her know what you want in it: cheese, mushrooms, tomatoes, peppers .... She also makes scrambled eggs. There's a waffle iron over there. The batter's all prepared, so you just make your own. Over here are the dispensers for cold cereal, but we don't have Coco-puffs." Amy made a pouty face to show it was a great disappointment. "At the juice fountain we have apple, orange, and grape. If you're like me, you'll just grab a pastry and a cup of coffee. Oh, and I forgot, they always have cooked cereal: oatmeal, cream of wheat, that kind of thing."

Eva set her tray down on the counter and ran out of the cafeteria. Amy placed her own tray on top of Eva's and ran after her, catching up just inside the entry doors. "What is it? What's wrong? Are you sick?" Amy asked.

The commotion caught the attention of Mrs. Henry, a Higher Education Opportunity Program (HEOP) advisor, who was entering the dining hall. She stopped by the two girls and touched Amy's arm lightly. "Give us a minute, okay? We'll meet you back inside the cafeteria in a bit." Amy nodded, and walked toward their abandoned trays, turning once to look back at Eva.

"What is it, dear?" Mrs. Henry asked Eva when they were alone.

"It's nothing. I'm just tired, you know, up all night chatting."

Mrs. Henry nodded. "When I first went to college, I found all the food choices overwhelming. And no one else seemed to think such abundance was out of the ordinary. I guess they weren't from a family like mine who had a single pot of pasta on the table night after night. Of course, that's when Dad was working and things were going well. I still have a

50

difficult time seeing students take twice as much food as they can possibly eat and throwing half of it out."

"It was the oatmeal," Eva confided, lowering her head to look at her shoes. "Someone had given us a case of it because the box had been damaged on the truck. It had gotten damp, so the oatmeal tasted a little moldy. But we ate oatmeal for weeks and were happy to have it." Eva looked up at Mrs. Henry and gave her a small smile. "This was back when I lived with just my sisters. There's always plenty of food at Penny and Michael's, I don't know why it felt overwhelming today. I have a feeling I'll gain more than the standard *Freshmen fifteen* when I come here, either that or I'll be too overwhelmed to eat anything."

Mrs. Henry smiled back at Eva, "I don't think you have to worry about either of those things, Eva," she said softly. "Just try to enjoy the pleasure of having choices. Later on in life, your pleasure will double when you also help others to have more choices. It's a wonderful thing."

Eva nodded. "I should get back before Amy thinks I'm a total freak."

It was comforting that Mrs. Henry understood about food and being poor, but Eva doubted Mrs. Henry or *anyone* outside Eva's family could possibly understand that her father went to jail *because* he loved his daughters. Lest they judge him and her, Eva didn't mention the situation to anyone. How could Eva say that some of her weekends included a visit to *Copper John*, the nickname Eva and her sisters gave to the Auburn Correctional Facility in honor of the statue of the colonial soldier looking down from the facility's apex?

Why a colonial soldier? Eva often wondered. It was as if he guarded the Hessians and not her gentle father who had tried to rob a convenience store with a chocolate bar. It was wrong what her father had done, but why give a man who had never been in trouble before the maximum sentence?

The courtroom experience had been a nightmare. Her father's shame was so great, he wept. It was the only time Eva had ever seen her father cry. The court appointed attorney kept forgetting her father's name, referring to him as Mr. Mentos instead of Muñoz. *As if our father was a breath mint,* Eva thought. His lawyer yawned throughout the trial until the judge finally asked if the defense was in need of sleep. The attorney apologized profusely to the judge, but didn't seem too concerned about his client's fate. The girls had compiled lists of the good deeds their father had done. Several of her father's friends and the local priest had come to give testimony to Mr. Muñoz's good character, but the lawyer didn't call them to the stand. It was obvious the bored attorney was ready to go home, put his feet up, and have a drink.

After family visiting days, Michael often took Eva to Harriet Tubman's last home which was a few miles away from the prison. He said there were always different points of view to photograph, but Eva knew what he was doing. He was showing her that everyone has their trials. It's how you handle adversity that reveals your character. Eva knew it was stupid and she never told her sisters, but Eva often prayed to Harriett Tubman to watch over her father.

With her book bag organized, Eva shouldered it. She took a brief look into the mirror next to the door and frowned at her reflection. *Will I ever lose those plump baby cheeks?* Eva asked herself as she quietly closed the door behind her. Once she was in the hallway, Eva spoke into her phone with a smile in her voice, "Aren't you the early bird. What's up?"

"Listen, I've got something to tell you and I don't know how to say it except to just blurt it out. Penny's in the hospital again. She'll be fine, but she mixed sleeping pills with alcohol. Something you should never do. It's dangerous."

"Penny, did what?" Eva exclaimed as she leaned against the wall for support, her shoulders drooped in shock.

"You okay?" asked a girl who lived down the hall.

Eva nodded a yes.

"Are you sure?"

"It's okay," Eva said. The girl nodded and moved on.

"Yes, she'll be fine," Michael confirmed.

"What happened? She wasn't trying to ... She must have known. What was she thinking?"

"She didn't mean to. She hasn't been sleeping well and she just, got careless."

"I'm taking the bus home. I can be in Schenectady by nine."

"No, don't do that E, Penny would feel awful if you missed classes. I'll come and get you on Saturday. Really, everything is under control."

"I thought you were coming to get me on Friday evening so I can help out."

"Friday?"

"Penny's birthday party. Don't we have thirty-some people coming on Saturday?"

"Damn!" Michael exclaimed. "I completely forgot about it. I don't know if Penny will be released from the hospital by then, and even if she is, I doubt she'll feel like attending a party."

"I really think I should come to the hospital. I'm not going to be able to concentrate in class anyway."

"The best thing you can do for Penny today is to go to class and focus on your studies."

"How can I possibly do that?"

Michael sighed, "When does your last class end?"

"12:30."

"Okay, here's the deal. Go to your classes and I'll pick you up at 12:45. You can visit with Penny, and then I'll drive you back to Siena. You'll feel better seeing for yourself that she's okay. I hated to call and tell you, but we felt you should know."

"We?"

"Your sisters and I decided we needed to be up front; but you can't, I repeat *can't* let this affect your studies."

"I know. I won't let it. I'll meet you outside Siena Hall at 12:45."

"I love you, E. We all do. It's going to be all right. It was just an accident."

"Love you too," Eva said as she ended the call. She ran to class, but Eva was late and her professor hated that. As unobtrusively as possible she slid into a chair and got out her textbook. It opened to a bookmark with green printing and a gold tassel, the college's colors. Penny had made the marker during the end of summer when Eva started getting butterflies about going to college.

"What if I can't manage all the work? What if I don't fit in? What if my roommate doesn't like me?" Eva had fretted. Penny had listened to Eva's apprehensions for days and had tried to calm her fears.

"Remember you have an advisor with H.E.O.P. *and* an academic advisor," Penny told her. "You had those classes in July to help you get acclimated. You'll do fine."

Still Eva carried on, her anxiety level at an all-time high. Finally, Penny said, "Look, you have never been a sissy. I can't believe you're going to turn into one now. The future doesn't get any easier by worrying about it. Always face the day with courage, Eva."

Eva rubbed her finger over the raised letters of the bookmark.

I can't believe it, Eva thought. *Penny mixed drugs and alcohol. Penny!*

Eva grew up in a rough part of town where drug and alcohol use was rampant. One of Eva's earliest childhood memories involved her mother and a frightening drug deal. As an adolescent, Eva had hated her mother for abandoning them until Penny convinced Eva that she should look upon her mother's leaving as a selfless act.

"It could well be that she left *because* she loves you. She didn't feel strong enough to break the addiction, but she didn't want to expose her daughters to it. In her own way, she was protecting you."

Eventually, Eva believed it. But today Penny's theory seemed too Pollyanna, and Eva wondered if Penny really believed it herself. Maybe she was just trying to help heal Eva's hurts. A tear dropped on her textbook page.

I can't have this, Eva thought. *This is my chance to build my life. I have to pay attention.*

Eva concentrated on Dr. Ferte's lecture. She raised her hand and answered questions from last night's homework. Taking notes, she kept reining in straying thoughts. *This afternoon,* Eva reminded herself, *not now, I'll learn what's what this afternoon.*

The clock clicked to 9:00. *One class down, two to go,* Eva thought. As she started to the door, Dr. Ferte called to her.

"Eva, can you stay for a minute?"

Eva was full of apprehension as she approached her professor. *He's read my homework, and he doesn't believe I'm college material,* Eva thought.

"Eva, I read your homework last night. You had many interesting opinions. You obviously completed the readings and thought through what you wanted to say. However, your paragraphs were disjointed, and you didn't write in the format we discussed. I'd like you to go to the Writing Center with your next assignment."

"Okay ... I will," Eva said with a meek voice.

"You'll like the folks at the Writing Center," he encouraged. "And come and see me during my office hours, and we'll talk some more."

Afraid her voice would break if she spoke, she simply nodded and turned to leave.

"You dropped something," Dr. Ferte called out.

He picked up the bookmark and read it out loud, "Lord, I'm going to hold steady onto you. And you've got to see me through." He frowned. "I know the quote, but I can't place the author."

"It was someone who was brave, good, and true," Eva said, her voice indeed breaking. "Someone people could count on."

Chapter Ten

Live Right

"I'm sorry to awaken you Penny, but it's time for your CT scan," Liv said.

Penny gave a look of disbelief as she ran her fingers through her hair.

"I'm hospitalized because of insomnia, but when I get a moment of sleep, I'm awakened."

"A hospital is not a fun place to be, that's for sure," Liv replied. "You need to get better so you can go home, having a decent breakfast is a good place to start."

"I just don't have an appetite."

"Come on, get your skates on or you'll miss your time."

Penny regarded the nurse's face and reflected that the liberal sprinkling of freckles across her cheeks and nose gave her a youthful air and that the faint lines at the corners of her eyes and mouth seemed complementary, rather than telltale. The nurse was of color, tall, and slender leaning towards statuesque. A person of integrity was Penny's initial impression. It was those eyes. The nurse's large, dark eyes stood out on her petite face like beautiful illuminated letters on a page of scripture.

A page of scripture is probably what she reads every morning, Penny decided; then quickly questioned her own evaluation. Was she stereotyping? Penny knew she didn't think of all people of color as Bible reading enthusiasts. No, it was because this woman carried with her an aura of Christian moderation in dress, makeup, calories, and scent. The scent being that of primroses, a smell that comforted Penny because it reminded her of Margaret.

As they walked down the hall, Liv pulled her cell phone out of her pocket. "I'm calling the kitchen and ordering you some food. I saw the tray they took out of your room; you hardly ate a thing. Do you like grits?"

"Yes, actually I do, if they're cooked properly. I lived in New Orleans for a while; they make the best grits in the world."

"Second best. No one, not even my Mama, cooks grits better than Norma. Well, here we are. They'll call me when you're done, and I'll walk you back."

"At least I'll be able to sleep while I'm in there."

"You'll be able to sleep through a CT scan with its buzzing, clicking, and whirring sounds? Don't get me wrong it's not as bad as an MRI which sounds like machine guns going off in a barrel. Well," Liv said with a shrug, "maybe you will be able to sleep through it. God knows you're tired enough."

"So, how'd it go?" Liv asked when she returned to retrieve Penny.

"You were right; it was O.K. but it's really no place to sleep. Plus, it was over almost before it began."

"Hey Liv," one of the nurses said as they passed in the hall. Liv smiled a greeting in reply.

"Is Liv short for Olivia?" Penny asked.

"It's not short for anything. My mother was forty when I was born, her first and only. She was way past hope of ever having a child. When her friends came to call, they told her she must be living right to have such a healthy, pretty baby at *her age*. Some folks are just not known for their tact, are they? Anyway, my mother decided to incorporate our last name, Wright with Liv. It's served me well, reminds me of how I started out in this world – loved and wanted."

"Sounds like you had a golden childhood."

"I wouldn't go that far, but I always felt loved even when my folks made choices for me that *they* thought were for the best, but *I* knew were not. I promised myself I would do better by my kids. Of course, that's what each generation says. You'd think we'd get it right eventually, wouldn't you?"

"You have children?"

"Three boys. Men, really. 36, 34, and 31."

"If they take after you, they must be heartthrobs."

"They're all the spittin' image of my husband; you'd think I had no involvement at all. And yes, they are handsome men," Liv smiled. "Martin, the eldest, is an engineer, currently working in Stockholm. The middle child, Mathew, is a doctor, an internist. The youngest, Merrill, is in construction and getting married next summer."

"Three sons! You were outnumbered. What does your husband do?"

"He's a police officer, detective."

"How did you meet?" Penny asked. "I love to hear about romance."

"Oh good, your tray arrived. Well, what do you think, Miss Penny?"

"It looks like it belongs in a fancy restaurant. How *ever* did you arrange this?"

There was a steaming bowl of grits with a sliced banana, maple syrup in a small stainless steel pitcher, buttered wheat toast with strawberry jam, and a mug of hot chocolate with a swirl of cream. A white napkin with blue piping was wrapped around the silverware.

"It's just so comforting – the aroma, the presentation. It just makes me want to sigh," Penny said.

"But does it make you want to eat?"

Penny picked up the spoon and sampled the grits. It was divine. Penny looked at Liv to say so, but the nurse was already nodding. Penny's expression had said it all.

"Thank you, Liv. It's just what I needed."

"When you're done, I'll pay close attention to your door, and let no one bother you until you get some more sleep. You shouldn't sleep too much during the day, but if you don't get some rest you'll be too tired to sleep tonight. I'll watch the monitor and if I see you're starting with a nightmare, I'll awaken you. Does that give you comfort?"

Penny nodded.

"We want you fresh and alert for when you meet with Dr. Allen," Liv said. "He's an excellent doctor, Penny. He can help you, if you let him."

When Michael and Eva walked up to the nurses' station, Liv informed them that Penny was sleeping.

"She's doing much better," Liv told them. "But I'd like her to sleep a bit longer. Could you come back at two?"

"Sure," Michael said. "Eva and I can grab some coffee."

Liv got up from her desk and watched Michael and Eva go down the hall. Liv believed she was a good judge of character, but she hadn't fully formed her opinion of Michael.

"Penny," Liv said softly, "You need to wake up now. You've been sleeping for a couple of hours. Michael and Eva will be in to see you soon."

"Eva? Eva's here? How does she look?"

"She looked ... concerned," Liv answered. As Michael and Eva entered the room, Liv went out but she kept a close eye on the monitor.

The visit started out easily enough when out of the blue, Eva started crying.

"What is it, sweetheart?" Penny asked.

"How could you have done such a thing? You could have died!" Eva angrily sobbed.

"Eva, I didn't mean to –"

"Do you think that makes it okay, that simply being *careless* makes it any better? The results would have been the same."

"No, it wasn't okay," Penny replied.

"You don't care about me. I used to think you did, but you're just like everyone else."

Liv saw Penny looked genuinely distressed. With professional decorum, Liv entered the patient's room in time to hear Michael say, "We're all upset, E, but your anger isn't helping anyone, is it?" as he handed her his handkerchief.

"I have no idea what to think about anything anymore," Eva said as she ran out of the room.

"Go to her, Michael," Penny said. "Make her understand that I –"

Penny didn't finish the sentence as her worried husband was already out the door. She looked over at Liv and said, "Eva's not normally like that. I'm sure it was a shock."

Liv sat down and held Penny's hand. "Your Michael seems like a good father figure," Liv said.

"He really is, so caring," Penny replied.

"How long has he been involved with the fair trade projects?" Liv asked. She looked over and saw two young women standing hesitatingly in the doorway. Liv gestured it was all right for them to enter.

"Annalise, Mayra-Liz," Penny called to them as lovingly as naming beads on a rosary. "Come in!"

They were strikingly beautiful. Annalise was a bit shorter, but still tall by any standard. Their glossy, dark hair flowed in long, full waves down their perfectly-postured backs. They were impeccably dressed on thrift store finds. Their skin looked like milk chocolate in color and texture, setting off their eyes that were fringed with dark, full lashes. Yet, they carried their beauty like exotic butterflies, oblivious of their dazzle as they focused on family and responsibilities. For the past couple of years, gratitude for their many blessings showed in their happy countenances. But today, they wore worried brows. The sisters stepped into the room, one on each side of the bed, and hugged and kissed Penny. They brought flowers and chocolate embossed with the shop's name, *Ruth and Naomi*.

"How are you feeling?" Annalise asked as she hugged Penny close a second time.

"I feel *stupid;* I've upset Eva," Penny said in a self-berating voice. "She ran out of the room. Michael went after her. I'm surprised you didn't see them in the hall."

"I'll go see if I can find them. Mayra-Liz, you visit with Penny," Annalise ordered with big sister authority.

Liv went back to the nurse's station, while Mayra-Liz pulled a chair close to Penny's bed, sat down, and held her friend's hand. "Are you okay?" she asked quietly.

"Yes," Penny said brushing Mayra-Liz's concern aside. "I just feel so awful that I've upset Eva. She must feel like she had another parent abandon her."

Mayra-Liz winced.

"I'm sorry! I shouldn't have said that."

"It's okay."

"How can I convince her that I'm not going anyplace?"

"Don't go anyplace," Mayra-Liz said looking off into the distance.

Eva, Michael, and Annalise returned. Eva looked less angry, but still distraught as she apologized. "I'm sorry, Penny. It was unfair of me to be critical when you're not feeling well. I'm sure we can sort out our feelings about this later."

Penny heard Eva's voice, but they all recognized Annalise's tone. It must be what she prompted Eva to say. An awkward silence filled the room until Liv poked her head in.

"I hate to interrupt," Liv said, "But Penny will be meeting with Dr. Allen soon."

There were hugs and kisses goodbye with last minute advice about the shop and encouragement given to Eva to study hard. Penny gave another round of apologies, and then her visitors were gone. Penny settled back on the pillows and heaved a deep sigh.

"It feels like out-of-town company that just left after a three week visit, doesn't it?" said Liv.

"Yes, and it's really wrong of me to feel that way, after the way I upset everyone."

"You never let up on yourself, do you?" Liv replied.

"What I did was just awful, even though I didn't mean for it to happen. I must be more responsible. People count on me. I can't imagine what this has done to Eva. She had been doing so well. She had learned to trust and rely on Michael and me, and now this!"

Liv's cell phone rang. When she ended the call, Penny said, "So, I guess I'll be seeing Dr. Allen now."

"Well ... no. That was the front desk. Dr. Allen can't meet with you today. He has a family concern, and won't be in. Dr. Reed will cover. You're scheduled to meet with him in an hour."

"Oh, that's too bad. I liked Dr. Allen, but I'm sure that Dr. Reed is good too."

Liv looked away.

"Liv? Do you not like Dr. Reed?"

"He's certainly qualified, as educated as they come, well published."

"But you don't like him."

"Oh, I wouldn't say that."

"So, you do like him?"

Liv gave a brief smile. From there, her facial expressions ranged from deliberation to decision. Liv punched in a phone number. With professional decorum she said, "Hello, this is Liv Wright; please inform Dr. Reed that Penny Morgan may be coming down with a cold."

"I am?" Penny started to ask. "Because I don't think –" Liv's expression would have stopped a naughty preschooler in her tracks.

After Liv hung up, she explained, "Dr. Reed suffers from mysophobia."

"From what?"

"He's afraid of germs." Liv shook her head and the rolling of her eyes said, *oh the fools we are required to endure.* "Reporting an alleged cold is what my mother would have called, *considerin' the greater good.* You need to talk. I'm worried that you're going to spend ten minutes with that ... with Dr. Reed and decide it's a good idea to keep your thoughts to yourself. But I can tell that you're going to positively explode if you don't share what's going on inside that head of yours."

"What makes you think something's going on? I just need to sleep."

"Yes, you do need to sleep, but you told me when you first awakened that you needed to make him stop. Something is going on. If you want, you can confide in me."

Liv's phone rang. After a brief one-sided conversation Liv hung up the phone and reported, "Okay. That's taken care of. Dr. Reed won't be seeing you today; he's ordered you to bed rest. My shift ended, but I'll tell the next shift nurse that I'll stay on for a while. You can tell me your whole story, if you wish, without interruption."

Penny stared at the nurse in amazement. "Good thing you use your powers for good, Liv Wright."

Chapter Eleven

Hell to Pay

Earlier that day, Drs. Patrick and Judith Allen were hurrying to their car from the nursing home in a cold, biting wind when they were approached by a woman who held up Judith's fifth self-help book.

"Aren't you?" the woman asked pointing to the author's photograph on the back dust jacket. "I had heard your mother is staying here, too."

"Mother-in-law," Judith corrected.

"How is she?"

"She had a rough night, but she's sleeping now." Judith said as she continued towards the car.

"I think your book is just ... but in chapter eleven I wonder if –" the wind carrying the ends of her sentences away. Judith gave a nod and a forced smile, but didn't slow her purposeful stride. She was cold, exhausted, and worried definitely not in the mood to chat with an opinionated stranger. Neither Judith nor Patrick were dressed for the cold. When the nursing home had called late in the night to report that Mrs. Allen was distraught, Patrick and Judith grabbed the first jackets they found, both of which turned out to be too lightweight for the change in weather. Patrick shivered as he unlocked the car doors.

"Would you like me to drive?" Judith asked.

"Why?" Patrick asked, as he slid into the driver's seat.

"I thought you might be feeling –"

"I'm fine."

They rode in silence during the short drive to their home. Patrick pulled up to the front to drop Judith off.

"I'd like you to come inside," Judith said, her hand resting on his arm. "I'll make breakfast."

"I have to get to the hospital. I'm already behind."

61

"We have to talk about this."

"We can talk tonight."

"Who is your mother afraid of?"

"You know my mother has dementia. She lives in her own frightened world."

"But you looked frightened, too."

"Of course, it's upsetting for me to see my mother like that, screaming like a banshee," Patrick's voice sounded weary with a touch of condescension. Apparently, he had forgotten in that moment that he had more than *met his match* in the woman he married. When faced with something she cared about, Judith didn't back down, not an inch. And Patrick was on the top of her list of what she cared about the most.

"'He'll find me, he'll find me, *and then* there'll be hell to pay.' That's what she said and you went positively pale. Patrick, what *is* it?"

Patrick started to shake his head indicating that it was nothing.

"Patrick, *tell* me," she insisted. "You're upset and it's something more than your Mother's health. What is going on?"

Patrick took off his glasses and rubbed his eyes.

"All right," he said as he replaced his glasses and turned off the car engine. "I should have told you years ago." The doctor paused, collecting his thoughts, and began with a deadpan voice. "My mother believes completely in the afterlife. She believes all who confess their sins will live forever. She also believes her husband, my father, prayed for forgiveness before he died." Patrick squinted his eyes, grit his teeth, and continued with an angry tone of voice Judith rarely heard from her husband. "He was a mean son-of-a-bitch. But my Mother believes, by prayer, he was spared the fires of eternal damnation. She also believes my father could never truly change. I know the logic is flawed, but my mother believes when she and I die, my father will take his revenge."

"Revenge? For what? What happened?"

Patrick looked away.

"Patrick?"

"We killed him."

Chapter Twelve

The Beginning

"I don't know where to start," Penny said. "And there's so much to tell, much of it will seem unbelievable."

"I always favor the beginning. Just start there and work your way through," replied Liv.

Penny took a deep breath. "Okay. Well, it started in high school. He was the most handsome boy there. Not a boy really; he seemed older than the rest of us, like he had already experienced life. There was something about him that was just intriguing. All of us girls felt it. He seemed strong and self-assured, and yet there was something vulnerable about him that lay just below the surface. He was Native American. Cherokee, the kids said. He didn't talk about that either."

"This isn't Michael, you're talking about."

"Gosh no, I didn't meet Michael until I was 32. So, this boy and I both worked at a neighbor's farm one summer, and just like that, I was in love. We both felt it. I guess I still believe that. Before we knew it, the hay was in, the summer was over, and it was our senior year with graduation approaching. Neither one of us had any idea of what we were going to do after high school, except we wanted to do it together.

"His grandparents gave him an older car for graduation. It was a pale yellow Chevy station wagon with fake wood panels. Our friends teased him; they called the car The Queen Bee. Someone put a Navy Seabee sticker on the bumper. You know the design? A muscular bee with his sleeves rolled up holding a machine gun and tools. Anyway, folks started asking him if he planned to enlist. An elderly man came over once, thumped him on the back and said, 'Thank you, Son for serving this great country.' It's crazy when you think about it, that a bumper sticker would be the start of it all, because he did join the Navy. Since he had a steady job in the military, the start of a career even, we saw no reason not to get married right away. Margaret was against it. Well, that hardly describes it. I had never seen her in such a state," Penny shook her head as she revisited some long ago scene in her mind.

"Margaret was my great-aunt. She raised me. My parents were killed in a car accident when I was a baby. Margaret had been an Army nurse in the prime of her career when it happened, but she took a hardship discharge when she saw there was no one else to step up to the plate. Anyway, Margaret couldn't understand why we had to get married right away. 'Give it a year; see what happens,' she had encouraged. Margaret had already tried the, 'you're too young to know what you want approach' and had gotten no place. Then, Margaret wondered if I was in the family way. 'Pregnancy doesn't have to mean marriage. I don't want you to think you have no choices. You do.' But I wasn't pregnant and I wasn't changing my mind. Margaret fussed about it for days and days until I grew weary of it, so I uttered the name that stopped the argument cold .... Uncle Damiano," Penny said with a grimace, as if the name itself made her stomach flip.

"I was six years old when Margaret and I went to London to visit her old friend, Jackie and her new husband. Aunt Jackie had married late in life to a man she had met in Italy. Uncle Damiano had a constant five o'clock shadow. He had been one of those dark, handsome fellows who aged well. It was obvious to Margaret that Jackie and Damiano adored each other, and Margaret was happy for her friend.

"One lazy afternoon during our visit, Aunt Jackie got out a deck of cards. I was all ready to participate. Margaret had taught me how to play crazy eights and hearts and at the ripe old age of six, I thought I was a card connoisseur. But Margaret said no, I wouldn't understand the rules as they had designed their own, why didn't I go play in the back yard.

"'I don't like the neighbor's dog,' I had whined."

"'Penny, he's behind a fence. He's not going to hurt you.'"

"But I just shook my head."

"'Come on, Kiddo, bring your jacks,' Uncle Damiano said. 'You can join me in the garage. The girls want to talk.' Aunt Jackie had given me a set of those metal Xs and a rubber ball when I arrived. It hadn't occurred to her that it wasn't the best thing for indoor play, especially in a house filled with precious memorabilia from exotic travels.

"Their garage wasn't a place to park a car since neither Aunt Jackie nor Uncle Damiano owned one, preferring the ease of London's public transportation. The garage was 'Damiano's place to read and smoke his pipe,' so said Aunt Jackie when she gave the nickel tour. The garage was a miniature of the house, stone walled with a slate roof. It was a place that invited reading. There was a coal stove and twin overstuffed chairs.

A huge, manly desk was set under a large bow window that overlooked the gardens, a black swivel chair placed in front of the desk. I adored the room on sight with its rows and rows of hardbound books arranged on shelves, and thought I'd like to live in a house just like it when I grew up. I ran and got my own books, tucking them under my arm. Childish jacks didn't belong in the garage, I thought. Uncle Damiano took my hand as we walked down the stairs. As we started to enter the garage, he brushed my hair back over my shoulder. I looked up at him and he smiled. Then, something in Uncle Damiano's eyes turned mean and he reached his hand up my skirt and tugged at my panties with his fat cigar fingers.

"Uncle Damiano," Liv echoed the name. "Why is it so many women have an "uncle" who affected their lives in such a despicable way?"

"The pit of my stomach lunged. I got away from him and ran to the house. Margaret who normally had the patience of a beloved Irish nanny, looked up. 'What is it?' her exasperated brows asked above her fanned playing cards.

"'I'm going to the drugstore. I need my change purse.'"

"'You tell Uncle Damiano he's to buy you ice cream,' Aunt Jackie called out.

"'Men!' Jackie and Margaret exclaimed, and then howled with laughter.

"I grabbed my change purse and went out the front door, crossed the busy London street by myself and devoured ice cream, a huge dish of it with chocolate syrup, over-sweet pineapple topping, and maraschino cherries. It finished off my stomach's defenses. I ran out of the store in time to throw up on the sidewalk. To this day, ice cream still makes my stomach flip."

"I'm not surprised," Liv said. "Uncle Wilton gave me my first sip of whiskey. Today, I'd sooner drink windshield cleaner than Jack Daniels."

Penny nodded her understanding. "It must have been a year later when Jackie called with her distressing news. We had been eating dinner, and Margaret sighed at the rudeness of the ring. She maintained that no one should place phone calls between six and seven and risk interrupting the sacred dinner hour. Her annoyance was gone when she realized it was her good friend. A smile spread across Margaret's face, but the smile froze as her eyes clouded with confusion, then shock. Margaret listened, barely saying a word, while she kept shaking her head no, silently communicating that she couldn't comprehend what was being said. Finally Margaret said, 'Of course, it's not true. Damiano would never ... I'm here for you, Jackie. For whatever you need.'

65

"'I don't believe it,' Margaret said to the room after she had replaced the receiver.

"'Did Uncle Damiano hurt a little girl?' I asked, my chin quivering."

You know, Liv, I wish with all my heart that we had never visited Jackie and Damiano that year. If we had just waited, a year later he was in prison. I think my life may have turned out differently," Penny said and in spite of the emotional topic, gave a great yawn.

"You blamed yourself?"

"At first, that was my reaction. But Margaret was wonderful at convincing me that little girls were not responsible for adults' behavior. No, the problem was that later I used that incident to think I was more perceptive than Margaret. It was stupid of me. I know that now. Margaret had seen the world, had real insight. But as an eighteen-year-old, I thought I had all the answers," Penny said as she rubbed her eyes. "I had one encounter in which I had guessed correctly, and before I was even grown up, I thought I could look into people's eyes and see their souls."

"You and George W," Liv quipped.

"But he had more insight than me. He didn't marry someone who ... Well, I've gotten off track. Goodness, I'm feeling so sleepy. So, after I invoked the name of *Uncle Damiano*, indicating that I was perfectly capable of making my own decision, hadn't I been making sound judgments since the age of six, the wedding plans moved forward. Margaret wasn't silent on the subject, but I could tell she was resigned.

"After the rice was thrown, my husband and I drove straight to New Orleans where he would be stationed, but it seemed like the fates were against us from the start. Margaret would hate hearing me say something like that. She always said people resorted to blaming fate when they weren't adequately prepared or organized. Well, that was certainly the case for us. We thought we'd live in military housing. I was really looking forward to it – imagined a welcoming committee complete with a warm pecan pie. When we arrived, we learned that only service people of a high enough rank could live on-post. Since he was only an E-3 Seaman, we had to find our own accommodations. Apartments we could afford were decrepit. Have you ever been to New Orleans, Liv?"

"It's on my bucket list."

"Well, parts of the city are beautiful and others are downright scary."

"I suppose that's how it is with most urban areas," Liv countered.

"Well, you see that was part of the problem. I had never lived in a city before. I had no idea what to expect. However, we thought our luck had changed when I spied a "for rent" sign in the window of an old Victorian

66

with a wraparound porch in a nice part of town. When we learned the rent was within our tight budget we were ecstatic."

"My mother would have said that was Jesus watching over you," Liv said.

"Well, if that was the work of Jesus, I'd be sore afraid. Scary, inexplicable things happened in that house almost from the day we moved in."

"What do you mean? Are you suggesting the house was haunted?" Liv asked, keeping her voice neutral.

"I don't know. As with almost everything that happened with *him*, I don't know *what* to believe. But yes, I do believe something evil was in that house," Penny said as she closed her eyes.

"Why don't you try to sleep? You look like you're halfway there already. We can talk some more tomorrow night."

"Okay, I'll try to sleep. Are you staying?"

"No, my shift ended some time ago. And I still need to file a report," Liv said as she glanced at her watch. "But I can ask the nurse at the station to awaken you if it appears you're having bad dreams."

"Do you think he thinks about me?" Penny asked with a groggy voice.

"Who?"

"You know, my first husband."

"I don't know, Sugar. I believe most of the time people don't think nearly as much about us as we give them credit. Do you worry about that?"

"I do. I most certainly do," Penny said, but her eyes were closed and her expression slack.

A few moments later, Penny was softly snoring. Liv went to the hallway and pulled out her cell phone and texted: Nothing to report. As Liv put her cell back in her pocket, she glanced at Penny. Liv had grown fond of her in a short length of time. *I feel protective,* Liv realized with a jolt. *I wonder if it'll be difficult to give a full report if something turns up. It's your job, Liv,* she informed herself. *Let's not forget why you're here.*

Chapter Thirteen

Son of Mack

It's unbelievable I can't sleep, Jack thought. Even when he first went to prison he fell sound asleep as soon as his head hit the pillow. Then, it had been a liability. During the first few weeks, it's best to sleep with one eye open. Like war, it's the beginning and end that's the most dangerous, when the rules change and you don't know the boundaries or the score. Yet, here he was back on the outside, with relatively few worries, and he couldn't keep his eyes shut. *Must be the adrenaline. Every time I close my eyes I see the fire. I can even smell the smoke, which is ridiculous. I showered twice and got rid of the clothes.*

"I hadn't planned for it to go the way it did. It just happened," Jack said out loud to the dark room as if someone was listening and actually gave a shit. He punched the pillow, trying to make a comfortable nest. "Nobody cares about me. *She* doesn't even care. I bet she calls me her Ex, doesn't even say my name, like I meant nothing to her. Well, I'm not thinking her name either."

Maybe no one cares about anyone else in this life, Jack thought philosophically, *even when you're good to them. Like the news interview I saw this morning when the old lady was talking about her ex-neighbor.*

"I just can't get over it," she had said. "My neighbor had been a burglar and a jail bird. He'd been in my *home,* came over when I hadn't gone to the mailbox in days. I had gotten the grippe, ya see, so he went to the drugstore for medicine. He came in, made me a cup of tea, and scrambled up some eggs – making sure I ate," her eyes softened at the memory, then hardened again as she continued, "I have lots of nice salt and pepper shakers; I'm lucky he didn't steal them. Do I think the punishment was fair? Well, don't do the crime, if you can't do the time!"

Like she has any idea what it's like for an ex-con, Jack thought. *She probably thinks a friggin' rainbow comes out on release day, with job offers in the pot at either end. Shit. No one would ever hire you if you told the truth. So you lie. "I have never been convicted of a crime, Mr. or Ms. Hiring Person," and hope to hell they don't find out. They usually don't. As long as the job pays low enough, and you don't handle money, they don't bother with a security check. And you learn to keep your mouth shut.*

For a time, Jack worked three jobs and still couldn't cover his modest expenses. He finally got a job as the security and maintenance man in a retirement community. The under-the-table pay was the use of a studio apartment within the community. With that work, and the other job at the furniture store that included overtime for working weekends, Jack was able to make ends meet, sometimes with a little to spare. He kept his nose clean and always came to work on time. Jack knew Albert, the store manager, liked him. Most of the customers gave him a tip. Jack knew how to be friendly, but not too friendly. *And polite, yeah customers like their laborers nice and polite,* Jack thought as his eyes narrowed.

The furniture store owner's daughter, Bethany, was a girl whose name Jack could never quite seem to remember. She was a chubby girl with a crush on the Jack, the furniture mover. When she came home from college during the holidays, she was constantly in the store. Not really working, just there to make eyes at Jack. She even made him chocolate chip cookies. He thanked her, told her how delicious they were, but if Bethany had looked closely, she would have seen that his eyes said, *My life may be shitty, but there is no way I'm taking you out. I mean come on! I haven't given up on all standards.*

Bethany lingered in the parking lot after work so she could tell Jack how much she liked his bike, obviously hoping for a ride. She probably thought Jack was the perfect combination: bad boy looks with a good boy heart. Bethany would have been shocked if she knew what she had really found.

I had found what I wanted, Jack reminisced. *I still can't believe how it all fell apart. Life is fuckin' fragile, it really is.*

When Jack first got out of prison he tried to find his ex-wife. He didn't think it'd be a problem – just call up a few of their old friends, ask them where she was, and that would be that. But as soon as he said his name, click went the phone. He tried other people they knew, pretending to be a lawyer who had inheritance information – and the phone still went dead. Once he even spent rent money on a road trip to go back to their hometown, but no one knew anything about her other than she had

70

returned, kept mostly to herself, sold her aunt's house, and then left without saying goodbye to anyone. Jack tried every trick in the book and found nothing – not hide nor auburn hair. After a while he gave up looking, figured it was probably better that way. No good could come from finding her.

A few months ago, the furniture store workers started talking about the Internet in the break room. All the men had been in prison. While they served time, technology had marched on without them. They were shocked that no one could go underground anymore because everyone's information was out there on the Web. Gus said, "You can't help but leave a trail, everybody now knows everybody else's business."

"Hell," Nate said, "If you type in my name, my address appears, and it shows a map to my goddamn house!"

Wow, Jack thought, *a map to her goddamn house ... That really would be the last word.* The next time he went to the library, Jack saw a flyer about a computer skills class. The gothic-looking librarian with dyed black hair and piercings in her nose and eyebrow looked up from her computer to say, "Oh, you should come. I'm teaching the class." She gave him one of those *you should get to know me because I'm really hot* smiles.

"Is that so?" Jack said flirting back before he had thought it through.

"I'm Lydia. I see you in here a lot. You take out a lot of books."

"It's good to read, keeps me out of trouble," Jack told her as he leaned in closer to her.

"What fun is that? We're going out Saturday night for some *real* fun at The Blue Jay. Wanna *come*?" Lydia asked, giving him a wink.

Jack wasn't sure if she meant it as a double entendre like some Mae West line, but she certainly had his attention. *Did he want to come? Hell, yes!* he thought. *It had been way too long ... at least a month. Besides, Lydia was cute in a crazy, wild kind of way.* He returned her smile and asked what time.

Lydia put her hand on his. Jack looked down and saw chewed off nails and swollen fingers. *A user?* he wondered. Jack looked up at her dilated pupils and knew for sure. He made himself think with his big head, not the small one that was standing at attention and panting. Jack struggled to think dispassionately. *Isabella from the gym will probably be up for another go around after her private lesson. Sure, I like variety, but I have no business tempting fate by hanging around a user. The twelve steps are no joke.* Jack slid his hand away and stepped back.

"You do that a lot," Lydia said.

"What?"

"Toss your hair out of your eyes. It's really sexy."

With the computer skills course under his belt, Jack thought he'd do research at the library, but Lydia wouldn't leave him alone. Being stood up didn't seem to put her off. She'd sneak up behind Jack, lean over his shoulder and say hi while looking at his computer screen.

Jack didn't need Lydia becoming a witness later on, stating in court whose name he had googled. He had to get his own computer.

The laptop just fell into my lap, Jack thought as he snorted a laugh. He was delivering a bed to one of those new homes, the type that's been springing up all over the place: a monstrosity with white Greek columns like they have in the south.

But we aren't in the south. None of our trees have Spanish moss swaying from their branches. To my way of thinking, the southern-styled McMansion looked just plain silly planted among the maples in Massachusetts. The grounds of this delivery stop were beautiful, woods on three sides. *A nice barn-red Colonial would have been just right,* Jack had thought. *If I had their kind of income, I would have added a pole barn to house a dozen horses. Call me crazy, but an airplane hangar to house a private goddamn plane just seemed a bit over the top. But it's not for me to say what kinds of houses get built. I'll never be able to accumulate the kind of money needed to buy land, let alone build on it.*

The lady of the house was on the phone when Jack arrived. She was all legs. She wore faded denim shorts, a sweatshirt, and tennis shoes with the toes worn through like she was at summer camp. She was good looking and knew it. You could tell from the way she tossed her beautiful blonde mane. Her kid had let Jack in, and they stood politely in the kitchen doorway waiting for a break in Mom's phone conversation. *Hadn't she heard the doorbell? Could she possibly not know he was standing there?* Jack thought. Finally, he cleared his throat to get her attention. She glanced at him raising her index finger to show she needed one more minute.

"Yes, I'm serious," she said. "Turquoise. The dress was *turquoise* and at least a size too small. That tremendous bosom of hers was all but spilling out – I know! And to a family wedding! But the worst part, she had a heart tattooed on her shoulder with my brother's name in the center! Can you imagine?"

A tight dress, big tits, and a tattoo, what's not to like? Jack had thought. He wouldn't have minded hearing more about how the brazen babe irritated the shit out of Miss Priss, but Jack had a schedule to keep and made a show of looking at his watch. The kid noticed, and whined, "Mom-m-m! The guy's here!"

Heaving a sigh, the woman said into the phone, "Hold on a minute, I've got the furniture delivery man here." She turned to him saying, "It's to be set up in the master bedroom. Here, I'll show you." He followed her shorts and tanned, bare legs up a grand staircase that was meant to look like something from a southern plantation. The staircase was brand-spanking new and no doubt manufactured in China. Its charm was as contrived as a plain woman trying too hard.

"Yes, I'm still here, Beth. What was I saying? Oh *her*! I shouldn't talk about her anymore. It only upsets me. I'm sure my brother will move on. He's just doing a bit of slumming. Are you going to the Follies Jubilee on the 15th? No? Don't say you and Alex aren't coming! Who will Martin and I sit with? It's to benefit Juvenile Diabetes. See, you must come."

The lady of the house stood at the master bedroom doorway, gave a vague wave at the center of the room, and turned away while saying, "Oh, *that* benefit isn't even worth attending. It's not even black tie."

Later, when Jack came back through the living room, lugging the huge mattress, their eyes met. She turned and lowered her voice into the phone, but he heard part of it. "Ought to see ... *really* buffed ... I guess handsome ... if you like the *just got off the reservation* look."

Her friend said something that made her giggle and the lady of the house looked him over again, giving his hard body another good hard look.

Yeah, take it all in, Sweetie, Jack told her in his head. *It's all bought and paid for. Nothing you know anything about. I bet you get your workout by playing tennis or doing boot camp for ladies, not hauling heavy bags of potatoes up three flights of stairs and sweating your ass off in a prison kitchen. Then when the work day's done, it's time to let off steam by doing a hundred pushups in the cell.*

Normally, Jack was happy when the ladies gave him the look over, but that day he didn't want to draw attention to himself. So far, he'd seen computers in the kitchen, den, and living room. And to top it off, there was even a laptop left haphazardly on the friggin' bathroom counter. That had been the tipping point; when he decided the obscenely wealthy, not to mention *rude*, lady of the house was going to get in a sharing mood and make things a little more even for the have-nots in this world. It was a perfect set up – a house out in the middle of nowhere, with wires hanging out of the walls waiting for the burglar alarm to be set up.

After Jack dropped the mattress to the bedroom floor, he noticed a man's organizer on one of the dressers. Now, apparently well-to-do men need an organizer to stash their wallet, watch, and change when they come home, while Jack seemed to manage just fine with emptying his pockets onto a table. He took a quick look under the lid. This organizer held jewelry: cuff links, rings, and five watches. It looked like expensive stuff. Jack couldn't even imagine having different watches for different occasions. But he could imagine this rich idiot asking his wife which looked better with his suit, the green face or the blue moon-phase? *What a fag! No wonder his wife looked me over.*

Jack propped up the mattress and looked for any mirrors that could give him away. All clear. The bureau mirror was on the other side of the room. Using the mattress as a shield, Jack pulled open the bedside table drawer. There was an assortment of condoms, lubricant, handcuffs, and a riding crop. So, the little Priss downstairs likes to be ridden hard, huh? Or maybe she doesn't like it, but gets it anyway. The thought made him hard. He dug around in the back of the drawer and found a thick wad of cash.

Bingo! Oh yes, with a little luck the cash will still be there when I come back for the laptop. I can't risk taking it now. It would be too obvious. Albert would go ape shit if there was even a hint of impropriety, let alone theft while a delivery was being made.

Jack carefully assembled the bed, making sure the joints were tight and the legs didn't wobble. *I really do take pride in my work. Just because I get paid shit, doesn't mean I do shit work.* It took a bit of doing to get the pieces to match up; even expensive furniture gets slapped together at the factory these days. Jack had to go back out into the truck and find the right piece of wood to shim the leg so the headboard was steady. The bolts that came with the bed were short. Jack could have made them do, but he made another trip down "Scarlett's" staircase and got longer ones from the truck.

By the time Jack was done, the bed was solid. He pictured the lady of the house inspecting the bed and being impressed with how well it was assembled. When he went to the kitchen doorway to tell her the bed was all set up, Jack saw a magnetized calendar on the fridge with "CAMP" written in marker across the following week. He stood there for a bit waiting for her to finish her saga about how long the painters were taking to finish the living room. With the phone to her ear and her mouth still running, she fished a five dollar bill out of her purse and handed it to him.

"Do you want to take a look at it?" Jack asked.

She gave a surprised look, and shook her head no. He could tell she thought a bed installation wasn't worth another trip up the stairs. As Jack went out the door, he thought how much people like her really pissed him off. He had gone out of his way to do a good job, and she didn't even know it. *People like her deserve to get ripped off,* he thought.

Two boys, sons of the manor, were playing catch with a football. One of them missed, and the ball bounced off Jack's shoulder. He picked it up, tossed it back and forth in his hands while he gave them a challenging look. Jack was so pissed he considered taking the ball with him. What could they do about it? But they looked like nice kids. Their parents hadn't turned them into brats, at least not yet.

His contemplation must have concerned the boys, for they looked like they were trying to decide whether to make a run for the safety of their home or stand their ground and ask for their ball back. Jack gave them a hard look. *Things shouldn't come easy to people,* he thought. The boys' brows furrowed as they took a step back. Then, Jack gave them a smile, because ... well, why not? They couldn't help who their parents were any more than he could help being the son of Mack.

Jack back-pedaled a couple steps with the ball between his hands, shouted "go deep", and lobbed the ball over their heads. They scrambled and made a game attempt, but missed the first throw. The kids immediately got into the fun, excited to have an adult's interest. Jack played longer than he should have. Finally he said, "Thanks kids. That was fun, but I've got to get going. I'm going to be late with the rest of my deliveries."

Jack was out of breath, even wheezing a bit as he walked to the truck. He fished a cigarette pack from the dash. Albert hated drivers smoking in the truck; stinks up the furniture. As Jack smacked the pack against his hand, tapping down the tobacco in their sleeves, he looked up and saw the boys had meandered over.

Yeah, he thought, *these kids like me. And why wouldn't they? I'm the real deal, not like their phony parents.*

"Your old man smoke?" Jack asked, as he continued to smack the pack against his palm; sounding like a fish's tail slapping the water. The boys shook their heads no, and then the older one said, "But Uncle Erick smokes. He's really cool, drives a Porsche, 718 Cayman S!" Jack leaned against the truck while his back bitched about mistreatment. He shook out a cigarette, lit it, and took a long draw. Jack glanced at the *manor's* windows, but didn't see anyone.

"Want one?" he muttered.

The older kid also looked around to make sure no one was looking. "Yeah," he breathed in amazement, not believing his luck.

"Andy!" the younger one exclaimed.

"How old are ya?" Jack asked the taller one.

"Twelve," the kid said standing up straighter.

"Are not," the kid brother said.

Jack shook out two cigarettes, dropping them on the lawn.

"Thanks," almost-twelve said beaming up at Jack like he was a hero.

"I didn't give them to you," Jack said giving them a warning with a raised eyebrow. The kids solemnly nodded their agreement that this little transaction would remain between the three of them.

Jack took hold of the steering wheel and used it to pull himself back up into the truck's cab. He leaned back in the seat trying to find a comfortable place for his spine, but it just wasn't happening. As Jack pulled the door shut, the kids pocketed the smokes. He rolled down the window and said, "There's a display of football memorabilia at the Y this Saturday. You should go."

"Can't," the kid said, "We're going to Maine."

"Too bad. Well, take it easy,'" Jack replied with a hidden smile.

Jack hadn't planned on trashing the place. He was just going to grab the *bathroom* laptop and money, and make a beeline out of there. But when he got there, the money was gone. *They're probably spending it in Maine, the jerks!* He had the laptop in his backpack and was at the front door when he remembered the jewelry and thought, *Why not? It was already breaking and entering, might as well make the most out of the risk I'm taking.*

But this time as Jack walked through the living room, he noticed the framed photos on a table. He picked up their wedding picture with gloved hands: the beautiful couple with their perfect, white teeth. The frame was heavy, probably silver; not plastic with silver paint like the one he had kept from years ago. They also had framed photos of summer vacations at Disney, a camping trip with autumn leaves on the ground, a winter holiday when the boys were learning how to ski. The photos told the story of a privileged life with healthy children.

Why do some people get all the luck? It was then that Jack saw the paint cans neatly arranged on the drop cloth next to the window. *Their* biggest problem was how long it takes someone *else* to finish painting the room. It just irritated the shit out of him.

They have no idea how hard it is for people like me: back and arms burning from overuse, second and third jobs to pay for luxuries like electricity, heat, and a carton of smokes. Bastards! Before Jack knew it, he had opened the cans, hurling *Mourning Grey Dove* at the furniture and walls. The first splash sent a wave of euphoria through him. He took their picture-perfect house and turned it on its ear.

"Yeah! Yeah, Baby!" Jack yelled like he was riding some woman. But his euphoria was quickly replaced with rage when he thought how the owners would simply hire a cleaning crew. Then the leggy lady of the house would redecorate. Jack could just picture her on the phone saying, "You know I was going to get a new living room suite anyway. And don't get me started on that stupid chair of his. Many times I've wanted to throw paint at it myself. Of course, insurance covered everything, and then some." She would give a high society laugh, not shrill or nervous just a relaxed, natural sound of amusement. The lady on the other end of the line would answer with the same call of the rare and exotic birds who live in the faraway land of the upper crust where things rarely go badly, but when they do, after it gets turned around, life is even better than it was before. They have more than a safety net; they have the magic of compound interest.

"Stupid, stupid assholes, always getting whatever they want," Jack yelled. His face started to crumple. "No one makes me cry, not anymore," he said to the empty room. He touched his lighter to the throw draped over the back of the sofa. It flamed like a bottle rocket. Jack ran into the kitchen and grabbed a roll of paper towels and made a path from the flaming couch to the drapes. By the time Jack ran out the door, the living room was crackling like a bonfire.

Jack tossed in his bed thinking about what he had done. *Those kids will come back to a ruined home. Kids should have security. The image of their burned out home will follow them.* As he forced down a sob, he said in the dark, "Oh, buck up, Jackie Boy and remember what your old man would have said, 'them's the breaks.'"

Now I've gone and done it: thought about my old man. If I'm not careful I'll start hearing his breathing. Shit! There it is ... like some piece of antique machinery: gasp ... cough, cough, cough ... gasp ... cough, cough, cough. The signature sound of emphysema.

"LaaaaLaaaaaLaaaa," Jack sang out as he put the pillow over his head. But it was no use, just as he couldn't avoid the sound when his father was alive. The County brought in a hospital bed making it easier for the old man to sit up. They assembled it in the living room so it would be more convenient for the twelve-year-old caregiver. Yeah, convenient. The sound of his father's wheezing breaths filled every nook and cranny of their matchbox-sized house. And the smell ... it was the worst. Even now, as he kicked at the memory, the stench permeated his mind.

Will I ever learn to stop kicking it? It's like a pile of old dog shit; it doesn't smell unless it's disturbed, he thought. But Jack couldn't stop the thoughts now, they were off and running. He could see himself changing his father's bedding. The last few months he changed them twice a week. Okay, sometimes it was less often, and it should have been done every day. The old man used the top sheet as a hanky for his hacked up bloody loogies even though there was a roll of paper towels next to him. The routine was supposed to be the sheets got changed after his sponge bath, but the father never wanted one. "Not today," he groaned. "Tomorrow, I'll be up for it tomorrow." But the next day Jack got the same story.

"Come on, Mack, you're smellin' ripe. We need to get this done," Jack would say when he caught a whiff of the stench on the front porch when he came home from school. He didn't know when or why he started calling him Mack. It wasn't his given name; Jack never used any of the standard paternal names: not Dad, or Daddy, or Father. It had always been Mack.

The County also gave them disposable diapers, but Mack refused to wear them. When Jack was at home, he could usually get his old man on the bedpan in time, but when he had a coughing fit, the shit just dribbled out. And when Jack was at school, all bets were off. That really added to the stench.

That last week, Mack kept inhaling and inhaling and inhaling, but didn't have enough lung power to push all of the breath back out. Jack imagined his father ballooning and floating away on his own oxygen like a cartoon guy with a gas station air hose stuck in his mouth, filling cheeks and belly round and full, floating up, up, and away. *Well, the man can go in a clean bed,* Jack thought as he held a pillow under his chin pulling on a fresh pillowcase.

Mack wheezed, "Jackie."

"Yeah?" he didn't look at his father. It was easier that way.

"Hey," Mack gasped.

The boy looked over and saw his father was crying. Not sobs. Mack couldn't have physically managed those, but tears leaked out of his eyes.

"Do it." Mack nodded at the pillow. "Just ... do it."

Jack looked at the pillow and back at Mack. Jack remembered the times his father had swung his belt when he was little, leaving welts on his backside. Jack dropped the pillow to the floor and stared at the worn out bastard. Mack wasn't stupid. He had worn sergeant stripes. Mack

78

knew what would happen to his son if he followed through. But Mack didn't care.

Jack went to the kitchen cupboard and dug around behind the cereal boxes where Mack had stashed his last bottle of whiskey when he was still able to get around. Jack walked back to the bed, chugging from the bottle. He gagged, nearly brought it back up; but it stayed down, warming his belly. He took another pull. The old man's eyes glowed like shiny bits of coal as he anticipated an alcoholic haze. Jack walked closer to him. Mack opened his mouth like a baby robin about to be fed a worm. Jack slowly poured the golden liquid into his father's mouth. He swallowed with difficulty, and then opened his mouth for more.

Jack walked over to the TV stand they used as his father's night table. Among the clutter was a pack of cigarettes and a lighter. He knew Mack was getting towards the end when he could no longer smoke. Jack shook out a cigarette, lit it up while taking a deep drag. He was an experienced smoker having risked the possible severe consequences of cigarette theft for the past year. Jack blew the smoke over Mack. Even though he coughed and hacked, Mack closed his eyes savoring the nicotine cloud. When he opened his eyes, Jack gestured at the pillow at his feet and asked, "You sure about this?"

Something in the Jack's voice must have given him away. Mack looked suspicious. And for the first time, he seemed wary of the boy, like he knew the tables had turned. Mack bit his lip and sucked at his blackened teeth, as he looked away from his son.

Jack gave Mack a hard smile as he pulled on the cigarette. "That's right. It's tough to be the one of the receiving end, to hope the one in charge will do right by you."

Jack pocketed the lighter and picked up the pillow. "How often did you do right by me, Mack?" Now the father was worried. He tried to lunge at the phone which was comical to watch. The man could barely turn over on his own. Jack moved the phone just out of his father's reach. Mack's eyes grew huge with fright. Jack patted his father on the shoulder in a mock show of comfort.

"You look like our Jack Russell, the day you dragged him into the backyard."

Mack was in a panic now, like a cow slotted for slaughter.

"Come on, you remember the family dog, don't you?"

"Don't," Mack whimpered.

"Don't what? I thought you wanted to check out. And don't I always do what my old man says? Didn't I learn at a tender young age that I had better do as I was told or get what's coming?"

Mack started coughing to beat the band, gasping and wheezing for breath and Jack thought he'd better get moving before he lost his chance and nature beat him to it.

"Yep," Jack said as he sloshed whiskey onto the soiled sheets. "Eventually, everyone gets what they have coming." Jack closed his eyes, took a long, slow pull on the cigarette and held his breath for a moment. He opened his eyes and let the smoke curl out of his mouth. Jack lowered his hand and touched the cigarette to the whiskey soaked sheets. The flame made a little *fump* sound and took off. Jack dropped the cigarette next to his father's hand so it would look like the old man had fallen asleep smoking. Mack tried to pull his withered legs up away from the scorching fire, but he was no longer the master of his own muscles. Jack watched the show for a while as his father made a valiant effort to get away until Jack realized his father's screams might be heard from the outside. Jack ran out the door and to the neighbors.

"Call an ambulance! Call an ambulance! My Father!" was all Jack said. Even at the age of twelve, he knew the less said, the better. When help arrived, Jack went running back towards their house, acting as if he was going to rescue his father. Someone grabbed the boy and held him back. Jack sat down on the ground and cried. It started out as show, until it wasn't, and Jack sobbed for every miserable day he had spent with Mack.

But that was a long time ago, the now grown and *orphaned* son thought as he got out of bed and walked over to the kitchen counter for his smokes. Jack doesn't allow smoking in his apartment, by himself or others, but he'd make this exception. He needed a smoke and wasn't going to get dressed and go out in the night. He dug an ashtray out of the bottom of the cabinet under the sink. He picked up the Zippo, the weight and shape comfortable and familiar in his hand. He flicked open the lid, enjoying the sound, thumbed the flint wheel, and lit the cigarette, the first drag, pure cerebral pleasure. As he clicked the case closed and placed it on his desk, Jack thought, *Tomorrow, I'll need to air out the place.* As he smoked, he closed his eyes, waiting for the nicotine to sweep across his brain and quiet his nerves. But it was no use. The image of his father's wasted body, blotched white and red like a scalded pig, waited behind his lids.

"Ah, ah!" his father had moaned as the paramedics carried him past Jack. An accusatory stub of a finger with curled, crisp skin pointed at the boy. The paramedics kept saying, "It's okay. Your son's okay." At Mack's funeral they made him sound like the friggin' father of the year.

80

"He had third degree burns over ninety percent of his body and his only concern was for his son."

Jack held his old man's lighter with its emblem of an Army war eagle clutching a laurel branch in one talon and arrows in the other. He used the lighter so much, he often forgot about its history, the missing piece of the crime that no one knew was a crime. Young Jack had a few nervous nights when he realized he had taken the lighter with him.

How no one thought about how Mack's cigarette got lit during the investigation, I'll never understand, Jack thought as he ran his thumb over the lighter.

"I guess that just proves it's true; most of the time people get what they deserve, often tenfold. I needed a break and Mack needed to pay. Which brings me back to *her*. Yeah. Someday, I have no doubt, she'll pay," Jack said to the quiet room.

.

Chapter Fourteen

Reality Check

Mayra-Liz stood looking out the shop window. The streets were dressed up in their finery: colored lights, greenery draped over store doors, and windows with red velvet bows. Banners hanging from light posts wished shoppers "Happy Holidays." The shoppers were dressed in casual, yet stylish clothes. It was amazing to think, just a few streets down, shoppers weren't looking for gift wrapping. They mainlined, snorted or smoked their purchases as soon as possible. Mayra-Liz knew just what she'd buy if she were in the market and just where to find it. She abruptly turned away from the window and cleared the café tables, scrubbing the tile with extra vigor.

"I'm *not* in the market," she told herself out loud. "I never will be again." She tossed her long hair over her shoulder giving it a little tug as if to make herself pay attention. It was her mind that caused the trouble. It itched to get high.

As she pulled the green window shades down, Mayra-Liz gave a sad smile when she remembered how they had teased Penny about stenciling both sides of the shades with red Christmas bows and bells.

"Do you think I'm going overboard with the decorating?" Penny had asked.

"No, not at all," Annalise replied, trying to hide her smile. "I'm just going to keep moving lest I have a pinecone stamped on my forehead. As it is, we're wearing these ruffled Christmas aprons."

"But those aprons look darling on you!" Penny had replied. "Do you really not like them? They've been a big seller this year. The sixties look has made a big comeback."

"They're fine. We're just teasing you!" Mayra-Liz had said as she gave Penny a hug.

Mayra-Liz stacked the mugs and plates on a tray, carried it to the back, and filled the dishwasher. It had been her idea to create a café section in the shop. They served Fairtrade spiced tea, hot chocolate, and coffee. Some customers took their beverages to go, but others found the rich aromas so enticing, they pulled up a chair and added a freshly baked pastry. Recently, their sale of Kenyan whole bean coffee was so brisk, they had to place a rush order. The shop became a meeting place which increased the gift sales as well. Penny complimented Mayra-Liz on her creativity and insight. The words had filled Mayra-Liz with pride. The plan had been for Mayra-Liz to accompany Penny this spring to South America on a buying trip. Mayra-Liz had been looking forward to it; she rarely traveled out of the state, and had never been out of the country.

I wonder if we'll still go, Mayra-Liz thought. *What if Michael decides the shop is too much to manage and they sell it?* When Michael told Mayra-Liz and Annalise about Penny's accident, he said his wife had been doing too much, and he was going to make sure she slowed down. When Michael made this pronouncement with his arms crossed, Mayra-Liz felt as if she had had her legs swept out from under her, worse than when her mother had left. Almost as bad as the day her father had been arrested. At least with Penny's hospitalization, Mayra-Liz didn't need to feel like it was her fault.

Mayra-Liz paused as she thought back to the day they learned of their father's desperate attempt to solve their problems, and she realized weeks had passed without her reliving it. It had taken a year before she went from replaying the news announcement constantly in her head to just frequently: "Forty-eight year-old Albert Muñoz was arrested this afternoon when he attempted to rob a convenience store on Erie Boulevard. He was shot when police mistook a chocolate bar he brandished for a gun. His medical condition is unknown at this time."

Annalise had been stirring chili. Mayra-Liz had been helping Eva with her math homework at the kitchen table. The girls were stunned as the radio went on to play disco music. When she caught her breath, Annalise looked up and cast an accusatory look at Mayra-Liz whose face was purple and yellow with one eye swollen shut.

"I know, I know! It's all my fault! He was trying to get the money to pay off Rafael," Mayra-Liz cried.

Trying to smother her anger, Annalise said, "It wasn't your fault. It was a stupid thing for Dad to do. We could have figured something out. Holding up a convenience store with a chocolate bar, my God!"

"Would you have preferred he used a gun?"

"I would have preferred he used his head! We should have gone to the police."

"But Rafael said he'd kill me if we reported it," Mayra-Liz said, fear coating her words.

"Of course he said that. He didn't want the police involved; people who could have actually helped us," Annalise said hotly.

"Do you think Dad's dead?" Eva asked in a small voice.

"I'll go to the neighbors and use their phone," Mayra-Liz said as she hurried to the closet to get her coat. As Mayra-Liz jammed her arm in the sleeve, she wondered out loud, "Who do I call?"

"Go to Maria," Annalise directed. "She works at the hospital. See if she can find out if he's there, and if so, what his condition is. We need to be careful. We can't let it be known there's no parent here."

"Well, there *is* no parent here," Mayra-Liz said with sarcasm, showing that she minded the obvious statement. "We can take care of ourselves. We've been doing it for a long time now."

"We can take care of ourselves; but Dad had taken care of most of the bills. We'll need to figure out how we can carry on without making it obvious that we're doing it on our own."

"I tell you, Annalise, I have never met a person like you who works to borrow trouble. We have enough problems right now without worrying about what the neighbors think."

"Not the neighbors, the authorities: Child Protective Services." Annalise nodded at the youngest sister. "Eva's a minor. Our first and foremost concern must be for her. They won't let her stay with two slightly older sisters who don't have jobs on the books. Eva would be sent to foster care."

Mayra-Liz started crying. "If only I hadn't gotten caught up in it, that whole drug scene. I thought I'd try it just once. Rafael kept saying not to worry; he'd just add it to my bill. I didn't even think he was keeping track. I wasn't keeping track. Then –"

"Then he wanted you to be his whore. Great guy this Rafael," Annalise said interrupting Mayra-Liz as her anger boiled over. "One thing I know for sure, you are never using again. We can't hold this family together with you using. Didn't you learn anything from Mom? I mean it, Mayra-Liz, if I ever see you messed up again, you're out of here and I'll take care of Eva myself."

"Stop it! Stop it!" Eva sobbed as she jumped up from the table so quickly her chair fell backwards to the floor with a crash. "I can't stand it! Dad's been shot and you're threatening to throw out Mayra-Liz. What's happening to us?"

The older sisters came to Eva and held her. "It's okay," Mayra-Liz said to Eva. "I'll never touch the stuff again. I swear to you."

The sisters worked hard to keep the household running. They managed the expenses for over a year with their numerous part time jobs and babysitting. Then, Eva fell while rollerblading and needed surgery on her elbow. There was nothing to do, but ask for help.

If only God had whispered in our ears and told us everything would turn out all right, Mayra-Liz thought. But He said nothing, and Eva had gone to a group home. It wasn't the best, but it wasn't as grim as they had imagined. The City Mission isn't a place where anyone hopes to end up, but Mayra-Liz and Annalise made the best of it, continuing with their part time jobs, and Mayra-Liz got her G.E.D. They were surviving. It had been much better than they had feared. The girls had expected life to continue on this course when Penny walked into their lives.

"The pay is modest, but the person can live in the apartment over the shop," Penny told the City Mission's job coordinator. "It's called *Ruth and Naomi* because my husband and I are dedicated to improving the lives of our fellow sisters. We need someone who is sympathetic to the plight of impoverished women. We believe what we do in the shop is more than sell quality gifts. We sell products made by women in mostly underdeveloped countries. We only purchase from women who are in need. The person who works with us needs to think of the position as more of a calling than a job."

Mayra-Liz had been mopping the hallway outside of the office, listening to this. She propped the mop against the wall, walked into the office, and turned to Penny saying, "I want the job. I understand the plight of impoverished women. I'll work so hard. I mean me and my sister, Annalise will work so hard. I can't leave here without her."

"Do you have any experience?" Penny asked.

"In being impoverished?"

"I meant in retail sales. Do you have computer skills?" Penny clarified, with a faint smile.

"I do. I attended a training program through The Mission," Mayra-Liz said proudly, "And I'm a quick learner and hard worker."

"True enough. I can vouch for that," The Mission's coordinator said.

"Well, I wasn't planning on hiring two people, though I expect we'll have enough work for two before long. Let me meet your sister. How old is she?"

"Twenty-one, almost twenty-two"

"And how old are you?"

"Nineteen. Almost –"

"Twenty," Penny finished for her. "You're very young to be on your own."

"We're old souls. We made our mistakes early. But we've already learned from them. We're responsible. You won't regret hiring us."

"One thing I will not tolerate is drug use," Penny said.

"We don't tolerate it either," replied Mayra-Liz honestly. She had been clean and sober for fourteen months.

Working in the shop had been the best experience of Mayra-Liz's life. She knew how selfish it was to consider her own future at a time when Penny was at her lowest, but she couldn't help it. What if Michael made Penny give up the shop? Mayra-Liz had never heard him sound so high-handed, but then again his wife had never had a drug overdose. Would Penny stand her ground if Michael insisted?

She looked pretty worn out to me, Mayra-Liz thought, *like someone who would just take direction and be thankful for not needing to make decisions.* Even before this overdose, Mayra-Liz knew something was troubling Penny. More than once Mayra-Liz had gone to the storage area to find Penny crying. Mayra-Liz tried to get Penny to confide in her, but Penny just said she was overtired.

If the shop closed, what would Annalise and she do to support themselves? They had become acquainted with the finer things in life: decent pay for rewarding work, a safe place to live, nutritious food, health insurance. With Penny in the hospital, it became painfully clear how much they relied on her. Too many times, the sisters had depended upon someone only to have them leave. Mayra-Liz knew she needed to find a way to stand on her own two feet because, after all, the only one you can really count on in life is yourself. For a while, she had allowed herself to forget that hard, cold fact. It was now time for a reality check.

Chapter Fifteen

Fifth Catholic Child

Patrick took the keys out of the ignition and pocketed them. He pulled out his cell phone, hit the speed dial, cleared his scratchy throat while the call went through, and then said, "This is Dr. Patrick Allen. Due to a family situation I won't be in today. Thank you, I appreciate your concern. Who's on call? Oh, well, it can't be helped. If you could let my patients know I'll be in tomorrow. If it's necessary, you may call my cell."

As he pocketed his phone, Patrick looked at his wife and said, "I'll fix you breakfast."

Judith took their dog out for a needed walk; when she returned, plates of steaming scrambled eggs where on the counter. Patrick was buttering toast and sipping coffee.

"There's hot water and a pot of coffee ready. I wasn't sure if you wanted herbal tea or caffeine," Patrick said as he brought the plates to the breakfast nook.

Judith poured herself a cup of coffee and sat down across from him. Patrick said a silent prayer of thanks as he did before every meal for as long as he could remember. He took a sip of coffee and looked into the concerned eyes of his wife.

"Right. Well – it's difficult to know where to start." He gave a humorless laugh and stroked the top of his head. "I sound like my patients."

He looked down at his plate and studied his eggs as if they had the answer of how to begin. When the silence continued, Judith prompted him by saying, "You said your father was a mean, brutal man. I've never heard you describe him in that way. You had said your father had been a present, yet uninvolved parent, but before today you never said he was abusive."

"He was," Patrick said simply.

"Why didn't you tell me?"

"I don't know. He had been dead for a while when we met. The luck of meeting you in the medical program ... falling in love .... It was so ... *nice*." They both smiled at this huge understatement. "My father was the last thing I wanted to talk about."

"Were you concerned that if I knew about your childhood I'd analyze it and somehow judge you? Or maybe try to figure out how it affected you as a person."

"That probably had something to do with it. As a psychiatrist, you would have been unable to discount the influence."

"And you didn't want me to see you in a vulnerable light," Judith said.

"I didn't like seeing *myself* in that light. I've done my best to not think about it on almost a daily basis."

"Patrick, it wasn't your fault."

"I know that," he snapped and just as quickly, Patrick apologized.

Judith brushed the air with her hand, showing she didn't take it personally. With a professional demeanor, as if her husband were her patient, she probed, "You said you killed him? You didn't mean that literally."

"Could I be found guilty of murder in a court of law? No. Am I morally responsible for his death? Without a doubt." Patrick's eyes narrowed as he said, "I get so angry when I think about it. He never should have put my mother and me in that situation." He took another sip of coffee and said, "You know there are days I still long for a cigarette. How long has it been since I quit? Thirty years?"

"And you'd like one now?" Judith asked.

"I'd *love* one now," Patrick replied.

The sound of the ticking clock in the dining room filled the room.

Judith reached over and took Patrick's hand, "Have you ever talked with someone about this? A professional?"

Patrick shook his head, "No, no one," he said.

"If you're finding it especially burdensome to talk about it with me, we can set you up with Andrew Schultz. People say good things about him."

"No, I want to tell you," Patrick said as he sighed deeply and rubbed his forehead. "It just feels unnatural talking about it."

"Take your time," Judith encouraged.

Patrick took a deep breath, rubbed his head again and said, "I can't remember a time when my father wasn't angry. I was the fifth Catholic child, born twelve years after the fourth, obviously not planned. Of course, I was never left to wonder about that. My father told us all the time that rich men get richer while poor men have more kids. And it wasn't like he thought of us as a blessing. There was a sixth child, Matthew; he died when he was little, but I've told you that. My father criticized everything I did. But I found ways to make life bearable. I participated in softball, boy scouts, any school and church sponsored activity that kept me away from home. Even my paper route was its own special kind of deliverance.

"When I was in sixth grade, my father dropped a twelve-foot steel pipe from a crane he was operating. A co-worker's hand got crushed. It was fortunate the man wasn't killed. My father had liquor on his breath and was fired. He had always been a drinker, but after he lost his job my father made drinking his full-time occupation. He was a mean drunk, slapped my mother around and when I tried to intervene, it got really ugly. He was such a big bruiser of a man and I was a scrawny thirteen-year-old kid.

"One night, when we heard him coming up the porch stumbling drunk, my Mother said, 'Lock the door. We can't go through another night of it.' The chained door unleashed his Furies. He was hollering, demanding we open the door or he'd kill us. My mother shook her head no. The neighbors' dogs started barking and one by one the neighbors' lights turned on, and one by one they turned them back off. I guess they thought it wasn't their business to intervene in what was considered a "family matter." It's ironic. Had it been a stranger trying to terrorize a family, every one of those strapping Irish blokes would have been over with a shovel ready to take him on. We didn't call the police. We had tried that before. His drinking buddies weren't interested in arresting him."

Seeing Judith's shocked expression Patrick said, "It was 1964, a different era. A call to the authorities only added fuel to the fire after they left. It was cold that night, below zero. I was terrified he'd just break a window and climb in. My mother held a rosary in her hand with her arm around me as we sat waiting on the couch all night with the lights off. At some point, we fell asleep and awoke to see it was morning, past the time I should have left for my paper route. We peeked through the curtain and saw his car parked out front. We carefully unchained the door and worked the latch, all of which made an unnerving racket. We cracked opened the door, half expecting to be grabbed on the front porch. We saw his footprints in the snow leading back to the car, his stupid, '41 Lincoln Continental. I truly believe that car was the only thing he ever loved. It was still running; he was in the driver's seat asleep. My mother started towards the car. I grabbed her arm, 'Let him sleep it off,' I begged. But she kept walking and I followed. I suppose she didn't want the neighbors to see him like that. She walked up to the driver's door and lightly tapped on the glass.

"'Thomas?' she said. When she received no reply, she tapped harder. When he continued to sleep, she curled her fingers through the chrome door handle and pushed her thumb on the door button. The door popped open against his weight. His body shifted and his head nodded down further, but he still didn't wake up. I was sure he was trying to trick us into coming closer, so he could grab us. In spite of her obvious apprehension, my mother leaned in front of him, reached through the steering wheel, turned the key, and killed the engine. His left hand rested on his left knee. I can still see it clearly: the dirt in the edges of his cuticles, his fingernails cyanotic, and the crucifix he always wore dropped to the car floor. She tried to straighten him up, but his head gently lolled back and to the left. I looked into his face and his empty eyes stared back.

"At first Mom was silent, but her mouth moved to form his name. When her voice engaged, she didn't worry about attracting attention. Mom screamed her husband's name until she was hoarse and sunk to the sidewalk scaring the local school children. As I helped Mom up, she continued sobbing, 'Oh Thomas! Thomas! I didn't mean it! I didn't mean it!'

"I held her close to me and said, 'It's over. It's over.'

"She grabbed my arms and sobbed into my shoulder, 'Oh Paddy, I prayed for him to die. I begged God to take him away from us.'

"'I did too,' I admitted.

"'Then we're responsible,' Mom said, her face horror-struck. 'Guilty in the eyes of God. How can we ever be forgiven for such a horrible sin?'"

Patrick, the adult, took off his glasses and rubbed his eyes. Judith reached over and took his hand. "But, you weren't responsible. That doesn't make any –"

"Sense. Of course, it doesn't make sense."

"But you don't really believe you're in some way morally responsible for your father's death, do you? I know you said that earlier, but you can't possibly believe that."

"I'm very tired," Patrick said, evading further consideration of guilt.

"You must be exhausted," Judith said as she came around the table and held her husband, stroking the back of his neck.

92

"I don't know the cause of death," Patrick said as if Judith had asked. "It could have been alcohol poisoning, carbon monoxide poisoning, maybe a heart attack. Who knows? I never saw his death certificate. When I cleaned out my mother's house I found all her important papers carefully organized in a safe box. The birth records of all her six children were there as well as Mary and Matthew's death certificates. But my father's death certificate was no place to be found. How can that be? She must have it someplace. She would have needed it for his Social Security benefits. It must be in a safety deposit box someplace. It was as if she didn't want me to see it. She must have known I'd be the one to organize things when the time came."

"It's impossible to know what she was thinking," Judith murmured.

Patrick nodded and stared at his untouched breakfast.

"Do you know that until she gave up driving, she drove that Lincoln? That's how good she was at compartmentalizing. My mother hated that car. Never mind that her husband died in it, her contempt for the vehicle went further back than that. While she was buying week old bread and canning tomatoes, he went out and paid good money for his dream car. Even though he didn't pay top price for it, it was still too dear for their budget. The car had been in an accident. My old man had been working as a mechanic at the time and proudly told anyone who would listen how he exaggerated the damages and got the car at a bargain price. He couldn't understand why his customer base then dwindled. All he enjoyed doing was polishing that stupid car –" Patrick's voice broke. "I hate thinking about him. I have spent my entire life trying *not* to think about him."

"I'm here for you," Judith said. "You know that, don't you?"

Patrick nodded.

"Do you think you could rest?" Judith asked taking in the tired lines around her husband's eyes and mouth.

"I should at least try. It's difficult to tell when we'll be called to the nursing home again. I don't think she'll live much longer."

"Why do you say that? Your mother's heart is strong; her lungs are clear."

"It's just a feeling."

Judith stared at him. She wasn't used to her husband diagnosing a patient's condition based strictly on feelings rather than medical observations.

"You know he can't hurt you anymore," Judith said.

"Of course," Patrick replied, but he looked like a man who didn't believe it.

Chapter Sixteen

The Blue Sheep

When Penny awakened there was a new nurse in her room and a tech who wanted to take some blood. Judging by the sounds coming from the hallway, she knew the hospital was in full swing.

"What time is it?" asked Penny.

"Seven, o-two," the new nurse replied, all business as she took Penny's vitals. "My name is Denise; I'll be your nurse for the day shift. How are you feeling?"

"Just ducky," Penny said through gritted teeth as the tech poked her arm for the third time trying to find a vein.

While Penny tried to watch the morning news, her thoughts kept straying to Liv. *What a good and kind person she is,* Penny thought. *I can't believe that I talked about my past with her. It's so unlike me.*

Penny knew that Liv would want to hear more when she returned this afternoon. Penny contemplated how much she should say. In the past, the answer had been easy – say nothing. But Penny found that she wanted to talk with this nurse. Liv had been able to loosen the emotional knot that had been around her chest for a long time. Of course, every action has a consequence. Was Penny ready for what could happen if she continued to talk about her past?

Michael walked into the room, carrying a small blue stuffed sheep and Penny's overnight bag filled with clothes and toiletries. "To help you sleep," he said as he handed her the stuffed animal, rolling his eyes to show how corny he knew it was.

"Thank you. He's very sweet," Penny said as she gave the sheep a kiss, tucking him under her arm.

"How's your forehead? Does it still hurt?"

Penny touched the bandage that had been recently changed.

"Just a dull throb. Sometimes I forget it's there. Is everything okay at the shop?" Penny asked. "How is Eva? Don't you have a photo shoot today?"

"Hold on!" Michael replied. "You're here to relax, not to worry about everything and everyone."

Penny's raised eyebrows said, *you might as well just tell me because I'm going to keep asking until you do.*

"Okay," Michael said resigned. "Here's the rundown: Everything is fine at the shop. I stopped in last night after Mayra-Liz closed up. She had everything under control, all clean and organized. Annalise was out buying supplies so I didn't see her, but Mayra-Liz said Annalise is the rock that she always is. I called Eva last night. We didn't talk long. She was doing her homework. I won't lie to you; Eva is upset, but she'll be okay."

"Your photo shoot?" Penny asked.

"Yes, I cancelled it. I rescheduled it for next week."

Penny frowned. Michael sat down on the bed next to her. "You've got to learn to relax," Michael said stroking Penny's hair. "I need you home with me. Now, I'm not sleeping."

"You do look tired," Penny said as she traced the lines next to his eyes that looked more defined after his restless night.

"You look better. Did you get some sleep?"

"I did. I think it was about twelve hours' worth. It was so wonderful!"

"That's good. Really good. Maybe they'll let you go home soon."

"Hmm, that would be nice," Penny sighed.

"Speaking of home, we need to talk about how to make your life less stressful," Michael said.

"What do you mean?"

"You're doing too much. You're working, what? Fifty, sometimes sixty hours. That's too much. I think we should hire another person, at least during the holiday season. And we should definitely hire someone year-round to manage the books. Don't you think letting someone else do the taxes and all the record keeping would take a huge burden off your shoulders? Haven't you said the only part you don't enjoy about the shop is all the paperwork? Let's just have someone else do it."

"Can we afford that?" Penny asked as she chewed her lip.

"Yes," Michael said simply. "I crunched the numbers last night, and we'll be fine. I know we both believe in this cause, but we can't do it at the expense of running you ragged. We should have hired extra help years ago. I don't know what we were thinking. You mean everything to me, Penny. I can't imagine my life without you."

He leaned over and kissed her soundly on the mouth.

"Penny, you have a group counseling session scheduled in fifteen minutes," Denise said as she walked into the room, startling both Penny and Michael before she backed out again.

"I guess I shouldn't be kissing you like that in here," Michael whispered.

"It's the sexy blue hospital gown. You couldn't help yourself," Penny whispered back. "And if you don't want me to turn all of my 'group' on, I'd better get changed."

Penny watched her husband leave. She picked up the blue sheep, "What do you think?" she whispered in the sheep's ear, "Will he still love me after he learns who I am?"

Chapter Seventeen

The Music Box

Shortly after one in the afternoon, Liv walked in as Penny's lunch was set on her tray.

"You're early," Penny observed. "Doesn't your shift start at three? I think you've had a different shift each day I've been here. Goodness, you look so tired. Sorry, that was blunt."

"It's not called the swing shift for nothing. All those different hours just swing you right into the ground."

"Do you still need to do that? I mean, don't you have enough seniority to —"

"I'm one of those on-call nurses. I'm hired through an agency, so I work when I please. And it will please me to take most of the summer off when my son, Merrill gets married. Do you want company? I'm not on duty. I came in early so we could chat. I bought a tuna fish sandwich," Liv said holding up a lunch bag.

"Sure, I'd love the company," Penny said.

"What did you order for lunch?"

Penny lifted the warming lid.

"Turkey and fixings. Comfort food, what a good choice. Besides, you could stand to put some meat on your bones," Liv informed Penny. "Now then, we left off with you telling me about that place in New Orleans that may or may not have been haunted."

Penny took a bite of turkey with a bit of stuffing. She chewed slowing, deciding whether to share her story with Liv. Penny took a long, slow drink of milk. When she set the glass back down Penny said, "We parked the car in front of the house and just sat there, admiring it for a bit. It had a large yard that badly needed mowing. The flower and vegetable gardens had long since gone to seed, but we knew we could bring it all back to its former glory. An ornate wrought iron fence topped with fleurs-de-lis marked the property lines. A porch swing creaked in the breeze."

"'I told you we'd find the right place,' my husband said as we got out of the car and hurried to the front door as if we couldn't wait to get our new life started. He put the house key into the lock, and then stopped."

"'Is it stuck?' I asked."

"'No,' he answered as he jerked his head back and to the side. It was an old habit. His dark hair had hung low over one eye, and he would jerk his head to toss his hair back. It was a habit Margaret had found maddening. 'Why doesn't he just cut his hair?' she used to say. She didn't understand how cool it looked. After he had joined up, he still jerked his head even though his hair was short, nothing to toss."

"'I felt a chill,' he said."

"'A chill? It must be 80 degrees!'"

"'Maybe we should look around some more. There could be another place –'"

"'You're kidding, right? This house is perfect.'"

"'Right,' he said, and with a deep breath he turned the lock, walked inside, and started down the hall."

"'Wait a minute! Aren't you forgetting something?' I called. He stopped, turned, and looked at me blankly."

"'The threshold ... a new bride ...' I said pointing to myself. He walked back, picked me up, and carried me through the house to the bedroom."

"'But there are no sheets or flowers. I was going to –' but when he kissed me, it no longer mattered. Later, we walked hand in hand through the house. There was a fireplace in the living room with a magnificent mirror over the mantle. We talked about how nice it would be at Christmas time to have a roaring fire and drape the mantel with greenery."

"'We'll have the tree over in that corner so the lights can be seen from the street. We'll meet other couples and throw parties.' There was a formal dining room with a round table large enough to seat eight."

"'Solid wood,' my husband said as he picked up one of the chairs. 'They don't make them like this anymore.' There was a mahogany sideboard and matching china cabinet. They were remarkably unscarred for furniture in a rental apartment. The kitchen window looked out over lilac bushes that smelled divine. An ancient combination gas and wood cook stove took up one side of the room. In the letter that I started to Margaret, I wrote the stove was large enough to hold a body. I stared at the page wondering *where* in the world *that* description had come from before I crumpled the stationery. On a fresh page, I wrote the bathroom was the size of my bedroom back home, with an enormous clawfoot porcelain bathtub, a pedestal sink, and a toilet with a wall-mounted water tank, just like my doll house furniture. The bedroom had eight windows, its own fireplace, and a bed so ornate, we were certain inventory from Windsor Castle must be missing.

"My husband and I had a rather restless first night. So did the house. It seemed to do a lot of creaking and groaning. Well, of course it would make some noise, we said to each other in the morning. After all, it was over a hundred years old, and old houses made noise when they relaxed after the heat of the day. Plus, the humidity. That probably accounted for some of it.

"We went out early to the grocery store. We bought eggs, bread, sugar, vanilla extract, coffee, bacon, and some pancake syrup, and I made French toast. He said it was the best he ever had, even though the pancake syrup wasn't the same as the real maple syrup from back home. It made me think about our old neighbors who tapped trees every spring and boiled the sap down in large vats over wood fires, making the entire valley smell like breakfast. I felt a momentary stab of homesickness. He must have noticed because he tried to distract me by continuing to heap praise upon my rudimentary cooking skills."

"'The bacon was just right: crisp, not burnt.'"

"'Well, the ends were a little burnt.'"

"'No. It was perfect.' He said as he kissed me."

"'What do you want to do next?' I asked. My husband arched an eyebrow and smiled."

"'Again?' I asked, sparkling eyes belying the feigned tone of puritanical shock."

"That afternoon we called our folks from a pay phone and told them how well we were doing. How lucky we were to find such a nice home. Cleaning, unpacking, and settling in kept us busy for the rest of the day and we were bone tired when we fell into bed at midnight. Sleep washed over us within moments."

"'What was that?' I whispered after being startled awake by a loud crash, then muffled voices."

"'I don't know,' he whispered back. 'Stay here.'"

"The heavy draperies made the room pitch black, but I could feel him pull the covers back and slip out of bed. I heard him pull on his jeans and then heard the retreating creak of the stairs as he went down to investigate. Then, it was deathly quiet. Even the house seemed to be holding its breath. Shortly, the stairs signaled his return, and I felt him climb back into bed."

"'I didn't see anything,' he reported in a low voice. 'Maybe it was just some kids in the neighborhood.'"

"'But it sounded close, like it was in the house. In the kitchen.'"

"'I know, but the windows are open. It just sounded like it was close.'"

"I wasn't convinced, and neither was he. We cuddled up, and fell back to sleep. But it was a watchful, troubled sleep, no longer a warm and secure surrender. In the morning, I found the couch pillows on the dining room table. Why are these here? I wondered as I put them back on the living room couch. I put it out of my head since it was Sunday morning and decided to go to church. I looked forward to meeting other people in the community, making friends. I wore my blue going-away suit. My husband wore his dark grey wedding suit, his only suit. I suppose we made an attractive couple, in the way most young people are effortlessly good-looking.

"Several members of the congregation turned and smiled at us when we walked in. During the meet-and-greet portion of the service, a small group of them gathered around us and extended a warm welcome."

"'Always nice to see young people here. Military are ya?' they asked, taking in my husband's crew cut."

"'Yes, we're from Pennsylvania, just arrived a few days ago. We moved into a place on Second Street,' my husband said."

"'Which one?'"

"'1214. The big Victorian.'"

"No one replied. All the happy faces vanished, replaced by raised eyebrows and wide-eyed surprise. Before I could ask what was wrong, the minister pulled the congregation back for the Bible reading. I wanted to speak to them, but we were left to ourselves when the service ended."

"'They weren't very friendly,' I pouted."

"'Yeah, people are jerks,' my husband said."

"'Perhaps one of them had their eye on the house for someone they knew and were disappointed that we got it first. If they had waited around we could have told them that the attic apartment is still available.'"

"I didn't brood about it for very long. I got busy cooking our first Sunday meal as soon as we got back home. I had mixed results. The pasta was cooked al dente. I had mixed dry mustard and thyme into the cheese sauce and was pleased with the tangy flavor. But the sausages were overcooked and the green beans undercooked. I would need to figure out the trick of timing everything so the entire meal was ready at the same time. As I washed the dishes, I inhaled the summertime scent of lilacs and felt grateful to have this old house as our first home. We would make lovely memories here. That night we were awakened to what sounded like footsteps in the attic."

"'Perhaps it's the landlord,' my husband whispered."

"'At two in the morning?'"

"'Could be he's got a mistress.' We both giggled at the thought of spindly, old Mr. Wesley having sex. We listened for further sounds from upstairs, but any sounds of old Mr. Wesley were replaced by the usual creaks and groans of old Mr. House, until we finally fell back to sleep."

"My husband got up early, as it was his first day to report to duty. He came into the kitchen wearing his uniform and carrying the couch pillows. 'Do these look different to you?' he asked, presenting them to me for close inspection."

"I looked at them, turned them over in my hands. 'I don't know. Somehow they don't look as worn as when we first arrived, but that's must be my imagination. Why do you put them on the dining room table?'"

"'I don't.'"

"'Well, I don't either.'"

"'I could have sworn that when we moved in these pillows were faded – I mean more faded. The same green vine pattern, just lighter.'"

"I shrugged as I put the pillows back on the couch. I didn't want to say so, but I thought my husband probably walked in his sleep. I walked him to the front porch and kissed him goodbye."

"'Hurry home. I'll make something special for dinner.' As I turned and entered the house I realized I sounded like a wife. I had gotten used to being a bride, but it was then that I fully realized I was a married woman. The thought pleased me."

"You were so young," Liv said.

Penny nodded. "I'm sure that was a big part of the problem, I wasn't mature enough to know how to handle new experiences: like deceit. I can still remember that evening so well. He said he smelled the roast pork from outside. I also made apple sauce, roasted vegetables, and my first loaf of homemade bread. My husband kept praising the meal, and I kept saying how much I enjoyed fixing it. After dinner, he said he had a surprise and retrieved a bottle of whiskey from his knapsack."

"'You spent money on *liquor*! You know how tight our budget is.' I was sorry I said it as soon as the words were out of my mouth. I saw that he didn't like being questioned like that. I don't suppose anyone does."

"'No,' he said coldly. 'It was a gift from someone I met at work. He invited me for lunch to his place on-post. When I told him we were newly married, he dug around in the back of his cupboard, retrieved the bottle, and said take it home to your new bride and celebrate. He didn't know that my old lady was going to jump on me about it.'"

"'Who's old? Look, I'm sorry, really I am. Here! Let's have a toast.'"

"'Never mind,' he said as he walked out the front door and onto the porch.'"

"I wasn't sure what to do. Margaret had been worse than any Baptist preacher when it came to drinking. 'It's a slippery slope, Penny,' she used to warn. 'I saw it plenty when I was in the military. Men and women both, who started out as social drinkers, just a glass of wine on a Friday night, turned into people who couldn't wait to get home and get a buzz on. It's no way to live, Penny. It's expensive and ruins your health.' But I had already offered to have a drink with my husband. Well, just one celebratory drink wasn't going to turn us into alcoholics, I decided. I poured a small amount of the auburn liquid into water glasses. I was on my way to the porch when I noticed a piece of paper on the floor. I picked it up. It was a sales receipt. The bottle had been purchased a couple of hours ago. But he had said it was a gift. The new friend had retrieved it from the back of his cupboard at noon. He wouldn't lie to me. But what was the explanation for the receipt? I had to know."

"Of course, you needed to know," Liv replied. "There's nothing worse than a lying husband."

Penny nodded as she played with the hem of her sleeve. "I left my glass on the table and walked to the porch trying to figure out how to ask without sounding confrontational."

"It was a beautiful night. The Magnolia trees in the front yard were blooming and the air was heavy with their scent. He sat still on the porch swing with his face turned away, yet I could see in the dimming light that his jaw was set. 'No drink for you?' he asked causing me to jump."

"'No ... no,' I stammered. I handed him his drink and sat next to him on the swing. 'I need to ask you about this.' I handed him the sales receipt. He took the receipt and looked at it. He showed no emotion. No telltale color rose in his face as I'm sure it would have in mine, if I had been caught in a lie. 'We really need to have our marriage built on trust.'"

"'What are you talking about?'"

"'That bottle of whiskey wasn't retrieved from someone's cupboard at noon.'"

"He just looked at me, shaking his head as if he couldn't *believe* we were having this conversation."

"'The sales receipt says Culotta's Liquor Store, dated today, April 17, 1997 at 5:17,' I continued, hoping there was some explanation, other than the obvious."

"He threw the rest of the drink down his throat. 'I only said that because you were going on about the damn budget. I was trying to do something nice and you spoiled it.'"

"'You lied to me.'"

"'It's a sad state of affairs when a man can't come home from a hard day's work, and have a drink without a shit storm.' He crumpled up the sales receipt and threw it on the floor. 'I'm the one earning the damn money and you're bitching about six dollars.' He got up and allowed the screen door to slam shut behind him."

"I wandered back into the house, cleaned up the kitchen, did some reading without knowing what I had read until I finally went upstairs. He was propped up in bed reading the book, *To Kill a Mockingbird*."

"'I love that book,' I told him as I got my nightgown on."

"'Don't tell me the ending,' he mumbled."

"'Did you get a library card?'"

"'No, a guy at work gave it to me,' he said as he closed the book and turned out his bedside light."

"The same guy who gave you the whiskey? I wondered. As I got into bed I realized how exhausted I was. I turned off my light and fell asleep as soon as my head hit the pillow. My sleep brought me back to the county fair, and we were on a roller coaster. Only this ride didn't have any loops. It climbed higher and higher until it came to a peak and then dropped straight down. In my dream, we were holding onto the handle bar for dear life, screaming our lungs out."

"'What the hell?' he growled, awakening me."

"'What!' I panted. I was already sitting up; my hands clenched out in front me. It was a relief to be awakened and realize that I was in bed and not falling to my death. 'I had the most horrible dream! Did I cry out?'"

"He ignored my question and said, 'I have to get up and go to work in the morning, so if you don't mind, how about turning off whatever it is you left on.'"

"I strained to hear what he was grumbling about and faintly heard music playing. He's gotta be kidding, I thought. That woke him up? I didn't relish the thought of walking through our darkened house, but I wasn't going to ask my husband to check it out. I didn't want to sound like a scared little girl. I got out of bed, my hands out in front of me as I groped the air in the darkened room. When I came to the hall, the light of the full moon entering through the stairwell window lit the way. A century of use made the stairs creak and worry; each step caused my nerves to splinter a little more. I entered the living room and saw an apparition looking at me from across the room. I put my hand to my mouth to smother a scream, and the ghost did the same. I heaved a sigh of relief when I realized I had been frightened by my own reflection in the mirror over the fireplace. I continued across the living room and as I entered the kitchen, the music stopped. I looked around and saw nothing amiss. That was good enough for me, and not wanting to tempt fate, I turned to retrace my steps and return to the safety of my husband.

"Just as I started out of the room, the cellar door swung open on creaking hinges. I rushed over and slammed it shut. Leaning against the door, I felt a cold draft against my ankles. Fear swept through me. I wanted to run away, but I needed to bar the door. Had there been a lock, I would have used it. Keeping one foot pressed against the bottom of the door, I leaned over toward the kitchen table and was just able to catch the back of a chair with my outstretched fingertips. As the chair tipped back, I dragged it over to me, and wedged it under the door knob. As I breathed a sigh of relief, something tickled my ankle. With my heart beating out of my chest, I outran my reflection back through the living room, up the stairs, and threw myself into bed, wrapping my arms around my husband. He wrapped his arms around me in return.

"'I'm sorry, too,' he said."

"In the morning I moved the chair back to its place at the table before he came downstairs. I didn't want him to know it was fear that had ended the argument."

"Later in the week as I was baking, I started singing this happy tune without remembering all the words. Margaret used to sing it when she was getting ready to go out –
Heart and soul/
La, la, la, la, la/la/
Heart and soul/
I fell for you/
La, la, la/
You are the one for me/
Kisses/
La, la, la, la, la/

"I froze, wooden spoon in hand, when I realized it was the song that played from the phantom music box. It gave me the shivers. This is ridiculous, I thought. Am I really going to allow myself to be afraid in my own home? I glanced over at the door. I hadn't heard the music box except that one night. Maybe I hadn't heard it, I tried to reason. Perhaps it had just been a song going through my head. But no, my husband had heard it too. I took the first batch of blueberry muffins out of the oven and put the second batch in. I looked them over. They smelled heavenly and looked delicious, all golden brown with sparkling sugar on the top. Maybe I was getting the knack of it. I looked back at the basement door. I should just go down there, I thought; but remained where I stood. Come on, what are you a Fraidy Cat? That self-taunt made me move my feet. I hit the light switch, strode to the door, swung it open, and marched down the stairs before I allowed myself to get cold feet. The next thing I knew the smoke detector was blaring. I was standing in the basement and looked up to see smoke filling the kitchen. I ran up and pulled out the muffins that were burnt to a crisp. How could that be, I thought? They took twenty-five minutes to bake. What had I been doing in the basement all that time? I thought back and couldn't even remember what the basement looked like."

"The following week we were working in the yard when our neighbor, Mr. Green, came over with an invitation for coffee. Being an antique dealer, his kitchen and dining room were overflowing with mismatched cups and saucers. Just choose a pattern you like, he told us as he brought the coffee pot over. 'This is a particularly nice one,' he said as he handed me a rose-designed cup with gold edging. 'It's Royal Doulton. I was really pleased to see that you two have stayed on so long. I must say, my curiosity got the better of me and I had to know how things are going.'"

"'Fine,' I said. 'I must admit I'm missing home a bit, but we're good.'"

"'I mean with the house. No weird things going on? Stuff moving around on its own? Footsteps from empty rooms?'"

"I nearly choked on my coffee and my husband said, 'What are you saying?'"

"'The house is haunted,' Mr. Green said simply, shrugging his shoulders. 'No doubt about it. I never would have thought I'd be saying such a thing. I never used to believe in all that superstitious, hocus pocus stuff. Except what went on in that house changed my mind.' Then he lowered his voice as if he didn't want any lingering spirits to overhear, 'There was devil worshiping going on. It started in 1962. All kinds of weird noises going on in that house all night long. Soon some of the neighborhood cats went missing, only to turn up dead, mutilated, and bloodless,' he almost whispered, leaning in closer to us and arching his eyebrows at the last words. He sat back, his face pensive as he relived the experience. 'I tried to get the police involved, but they said no crime was committed so nothing could be done. I'm not sure that's how the cats felt about it. Anyway, in February 1963 a man turned up dead in that place. Somebody called the police and said to look in the basement. And there they found him. Never did find out just who he was, who made the call, and no one was ever charged. For a long time, the house stood empty. It got inherited by some fella who thought it would be best to just sell the thing. Only he couldn't get a taker. Who wants to buy a house with that kind of history? So, he got the real estate agent to rent it out, trying to get some income out of the place. Only problem, no one lasts but a day or two. Most run out in the dead of night. Sometimes months go by with no one moving in. But you say you haven't experienced anything?'"

"My husband started to answer, but I blurted out 'No! No problems at all.'"

"'Nothing weird?' Mr. Green asked, raising a questioning eyebrow."

"'Not a thing,' I lied. 'Well, thanks for the coffee.'"

"'Oh, you're welcome, Miss. Now, you be careful. Just because nothing has happened, doesn't mean it won't start.'"

"'Why did you say that to –' my husband started to ask when we were outside. But I interrupted him. I wasn't scared, I was livid."

"'I see what's going on here. Mr. Green wants our home! He scares people away. If the owner can't rent it, Mr. Green will be able to buy it for cheap. He probably does it all with wires and string and mirrors and such! When I think of how he scared me! What kind of person would do that, especially to a young couple just starting out?'"

"By the time I was done with my rant we were back at the house. We entered through the back door into the kitchen and there to the left was the door that led to the basement. We stared at the innocent looking, plain white door as if it was the camouflaged entrance to hell. My moxie had run away as I pressed my lips together into a tight, straight line lest I started blabbering about how the tinny music had stopped when I entered the room, how the basement door had swung open seemingly on its own accord, the cold touch against my bare ankle, and the loss of time when I went to investigate. Where would we go if we left this house? I asked myself. It was rather like glib talk about giving up birthdays, fine until you considered the alternative. Our meager savings wouldn't cover another security deposit and all the rest that went with renting a new place. I shuddered when I remembered the places we had looked at before this one.

"'Why don't you start looking around for someplace else?' my husband said fulfilling my fear. 'This place has given us the willies since we moved in.'"

"I continued to stare wide-eyed at the door."

"'Well, say *something*!' he demanded."

"I turned away from him and the basement door, ashamed that I couldn't rally and say in a gay voice, 'There's no need for us to get silly about this. I'm sure we just need to get used to the place is all.' If I had, he might have joined me in laughing it off. Instead I mumbled, 'It's only Mr. Green, you big Fraidy Cat' as I tried to taunt myself into moving towards the door. I saw him flinch out of the corner of my eye."

"He lunged at the basement door and yanked it open. He looked over his shoulder and scorched me with a look of utter contempt before he stomped down the stairs."

"The cause of his angry reaction dawned on me. 'I didn't mean you!' I hollered down to him. 'I was calling *myself* a Fraidy Cat! Not you!'"

"I followed him down the steps, with unwilling feet. I couldn't believe this stupid turn of events. Damn Mr. Green for nurturing our unease about the house. Somehow I must not show fear so we could stay put until we saved enough money to move. I didn't want to ask Margaret for funds. She would be gracious about it, but I didn't want her prediction that our nest egg was inadequate to be true. It would make me wonder if she was right about other things, and I couldn't start going down that path.

"There was nothing special about the basement. There was no fake, dried blood sprayed on the walls or a turned spot in the dirt floor where a body had been dug up and removed. Really! Our story-telling neighbor missed an opportunity here. If he was going to scare people, he should have done some staging. We stood at the foot of the steps for a moment looking around, breathing in the damp cellar air. A pile of lumber on the floor caught my attention. I was considering whether we could use the scraps to make a bird feeder when I realized my husband had walked to the far side of the room and was staring at the walls."

"'What is it?' I asked."

"'There's something not right about this space. It doesn't fit the footprint of the house.' He started tapping the walls."

"'Look,' he said. 'This wall was added on. The rest of the outside walls are masonry, but this one is smooth and sounds hollow.' He grabbed a short length of 2x4 and used it like a battering ram against the center of that section of the wall.”

“‘What are you doing?’ I yelled. But there was no stopping him when he wanted to prove a point. After a couple blows, he punched a hole in the wall. A couple more blows and a chunk of broken sheetrock disappeared from view leaving a black gap in the wall. A cold current of air escaped from the void beyond the hole, accompanied by what seemed to be a barely audible sigh. He reached in behind the opening and tugged at the edges until several more small pieces of sheetrock broke off and fell onto the dirt floor on our side of the wall. He peered into the hole but of course it was too dark to see anything.”

“‘Let’s go!’ I begged my husband. Suddenly, I felt terribly anxious. But he ignored my plea as he tore more pieces of the sheetrock away until he had an opening big enough for his head and upper body to fit through.”

“‘There’s something here,’ he exclaimed as excited as a boy on a treasure hunt. ‘I ... can almost ...’ he pulled his body further into the hole. When he came back out, he had a round metal box grasped in his hands. He was all smiles as he dusted it off with his sleeve.’”

“‘Put it back!’ I told him.”

“‘It’s like getting a gift from Boo Radley! It looks like it’s silver ... and old,’ he said, examining it.”

“‘And not ours!’ I told him.”

“‘It’s a music box!’ he exclaimed as he turned the key at the bottom of the box. The same song that had waltzed through the house now filled the basement. I took a step back away from it. ‘Here,’ he said moving forward and thrusting it into my hands, delighted to make it a present. ‘You can keep it. No one’s going to know we took it.’”

“The music box felt burning cold in my hands, like a block of ice. It did look valuable. It had entwined hearts carved in the silver with a deep ruby stone in the center. I turned it over and saw engraved initials: MST to JVT and a date that was too worn to read. What if it had been someone’s cherished possession? What if that person didn’t like us touching it? I hurried to the opening in the wall with the intention of placing the box respectfully inside. But as I drew closer, I grew more afraid, and I threw it through the opening to get it out of my hands as quickly as possible. I heard the silver box hit the back wall and the music stopped.”

“‘I can’t believe you!’ my husband snapped. ‘If you didn’t want to keep it, we could have pawned it. I bet it was worth something; now it’s broken.’”

110

"What was going on here? I thought. He was no longer concerned, but I was scared out of my mind. What on earth had we gotten ourselves into? I ran to the stairs. As I reached them, the single light bulb hanging from the center of the basement ceiling went out."

"'Hey!' my husband called out, annoyed, as if someone in the kitchen had accidentally turned the light switch. I, on the other hand was terrified, and started bounding up towards the daylight at the top of the stairs. I watched in horror as the basement door slammed shut, barely missing my fingers. I groped around in the darkness for the doorknob. When I found it, it wouldn't turn. But there was no lock. It was as if someone held it in place. My husband pushed me aside. He twisted the knob with all his might and threw his weight into the door."

"'Get us out of here! Get us out!' I screamed. And with that, the door flew open, and we fell into the kitchen. We slammed the door shut behind us. While I braced the door, he raced to the back porch, grabbed a hammer from his tool box, a handful of 10 penny nails, ran back to the basement door, and nailed it shut. He was out of breath when he finished and dropped the hammer to the floor. Twenty nails toed into the door and frame guaranteed nobody or nothing could ever come up from the basement."

"But we knew it wouldn't help. Whatever it was, wasn't in the basement anymore. We could feel it. Everything *looked* the same, but the very air felt charged with rage and a putrid smell swept through the house."

"'We're moving!' my husband announced."

"I nodded yes. I was so terrified I couldn't speak."

Liv had taken three distracted nibbles from her tuna fish sandwich before setting it down and leaving it on the waxed paper. The nurse had begun listening to the story with a professional ear. What was the patient's credibility? Why was she telling the story, and what did the patient want her to hear? What was *not* being said? However, when Liv was distracted by a commotion in the hallway, the nurse realized she had ended up listening to the story as intently as a child in her Grandma's kitchen. Penny's attention was also diverted as she paused and followed Liv's gaze. Mayra-Liz burst into the room. "Is Eva here?" she asked out of the breath, as she looked around the room.

"No," said Penny. "I haven't seen her since yesterday. What's happening?"

"Siena called. Eva's missing."

111

Chapter Eighteen

Rose-Colored Crayon

"I see that you've been writing in your notebook," Dr. Allen said with an approving nod as Penny and he settled down in the small counseling room.

"Yes, but I can't say how helpful it will be."

Dr. Allen went through some papers in a folder, brought out a report and said, "Your CT scan came back fine, but for some reason your blood wasn't drawn until this morning, so we'll have the results tomorrow. On a scale of one to ten, how was your sleep last night?"

"It was fine," Penny replied distractedly.

Dr. Allen kept his pen raised above the paper.

"Nine," Penny answered. "I can't give it a ten because I didn't awaken in my own bed, next to my husband."

Dr. Allen nodded and made a note.

"Why do you think you slept so well? I saw in your chart that you refused a mild sleep aid. Patients don't normally sleep well with all the hospital commotion."

"I don't know," Penny shrugged.

"You didn't write anything in your journal about having a good night's sleep after months of not sleeping well?"

"I had planned on writing about it in my journal this afternoon, but I had lunch with Liv and –"

"You had lunch with Liv?"

"Yes. She came in early so we could finish the talk that we had last night, but we weren't able to because Mayra-Liz came in and said that Eva is missing and I –"

"I'm sorry; we're talking about the nurse that was on duty when you first came in, Liv Wright?"

"Yes, we ... I guess, we connected. I told her lots of things that I hadn't told anyone else, and she came in early so we could continue talking."

"I noticed in the charts that you didn't meet with Dr. Reed yesterday because you were ordered to bed rest for your symptoms of nasopharyngitis."

Penny gave a questioning look. "A head cold," he explained. "You look well. Are you feeling better?"

"Hmm. Yes, much better. In fact, I'm fine now."

"That's good," Dr. Allen said as he gave Penny a questioning look, and then made a note for the charts. "You must be a quick healer. So, you said you spent time with Nurse Wright, had your lunch with her?"

"Yes. It's all right, isn't it, if a nurse makes a friendship with a patient and comes in early because she's concerned."

"I trust Liv Wright completely to follow professional protocol. It's just a bit unusual. Now, what is this about someone missing?"

"Eva. I talked about her yesterday. Michael and I, we ... well, I don't like to call her a foster child, but she came to us through the Foster Care system. She's now at Siena College, but her roommate reported that Eva didn't sleep in the dorm last night, and she didn't attend her morning classes."

"Has she done something like this before?"

"Never. And she's in the HEOP program. It was very competitive to get in. Eva signed a bunch of papers promising to follow rules and protocol. Skipping classes, staying out all night during her very first semester," Penny shook her head. "I don't know what the ramifications of that will be."

"What did you write about?" Dr. Allen asked, nodding towards Penny's notebook.

"Thirty-seven places where Eva might be. I know that it's not helpful toward my counseling session, but it was all I could think about."

"May I?" he asked, nodding towards the notebook.

"Sure," Penny said as she handed it to him.

Dr. Allen scanned the page. "Paris?" he asked. "Would she go to Paris?"

"It's where I would go, if I was running away. Eva has a passport and just about enough money in her bank account to cover a plane ticket."

"Do you think it's likely Eva would leave the country?"

"I don't know. I didn't think it was likely Eva would ever skip a class. Her roommate said Eva was sobbing in the library yesterday. That's not like her. She's a very private person."

"I assume people are looking for her."

"Yes, her friends wrote something on her Facebook page. Her sisters are calling everyone they know. Michael is driving around Schenectady in case Eva went looking for her mother. The girls' mother left when Eva was young, I think she was ten."

"And Eva misses her," Dr. Allen said.

"When Eva first came to live with Michael and me, she was very angry with her mother. I convinced Eva that her mother did the noble thing by leaving and not subjecting her daughters to her drug addiction."

"Do you know that for a fact?"

"That she was a drug addict?"

"No, that the mother left to do the right thing."

"Of course, I couldn't know that for sure, but it was a positive way to look at it, and it helped Eva cope with her mother's abandonment."

Dr. Allen frowned as he wrote something on the note pad.

"Was that wrong?" Penny gasped. "I'm *so* new at parenting. I never really know what the right thing is."

"I have never parented, Penny, and I would never suggest that I have all the answers. However, I would be careful coloring in reality with either a rose-colored crayon or a black one."

Penny shook her head. "I sometimes feel that I'll never get this right. What am I doing trying to be a role model for three young women? I can barely keep my own head above the emotional waves."

"Do you know of the book, *The Five Encouragements*?"

Penny shook her head no.

"It's a self-help book. My wife was a contributing writer. One of the encouragements is *I will take life as I find it*. That means we don't pretend that a situation is worse or better than what it actually is. They say it's a good way to deal with life."

Penny nodded as she stared into the hallway. "Is the book in the hospital library? I could check it out."

"I don't know," he replied. "But I'll bring you a copy if you want to read it. I do feel it has a lot of helpful information."

Penny nodded.

"Perhaps something in the reading will help jumpstart our counseling sessions. You know you can talk to me about anything, Penny. I will certainly keep it confidential."

"I know," Penny smiled her thanks.

"We'll meet tomorrow. Try to write in your journal about something other than Eva. Oh, and I'd like you to go to the sleep clinic tonight so your sleep can be monitored. Let's figure out how we can get you to sleep as well at home."

Dr. Allen walked Penny to her room where Liv waited for them.

"How'd it go?" Liv asked.

"Good," Penny replied absently. "Has anyone come in? Did you hear anything about Eva?"

"Not yet," Liv replied.

Dr. Allen looked at Liv. She looked tired and with good reason. Liv had worked a swing shift for the past three weeks straight. *Why would she do that?* Dr. Allen wondered. *Why would someone who was offered a full-time position with benefits continue to work through a temp agency with no benefits? Was the flexible time off that big of a pull?*

"You look tired, Liv," he said.

"Now, you know that's nothin' a lady wants to hear," Liv replied with a wry smile.

"I just meant that I could ask the head nurse to try and arrange the schedule so that you aren't working a swing shift."

"But that's what the temps do."

"I just meant I could ask if –" But Dr. Allen stopped when he saw the closed expression on Liv's face which said she didn't want Dr. Allen to intervene. "I'll see you tomorrow, Penny," Dr. Allen said. "I hope you sleep well. She's scheduled for the sleep clinic at nine, Liv."

"I'll make sure to walk her down."

Dr. Allen walked out of the room, but in the hallway he paused and looked back at Liv. She had been watching him. When their eyes met, it briefly startled her. But she quickly recovered, gave a nod, and returned to the chart she was reading.

It was odd for a nurse to have lunch with a patient she doesn't know. Dr. Allen remembered the last time Liv had taken a personal interest in a patient; the man was later arrested for bank fraud and embezzlement. Penny certainly didn't look like an embezzler, but then again neither did that man. Dr. Allen glanced back at Liv for one more look, and then shook his head. *Really,* he thought. *I must get some more sleep.*

Chapter Nineteen

The Home Front

As Edward parked the car, Eva looked up at their destination: The Home Front Cafe. The building suited its name. It looked like it had been someone's home in the 1940s. Ruffled country curtains hung at the windows. It had white clapboard siding, and the trim was painted red and blue. There was a tiny plot between the sidewalk and house that had been prepared for a flower bed. Eva imagined that in the summer red geraniums, white petunias, and blue bells grew, matching the American flag that hung next to the scallop-edged front door.

"It's sweet," Eva said with a smile, one of the few she had sported in the last few days.

"Yeah, and the coffee's great," Edward said.

A stroller and a blue plastic tricycle were parked at the edge of the sidewalk. "Creepy," he said as they walked around them.

"What's creepy?" Eva said, looking around.

"The tricycle, or rather the big wheels. It's like the one Danny rode in *The Shining*."

"Oh! That's right! Do you think this place is wooooo haunted?" Eva teased.

Edward messed his dark hair across his forehead, and flashed a crazed smile and said, "Herrreeee's Johnny!"

"Stop!" Eva said as she reached for the door. "You'll scare the women and children."

As she pushed the door open, a bell jingled. They were greeted by the Andrew Sisters harmonizing about fidelity and an apple tree. Eva paused to take in the clientele: a half dozen children ranging from newborn to pre-school and not a mommy in sight. The children were cared for by a group of what looked like seasoned veterans ... of wars, not parenthood.

"Come in and shut the door," demanded a lean and fit, older gentleman. "You're letting the cold air in; we've got an infant here."

"Sorry," Eva mumbled as she and Edward hurried in.

"I'm Sammy!" a preschooler with a cereal bowl haircut and a head cold informed them.

"Hello, I'm Eva," she replied as if formal introductions were being made. Eva didn't go in for kitschy coo talk.

"Sam, get over here and let me wipe your nose again. Runs like a faucet, doesn't it, Buddy."

"They're short staffed," the man with the newborn informed them. "Just take any table. And help yourself to coffee if you want a cup. The waitress is currently in the back cooking. Jacob, you share those cars or I'll put them away."

"You want coffee?" Edward asked.

"Sure," Eva said as she chose a table next to the window.

Edward set the big, white mugs with American flag decals down and sat next to Eva. "Looks like an interesting group of caregivers, huh?" Edward whispered as they watched an old timer make airplane noises as he dive-bombed scrambled eggs into a little girl's mouth. "Thatta girl," he told her with a booming, masculine voice for every bite. She responded with a baby tooth grin.

"It sure as hell could be worse," Eva whispered back as she leaned across him to pick up the sugar dispenser. She held it over her coffee mug so that the little flap on the silver cap remained wide open. Eva glanced at Edward defying him to say something as nearly five teaspoons flowed into her coffee. He did. "Your hair smells like wood smoke and leaves."

"So?" she asked defensively.

"So, it's nice. It reminds me of camping on an autumn day."

"What are you having? I'm starved. I want the Eisenhower stack of pancakes," Eva said as she closed the menu that was inserted in a red plastic cover. "How did you find this place? It's so cool with all this memorabilia stuff under the clear plastic tablecloths."

"My buddies and I threw a party here for Aaron before he went to Afghanistan. It was fun. We all dressed up in vintage clothes. Look, before we order, we need to discuss finances. I have exactly six dollars and seventeen cents. I have a half a tank of gas, so we're okay in that regard, but the most we can order besides the coffee is a bagel that we share. And don't order extra cream cheese."

"It's okay; breakfast is on me. I have fifty dollars that Michael insists I carry for emergencies."

118

"This isn't an emergency. We can get breakfast on our meal plan when we get back to campus."

"I want to treat you to breakfast. Please. You were so great to pull me out of the library before I made an even greater fool of myself. I can't believe I fell apart like that. I'm no baby, and I was *bawling*. I don't know how you could stand being around me when I'm like that."

"It was fun. I mean, after you stopped crying and stuff. Thatcher Park is always great in the winter, once you get a campfire going."

"Yeah," said Eva almost smiling. "It was nice."

They looked out the window remembering the night. Eva had cried most of the thirty minute drive from Latham to Altamont. It wasn't until the car started climbing the steep road that Eva looked out at the inky darkness and asked where they were going.

"Thatcher Park."

"Really?" Eva asked. "It's open now?"

The question was answered by Edward parking next to a chained road. He went around back and got out two folded lawn chairs and a couple of red plaid, woolen blankets. As Eva got out and joined him, she said, "You look prepared for anything."

"I like to keep these in the car for when I go train watching."

"You watch trains in a chair next to the tracks?"

"Yeah, it's better than sitting in the car. Next to the track, you can really feel the energy of the engines when they roar past, turbochargers whining. It's so cool."

"What'll you have?" asked the harried waitress/cook, "Do you want breakfast or are you all set?"

Eva looked at Edward beseechingly; she wouldn't order breakfast unless he did too. "Okay," Edward replied, "I'll have the F.D.R. omelet, please."

"And I'll have the Eisenhower stack of pancakes and a Judy Garland orange juice," Eva said, reading from the menu.

"Coming right up," the waitress said, taking a moment to give them a smile before she hurried back to the kitchen.

"She's nice," Edward said.

"Yeah, she's okay."

Edward glanced at his watch. "I need to get back by 1:30 for Cell Bio. When's your next class?"

Eva glanced at her watch. "In forty-five minutes."

Edward's mouth dropped open. "We could just about make it if we left right now. Did you miss other classes?"

"Two."

"Two? Are you kidding?" Edward said.

Eva shook her head no.

"Where did you tell your roommate you were going?" Edward asked.

"I didn't. Look, this table has a little drawer in it ... And there are glass marbles inside!" Eva said as she held up a blue and green one.

"What do you mean, you didn't? You didn't call Emily or anything?"

"Nope. I just didn't want to get into it with her. Emily wouldn't have wanted to let me off the phone without me telling her what's going on. I mean, I haven't even told *you* what's wrong, and we spent the night together."

"But what if she gets worried and reports it to the R.A.? Would she do that?"

"I don't ... know."

"Gees, Eva, call her. See what's happening. Make sure they don't have a search party, I mean with you being so upset and everything yesterday, they might be really worried."

"All right," Eva said as she dug her phone out of her backpack. "I don't know why we couldn't have had breakfast before getting into this …. It's ringing."

"EVA! OHMYGOD, where are you! I have been worried sick," Emily said.

"I'm fine. I just needed to get away, get my head straight."

"Get your head straight? What a way to go about it! Your sisters have been calling me constantly. Michael is really upset. He's out driving around looking for you! I had to report your absence. I'm sorry, but what was I to think? I heard about your melt down in the library, and then you don't even –"

"I'm fine and I'll be back soon," Eva said, just before she hung up. "Yep, you're right. Things are really bad at the home front and I don't mean here."

Chapter Twenty

You're Scaring Me

Penny stared at her lunch without an appetite, a plate of chicken pot pie. She had hoped that running on the treadmill for the stress test would make her feel hungry, but no such luck.

"Hey," Liv said as she walked into Penny's room. "Any word yet on Eva?"

"Not a one," Penny said.

"I'm sure she's fine, just went off to give herself some time to think."

"That's such an optimistic view. How do you do that? I mean you must see some pretty depressing stuff in the hospital on a daily basis. How do you stay so upbeat?"

"I wasn't always. Then, there came a time when I just decided I had to turn myself around. It was either that or go around with a cloud over my head." Liv paused and reconsidered. "Well, I guess the cloud is always there someplace, but I try to not let it affect my outlook. We all have something that's our personal burden to carry around. I brought my lunch, if you feel like company," Liv said.

"I'd really like that," Penny told her.

"It's time for group, Penny," Mary announced. "Oh, sorry, Liv. I didn't know you were in here."

"I think it would be fine if Penny skipped group today, unless you want to go, Penny. Have you found it helpful?"

"Not at all. Everyone there has a substance abuse problem. It's like they have a romantic relationship with cocaine."

"Oh, okay. If that's what you want," Mary answered hesitantly. "You're not required to go."

"I'll square it with Dr. Allen," Liv said.

"Okay, I'll just check in with you later on, Penny," Mary said.

"I've got this, Mary. You don't have to check in," Liv told her. "I'll fill in the log when I'm done."

"Ahem, okay. I mean, is that okay? I've never had someone do that before."

"It's fine," said Liv.

"O-kay, then," said Mary as she backed out of the room while giving Liv a peculiar look.

"You're amazing," said Penny. "And I think a border-line con artist!"

Liv was poised to take a bite out of her sandwich when her head shot up.

"I'm joking," Penny laughed.

"So tell me the rest of your New Orleans story. The story stayed with me all night. And that music box –"

Penny's cell phone rang. Looking at the caller I.D. she said, "Its Michael."

"You want me to step out?"

Penny shook her head no.

"We found her!" Michael announced. "Rather, Eva called her roommate and said she's okay. Mayra-Liz called me. I'm in Schenectady now, but I'm on my way to Siena. I'm assuming Eva's on her way back there."

"But why did she leave? Where did she go?"

"All I know is that the roommate ... what's her name?"

"Emily."

"Emily. That's right. Eva called her and said she was okay, but needed to go someplace to think."

"Where would she go without a car?"

"I don't know. As I said, I hope to meet up with Eva at Siena. I really don't have much of anything to report other than our girl is safe and sound. You can put your mind at rest. Eva may be upset, but she wasn't abducted."

"Abducted!" Penny said with alarm. "I hadn't considered that."

Michael heaved a sigh. "I'll call you later."

"I'm sorry. I should be rejoicing in the good news, not –"

"It's okay. We all have fried nerves at the moment. Talk with you soon."

As Penny put her cell phone down, she met Liv's eyes. "I really must learn to not have the clouds color my life or whatever it was you said."

"Eva's okay?" Liv asked.

122

"Yes, thank God, and I'm going to try and not worry about what caused her to run off like that. Michael will tell me when he knows. I can't imagine that it was solely because I landed in the hospital, but maybe it was."

"I thought you weren't going to worry about that. Besides, I think you have been frying bigger fish. As I said, your New Orleans story just stayed with me last night. You've just got to tell me what happened."

"Yeah, that's certainly a bigger, darker cloud, and one that's followed me for a long time. I've got to say, it's been a relief to talk about it. Where did I end off?"

"You had thrown the music box back into the sealed area, the basement light went out, and you decided that you had to move."

"Jeez, look at my arms. Just remembering that time gives me goose bumps. What we did next was sign up for the first place we could afford without calling Margaret. The rental agent showed us a tired-looking, swaybacked trailer which would be available the following week when the young couple living there moved on to Germany, their next assignment. The following morning, when I put my husband's lunch in his backpack, I found a knickknack that had been sitting on the kitchen counter in the trailer. It was a ceramic brown and white dog with short ears, like a Jack Russell terrier. His paw was raised, poised to shake hands. Why did my husband steal it? I left the figurine where I found it. I had enough on my plate, like how I could remain in an angry house for seven more days. I didn't need an angry husband on top of it, well, angrier.

"The next morning I heard my husband shout, 'Good God in heaven!' I rushed into the kitchen and saw all the nails pulled out from the basement door and scattered on the floor. The door was ajar. In a daze, I walked to the open door and saw the light from the basement's single bulb dimly illuminating the bottom of the stairs. I looked across the room at my husband's grey face. For the first time, I noticed how much his appearance had changed. He looked gaunt, like someone with a terminal disease. He worked his jaw, as if he was in a rage that he could barely control. He grabbed a red and orange vase by its neck off the kitchen table. It was a wedding present, an ugly thing that looked like it had been made by a child, but with none of the charm. Since my pastor and his wife gave it to us, I cherished it.

"'What are you doing ...' I started to ask as he stormed in front of me."

"He flung the vase down the stairs, shouting, 'Go to hell, you bastard!'"

"'I think you shouldn't have done that,' I whispered."

"'I will not be *bullied*, not by anyone,' he said as he slammed the door so hard, the windows shook."

"'That was impossible," I said, gesturing at the nails on the floor, 'and I think a warning. And you just ... I don't think he likes being bullied either!' My voice was shaking and I had broken into a sweat. The last thing we needed was to enrage whatever was down there. 'We can't stay here now, not another day. Ask someone you work with if we can stay with them for a few days until the trailer's ready. I'll go to the shops once they open and meet you back here at six.'"

"'Why can't you ask someone? '"

"'Because I don't know anyone except Mr. Green, and he's gone on an antique buying trip.'"

"Later that afternoon when I returned from the stores, I quickly packed an overnight bag, and waited on the front porch. As it grew late and night fell, I became scared out of my wits. Perhaps I should wait in the gardens. I took the bag and hurried over, but the grounds with their shadows and night sounds scared me worse, and I quickly returned to the safety of the porch light. It was after midnight when I finally saw the Queen Bee pull up. I picked up the bag and hurried towards the car. He climbed out on unsteady legs, held up a hand, and snarled, 'Turn around. We aren't going anyplace.'"

"'There wasn't *anyone* who would let us stay for just a few days?' I asked heartsick as I dropped the bag."

"'No! They all had some stupid reason why. The kids have colds. Wife had a Tupperware party. Their house was messy .... They're assholes, every single one of them.'"

"'Did you tell them how important it is that we leave?'I asked as I picked up the bag and dragged my feet back to the house."

"'No, I said that we felt like a night out and especially hoped to sleep on someone's ratty couch or hard floor,' he said sarcastically. Then his voice exploded. 'I practically begged them. I told them how this house is evil. Goddammit to hell, I told them if I don't report for duty some morning, you can safety assume that my wife and I are both dead. Just have someone come by and scrape up our bodies.'"

"'Jeez!'" I said with a heavy sigh. "'What must those people think?'"

"'They think I'm frigging nuts! That's what they think.'"

"He tripped going up the front steps and fell into me. His breath told me he had found a friend with a whiskey bottle. 'You're drunk!' I said with anger. 'I can't believe it. I've been out of my mind with worry, left alone in this horrible house, and you've been out drinking!'"

"'I can't believe it either,' he shouted. 'I could have stayed in the men's barracks, but I came back to you. And what thanks do I get?'"

"That night there was a tremendous thunderstorm. The sheets of rain seemed like a barrier, closing us off to the outside world. We both let out a yell when lightning struck the locust tree out front and a branch smashed an upstairs window."

"'You'll need to call the realtor in the morning and get the window fixed,' my husband hollered over the raging storm. When I called Mr. Wesley he said he'd send someone right over. Of course, no repair person found their way to the house, but mice sure did. The next evening, the little critters were scurrying across the kitchen. I screeched at the sight of them, causing my husband to come flying into the room, his eyes blazing, battle-ready, carrying my grandfather's pistol that Margaret had given me years ago. Seeing it was just another mouse, he shouted, 'God *damn* it! You've got to stop doing that! I swear to Christ I can't take much more.'"

"'You've got to stop waving my gun around. You're going to kill someone, namely me!' I shouted back."

"'Then stop your *screaming*!' He turned away from me, but not before I noticed he had blood on his tee-shirt."

"'What is that?' I asked."

"'It's just a nosebleed,' he said as he put the back of his hand to his nose and more scarlet-red blood came out. 'I used to get them all the time when I was a kid. It'll stop.'"

"'But why did it start again? What's happening to you?' I wailed."

"'I'm sure it's just from being so tired. I'll be fine after we leave here and start sleeping again. Let's not overreact.'"

"I let out a snort and then a giggle. At first he looked at me like I was crazy, then he started laughing too. *Not overreact* was the funniest thing we had ever heard! But when he continued to laugh with great booming howls, the light-hearted moment turned ominous. He sounded like he belonged in an asylum."

"'Don't. You're scaring me,' I told him as I put my hand on his arm."

"He shrugged my hand away, gave me a sneering smile, and said, 'I wouldn't want to do that, now would I? After all, you're the one who got us into this mess.'"

"'*I* am?'"

"'You're the one who saw the For Rent sign in the window.'"

"'You can't blame this on me! How could I have possibly known?'"

"'I knew. When I put the key in the lock, I knew something was wrong, but you were all hot and bothered to be carried into the house, dying to get in bed. If I had followed *my* instincts, instead of *yours,* we wouldn't be in this mess.'"

"'Stop it! We have to stick together through this. We haven't even had our first month's anniversary!'"

"But he moved close to my face, popped his eyes wide open, and gave a blood curdling howl, causing me to shutter. For the first time, I was afraid of him. Had he lost his mind? I listened as he went through the house and up the stairs, howling and laughing. I sat down hard on a dining room chair and sobbed as another thought occurred to me. It came in the sound of Margaret's voice, 'I know you love that boy, but there's something wrong with him. Deep down where no one can see, he's wounded, perhaps damaged beyond repair. *Listen to me, Penny.* I know what I'm talking about,' she had said in a stern voice that I rarely heard before he came into our lives. Hearing my husband's mad barks somewhere on the floor above me, I wondered if Margaret was right. Maybe it wasn't just the house that was making him act this way. The lying, stealing, and explosive temper. What if Margaret was right?"

"The following day he came home from work and told me he had field training the next two days *and* nights. 'How can I possibly stay in this house alone?' I wondered out loud."

"'I don't have any choice in this,' he said hotly."

"'I know, and I'll be okay,' I said with a sigh of resignation. Secretly, I wondered if I might do better with my husband away. Plus, I had my cross. Nothing evil was going to hurt me while I had it. My cross had been a going-away present from my church group and had been blessed with holy water to ensure a safe trip to New Orleans. It had been hanging from the car's rear-view mirror, but I started wearing it around my neck shortly after we moved in.

"My husband got up in the morning, packed his gear, and left. We were angry with each other, and barely spoke. A few moments later, he came back in. 'I'm sorry,' he said, gesturing to the room and the house at large. He took me in his arms and held me close."

"'It'll be all right' I told him. 'After we get away from this house, things will get better. We'll start again.' Weeks later it occurred to me that he apologized for the *house*, not his crazy behavior."

"I spent the day outdoors doing yard work. When I came into the house for water or to use the bathroom, I held up my cross and said in a quivering voice, 'I'm not afraid. I have my cross. You mess with me, and you'll be asking for trouble.' At nine o'clock that night I practically collapsed into bed from fatigue and fell immediately to sleep, only to tumble into a horrific nightmare about a pillow forced over my face and held there. I woke up gagging and gasping for air."

"'It's only a dream. It's okay. I'm *okay*,' I reassured myself as I sat up and tried to slow my breathing and out-of-control, racing heart. I brushed my hair out of my face and saw one of the living room pillows next to me. The vine pattern was no longer faded, but a verdant green. I grabbed the pillow by a corner as if it could bite or infect me, and threw it. It hit the floor and took a bounce forward towards the bed. I screamed. The sound bounced around the walls and echoed down the hall, scaring me even more. 'Dear God!' I cried out and with a shaking hand, reached for my cross. It was gone. My silver chain was still around my neck, but the cross was gone. It took a moment for the thought to settle in. My mind explained it to me in slow, deliberate words, as if I was a small child: *Your ... cross ... is ... gone*.

"'No!' I cried out loud. Without my cross I felt exposed. I leapt off the bed and pawed frantically through my clothes, shook out the sheets, and tore the cases from the pillows. 'Where is it?' I pulled the mattress off the bed springs. I crawled along the floor, checking every square inch. 'Where is it? Where is it!' I looked across the room. Had the pillow moved closer to me? Had it? Had it! I couldn't be sure. What would happen tomorrow night? Would I be smothered in my sleep? Well, I wasn't going to wait for that to happen. I flew downstairs into the dining room and grabbed the shears from the side board. I saw the other couch pillow on the table. It looked bold and mocking in its deep green color. I had had it! I grabbed that pillow and stomped my way back up the stairs."

"'I'll show you!' *Snip went the shears.*"

"'You stupid ...' *Snip*"

"'Moving on your own ...' *Snip*"

"'Color-changing ...' *Snip*"

"'Pillows.' *Snip. Snip, Snip*"

"My breathing was ragged, but I felt superior as scraps of fabric and stuffing fell to my feet. Why hadn't I done this days ago? Just who is in control here anyway? I thought as I squeezed down hard on the shears only to nick my finger with the sharp point. I held out my hand and watched in fascination as blood ran down my arm forming crimson drops on the floor.

"Somewhere in my mind, I knew I was in a dangerous state. An inner voice of self-preservation commanded, *Put the shears down. Do it now!* I put them down. *Now, pull yourself together.*"

"'I have to get out of here,' I cried aloud."

"Where would you go? I asked myself. "Mr. Green, the only neighbor you know is away. It'll be hours before the stores open. What you need to do is *calm down*. Go get a band aid, wash your face, and pull yourself together.

"Okay. Good. Now, find something to do, get your mind off of this. Go down to the kitchen and bake some bread. That will relax you. Besides this is your place for now. You paid good money to live here. Sure, whatever is in this house has managed to drive you out and into a tin can of a place in *Crime City*, but for today you just *stand your ground*, I thought with false bravado."

"'Okay. I'm getting out the ingredients. I've got my mixing bowl and measuring cup,' I encouraged myself as my entire body shook and teeth chattered. I kept looking around, to make sure nothing jumped out at me. This is ridiculous, I thought as I breathed into my cupped hands to help control the hyperventilation. I can't continue like this. I'm going to have an emotional breakdown. That's when it occurred to me, I had never tried to talk with this ... whatever it was. Perhaps if he knew I wouldn't hurt him, that I wasn't a threat, he'd be okay with my being here. Things couldn't get any worse, I reasoned. I cleared my throat.

"'Excuse me, sir. We need to talk. I know you had a *really* bad experience in this house, but my husband and I are not to blame. We would *never* hurt you. I'm sorry about the music box. And really, my husband didn't mean anything by what he said.'"

"A foul smell swept into the room. I was wrong, things could get worse. I froze, petrified. My flour-covered hands rested on the table. I held my breath and kept my eyes focused on the mixing bowl in front of me, afraid of what I might see if I looked up. I started crying."

"'I didn't mean to upset you,' I whispered. A chair was knocked over and slid across the floor. As I turned to look at it, something grabbed my shoulder. I screamed as pee ran down my legs, and pooled on the kitchen floor around my feet."

"'GET AWAY FROM ME!' I cried out. And in an instant it was gone, *completely* gone. The heavy presence vanished, the foul stench dissipated. I was in an empty house. Alone. I stood there without thought or emotion. All I felt was the throbbing in my shoulder. I'm not sure how long I stood there in a daze before I stepped out of my wet panties and left them on the floor. Like a bird with a broken wing I struggled out of my nightshirt. When I saw the scorched fabric on the shoulder of my shirt, I wasn't surprised. I'll never be shocked by anything ever again, I thought."

"Wait," Liv exclaimed. "Your nightshirt was scorched ... from where he touched you? Well, that's just –"

"Not possible? Yeah, I would like to think that, too. I dropped the shirt and used it to wipe up the puddle of urine. I walked upstairs and into the disheveled bedroom. I knew what I had to do. I got dressed as quickly as I could and then picked up an empty packing box and used my hip to hold it up against the dresser. With my good arm I swept everything except for the lamp from the top of the dresser into a jumble in the box. Easing the box to the floor I then ran from room to room and managed to pack up the entire house, working with the frenzy of a one-armed paper hanger, using my good arm and my feet to drag and shove the boxes to the front porch. When I was done, I wrapped myself in a quilt and sat on the porch swing and watched the empty road.

"I saw the Queen Bee turn the corner onto our street just as it started to get light out. He had managed to leave a day early! I threw the quilt aside, ran down the porch steps, and was yanking on the driver's door handle before the car had even stopped. As he got out, I pulled him to me as close as possible. I wanted to be inside his skin, to be safe. When he hugged me back, squeezing my shoulder, I cried out in pain."

"'What?' he asked. 'What happened?'"

"'I *cannot* go back inside that house.'"

"He looked over and saw all the boxes on the porch. 'I don't know what to say. Where would you have us live ... in a tent?'"

"Of course! That was the answer. Why hadn't we thought of it earlier? There were tents to rent for practically nothing at the state park, not an hour away. We could take the rest of our money and go there. We piled everything we owned into the back of the station wagon."

"At noon I awakened to the sound of children playing near our tent. I was stiff and sore, but the morning nap had felt like a luxury. My husband cuddled me close, but when he leaned in to nuzzle my neck, I gasped."

"'Let me look at it,' he said."

"'You have a horrible bruise,' he exclaimed. 'Can you raise it?'"

"When I demonstrated that I had mobility, he sighed and said, 'Good, we've got enough stuff to get done without going to the emergency room. Since I pulled field duty, I don't report back for two days. It'll give us time to get things settled with the realtor and get our security deposit back.'"

"'Will they inspect the house first?'"

"'I'm sure. You left it in order, didn't you?'"

129

"'I dropped a jar of spaghetti sauce as I was taking the last box out. I wiped it up but I was in such a hurry; I can't say how clean I got it.'"

"'I'll check it out,' he said. 'I need to go back anyway. I have to repair the hole in the basement wall.'"

"'We can't go back in there.'"

"'*We're* not going back in, *I* am. You can wait in the car or wait here. Look, it was a good idea to stay at the campground, but it's out of the way and we are flat broke. If I don't get money to gas up the car so I can report for work for the rest of the week, do you know the kind of trouble I'll be in? It's not like civilian life. We have to get the security deposit back.'"

"'Red sky at night, sailor's delight,'" my husband piped. "'Maybe it's a good sign for fighting the house villain.'"

"I started to cry."

"'What now?' he asked in exasperation.'"

"'I don't want you anywhere near that house.'"

"'It'll be all right,' his tone softened. 'Look, it left. You told it to, and it did. Remember?'"

"As we approached the house, the living room curtain next to the front door fell back into place, as if someone had been holding it aside just enough to peek out the window, and then quickly stepped back."

"'Did you see that?' I asked hoping he hadn't and it was just my overwrought nerves and the dim, evening light playing tricks on me."

"'See what?' he replied too nonchalantly, and I knew he had seen it too."

"'I'll call Margaret and ask her to wire us money. I know she'll send it,' I said as pride vanished and panic consumed me."

"'It's not just the money. I think the wall needs to be sealed up again. If it isn't ... I don't think it will leave us alone,' he said trying to sound logical, as if it was entirely possible that some apparition could trail us for the rest of our lives."

"'That can't happen!' I announced, trying to keep some semblance of sanity about us."

"'Who knows? How can we possible know what will happen unless we stop this thing,' he snapped."

"I watched my husband's faltering steps as he walked up the front porch carrying his heavy backpack filled with supplies to fix the wall. This isn't right, I told myself. I should be with him. I opened the car door and hurried up the steps."

"'All right,' he said, 'I don't have the energy to argue. You clean the kitchen, and I'll do the basement.'"

"When he pushed the front door open a rancid odor escaped the house making our eyes water. My husband gasped as he entered the kitchen. I looked past him and saw the room was practically dripping with spaghetti sauce. It was splattered on the walls like blood at a crime scene. A really violent crime scene. Across the room the stove was covered with it. There were thick red puddles of it on the floor. Even the ceiling dripped sauce."

"'It looks like somebody was murdered in here! How many jars did you break?' my husband asked."

"'One,' I said with a shaky voice. 'One,' I repeated, 'and I swear it didn't look like this when I left.'"

"He stepped around the mess and flipped the switch to the basement light, but it remained dark. He pulled a flashlight out of the backpack while saying, 'Why am I not surprised that the light doesn't work?' He took a deep breath and started down the stairs. As the second step creaked under his weight, the tinny music box started playing its melancholy song. My husband froze on the steps, turned and looked at me, the color drained from his face."

"'Let's go!' I cried.'"

"'I have to do this,' he answered. 'I know that for certain now. It'll never let go of us if I don't.'"

"I filled the bucket with soapy water, grabbed a sponge, and went to work. The music box had stopped playing, but I startled myself even further when I realized that I was humming the haunting tune to myself.

"The kitchen was almost clean an hour later when my husband hurried back up the stairs, as he pulled the backpack on. He closed the door and with a wild look announced that we had to go *right* now.

"As we rushed to the back door, we heard a loud crash."

"'Go! Go!' he shouted."

"When we got to the wrought iron fence, my husband grabbed my arm, pulling and dragging me in a panic over the jagged ornamental fleur de lis." I held up my arm and showed Liv the ugly scar that ran from my armpit to elbow. "I didn't even feel it happen."

Liv's eyes widened as she gently touched the roped skin as if she couldn't believe her eyes.

"Once we got back at the campsite, he placed something in my hand. I opened it to find my cross. He had found it on the bottom step to the basement. It was the first time in my life that I fainted."

"Dear Loving Jesus!" Liv said.

"I never told Margaret. She would have thought I was delusional. Our neighbors, who had a dairy farm next door, were all the time talking about strange happenings in a pasture that separated their property from ours: fox bodies mutilated, grass scorched, strange patterns in the ground created by ants. They wouldn't let their daughter take the shortcut through it to my house once it was night air."

"Night air?"

"You know, after the sun goes down and it starts getting chilly and damp. Our neighbors thought strange things came out then. They swore even the cows acted peculiar. Margaret thought it was just plain ludicrous."

Liv murmured, "What a terrible time for you, and just when you were starting out your married life."

"It was nothing compared to what was to come."

Chapter Twenty-One

The Boogeyman

Penny and Liv held each other's eyes until Liv's watch alarm started buzzing. "Whoa!" Liv said as she glanced down at her watch. "It's 2:30! You need to meet with Dr. Allen at 3:00 and I need to report to the front desk!"

"The time just flew by, didn't it? That's how it is when I talk with you, Liv. Thank you for coming in early and listening to me."

"I hope when you talk with Dr. Allen you're able to share what's haunting you. That New Orleans experience was something else, but if it was nothing compared to what's really bothering you, it's time you shared it with your doctor."

"I don't want you to think I was just filling time and avoiding the issue by talking about the New Orleans time. It's actually a very big deal for me to talk about my first marriage. Michael doesn't even know."

"Your husband doesn't know you were married before?"

Penny shook her head no.

"It's amazing, isn't it, the things we keep to ourselves," said Liv thoughtfully. "My mother's best friend, Annie back in Georgia, went to work every day cleaning houses after her husband went to work. He never knew until she passed and all these ladies showed up for her viewing. Annie didn't think Marcus would approve of her cleaning white ladies' houses, so she never told him. Seems to me a hard way to live one's life, keeping things bottled up inside."

"Michael and I made a pact before we got married to never share ancient history. I know Michael loves me. He respects me; he sees me in a certain light ... a good light. I can't bear to have him look at me differently."

"My, oh my, you really do have this thing screwed down tight on top of yourself."

"Well, I did. It really was a relief to talk to you about it. Maybe, maybe I can talk ... about ..." Penny hugged herself tightly and closed her eyes.

Liv reached over and gently squeezed Penny's shoulder. "Just take it one step at a time, Darlin'."

Penny looked up at Liv and gave a small smile. "I'm trying, Liv. I really am."

"I know you are." Liv gave Penny a thoughtful look, studying her face looking for the answer to a question without asking. "Don't answer this if you aren't up to it, but when you talk about your first marriage, you never say his name. Not once. It's always 'my husband' or 'he' or 'him.' Why is that?"

"I'll sound crazy," Penny said ruefully.

Liv raised her eyebrows in a 'Don't worry about me, I've heard it all' gesture.

"I'm afraid he'll hear me."

"Your first husband? You're concerned if you say his name, he'll hear it through what? Telepathy?"

"Something like that; I'm afraid he'll know where to find me."

"You've been hiding from him all this time?" Liv asked.

Penny nodded.

"Ah Sugar," Liv said, casting her eyes heavenward. "You've gone and made him into the boogeyman, haven't you? Come on, I'll walk you over to the counseling room."

"It's no wonder you're in such good shape," Penny said as they took long strides down the hallways. "You must walk miles every day. This counseling room isn't exactly in a convenient location, is it?"

"That it's not. Most of the time, I don't mind. As you said, it keeps me active. It's a rather depressing room though," Liv observed.

"And it smells like sauerkraut," Penny said whiffing the air.

"It does. Phew! Why don't we wait in the hallway? The chairs aren't the most comfortable, but it smells better out in the hall."

"What time is it?" asked Penny.

"Five of three," Liv said, looking at her watch.

"I bet you're the type of person who's early for everything, right?"

"Guilty as charged," Liv smiled.

A nurse pushed a bassinet briskly down the hall. A little bundle swaddled in a pink blanket was screaming her little lungs out. Liv glanced over to see Penny pressing her hand to her chest with a pained expression.

134

"You okay?" Liv asked.

Penny nodded as they listened to the baby's wail go down the hall.

"That baby's got a good set of lungs on her, doesn't she? When I work in maternity I always tell the new moms that bawling like that is a blessing. I know it doesn't always feel like it at four in the morning, but there's nothing more blessed than a healthy baby."

"And there's nothing worse than the loss –" Penny's words broke into a sob.

"I'm *so* sorry. I didn't know. Nothing was listed on your chart. You said you never had a pregnancy when we went over your medical history," Liv said as she studied Penny with a puzzled expression. "Oh, I see. That's part of the past that you don't talk about."

Penny turned and hugged Liv, sobbing in the nurse's arms.

"I know. I know," Liv said over and over.

Penny tried to control her emotions as she saw Dr. Allen in the distance taking his long stride down the hall.

"I'm never with a handkerchief," Penny said. "I should follow Michael's example instead of teasing him."

"Here you go, Child," Liv said as she produced a packet of tissues out her pocket, taking one to dry her own eyes, before she handed over the packet.

Penny wiped her eyes and nose. "I thought nurses were immune to patient's pain."

"We try to be. There'd be no way to continue to come to work every day if we absorbed all the emotional and physical pain that's all around us. But talk about losing one's baby, well, that tears me up every time."

"Then you?" Penny asked.

"Yes," Liv said with a nod, "In my own way, I know that loss."

"Hello there," said Dr. Allen. Looking more closely he saw that not only his patient, but Liv had a tear-streaked face.

"Do you need a few minutes?" he asked confused. He had never seen Liv emotional before.

"No," Liv said, "I need to report for my shift." She got up and gave Penny a hug. "It's going to be okay."

"Can't you stay?" Penny asked. "Please. Just for this session."

Liv looked at Dr. Allen.

"Ahem, well ... I don't normally," he started to say but seeing the bond that had formed between the two women he thought it might be worthwhile to break protocol. "I think that would be fine," he concluded.

"I'll call the front desk and see if they can cover," Liv said. Dr. Allen and Penny went into the conference room.

"Does it smell like sauerkraut in here?" he sniffed.

With all three seated around the table, Dr. Allen started the session. "I was told you slept well last night." Penny nodded that was true. "I'm glad to hear that Penny. I have your test results and they came back fine. I was told you participated in group yesterday, but not today –"

"Group doesn't really touch on my issues; everyone in there was a substance abuser and kept talking about how wonderful it was to be high. Plus, I really wanted to talk with Liv."

"Did you discuss what led to your overdose?" Dr. Allen asked, glancing over at Liv.

"Well, I couldn't sleep. Every time I closed my eyes I would relive something that happened in my past. No, that's not quite right. I don't *know* what happened so I kept imagining what happened and no scenario was comforting. In fact, they were all rather terrifying. It got to a point where my imaginings took on a life of their own. I couldn't *stop* thinking about them. It was awful. I just wanted to sleep, to stop the voices."

Dr. Allen studied Penny for a moment. "And these 'imaginings' that you call them, do you believe them to be real?"

Penny shrugged. "Probably one of them happened just the way I played it in my mind. But there are so many possible variances, it's difficult to know if I'm anywhere near the truth."

"I'm afraid I'm not following," Dr. Allen said. "Why don't we start with the facts as you know them surrounding this ... event?"

Penny closed her eyes and squared her shoulders as if she was going to take a physical blow. "When I was twenty I gave birth to a baby girl ... Nicola ... Nicola Rose." Penny reached over and took Liv's hand. "My baby died when she was almost six weeks old. Thirty-eight days to be exact."

Tears streamed down Penny's face, and Dr. Allen handed her the tissue box. "I'm very sorry, Penny," he told her.

Penny nodded, accepting his condolences.

"I never should have let him spend the night. If she had died when he wasn't there I would have known it was from natural causes which would have been horrific enough but he, perhaps an innocent man, wouldn't have gone to prison. If he did do it, then it's my fault for not keeping my baby safe. So you see any way you look at it, I am terribly at fault. Why didn't I listen to Mr. Bos!"

Dr. Allen looked at Liv who shook her head indicating she didn't understand Penny's musing either.

"Was your husband or boyfriend held responsible for your child's death?" Dr. Allen asked.

"Husband, ex-husband," Penny replied. She turned and looked at Liv. "While we lived in the New Orleans house he started drinking, just to take the edge off, he said. Then we moved into the beaten down trailer with the leaking roof and screaming neighbors, and he said drinking made it more bearable. By the time we moved on-post he was drinking heavily every night. He became moody and irritable, said he was sorry I was having a baby. In a day or two, he'd be apologetic, put on a happier face, and make an effort to get along, only to become angry and depressed again after a few days. It was like an out-of-control roller coaster ride. I had options. I could have gone home, but I wanted to make it work. There was a child to consider. I wanted us to be a family. I thought if I hung in there, things might turn around.

"The night he lost control – well, he didn't really lose control. It was deliberate. We had been arguing about money. I found out about his bar tab. It was tremendous, while I was counting pennies at the grocery checkout. I was angry; he was drunk and we had had the same conversation in three go-rounds with no resolution. I was big as a house and exhausted. 'I'm done,' I had said to him. 'I'm going to bed.'

"As I walked past, he grabbed me by the arm and swung me around to face him. I instinctively put my hand up to shield my face as if he was going to hit me. I don't why I did that. He had never raised a hand to me before. He gave me this small, quizzical smile that I interpreted as, 'Geez Honey, what are we doing?' I dropped my hand and he hit me square in the face, knocking me over. Then, he stormed out of the house. I stayed on the floor curled up in a ball, sobbing until I fell asleep.

"I awakened with an uncomfortable twinge in my back caused, I was sure from sleeping on the floor. I opened up the phone book and called the first attorney listed: William Bos, Esq. I showered, dressed, and trying to not look at my face, put on dark glasses. All I wanted to do was spend the day sleeping; but I was determined I would not let a day go by before I filed for an order of protection and separation. I wanted a divorce as quickly as possible.

"Mr. Bos was obviously a family man; pictures of his grown children and his grandchildren decorated his desk and walls. The floor was covered with an intricately designed Persian rug. Logs crackled in the fireplace taking the chill off the morning air. A row of Matchbox cars were neatly parked on the mantle. A white high-heeled Barbie doll shoe on the floor next to my chair gave further testimony to the fact that

137

grandchildren sometimes played in this attorney's office. I picked up and placed Barbie's wayward stiletto on Mr. Bos's desk.

"'Becky's,' he said as a way of an explanation and the attorney placed it into a paper clip holder for safe keeping. Mr. Bos had thick, white hair and a kindly face. He didn't wear the formal three piece suit and wingtips many attorneys seem to prefer. My pick from the phone book wore grey trousers, comfortable-looking black shoes, and a deep blue sweater with a cable knit design. The color of the sweater so closely matched his eyes I felt certain either his wife or daughter had chosen the yarn. Mr. Bos's first question was, 'Could you take your sunglasses off please?' I removed them and he regarded my face for a moment. 'Have you seen a doctor?'"

"'I have an appointment tomorrow. I spoke with the nurse this morning about my backache and she said as long as the baby is active and I'm not spotting, the baby should be fine.'"

"'Did you describe the injury to your face?'"

"'No. I spoke with my obstetrician's office.'"

"'You need to go to the emergency room now and have your eye looked at. We can fill out the paperwork tomorrow.'"

"'I need to have the papers filed today.'"

"Seeing that I wasn't going to change my mind, Mr. Bos shook his head but proceeded with the meeting. 'Please describe the events which led to this altercation as objectively and completely as possible.'"

"It was a catharsis talking with Mr. Bos. He let me talk and talk and talk while he jotted down notes. When I started crying, he came around his desk and held me like a daughter, stroking my hair saying, 'There, there.' Why are those words so comforting?" Penny rhetorically asked Dr. Allen and Liv. "They don't mean anything."

"Mr. Bos typed up the affidavit and slid it across his desk for me to sign. 'We'll file for full custody for you with no visitation rights for the father. Even if we get that, and that's not a given, with a man like your husband, I doubt he'll pay attention to the law. I recommend you leave the area as soon as possible. Change your name, start again. I suspect it's you and your baby's only hope for a decent life.'"

"I had stared at Mr. Bos. Change my name! He couldn't be serious."

"'I am serious,' he had said, reading my face. 'And you'll need to be smart about it. After you leave, you must contact *no one* you currently know. Don't use your current Social Security number. He could track you that way. I'll help you get a new one.'"

138

"That sounds like espionage, I had thought. And I wondered if I had chosen the wrong attorney. This family man had obviously escaped into too many novels."

"'You think I'm overreacting, don't you? Think about it objectively. A husband hits his *pregnant* wife and leaves her on the floor. What if it had caused her to go into labor? He showed total disregard for the welfare of his wife *and* child. If the wife allows him back into her life in any way, how will he interpret that?'"

"'I don't know,' I had replied."

"'He'll think that his abusive behavior will eventually be forgiven and in essence, accepted. You said this was the first time he hit you?'"

"'Yes.'"

"'It only gets worse. From what I've seen, each episode becomes more intense and he has started off with a bang. How would he react to a fussy baby who won't stop crying? I can tell you from experience even the most mild mannered among us feel like we could go off the deep end after endless nights with a wailing infant. Do you want a man like that in your life? Someone without self-control? Because I can predict your future if you remain with him: trips to the emergency room for you and probably for your child with your husband telling completely believable stories of his innocence. You'll become too traumatized and afraid to contradict him. Your husband's an excellent liar, isn't he?'"

"I nodded yes. How did Mr. Bos know these things?"

"'I know because I've seen it all before,' he answered my unspoken question. 'Too many times. If you allow him to have any part of your life or your child's life, he will use it. He will worm his way back in. He'll leave you wondering how it happened that you could have distrusted him. At first, it may even seem reasonable to allow him some role in his child's life. He's the baby's father, after all. It may even seem like the Christian thing to do. Don't allow yourself to think that way. He gave up his rights to remain in your lives the moment he raised his fist. You need to keep him away from you and I imagine it's going to take some doing, but I will help you.'"

"I continued to stare at Mr. Bos. It was true my husband's behavior had been horrific. But abandon everything familiar to me, the new friends I had made on post? Change my name? Wasn't that extreme?"

"Mr. Bos came back around his desk. He took my hand and helped me stand. 'Come with me,' he said. "He walked me to an elaborate mirror that hung over the fireplace."

"'Look there,' he said. 'Take a long hard look. Is that what you want for your future, for yourself and your baby?'"

"What I saw was a woman with auburn hair, pale face, and one eye nearly swollen shut. A deep purple bruise had formed from eyebrow to cheek."

"'I knew a boxer who looked like that and lost his eye. You need to go from here directly to the emergency room and make sure there is no internal bleeding or fractures.'"

"The enormity of my situation stared back at me. Mr. Bos wasn't overreacting to the situation. It was I who hadn't faced it. I turned and looked at Mr. Bos, reality ringing in my ears. At that moment my water broke. 'Your rug!' I had exclaimed."

"'Hang the rug,' he answered as he grabbed his coat and hat while fishing his keys out of his pocket. 'Which hospital?'"

"'Touro,' I had told him as he put his hand on my arm steering me out of his office to his driveway where his grey Chrysler Imperial was parked. He reached into the back, got a blanket, and placed it on the front seat. As I started to get into the car, the next contraction took my breath away. I grasped my middle, bent over, and cried out."

"'You're going to be fine!' he declared a trifle too enthusiastically."

"He got me to the hospital moments before Nicola was born."

"What kinds of complications did Nicola have when she was born?" asked Liv.

"Well, she was premature, almost four weeks early," Penny said. "She weighed four pounds, three ounces, 18 and a quarter inches long. We never forget those measurements, do we?"

"We don't," Liv agreed.

"Nicole remained in the hospital for almost three weeks because of her underdeveloped lungs. At first, my ex-husband respected the restraining order. He must have learned of Nicola's birth from our neighbors, and he turned his attitude around on a dime. Suddenly, he *longed* to be a father. He sent me letters begging forgiveness and a fresh start, said he had quit drinking and had joined A.A. He left little presents for Nicola on the porch. None of which softened my resolve to leave as soon as Nicola was cleared by the pediatrician to fly in a plane which I hoped would happened before Christmas. I told Margaret not to come to New Orleans. I brought Nicola home from the hospital and we were doing fine. We would meet Margaret at a place in Vermont where we had vacationed when I was a kid, and I'd figure out my next move. The only exception I planned to make to Mr. Bos's instructions after I left New Orleans was to stay in touch with Margaret. She was savvy.

Margaret would never let on to my husband or anyone else where Nicola and I ended up.

"It was Thanksgiving Day when my husband brought over a baby buggy. He was leaving it on the porch as I was leaving the house with Nicola. I hadn't realized he was there and literally bumped into him. I told him he needed to leave. But he just stood there, staring at Nicola. It was the first time he had seen her. He acted as if Nicola was the most magnificent thing in the world and she responded to it – watching him with her dark, beautiful eyes that looked like his. He suggested we take Nicola for a buggy ride. I'm sure I looked at him like he had lost his mind. The man had hit me!

"'All right,'" he said when he saw it wasn't going anywhere. "'Could I at least have a thermos of water for the two mile hike back?'"

"I went inside with Nicola, locking the door behind me. I laid my baby down in her crib, and filled the thermos. I came back to the porch where an assortment of cardboard boxes was stacked."

"'That my stuff?'" he asked as I handed him the thermos."

"'Yes, and you'll want to take it soon.'"

"'You going someplace?' he asked as he pawed through the boxes."

"'What are you looking for?' I asked."

"'My grandfather's watch,' he said. 'He's the only one who ever gave a crap about me. Well, him and my grandmother.'"

"'You should take all of your stuff,' I told him, as he continued to search."

"'I plan on it, but I need someone to help me move it.'"

"'Where's the Queen Bee,' I asked.'

"'Stolen. Look, the only thing I really care about is the watch. Here it is,' he said and put it in his pocket."

"'Our car was stolen! Never mind, it doesn't matter,' I said because it didn't matter. Who cares what happened to the Queen Bee. What I needed was to break all ties with this man. 'I'll be right back,' I told him. I ran into our bedroom and returned with a strand of pearls. 'Here, you should take these.'"

"'My grandmother gave them to you to wear on our wedding day. You should keep them.'"

"'They've been in your family. Please take them.'"

"He shoved them into his chest pocket. 'This has been one hell of a mess,' he said, his voice breaking. He stood there with his head bowed, his shoulders shaking, and then he kicked a box in a temper. The entire stack fell over on his foot. He swore a blue streak as he sat down, and pulled his boot and sock off. His big toe was badly swollen and I brought him ice."

"'Would it kill you to let me come in so I can prop my foot up while I wait for a cab? It's throbbing like crazy,' he said."

"It seemed like such a reasonable request, but I told myself if there was even a hint of a confrontation, I would call the police. We waited and waited for a cab to arrive, but none came even though I called several times. I wish I had called an ambulance. It wasn't really an emergency, but if I had known .... But how could I have known? He ended up spending the night. At the time it seemed like the only decent thing to do. Was I going to make a man with a broken toe and perhaps a sprained ankle walk two miles? In the morning Nicola was dead," Penny cried.

Liv held her, "I know. I know." she kept saying. When the crying slowed, Dr. Allen poured Penny some water.

"Are you all right?" he asked. Penny nodded.

"I can prescribe a mild sedative if you'd like."

"I don't want one."

"I have a few questions then if you're up to it, Penny," Dr. Allen said.

Penny nodded that it was okay to continue.

"Were there any signs of trauma to your child?"

"No."

"He was convicted of what exactly?"

"Manslaughter."

"There must have been evidence of this," Dr. Allen replied.

"It was circumstantial, yet incriminating," Penny said shaking her head. "I know, it sounds unbelievable."

"And that's part of the turmoil for you, the not knowing."

Penny nodded.

"You never say his name. Is he famous, a politician or something?" Dr. Allen asked.

Penny looked at Liv, silently asking her to explain.

"She's worried if she says his name he'll hear it, telepathically, and find her. She's been hiding from him since he got out of prison."

Dr. Allen finished a note, set his pen on the pad, slowly stood up and said, "Penny, I'd like you to stand with me."

She did: a slumped, defeated form still holding onto Liv's hand.

"I want you to stand up straight and strong. It's fine to keep holding Liv's hand. You don't have to do this alone," Dr. Allen instructed. "I want you to say this with me: He can never hurt me again."

Penny repeated the words.

"Again, louder, with feeling. Together."

The doctor and patient spoke as one, "HE CAN NEVER HURT ME AGAIN."

Dr. Allen's hands were in tight fists. His face was flushed with anger.

Well, I'll be, thought Liv. *The most emotionally sound person I know has something that haunts him too.*

Chapter Twenty-Two

Margaret

Liv's pager buzzed.

"I'll walk Penny back to her room," Dr. Allen said.

"I'll check on you later," Liv said as she gave Penny's hand a squeeze before she left.

Penny and Dr. Allen walked down the hall. "I think it would be helpful if you wrote down your thoughts now that you have opened the floodgates," Dr. Allen said.

"I've tried before. My thoughts on paper are just as confusing as they are in my head. It only succeeds in making me more anxious."

"Have you ever tried writing from someone else's point of view?"

"What do you mean?"

"I have a family in counseling now, a mother and teenage son who write down thoughts from each other's perspective. They don't share their writing; just thinking from the other's point of view can be insightful."

"You mean, you think I should write from my *ex-husband's* point of view?" Penny asked alarmed.

"It might be helpful."

"How?"

"Well, it might not reveal anything, but it's also possible something might come to light that helps you decide his guilt or innocence. I realize he has been tried in a court of law, but the legal process didn't give you any closure. And you need closure. You're a strong person, Penny. I believe if you decide in your own mind he went to prison an innocent person, you'll remind yourself that it was the court's decision, not yours. Also, I want you to keep in mind; he's not an entirely innocent person. He hit you, knocked you over, and left you there. It could be what caused you to go into early labor. If you decide he was responsible for Nicola's death, you'll learn that you can't hold yourself responsible for someone else's actions. I believe it's your ambivalence about his guilt or innocence that may be causing much of your anxiety."

Penny nodded in agreement.

"So," Dr. Allen asked, "do you think you can write from his perspective?"

"I can't," Penny replied. "I simply can't. I don't like to even think his name."

"Okay, is there someone else you could use, someone who knew about the situation, a friend?"

"My Aunt. She flew in right after it happened. I think I could write from her perspective."

"That's a good idea. Here's your room," Dr. Allen said. "Buzz if you need anything. I know today's session was very painful for you. Let the staff know if you need anything, even if it's just to talk. I can come back in."

"You've been very kind to me," Penny said gratefully.

Penny propped herself up in bed with a pad of paper and pen. It would bring her no pleasure to write about that horrific time in her life, but maybe it would help as Dr. Allen said. She couldn't go on living the way she had. Every year since Penny's baby died, her anxiety increased. Her sadness diminished. It was true, time healed. Well, maybe not *healed*, but at least scabbed over the hurt. Penny tried to imagine a life without anxiety. Then, she imagined never thinking about her first husband *ever* again. Penny frowned in concentration as she started writing. "Please let this help," she whispered.

Margaret Harris Smith absently looked out of her plane window. She rarely sat without knitting. She had been working on a baby blanket, but she knew that was one project she would never finish.

How quickly everything can change, Margaret pondered. Nicola was thought to be a healthy baby and Penny had been just delighted with her child. "She's such a good baby, Margaret. Wait until you see her. She's just beautiful!"

Then yesterday Margaret received the hysterical call from Penny informing her that Nicola was dead. One just never knows, Margaret thought, what the next day will bring. Margaret now wished she had driven all night to New

146

Orleans and retrieved both mother and child two weeks ago when Nicola was first released from the hospital, but it had sounded like Penny had everything under control.

Normally, Margaret loved flying, but today she couldn't wait for the flight to end so she could hold her grieving niece in her arms. Margaret closed her eyes and thought about Penny. Her given name was Kathleen Louise, but Margaret never thought the name suited the girl. When she went to school, the children called her Katie, and Margaret did too, except in private when she called her Penelope, or more often Penny, a nickname within a nickname. Margaret thought the name Penny was just right. It complimented her niece's copper-colored hair and faithful personality, like Homer's Penelope. Her niece had always been popular in her small school because she was one of those girls who kept her friends close and supported them always, occasionally beyond what Margaret felt some of her girlfriends deserved.

I know growing up with me as her only caregiver gave Penny a certain myopic view of the world, Margaret thought. But it had been a lovely world full of books, gardens, and travel. While Penny's friends spent their time screaming on amusement parks rides, my great-niece at the age of twelve strolled the parks of Paris with me. At the time I had thought I was giving Penny a most valuable gift. What could be better than travel and expanding one's horizons? Now I wonder if Penny would have been better served spending more time with people of her own age. Maybe she would have been better prepared to deal with immature young men or how to avoid them.

I didn't want Penny to work on that farm the summer she turned sixteen, but a neighbor suffered a stroke and my niece naturally volunteered to help out the family. I thought I was worried about her working around the farm equipment. Every year, at least a dozen farm kids in the community are rushed to the hospital after a moment's inattention around merciless cultivators and balers. I cautioned her to be careful every morning when we went our separate ways. I

147

know that sounds ridiculous, Penny was not a careless girl, and I was not a histrionic woman. Nevertheless, that summer I just had this feeling I couldn't shake. It must be how those poor anxiety-ridden people feel. Although my anxiety was not about whether or not I had turned off the stove, it was all focused on protecting my grand-niece. I worried I hadn't told her everything she should know. I started writing lists. I imagined something was wrong with me and that I would be leaving Penny alone in the world. I was no longer a spring chicken. I wondered if some part of my brain knew I was dying before any physical symptoms appeared. Nurses often encounter more peculiar cases than that. It never occurred to me that Penny would be the one leaving.

I had misgivings the moment I met that boy, the man Penny married. I believed no good would come of it. She wanted us to all get along and as much as I wanted to please her; I wouldn't, I couldn't pretend I felt any differently than I did. I believed it would have been a disservice to her. I had never lied to her and I wasn't about to start. It gives me no pleasure to know I was right. I felt as if there was a storm brewing behind his dark eyes. He was a boy that had somehow seen too much. I had seen that look while working in the V.A. hospital – soldiers who returned from war unscathed physically and on the surface seemed fine, even charming and happy. But with our trained eyes, we could see they were deeply scarred below the surface. Of course, I can't claim to have been a perfect judge of character of everyone I've met. There was that nasty business with Jackie's husband that I had missed. However, I felt I understood the attraction Penny and that boy had for each other – my niece wanted to save him, and he needed saving. And that surely wasn't a good basis for a marriage.

Margaret dozed off and was awakened by passengers dragging their luggage out of the overhead bins and into the aisle. For a moment she couldn't remember where she was or why. The memory of her niece's hysterical phone call reached up and shook her, literally taking her breath away.

Her heart raced and the sound of her blood rushing past her ears made her feel nauseous and faint. She put her head to her knees, hoping no one would notice.

"Are you all right, ma'am?" asked the young man with a strong Cajun accent who had been seated in her row. He had been standing in the aisle, but seeing her in distress, he sat back down next to Margaret.

"Yes, yes. I'm all right. Just got a little dizzy there. I'll be fine in a moment."

"Well, take your time. I'll wait with you."

"No need," Margaret had said, but she was glad he stayed. She closed her eyes and tried to relax.

Her anxiety attack subsided within a couple of minutes and Margaret thanked the young man for waiting. He stood up into the now empty aisle, fetched her suitcase and carried it out along with his own.

"Someone meeting you?" he asked as they walked out of the jet-way into the boarding area.

"No, I'm going to rent a car and drive to my niece's."

After assuring him numerous times she was perfectly fine and declining his offer for a lift, the Good Samaritan reluctantly left her. At the car rental she found a mostly empty lot with only a couple of trucks and a few vans. Margaret asked for a nice Impala or something of the sort. But it seemed there was no such choice available. It was after all, Margaret was informed by the car rental attendant, a Thanksgiving weekend near a military base. She was lucky there was anything left at all.

"All right, I'll take that red truck over there," Margaret said going the opposite extreme in rental choices.

"It's a stick. Can you drive a standard?" the young man asked raising a skeptical eyebrow.

Margaret found herself glaring at the attendant. Did he think she was a fool, someone who hadn't been around the block or did she look too old? Sixty-eight wasn't all that old, not for her it wasn't.

"Sorry," he mumbled. "Some people can't, you know."

149

His apology pulled her out of her reverie and her eyes and tone softened. "Of course, you should ask. I've always been amazed by the number of people who have never learned. Seems limiting, doesn't it? I learned on an army jeep in 1951. Dang near tore out the transmission." She shook her head at the remembering. "Not that you need to be concerned about your rental. I can assure you I'm good driver now."

"I'm sure you are, Ma'am."

It took Margaret no time to arrive at the navy base with her innate sense of direction. Military posts had always given her comfort. So clean, so orderly, so uniform. As she drove past the rows of nearly identical military housing units, Margaret thought about how every house has a unique story to tell. Every few years, one family moves out and another family moves in, and a whole new story begins. She pulled up in front of the address her niece had given her. It looked like all the other beige houses, yet Margaret could almost feel the sorrow ... her niece's sorrow. She turned the key, killing the engine, and slowly pulled the key out of the ignition. Margaret rubbed her forehead, a headache threatening. She glanced at the small, tidy front yard and noticed a two foot high, plaster of paris garden gnome with a floppy, red hat, pushing a wheelbarrow. Penny thought garden gnomes were weird and scary-looking, Margaret recalled; and yet her niece had one with a particularly mean-looking face standing next to a scarlet rhododendron bush. Margaret shook her head. Probably that idiot of a husband of hers gave it to her, Margaret thought as she reached over to gather up her silk scarf and handbag from the seat next to her. Her scarf had slid to the floor and when Margaret leaned over to retrieve it and her suitcase, she felt dizzy again. When Margaret straightened up, there was Penny, looking in through the passenger side window. It had been eighteen months since they last saw each other, and yet Margaret couldn't believe how much her niece had changed. It was like her light had been blown out and a mere shell of her remained. Margaret hurried out of the truck, and

150

Penny flew into her aunt's arms like she did as a child with skinned knees.

When Margaret went inside her niece's home, she was utterly taken aback. There were baby things everywhere, not messy of course, just a part of the house – an infant seat sat on the kitchen table with toys spread around it. There was a laundry basket filled with diapers waiting to be folded. She remembered Penny's long letter about saving the earth and her commitment to use only cloth diapers. Margaret knew if she picked them up, they would smell of Ivory Snow. Dr. Spock's Baby and Child Care book was open on a chair. Of course, Margaret knew Penny had a child. Their phone calls were all about Nicola, but it wasn't until she stepped inside the house that it struck her: Penny was a mother. Margaret looked at her niece in amazement, and Penny looked back.

"Yes, I was a mother," she said having seen Margaret's thoughts. "And now my baby's gone. I don't know how I will cope with the grief of it. I truly don't."

Chapter Twenty-Three

Jack Fox

Penny was so engrossed with her writing that she didn't hear Liv walking in. "Here you go," Liv said as she set down the heavy dinner tray on the rolling table.

"Whoa!" Penny exclaimed with a jump. "Goodness, you startled me!"

"I'm sorry. It's these dang nursing shoes; I could sneak up on a lion."

"Do they have you delivering meals now?"

"I was on my way in, so I thought I'd save Marcy some steps. You looked intent before I scared the daylights out of you."

"Dr. Allen wants me to write my experiences from someone else's perspective."

"Looks like you've written a lot."

"It's amazing how much has come back to me like that stupid garden gnome he gave to me. He knew I didn't like them. I wonder if he stole it," Penny mused. "It doesn't matter. I left it behind. I wonder if it's still there. It's painful reliving all this, like I'm watching an old, scratchy black and white film that's been transformed into Technicolor. But since it's coming from my Aunt's perspective I think it's easier, as if I'm not doing it all by myself. Speaking of which, thank you for all you did for me today. I didn't think I'd ever be able to talk about it."

"Losing a baby ... there's just nothing worse," Liv said.

"I was sorry to hear about your loss. You can talk about it with me, if you want," Penny said.

"That's sweet of you to offer. It really is; but it's best that I don't talk about it now. I don't want to get all emotional at work 'cause once I get started with the waterworks it's tough for me to stop. Even though, God knows, it was a long time ago. I guess some wounds are just more difficult to heal. I truly believe that the only ones who really understand that particular loss are other mothers who have ... Will you look at me?" Liv said as she pulled a tissue out of her pocket and wiped her tears. "Some other time, after you leave the hospital, let's get together, have some coffee. What do you say?"

"I'd like that," Penny said as she reached out and squeezed Liv's hand. "Why don't you come to our shop, *Ruth and Naomi*? It's a short walk from the hospital."

"That sounds like a fine idea," Liv said.

"The coffee's good," Penny said making the effort to talk about happier subjects. "Gosh, I hope we're still selling coffee. When Annalise called yesterday she said we were running low."

"How is Michael? How's he holding up through all this? The man was just a mess when you were brought in."

"I feel awful when I think about that. He's such a good person. I think he's fine now, but it's sometimes difficult to tell. He keeps his thoughts to himself so much of the time. Of course, Michael doesn't know the half of what's going on."

"Are you going to fill him in?"

"I feel like I should. It's weird; I had felt perfectly at ease with not sharing my past with him. I had told Michael from the beginning that I wouldn't. It's amazing he married me. I could have been a criminal, an embezzler, or a murderer! What a leap of faith he took when he married me. Now that I've opened up to you and Dr. Allen, it feels somehow dishonest to keep it from him."

"Well, I'm sure you'll choose the right time. Is Michael planning any buying trips in the near future?"

Penny was visibly startled. When had she talked with Liv about their buying trips? Goodness, was she forgetting entire conversations?

"Something wrong?" Liv asked. "I was just thinking it would be nice for you to have some time with Michael to sort things out before he has to go on some trip. I guess I just assumed you make the purchases for your shop yourself, not through some service. But you two probably travel together, don't you?"

"Whew! I'm glad you said that. I thought I had talked with you about some of our buying trips and had forgotten. I guess there's something about being in a psych ward that made me question my sanity. But to answer your question, Mayra-Liz and I are planning to go to South America this spring, maybe to Peru."

"I think that's great. Good for you to get back into the saddle, so to speak."

"Yes, but I hope I can also take a hold of the reins instead of being thrown around on the Bucking Bronco of Life," Penny said.

Liv let out giggle. "Oh, sorry, Sweetie. But really!" Liv said as she tried to control her laughter, "the Bucking Bronco of Life?"

"Yeah, that was pretty bad, wasn't it?" Penny said, and then she started laughing too.

"Bucking Bronco of Life!" Liv repeated just to tickle her funny bone. Soon, the women were laughing so hard they motioned to the other to stop.

"Stop or I'll pee my pants!" Liv managed to say between her howls which only caused both of them to laugh harder.

When they finally calmed down, Penny said. "Oh, that felt so good. I can't remember the last time I laughed until my sides hurt."

"It did feel good," Liv said as she wiped happy tears from her eyes. "Nothing as cleansing as a good laugh or a good cry."

"I'm tired of crying," Penny said, and the jubilant atmosphere ended.

"You know, I've been thinking about this, and I'm just going to suggest it. I think it would help if you just said the man's name. You know, your ex-husband's name. You've gone and made him bigger than life. It was a bad time; I have no doubt, but it's over."

Penny looked at Liv with a troubled brow.

"Just consider it," Liv said as she touched Penny's arm. "It might take some of the weight off. After you say his name and nothing happens, then maybe you can stop looking over your shoulder."

Penny nodded, "I'll think about it."

Liv's phone rang. "Gotta run. Don't forget you have the sleep clinic tonight. I'll come by at 8:45 and walk you over," Liv said as she hurried out of the room, the phone to her ear.

Penny stared at the notepad in her hands. Not once did she write her ex-husband's name. *Maybe Liv was right*, Penny thought. *Maybe by saying his name, I would feel like I have more control.* Penny took a deep breath, opened her mouth, but nothing came out as if her vocal cords refused. She closed her eyes, took another cleansing breath, but again Penny couldn't make herself say it.

It wasn't until Penny awakened in the early morning that she was able to whisper "Jack ... Jack Fox." The small, flat microphone that had been taped to Penny's neck to monitor snoring, recorded the whisper. Penny cautiously opened her eyes. Everything was, as it was before. *Did I really expect to see him appear before me?* Penny thought as she gave a snort of a laugh. *I can't believe I've been so silly.*

Chapter Twenty-Four

By the Sword We Seek Peace

Jack Fox decided he liked his state's motto "*By the sword we seek peace, but peace only under liberty.* He often went past the sign when he ran in the quiet streets of Braintree, Massachusetts before the morning traffic began. He was also looking for peace. Jack had hoped to find it through retribution; but the object of his rage was missing. *How was it possible that she could be so well hidden?* he brooded. *Don't they say that everyone's information is out there? Well, that doesn't seem to be the case with my ex-wife. Somehow she must have smartened up, a whole lot different from her days of burning sausages and constantly whining about alcohol.*

To stop himself from feeling like a schmuck that allowed a stupid-ass computer to consume his life, he concentrated on running faster. He was an endurance runner, always had been. He thought back to his high school days when his legs had been lean and stringy.

Now, I'm built more like a boxer: muscular and chiseled. The thought encouraged him and he started throwing punches in the air while he ran, like Rocky. He pretended kids were running behind, cheering him on. *Bum bum ba bum; bum, bum, bum, ba bum.* His sneakers hit the pavement in time with the song playing in his head.

Yeah, yeah, this feels good, Jack thought, even though his chest felt unusually tight. He knew the reason why. He normally limited himself to two cigarettes a day, and rarely smoked inside his home. But, during the past month and the height of his research frenzy, he accumulated overflowing ashtrays and dirty coffee cups throughout his studio apartment.

As Jack ran, he mapped out his reform: no more greasy takeout, back to whole grain and protein-packed food, cut out the smoking – altogether, and hit the gym, six days a week. *How could it be that even*

157

the prospect of seeing that pint-size, cutie pie with the dark ponytail and fantastic body at the gym wasn't enough to tear me away from the computer screen? I'm going to listen to the messages on the answering machine and hope to hell that one of them isn't telling me to take a hike from the instructor job. Not that I'd blame Diego. He had made it perfectly clear that instructors were to be at every class or find a good replacement. And I've missed my last four boxing classes without a call in. Time to get your shit together, Jackie Boy, he lectured himself.

"Jack … Jack Fox." He heard his name whispered. He stopped so abruptly that he almost fell over his own feet. He looked around, but the air was still and quiet. It didn't matter, Jack knew the sound came from inside his head, and he *knew* it was *her.* He raised his face to the sky and sniffed the air. His dark silhouette looked like the animal whose name he carried.

She's thinking about me, Jack thought. *She's lying in bed right now, stroking herself, and thinking of me.* Longing filled his body and determination filled his mind. *I can't give up,* he thought. *I must find her. It'll be a double-edged sword; chances are I'll get hurt in the process.* Jack narrowed his eyes as he set his jaw. *But what would be new about that?*

Chapter Twenty-Five

In Her Eyes

Saying her ex-husband's name gave Penny a new-found confidence. *I really think I'm making progress as they say in the psychiatric world. Even Liv would have been happy with how much I ate for breakfast. Maybe it really is possible to write this down and move on,* Penny thought as she picked up her pad of paper. Penny thought back to another time and place when she ate breakfast with Margaret and started writing from her perspective.

"Are you hungry?" Margaret and Penny both asked at the same time. They were used to it. Growing up, Penny and her aunt were more in synch than not. Margaret scrambled some eggs while Penny made cinnamon toast and poured orange juice. When she was little, Penny had considered it a treat to eat breakfast food for lunch.

"Can you talk about it?" Margaret asked as she set down their plates.

"I think so," Penny replied. But it took her a few more minutes before she could begin, "I had slept in on Friday morning. I awakened with my breasts heavy with milk. I remembered feeling surprised that the sun was already up. Nicola hadn't awakened for her early morning feeding. I got out of bed, cooing to her, saying, 'Oh, what a good baby you are, letting Mommy sleep in.' When I touched her, she felt cool. I thought I must start putting her in warmer sleepers.

159

When I went to pick her up, she was limp. I started screaming. Jack rushed in —"

"Jack! Jack was here?" Margaret asked, sounding like she was going to jump out of her skin.

"Yes, he stayed the night on the couch. He had come over to leave a baby buggy for Nicola, and a box fell over on his foot. He had hurt it badly. I got him ice and called for a cab."

"Where was his car?"

"It was stolen."

"Someone stole the Queen Bee?" Margaret asked incredulously.

"It happens in this part of the country. People steal cars and drive them over the Mexican border. Usually sports cars are the targets."

"But this time someone wanted an old, battered station wagon?"

"I guess," Penny shrugged. "So anyway, I kept calling for a cab, but none came. Jack couldn't possibly walk on his foot; his toe was swollen, his foot black and blue, and he was staying at a buddy's place that was two miles away. So I gave him blankets and a pillow, and he slept on the couch. Nothing happened. He knows we aren't getting back together. It was actually good he was here. He did CPR on Nicola until the ambulance arrived and the paramedics took over. Until ..." Penny gave a sob, "until they declared her ... dead." Penny nudged the plate of eggs away from her. "I don't know what made me think I could eat anything."

They sat quietly together until Margaret said, "I'll make you some tea."

"With lots of milk and honey," they said flatly, but in unison. As Margaret put the tea kettle on, she asked, "Where is Nicola now?"

"I ... I don't know. How unbelievable is that? They took her in the ambulance. They talked with Jack; but he didn't say. I think I was quite literally out of my mind. It feels like it happened years ago instead of yesterday.

"Where is Jack now?"

160

"I don't know. He left when the police arrived. Jack asked me not to tell anyone he had been here. It was a violation of the order of protection."

"Did you agree?"

"I just stared at him when he asked. I mean, really, who cares about a violation when their baby just died. I told the police everything I knew, which wasn't much. Nicola was fine when I laid her in her crib in the evening, and she was gone in the morning. Jack had tried to save her, but it was too late." Penny said as her voice broke. "If only I had awakened earlier, maybe he could have saved her. If only –"

"Don't," Margaret beseeched her, "don't do that to yourself."

"I imagine Nicola was taken to ...." Margaret stopped herself from saying "the morgue." Nurses can be too clinical. Instead she said, "We should call the hospital. There'll be paperwork you'll need to fill out. Then, we'll contact a funeral home. We should start writing a list." She looked over at her niece and saw a person ready to drop from emotional fatigue. "Why don't you go lie down for a bit? I'll start working on it."

Penny got up and went to her bedroom as if she were a child, relieved to have someone else in charge. Margaret created a long "to do" list on a yellow legal pad. Then, she wandered into the living room and sank onto the couch and dozed. When Margaret awakened, she went to her niece's desk and pulled open the top drawer in search of a phone book. What she found was Penny's grandfather's pistol. Margaret remembered teaching Penny how to load, shoot, and clean the gun. Margaret had always said if you were to have a gun in the house, everyone needed to respect it and know how to use it. Her niece was an excellent shot. Margaret picked up the gun and checked it. It was empty. The bullets must be in the locked box next to it, just as Penny had been taught. Margaret found the phone book in the top side drawer. I don't like this, not one bit, Margaret thought. It had alarmed her when Penny said Jack had been

161

over ⋯ stayed the night. I wonder how he managed that, Margaret pondered. Surely, he wouldn't have injured his foot on purpose so he had an excuse not to leave, or would he? I wouldn't put anything past that man. Penny had said she had called the cab company several times, but no cab came. Margaret believed her niece; but it just didn't make any sense. Margaret thumbed through the yellow pages and saw "Yellow-Checkered Taxi Service" circled. Margaret dialed their number.

"This is Margaret Smith calling, would it be possible to speak with the operator who was working Thursday evening."

"You've got him," the man intoned.

"I understand my niece called several times that evening to request a cab to her home at 1717 Meadow Lane, yet none arrived?"

"Ah yeah, I remember that. She kept calling, and some guy kept cancelling. They really should get their act together. It was a busy night being Thanksgiving and all. I didn't need the aggravation."

"Did you tell her someone had cancelled the cab?"

"Yeah, I said make up your mind, why don't ya!"

"I'm not sure she would have known what that meant, but thank you for your time."

Margaret hung up the phone and was surprised to see her hands were shaking. Her heart was racing and she got a pill out of her purse. The seed of a horrible thought buried in the back of Margaret's mind suddenly sprouted. She realized she had been trying to not let the thought germinate. But it had, and now she knew she must look at it. What if Jack had come here with the intention of ... No! The idea was too terrible to consider. Penny had said Jack hurt his foot. It had been black and blue. Bruises don't color immediately. Had he injured his foot earlier and then used it as a ruse to stay the night? Margaret tried to steady her thoughts. Was she really going to make a judgment about Jack's motives based on the color of a bruise?

162

Think objectively, Margaret demanded of herself. What you really need to consider is Jack's past behavior; it's the best predictor of future behavior. Everyone knows that. Just what do you think Jack is capable of? It shook Margaret when she recalled how he had hit his pregnant wife in the face, knocking her over, and then left.

Margaret suddenly felt like they were very exposed. She wondered if Penny had changed the locks. Margaret went to the front and back doors and fastened the chain locks. She came back into the living room and searched for the key to the ammunition box. Margaret found it on top of the door frame, the same place where she kept her own. With shaking hands, she loaded the pistol.

"What are you doing?" asked Penny, causing Margaret to jump out of her skin. "Are you all right? You're as white as a ghost. Why are you loading the gun?"

The doorbell rang causing Margaret to jump again.

"Margaret, are you all right?" Penny asked with alarm. "You don't look well."

"Did you have the locks changed after Jack left?"

"Of course."

The doorbell rang again.

"Don't open it," Margaret warned. "I put the chain locks on."

"Margaret, I've never seen you like this. You're scaring me."

Margaret went to the window and was relieved to see a police car.

"It's the police, Darling," Margaret said feeling like she was back in control again. "They're probably here to talk with you about Nicola, following up on the initial report. They may ask to see Nicola's crib."

"Oh!" Penny said as she swayed on her feet.

"I'll answer the door," Margaret said as she put the gun back in the drawer. "You go sit down."

Margaret ushered the Detectives McMillian and Andrews into the living room where Penny sat on the couch. Margaret

163

knew what they saw, a young woman with swollen, red eyes and lank hair. Grief is not pretty. Margaret sat next to her and the police officers sat in chairs across from them.

"Do you want to see her crib first?" Penny asked with a thick voice.

"The crib?" asked Officer McMillian.

"You're here about Nicola ... about my baby?" Penny couldn't go on. She started crying. Margaret reached over and put her arm around her niece.

McMillian, who had his notebook and pen out asked, "Has something happened to your child?"

Margaret responded, "My niece's baby died yesterday. I thought you were here ... Do you know the results of the autopsy?"

"I'm going to get sick," Penny said as she rose unsteadily to her feet.

"Penny, do you want me to come?"

Penny shook her head no as she hurried out of the room.

"It's just been terrible," Margaret informed the officers. "I'm an emergency room nurse. I had no doubt but what an autopsy would be performed, but I don't think Penny had considered it. I shouldn't have blurted it out that way, but I'm afraid fatigue has caused me to lose my polish. Although, there's no easy way to say such a thing, is there? If you're not here because of Nicola, then why are you here?"

"We'd like to talk to a Mr. Jack Fox. He's your niece's husband?"

"Yes, but they're separated. She's leaving and coming back with me to Pennsylvania."

The officer wrote a note and said, "Do you know where he's staying?"

"I don't. Perhaps my niece does."

When Penny returned she had the look of a pale, shaken child.

"I heard part of the conversation. I don't know where Jack is living," Penny told them. "I guess he's staying with a buddy who lives two miles away, but I don't know who that person is. It's Friday; he must be at work. He's part of the 159th Tactical Fighter Group."

"We went to the base first, but were told he had had a death in the family and was out. We assumed he would be at home. We're sorry for your loss, ma'am," said Detective Andrews. He paused for a moment looking at Penny's grief-stricken face and added, "Terribly sorry."

McMillian rose while saying, "Here's my business card. If you hear from your husba ... Jack Fox, I would like you to call me."

"Officers," said Margaret, "I believe you need to tell us what this is about."

"We're investigating a hit and run. It occurred the evening of October fifteenth. A seventeen-year-old boy who was killed while riding his bicycle. We found a station wagon not far from the accident that had gone over an embankment. We think this vehicle may have been involved."

Andrews showed Penny a photo of the car.

"It's the Queen Bee. That's what we called it. I'm sure it's our car. Jack told me it had been stolen."

"It wasn't reported as stolen. When was the last time you saw it?"

Penny took a deep breath, held her head in her hands and said, "October fifteenth. That was the day Jack hit me, then stormed out. It had been early in the morning. I think he had been drinking all evening. He left in the car."

"You're sure it was October fifteenth?" asked Andrews.

"I'm sure. I'm not accustomed to being hit. I filed for separation the next day. The date is listed on the paperwork with my attorney."

The phone rang and Penny answered it. She mouthed to the police that it was Jack. McMillian wrote on his notepad to tell Jack to come to the house. Penny did as instructed. After she hung up, Margaret said, "I don't want that young man anywhere near my niece."

Andrews held up a hand and said, "Don't worry, we'll park an unmarked police car down the block and wait for him to arrive. We'll approach him before he comes to the house."

"Will he be arrested?" asked Penny.

"As this point we just want to talk with him. We'll make it clear he isn't to bother you."

"Then, we really shouldn't have asked him to come here; that's sending him mixed messages. I don't want my niece involved in this," Margaret repeated. "She has been through enough,"

"It's all right," Penny said. "Let the police do their job. We'll soon leave here for good."

Margaret and Penny played Crazy Eights, both forgetting whose turn it was. Around four o'clock in the afternoon there was a knock on the back door. Margaret and Penny both jumped. They went to the door together and Penny saw it was her neighbor, Allison, with a cake carrier.

"Hi Sweetie," Allison said. "I brought you some brownies."

"Thank you," Penny said hurriedly. "Please come in."

"I can't stay. I just wanted you to know we're back and to bring you a little pick-me-up. We wish you had come with us instead of staying here by yourself with Nicola and no other family on Thanksgiving, it must have been – Oh!" she said as she noticed Margaret. "You have company."

"This is my aunt. Please come in, Allison. I want to lock the door behind you."

"So you heard about our theft. Doesn't it make you nervous? Really! Who would steal someone's baby buggy off their ... front ..."

Allison stopped when she noticed the buggy parked next to the stack of boxes. She stared at it in disbelief.

"Take it," Penny said.

"Why is it here? If you had wanted to borrow it, why didn't you leave a note? I called the police! I filed a report!"

"I don't know how to –" Penny started to say.

166

"Go lie down, my darling. I'll explain," Margaret said. "There's only so much you can withstand in one day."

It was dusk when Margaret and Penny saw someone slow down and drop off Jack. Niece and aunt stood at the kitchen window watching as the two officers approached Jack. It looked like polite conversation. Then, one of the officers gestured at the police car. Jack turned to walk away. Andrews put his hand on Jack's shoulder. Jack spun around and hit him.

"That's it," said Margaret. "He's done it now."

That night neither aunt nor niece slept well. Margaret and Penny kept getting up, roaming the house, double-checking the locks until they finally gave up, and read in the living room. By morning they were asleep, each curled up in opposite corners of the couch. It was just after nine in the morning when the ringing telephone awakened Penny. She quickly grabbed it hoping to prevent Margaret from awakening.

"Hello. May I speak to Mr. Fox?" asked a woman with a Cajun voice.

"He's not here," Penny said listlessly. "Who's calling, please?"

"Are you Mrs. Fox?"

"Yes."

"This is the Charbonnet Funeral Home. We're terribly sorry for your loss, Ma'am. A SIDS death is always so painful. Mr. Fox explained that you are unable to leave your home. It's understandable given the situation, but we hope in time –"

"I don't know what you're talking about. Jack said I was unable to leave the house? Never mind. I didn't even know that Nicola was moved from the hospital or morgue or wherever they took her. My great-aunt and I can come in today. I'd like to see my baby before the service. Today, if that's possible."

"See her?" asked the woman.

"Yes. I need to see Nicola by myself before the funeral. I can't have the first time I see her again be public. I can't have my grief that exposed. I'm sure you understand."

"I don't know how to say this to you. I thought you knew. I mean ... I thought there was an agreement ... your husband said –"

"What?"

"That you were so grief-stricken you didn't want to see your child ... deceased, and that you and he decided on cremation."

"Sweet Jesus!" Penny cried out.

"What! What's happened?" asked Margaret who now stood at Penny's side.

"I can assure you Ma'am in our over 27 years of business we have never had anything like this happen. He was so nice, so concerned for your wellbeing. He was crying. We had no idea that you didn't .... I am so very sorry, but we did follow procedures. It isn't a state requirement to have both parents' signatures."

"The state requirement! So, you followed the state requirement! Do you think that makes it okay? I'll never see my child again," Penny sobbed into the phone.

"When you come in, we'll help you plan a service. We –"

"I can't talk with you right now," Penny said as she disconnected the phone.

"What?" Margaret asked again.

"Jack had Nicola cremated."

"No!" Margaret exclaimed. Her aggravation was so intense that she started pacing across the room holding her arm which felt as if it was being squeezed to pieces. "How could he without talking to you?"

"Perhaps," Penny said, "that's what he wanted to talk about when he came to see me yesterday."

"Oh for God's sake, Penny! Will you just wake up! That man killed your child!"

Margaret watched Penny start to collapse before her eyes. She darted forward and had just enough strength to

168

support her niece into a controlled fall onto the couch instead of hitting the floor.

Penny chewed the top of the pen, as she read what she had written. Penny scribbled out Margaret's rebuke and accusation. Margaret never said that. She could never be that cruel. *But I saw it,* Penny thought. *It was in her eyes. She believed Jack was a murderer. It was what caused me to collapse. It had been too much to absorb, and continues to be too traumatic to consider. And yet there it is, day after day, the question that gnaws at me – what happened to my child?*

Chapter Twenty-Six

A New Perspective

"Good morning," Dr. Allen said as he entered Penny's room.

"Oh, hi," Penny replied as she glanced down at her watch. "You're late with rounds, aren't you?"

"You know it's time for the patients to go home when they start critiquing the doctors' schedules," he said with a wry smile. "How about it? Do you think you're ready to leave?"

"You mean just like that?"

"I think you had a real breakthrough yesterday. At least we now understand why you had a problem sleeping. I do feel convinced that your overdose was an accident. It appears, at least for the time being, that your insomnia problem has been resolved. The sleep technician said she *wished* she could sleep as well as you. Your blood work and tests are within the normal range. As far as insurance is concerned, we really don't have a reason to keep you any longer. However, that doesn't mean treatment needs to stop. I would like to see you continue counseling on an outpatient basis."

"That sounds fine," Penny said.

"Let's meet in the counseling room at eleven."

"I wrote from Margaret's perspective," Penny said as she handed him the notepad.

He quickly leafed through the dozens of pages filled with Penny's hurried script. "You wrote a lot," Dr. Allen observed as he handed the notepad back to her.

"Do you think you can read it before our session? I think it would help."

"I'll try," he said as he tucked the pad under his arm. "Do you feel ready to go home? You're one of the few patients who hasn't chewed my ear about being released."

"Actually, I was going to ask you about it today."

"So, you do feel ready?"

"I do. I suppose I should feel more elated, but I just relived some rather depressing stuff. Some of the details I had actually forgotten. But I do feel stronger, better than I have in a long time."

"We'll talk more at eleven, okay? As you observed, I'm running late."

In the counseling room, Dr. Allen asked Penny if she had called her husband.

"Yes, Michael was so pleased, said he'd be here at eleven-thirty. I told him I probably wouldn't be ready until twelve-thirty, but he said he would wait."

"There will be a nurse who'll ask you this when you sign the release papers, but I want to ask you too – do you have a safe environment at home?"

"Yes," Penny said simply.

"You don't feel in any way threatened or intimidated by anyone?"

"Are you asking me this because of my first marriage? You're concerned that I made the same mistake twice?"

"I ask this of every patient I release. I need to know that they are going to a safe and secure home. Now, it's a federal requirement that hospitals ask this question, but I've asked it long before it became law."

"I feel safe, secure, and *loved* at home," Penny said.

"I'm glad. I read it," he said gesturing at the notepad. "I'm sure that reliving those memories was difficult, but did it help you? Have you gained any insights?"

"I spent the morning trying to think along those lines as I thought you would probably ask me that. I do believe it was helpful looking at the past through Margaret's sensible eyes. I've concluded that if she were here today she would say something like, you loved your baby and you never tried to cause Jack Fox any harm. He caused it himself with his temper and drinking. If I can keep that perspective, I think it would help."

"A very wise woman, your Aunt Margaret, she must have been a great source of strength to you when you went through the funeral and trial."

Penny scoffed. "Margaret is really who I should feel guilt over – calling my *great*-aunt while I was hysterical, confident she'd fly across the country and take care of me like I was a child. I never gave her health a thought, never considered she might not be up to it. She was *Margaret* – you know, the woman was strong as an ox. She could work overtime at

172

the hospital, come home and spend hours weeding her gardens. It just didn't occur to me ...."

Penny closed her eyes and squared her shoulders in a gesture Dr. Allen came to recognize as something Penny did to gather strength.

"The day we went to the funeral home and they gave me Nicola's ashes was the worst day of my life. I really fell apart. My aunt tried to console me, tried to help me see that time heals all wounds, but I couldn't believe it. I asked if she thought I had been born under a dark star. I had lost my parents *and* my baby and I wasn't even out of my twenties. I thought it was entirely possible that disasters could just continue to swarm around me for the rest of my life. Of course, I was forgetting all the good things that had happened to me. Margaret had replied, 'You, my dear child, were born under a heavenly moon because you were loved. You were conceived in love by your parents, and I have loved you with all my heart; I always will. People who were raised with love have a foundation they can always build upon. It's my opinion that folks who don't receive nurturing love at the beginning often struggle for the rest of their lives.' We went to bed early and in the morning I went to the guest room and discovered that Margaret had died.

"I found it beyond shocking. For a day or so, I wondered if I would recover or if I'd become one of those women with straggly hair committed to an institution for the rest of my life. When I first met you, I said there had been a lonely and difficult time in my life; I wasn't kidding. If ever there was a time I could have put a gun to my head, it was then. Yet, I didn't consider it because it was as if Margaret was still with me. Every time I thought about what a self-indulgent brat I had been, someone who had killed her aunt by putting her through hell, I could hear her voice saying, 'None of that! We all have our time. And I had a good life. Don't you blame yourself. *I will not have it.*' Now I feel as if I have her voice back again, and she's telling me I need to put down *all* the guilt, and grief, and self-doubt. I mean if I was able to stop feeling guilty and anxious about her death, then why can't I stop feeling guilty and anxious about all the rest of it? Sometimes I think it's simply a matter of discipline."

"Well, discipline may have something to do with it, but don't be too hard on yourself," Dr. Allen said. "It was quite a traumatic experience, and you were handling it all on your own. You only heard your own conflicted self-talk on the subject. With counseling, I believe you'll be able to put it into a proper perspective. You have already made some good inroads."

Penny nodded.

"You talked about your anxiety and guilt," Dr. Allen continued. "Yesterday you also talked about your fear … fear of your ex-husband. Have you also been able to put that into a different perspective?"

"That feeling isn't as easy to change. Do I think he … *Jack* is capable of holding a grudge forever? Do I think he's capable of hurting me? Yes, I do."

"It's also possible he's changed or moved on and doesn't think about you anymore," Dr. Allen suggested.

"Yes, that's possible."

"But you don't believe it."

"I don't."

"You said his name," Dr. Allen observed.

"Yes," Penny said. "And you can't imagine what a big deal that was for me. I said it for the first time in years, earlier this morning."

"That really is wonderful, Penny. I hope this doesn't sound trite, because I do mean it – I'm proud of you."

"I'm pretty proud of myself," Penny admitted.

"I hope you try to keep in mind that society now views relationship abuse differently in this country. It's now against the law for someone in the medical, educational, and law enforcement fields to not report abuse. We're trained how to look for relationship violence and how to intervene. Plus, he's not your husband anymore."

Penny nodded. "That's all very well and good, but I will continue to keep a low profile. I'm going to work at feeling more secure, but I'm also not going to be careless about it."

"I don't think those are unwise choices. Just because we're better as a culture at identifying domestic violence, we still have a ways to go in protecting women from violators, and it's usually women who are abused. It's important to have a lifestyle in which you feel safe. The discharge nurse will let you know how many counseling visits are covered by your insurance. Most policies do not allot for many mental health appointments. I'd like to see you have weekly visits to start, but it may be self-pay."

"I'm sure that'll be fine," Penny said as she picked up the notepad.

"Try not to be so afraid. It's a difficult way to go through life."

Chapter Twenty-Seven

No Influence

Michael was waiting in Penny's room when she returned. He gave her a single pink rose surrounded by a spray of white baby's breath. When Penny smelled the flower that was the middle name of her child, a tear fell, but she resolutely wiped it away. "I have some things to tell you when we get home," she told Michael.

Penny didn't know when home had felt so good. She had always loved their sweet cottage, but today it looked especially dear. Their cat, Monty greeted her at the door as if she had been gone for years. Penny beamed her pleasure at Michael.

"The house feels different today," he told her. "It's as if it's welcoming you back. It was sad when you were gone. The clock stopped working."

"I missed our home too. I didn't realize how much until now."

"Do you want some tea?"

"That sounds good."

Michael turned to prepare it, but Penny stopped him.

"No, let me. I've been waited on for much too long. Coffee for you?"

When Penny returned, she saw Michael had lit the fireplace. It gave the room even more cheer. She placed the mugs and a plate of cheese, crackers, and grapes on the coffee table.

They settled down with their snack and Penny said, "I was married before."

Michael set his mug back down on the table.

"I didn't mean to blurt it out like that," Penny said. "I should have led up to it somehow. I should have said –"

Michael reached over and took her hand. "It's okay. I assumed. Way back when, the day you made me promise never to pry into anything that happened in the past." He brushed her hair back from her face, smiling at her. "I was just lucky to have met you when I did. You know, when you were between husbands," he said, trying to make light of it.

"There's more. I had a child, a little girl whose name was Nicola Rose." Penny said the words quickly in a single breath, as if said fast enough they wouldn't hurt, like ripping off a band-aide.

Michael looked shell-shocked. When he found his voice he asked, "Where is she?" He looked around the room in a distracted way as if Penny had kept her hidden on a shelf. And in a way she had.

"She died. Her ashes are in that urn."

"I thought they were Margaret's."

"In the center is a baby sock filled with some of Nicola's ashes. I buried the rest in Margaret's garden. I wanted Nicola to have some roots. It gave me some comfort to think of part of her there in that happy place. Margaret didn't need to be rooted. She was a free spirit. I knew she wouldn't mind traveling around with me."

Michael sat very still, staring at the urn for quite a while until he turned and looked at Penny. "But you always said you never wanted to have children."

"I couldn't go through the loss of another child."

"How did she … your child die? It was a genetic problem?"

"Maybe ... I don't know," Penny sighed.

"They weren't able to determine –" Michael started to ask.

"I wrote this last night," Penny said as she handed her husband the pad of paper. "It has most of what happened. If you don't mind, I'd like you to read it rather than have me tell it. It's from Margaret's point of view. While you read, I'm going to go for a walk by the river."

"Are you sure you're up to it? Do you want me to walk with you and I'll read this later?"

"I need to be by myself for a little while, and I think it would be better for you to read it without me here."

Michael was waiting on the back porch without a coat on when Penny returned, his face clouded with sadness and anger. He wrapped his arms around his wife.

"That bastard!" Michael grounded out the words.

"Don't," Penny told him as she stepped back to look at him. "Don't let him give you any kind of emotion. We can't allow him to control any part of this." Penny swept her hand wide meaning their home and their happy lives together. "He can't have any influence in our lives, not even in our heads."

Chapter Twenty-Eight

Morning Coffee

During the night, Penny had slept well while Michael prowled the house, too keyed up to sleep. In the early morning, Penny and Michael sat in bed sipping coffee while Monty purred at their feet. Michael drank his without tasting it as he studied Penny's profile.

"Go ahead; ask me," Penny said.

"I know you don't want the past to influence our lives; but there are some things I want to know," Michael said.

"Okay," Penny replied.

"Your name ... It's not really Penny?"

"It originally said Kathleen Louise Dunmore on my birth certificate. My school chums called me Katie and so did my ex-husband. Margaret called me Penelope or Penny when we were alone."

"Did you have it legally changed to Penny Smith?"

"Yes, so it would be difficult for him to find me. He didn't know me as Penny. I like the name. Margaret was right; it does suit me. I wish she had lived long enough to have known me as Penny Morgan."

"Is he out of prison?"

"His sentence is over. Time off for good behavior, if he was able to swing it, could mean he's been out for some time."

"Should we find out? It shouldn't be too difficult. We could hire someone."

"No! Let sleeping dogs lie."

"What happened with the hit and run? Was Jack responsible?"

"I don't know. He was arrested for it. That was his first hearing. The evidence was stacked against him. I testified that Jack had been aggravated and drunk when he left the house that night. Jack didn't have a good alibi for where he was. He said he had left the house, ran out of gas and walked back. No one had seen him. It was our car that was over

177

the embankment, not far from the accident, and there was gas in the tank. The prosecution said it was abandoned, never reported as stolen. The defense negated the impact of our car being near the scene by showing how the city was months and months behind in processing stolen car reports. Jack's lawyer maintained the theft had been reported and if the case hung on whether or not the car was stolen, the jury should take a long, hard look at the photo of the city desk with piles of undocumented reports.

"Next, the defense lawyer went after my credibility, stating I was a vindictive wife seeking divorce, and not an expert at determining alcohol levels. In fact, when asked, I couldn't remember a time when I was actually drunk. Isn't it interesting my sobriety was viewed as a negative! When the defense attorney described how Jack had bravely saved an officer from drowning the summer before, the jurors looked at Jack in a different light, and he wasn't convicted. One trial down. The next trial he stood accused of hitting a police officer, and again I testified."

"But you didn't have to, right? Spousal privilege or something like that?" Michael asked.

"That usually pertains to private conversations between married couples. This was something I had witnessed in public. I felt I had a responsibility to appear. He had assaulted a police officer. I witnessed it. His partner did as well, so of course I thought there was no way Jack could get off the hook, but then again he hadn't been convicted of the hit and run which had also looked like an open and shut case."

"Then there was the trial for Nicola," Michael said gently.

"He attended the court in prison clothing. It was quickly brought to light that Jack was serving time for assaulting a police officer. I'm sure it made an impression on the jurors. Of course, the prosecution wasn't allowed to bring up the hit and run, but it had been in all the papers. The jurors had to swear they had no prior knowledge about Jack, but I don't know how anyone living in New Orleans could have not known about the hit and run. The child was a minister's son. The funeral caught national press: a parade with a mournful-sounding jazz band followed by a weeping and singing congregation who walked behind an elaborate casket adorned with angels.

"The evidence in Nicola's trial was entirely circumstantial. Jack had been there when Nicola died and left when the police arrived. He had hit me when I was pregnant and left me on the floor. He had shown disregard from my health and that of his unborn child. One juror gasped when Jack admitted to ordering Nicola's cremation without my knowledge."

"It must have been very difficult for you to testify."

"It was. If anything I was a help for the defense. When I was asked if I thought Jack was responsible for Nicola's death, I answered as honestly as I could. I simply said that I didn't know. I answered all their questions in as straightforward and as unemotional as possible. He had hit me once when he was drunk. He hadn't been drinking the night before Nicola died. Yes, he had access to the bedroom and I might not have heard him enter it. Sometimes during my pregnancy he had expressed his resentment towards her. He later said and acted like he wanted to be an involved father. He had said she was beautiful when he met her." Penny shook her head. "I was shocked when he was convicted of manslaughter. He turned and gave me a look of unadulterated hate."

"That's when you became afraid of him."

"I had grown afraid of him *long* before that," Penny shivered.

Michael pulled Penny close in his arms. "You're right," he murmured. "We should avoid talking about him. He has no place in our lives. But I do want to ask you one more thing, if that's all right."

Penny nodded her head on Michael's chest.

"I do understand what you went through was horrendous. But we've been married three years now, and you had been able to sleep not well, but sorta okay, most nights. You'd have some days of melancholy, like the rest of us. But in the past few months, you just fell apart. What happened?"

"One night I had a nightmare, and then the next night, and on it went. It got so I was afraid to fall asleep. Medication made it worse. I worried that he could find me when I slept. Sometimes it felt like he was inside my head. It was stupid for me to feel that way. And I'm so sorry that I put you through all that, finding me on the bathroom floor –"

"Tell me what you did after you left New Orleans," Michael said, avoiding the painful memory of finding his wife nearly dead.

"It was amazing, for weeks after Nicola and Margaret died and Jack was imprisoned, all I did was sleep. No sleep problem then. One day, I just decided I couldn't do it anymore. It was an early spring and I packed a bag and caught a bus to Pennsylvania. I had my Aunt's place to get in order and sell. It sold quickly. It was such a lovely home with beautiful gardens."

"Was it difficult for you to leave?"

"No. Part of the place will always be in my heart; I don't have to live there to feel that way. But I couldn't stay there. Every time I went into town, people stared at me. They all knew what had happened. The town had followed all the newspaper stories. Don't forget Jack's grandparents had lived there, too. Although they didn't live long after their grandson was arrested. I think the stress of it killed them.

"My old neighbors had their hearts in the right place, they tried to be kind to me, yet it was obvious how uncomfortable they felt being around me. It was a family-oriented community and conversations were, more often than not, based around their children or grandchildren. Because I had lost my child, they felt as if they shouldn't mention children at all. I know they were trying to be sensitive to my loss, but I only felt it more deeply. The neighbors were good people, we just didn't connect anymore. I knew I had to leave. Besides it was best for me to be far away with a whole different life before Jack got out of prison. I traveled north with no destination in mind, but I knew I had had enough of the south."

"Did you have money?"

"Some. I had never thought about Margaret's savings until I saw her bank statements. I was surprised how modest it was. Of course, nurses don't earn all that much and we had traveled all over: France, England, Germany, Egypt, and Switzerland. I'm sure Margaret wasn't worried about a big savings account because she received a monthly pension from the army. The sale of her home brought a nice amount. Because of that I wasn't destitute, but I was certainly going to need to earn a living soon, and I had no idea what I would do."

"So you just drove north."

"That's right. I had Margaret's Oldsmobile, so I just drove. It was liberating to just roll down the windows without a destination in mind. It was August and I heard a radio advertisement for Saratoga Race Track. Margaret had taken me there one summer. We had had a great time and I thought, why not enjoy a little vacation? Goodness knows when I'd be able to take time off from work once I found it. But the track wasn't fun. I had remembered the excitement of the races, the horses with gleaming coats looking proud of themselves, and ladies with exquisite hats. Sitting alone in the crowded pavilion it seemed so sad and empty. I'm sure it was me who was sad and empty. In the evenings, I walked around the city as families and couples strolled past, and I felt utterly alone. I ate dinner each night at Hattie's Chicken Shack, the same place where Margaret and I had dined.

"One night Hattie, the cook and owner of the place, stopped at my table and said, 'How you doing tonight?'

"'Oh, the food was great, thanks,' I told her.'"

"'No, I mean *you*. This is what, your fifth night in here and each night you look a little sadder and eat a little less. You keep it up, you're going to tarnish this place's reputation.'"

180

"I looked at her stunned and felt insulted until Hattie gave a sympathetic smile and lowering her voice asked, 'You need a place to stay, Honey?'"

"When my expression turned to surprise, Hattie said, 'I have a pretty good nose for knowin' when folks need help.'"

"'I'm okay.' I told her. 'Thanks all the same.'"

"'But you're looking for work, am I right?'"

"'Yes, I am.'"

"'You want to do some kitchen work, wait on some tables and such? I don't give handouts. It's not in my nature, but I can't help but give a hand up to someone who needs it.'"

"I looked around the bustling room and for the first time noticed how much everyone was enjoying the food. It was a happy place with the Cajun music playing in the background. I looked up at Hattie's kind face and thought, why not? This place is as good as any. And it was work I knew how to do.

"'I'd like that, I told her.'"

"'Okay,' Hattie told me. 'I got a few rules. You arrive on time. You work as hard as I do and that's saying something. Don't let this old body fool ya. And there's no drinkin', druggin', or hanky-pankyin' going on when you're here. Are we clear?'

"'Yes,'" I said with a smile as I stood up to shake her hand.

"'That a girl,'" she told me. "'You've got a beautiful smile. Best not to be a sour puss. It don't help none with the tips.'"

"It was Hattie who got me thinking about going to college. I couldn't help but think about it. She started hounding me, said I had to start thinking about my future. The woman was connected to everyone. She introduced me to the Dean of the School of Liberal Arts at SUNY Albany who encouraged me to apply. Of course, once I started school and started opening my mind to literature, philosophy, and psychology, there was no turning back. It was like this magical world opened up. And of course, that's where I met you, my dear, sweet husband."

"And to think I almost didn't take the Artist in Residency position."

Penny wrapped her arms around him. "How lucky I was to find you," she said. They watched the snow falling lightly outside their window, the room a cozy cocoon.

"What do you have planned for today?" asked Michael. "You going to take it easy … do some reading?"

"I'm going down to the shop and thank Mayra-Liz and Annalise for holding down the fort. Then I'll go and get Eva. Her last class is done by

12:30. I'll see if she wants to go for lunch, then I'll bring her home for the weekend."

"Have you heard from her recently?" Michael asked.

"I haven't, and I've been calling and texting her."

"I'm supposed to go and get her at five. Maybe you should let me do that, and I can talk with her first."

"No, there're some things we need to discuss. We need to give it some air before it can heal."

Michael smiled.

"What?" asked Penny.

"Give it some air, so it can heal. I bet that's something your Aunt Margaret said."

"You know, I think it was," Penny said with a smile.

Chapter Twenty-Nine

Healing Air

Eva's face looked like a thundercloud as she waited outside of her dorm for Penny. Her book bag sat on the ground bulging with textbooks and notepads, and her laptop carrier was slung across her chest. Eva looked like she was preparing for a studying blitz.

I'll go home, it's Penny's birthday tomorrow and my sisters would be furious if I wasn't there, but I'm spending as much time as possible in my room.

"Hi Sweetie!" Penny said as she pulled up. Eva swung her things into the back seat and for a second contemplated sitting with them. *No, that would be too belligerent,* she decided. As angry as Eva was with the whole, wide world, she still valued her sisters' good opinion of her. However, Eva left no doubt of her state of mind as she slouched in the front seat, staring straight ahead.

"How are you?" asked Penny as she leaned over and gave Eva a kiss on the cheek.

"Fine," replied Eva with a tone that said she was anything but.

The car ride was silent until Eva reached over and turned on the radio. As they neared a coffee shop, Penny asked if Eva wanted a cappuccino, a treat they normally enjoyed together.

"No, thanks," Eva replied. "I had one at school."

"Lunch?" Penny asked. Eva shook her head no. The rest of the ride was silent except for the loud rock and roll. Once inside the house, Eva started to make a dash for her room.

"Before you go upstairs, I'd like us to talk," Penny said.

"I've got a ton of homework."

"This won't take long; there're some things we need to say."

"I don't think you want to hear what I want to say," Eva said evenly.

"Go ahead," said Penny, accepting the challenge.

"All right," said Eva as she dropped her heavy book bag to the floor and placed her laptop next to it. "What you did was so irresponsible and dangerous … I am so angry with you. I feel like I don't even know who you are! Taking an overdose of drugs and alcohol doesn't jive with the person I thought you were."

"It was an accident. I couldn't sleep. I was just trying to sleep. I never meant to hurt anyone … not myself, not you."

"And why can't you sleep? What's the big secret? We all know you have one. Mayra-Liz and Annalise were talking about it. They said they've seen you crying in the storage room. How is it we spill our guts to you about *everything*? Our past isn't pretty, yet we told you. You walk around saying, 'Everything is great. We're our own little family, as close as close can be' while you're keeping secrets and falling apart."

"I know how all this seems. There's just a lot in my past that I can't share with you. Not now. I think I'll be able to at some point. I'm in therapy and that's helping."

"That's such a cop-out," Eva lashed out. "You think there wasn't a lot in my past. You think it wasn't painful having my mom leave, my dad arrested? The truth is we aren't really the family you say we are. We can't be with all these secrets between us."

"We *are* a family!" Penny exclaimed. "I love you and your sisters like daughters!"

"How would you know? You never had one!" Eva shouted, raising her voice with superior indignation. *It was a low blow, but Penny had left herself wide open with that one,* Eva thought. Penny seemed to wilt while she held her face in her hands. At first she made sounds like a meowing kitten, then the storm broke, and Penny started sobbing. This game of "one up" had gone way too far and Eva's conscience called "game over."

"Penny! Oh Penny! I'm sorry! I shouldn't have said … You *have* been like a mom to us. Well, more like a big sister, but someone *very* important in our lives."

Eva's words only made Penny cried harder.

"Do you want something? Water?" asked Eva.

Penny nodded yes. Eva went to the kitchen for a glass of water and brought it back along with a box of tissues.

"I look like I need the whole box, don't I?" said Penny giving a weak smile, as she tried to control her emotions.

"Kind of," Eva said weakly, unsure of the right thing to say.

Penny took some deep breaths and pulled herself back together. "Okay, you have a point. These secrets as you call them aren't healthy for me to keep. It's not good for me to keep things bottled up, and it's unnerving for the rest of the family to not know what's going on."

"Yeah," said Eva contritely, "that's what I meant to say."

"Here, sit down with me on the couch. This is going to take a while."

"And that's what happened." Penny concluded.

"Your baby *died*! Oh Penny and I said ... I'm really sorry. I didn't know."

"I know," Penny said.

"So where is he now ... your ex-husband?"

"I don't know."

"Don't you want to find out? He could be dead. Then you wouldn't have to worry about him anymore."

"I suppose that's true, but I won't look into it. I don't want to know anything about him."

"But that doesn't make sense, Penny. Forewarned is forearmed."

"Eva, I couldn't even say his *name* last week. I want to know nothing about him. You've got to trust me on this."

"Okay," Eva said.

They sat looking into space, at a loss for further words.

"It seems so quiet here after spending time in the dorm."

"I bet it does. I'll put on a CD and light the fire. You're right. The house needs more life."

Penny joined Eva on the couch. Carla Bruni sang in the background.

"How's the French class going? Are you translating the lyrics? You look deep in thought," Penny said. "What are you thinking about?"

"Your ex-husband."

Penny eyes widened in dismay.

"I won't continue to, but I can't help it after just hearing about your life. I wonder why you sometimes doubt that he hurt your baby. The courts convicted him. There were times he was violent. Why do you have so much uncertainty?"

Penny rubbed her forehead as if warding off a headache.

"I'm sorry. I shouldn't have asked," Eva mumbled.

"It's because," Penny said with a faltering voice, "of the way he looked at her. I don't think it was a look that could be contrived."

"Which was?"

"Pure love."

"But sometimes people hurt the ones they love, don't they?"

"Yes they do, which brings us full circle. Don't you see how it was a continuous loop of painful thoughts for me? It kept me awake at night.

I'm going to try to change my thought process. I don't want to focus on the past. I need to put it down."

"There can be so much hurt in the world, can't there?" said Eva.

"Yes, but also so much love." Penny said as she put her arms around Eva. They leaned back again into the couch. Both feeling too tired to move. Carla Bruni cooed to her lover that he belonged to her. When the song ended and the silence continued, Eva asked Penny what she was thinking about.

"I was thinking that a trip to Paris would be nice," Penny replied without opening her eyes.

"Have you been there?" Eva asked her eyes closed as well.

"Yes, Margaret took me when I was a teenager. It was so beautiful." Penny opened her eyes and sat up straight. "We should go, you and me. Let's plan on it, for this summer."

Eva opened her eyes. "You mean it?"

"Absolutely."

"Oh Penny! That would be so cool!"

Eva snuggled in close to Penny and said, "You know, like your Aunt Margaret told you, I was born under the heavenly moon, too."

Chapter Thirty

Hundred Million Points

"Happy birthday to you," the girls and Michael sang out as Annalise carried a birthday cake from the kitchen, their faces brightly illuminated by burning candles that seemed to carpet the top of the cake.

"Oh my goodness," Penny said. "You didn't need to put on all thirty-eight candles!"

"Make a wish," Michael encouraged.

"I already got my wish," Penny said as she smiled at her husband.

"Ahhh," the girls said in unison.

While eating cake, Annalise and Mayra-Liz drilled Penny about her health. They had done research online and asked friends about insomnia. The girls had all kinds of remedies to help Penny sleep better.

"You both have got to stop," she told them. "I know you're concerned, but I'm so tired of thinking and talking about myself I could spit!"

"Spit?" asked Eva.

"I think it's an Aunt Margaret saying," Michael said.

"Honestly, I'm sleeping better now. There's more I'll tell you soon," she said to Mayra-Liz and Annalise, "but let's not get into it tonight."

"We know," Mayra-Liz said reaching across the table to take Penny's hand. "Eva told us, and you don't need to talk about it *ever* unless you want to."

Michael gave Eva a questioning look.

"Penny didn't tell me not to tell them," Eva said. "In fact, she said she was going to tell them sometime."

"I know E, but don't you think it would have been better to let Penny tell them herself?" Michael asked.

"I only told my sisters!" Eva said defensively.

"Oh, let's not worry about this!" Penny said. "Please! I want to hear all about what's going on in your lives."

No one spoke. "Come on. There must be something new," Penny said. "I haven't seen much of you in days. There must be something that's happened. Tell me anything."

"There is something to report," Annalise said. "Someone stopped by the shop today and asked that we 'pass on her regards.' Her name was Liz Wright. She must be a nurse or a doctor. She had scrubs on."

"Oh! It's Liv! How nice she stopped in!"

"She bought a lot of stuff too, said she was getting a head start on her Christmas shopping," Mayra-Liz said. "Liv asked if we provide Christmas wrapping. I asked if four dollars for a medium sized box was too much, and she said that was fine. Apparently, she hates gift wrapping, whereas I love it! I told her that I didn't have time to do it during the day, but if she came back on Monday, I'd have them all ready. The four dollar price was just a guess, but since then I've done a cost analysis and learned that we can wrap packages for about a dollar, that's 300 percent profit! Also, the department store in town charges five dollars. Maybe we'll get some of their business too, once the word gets out that we're cheaper. We could use banana fiber paper. It's better for the environment, and it looks exotic."

"Great ideas, Mayra-Liz! I don't know what we'd do without you!"

Mayra-Liz's face fell. She stared at her dessert plate where only the icing that she had scraped off her cake remained. Finally she said, "I wasn't going to say anything tonight, but I'm seriously considering enlisting in the army."

They all burst out laughing. "Oh, that was great," Penny said as she wiped tears away from laughing so hard. But when Penny looked closely at Mayra-Liz, Penny's face instantly sobered and she exclaimed, "You're serious!"

"I am. If I sign up, I'll receive college benefits. I'm not getting any younger and I need to start thinking about my future. How would I support myself, if I wasn't at the shop?"

"I thought you loved working at the shop."

"I do."

"Then what's the problem?"

"What if the shop closed?

"Why would you think that?"

Mayra-Liz glanced at Michael, causing Penny to also look at him. Michael shook his head and said, "I have no idea."

"You got me thinking when you said you were going to make sure Penny took things easier," Mayra-Liz said.

"Did you imagine I was going to tell Penny to sell the shop?"

Mayra-Liz nodded, her eyes glued to her plate.

"Oh Mayra-Liz, I'm not that type of man. I didn't mean to come across that way. I would never dictate decisions to my wife. I do want Penny to slow down. We talked it over and decided to hire another person during the holiday season and to hire an accountant to take care of the books. I'm committed to this project too."

"You're not going to sell the shop?" asked Mayra-Liz with hope and relief in her voice.

"Of course not!" Penny said.

"It's been awful thinking of leaving …. I just tried to keep myself super busy …." Mayra-Liz started to say before the tears came.

"Mayra-Liz," Michael said, as he got up from the table and came around to hug her. "I wish you had talked about this with me."

"I didn't want to add to what you had going on. It was selfish of me to –" Mayra-Liz gave a few more sobs into Michael's shoulder before she pulled herself back together.

"Goodness!" said Penny, "Do you have anything pulling on your heart strings too, Annalise?"

"I do," she answered with a secret smile. "I'm in love!"

Annalise was bombarded with questions: Who is he? How did they meet? What does he do? How long has she been seeing him?

"Does he have blond hair?" asked Mayra-Liz.

"Blond hair?" asked Annalise.

"I always pictured you with a blond-haired, blue-eyed farmer," said Mayra-Liz dreamily.

"That's uncanny and a tad bit spooky," Annalise said as she looked at Mayra-Liz with an astonished expression.

"I can't believe you haven't told me about him and when have you had time?" asked Mayra-Liz. "You're either at the shop or hanging out with Jen. The two of you have become joined … at … the … hip."

Silence filled the room.

"What?" asked Eva.

"You're disappointed," Annalise said to Penny.

"Not at all. I'm merely … surprised," Penny said.

"What's going on?" asked Eva again.

"I'm in love with Jen," Annalise answered simply.

"But why?" asked Eva. A heartbeat later she took it back. "I don't know why I asked that. I'm sorry. I know it's like being left or right handed. I'm ... I'm like Penny said ... surprised."

"Nothing to be sorry about," Annalise replied with a nonchalant attitude; showing that she took no offence. "I was surprised myself. I had always pictured myself with some tall, dark, and handsome guy, but it never felt right."

"But I got it right!" exclaimed Mayra-Liz. "Jen's blond-haired, blue-eyed, and operates a garden center. When I introduced you last year, I knew you'd hit it off. Of course I didn't know how much. But still ...." Mayra-Liz showed happiness in every pore. She loved to see her sisters happy; the only thing better for this middle sister was when she was a direct contributor.

"You look like a pleased Afghan Wolfhound," Eva said raising her hand for someone to "high five" and assign points. Like imaginative and impoverished families throughout time, the Muñoz sisters grew up with their self-invented parlor games. They awarded each other points for little known facts, amusing puns, appropriate metaphors, and for jobs well done. The points were good for bragging rights only.

"Doesn't count," said Annalise, "It's been used before. Besides it's too obvious: long silky hair, thin body, sculpted face."

"All right," replied Eva, not willing to give up, "She looks like an Afghan Wolfhound on her back, legs up in the air; slack mouthed while her belly is being rubbed. Mayra-Liz, you're such a praise whore!"

"Eva!" Annalise scolded while trying to hide her amusement. "All right, I give you 20 points. I subtracted 5 for vulgarity. Mayra-Liz, I award you a hundred million points for bringing Jen into my life. You deserve the praise."

Chapter Thirty-One

Poor Everyone

Michael found the shop bustling, customers three deep at the counter, and eight out of the ten tables filled. Kenyan Christmas music with its overtones of drums and steel guitars playing in the background, contributed to the lively atmosphere. The air was spiced with the smell of almonds and vanilla from the freshly baked cookies.

Mayra-Liz smiled at Michael as she cleared tables. She wore a red plaid bow tie that matched her apron. Michael smiled when he saw it. "Let me guess, a gift from Penny?" he asked.

"I like it, but wait until you see Annalise's present," Mayra-Liz rolled her eyes. "There's a table ready over here."

Michael threaded his way over to it and set up shop for himself, setting down two cameras, opened his laptop, and pulled some old magazine ads from his backpack. Sometimes Michael needed the quiet of his home office to do work, but other times he found the energy of the shop stimulated his creativity. 'How can that be?' Penny had once asked him. 'You're so immersed in what you're doing, a bomb could go off and you wouldn't notice.'

"Want some coffee, Good Lookin?" Annalise asked Michael. She was carrying a box of change purses to arrange on the shelves. The colorful purses had been woven by Kenyan women from discarded plastic bags.

"Yeah, but I can get it myself. Mayra-Liz thought I'd laugh at your headband, but I really like it."

"I do too," Annalise said as she adjusted the green plaid bow. We've sold a dozen already."

"Penny in back?" Michael asked.

"No, she went home. She had a headache and decided to lay down for a bit."

Michael reached into his jacket pocket and pulled out his phone.

191

"You know you're only going to wake her up," Annalise cautioned. "I really do think she's fine or I wouldn't have left her alone."

Michael nodded but continued to ring Penny anyway.

"Hello?" answered a sleepy voice.

"Did I awaken you?" Michael asked. Annalise rolled her eyes and mouthed "Men!" as she went to the counter for the coffee pot.

"It's okay," Penny said.

"You sound very sleepy. Did you take anything for your headache?"

"Aspirin."

"Are you okay? I mean … you haven't –"

"I'm fine, just tired. Not overtired, not drugged tired. Just tired."

"I didn't mean to imply –"

"I understand your concern, but really I'm fine. How did your photo shoot go?"

"I haven't looked at them yet, but I know I'll be disappointed."

"You always are, and they're always good."

"I'm sure they'll be flat. They won't evoke emotion. I need a different angle, a different perspective." Annalise brought over coffee and a sandwich. Michael mouthed a "thank you."

"I'm at the shop now, but I could work from home," Michael offered.

"It would be better if you stayed there, give the girls a hand at closing," Penny said.

"All right, I'll see you around seven. Feel better."

"Love you," Penny said as she hung up.

When Annalise returned to arrange the displays, Michael said, "Thanks for bringing over the coffee and sandwich. How did you know I didn't have lunch?"

"You had that crazy, 'I could eat a bear right after I wake up my wife' look about you."

Michael playfully threw one of the change purses at Annalise, and she threw it back.

Michael had been working on the photos for a couple of hours when he realized he hadn't seen Amanda, their new employee. "Is Amanda working today?" he asked Annalise.

"Yeah, she's the one who filled your coffee cup twice."

"Oh! I thought that was you. How's she working out?"

"She's great. Hard working, yet fun loving."

"The best combination," Michael said.

"It sure is. I don't know what we'd do without her. Look at this place!"

"I'm going to stay to help with closing, but do you need me to pitch in now?" Michael asked.

"Nope, we got it covered."

"What do you think when you look at this photograph?" Michael asked.

"Dorky, school picture."

"Anything else?"

"No."

They were looking at photographs when a handsome, nattily dressed man walked up to Annalise. "Excuse me, Miss," the man said, "I'm Damon Fremont. I'm here to pick up some packages for my wife, Liv Wright."

Michael stood up and extended his hand, "I'm Michael Morgan. Liv was a wonderful help to my wife when she was in the hospital last week."

"That's nice to hear," said Damon as he shook hands with Michael.

"I imagine you hear that often," Michael said.

"I do at that," Damon replied.

"Mayra-Liz has the packages all ready. They're in the storage room. We can help carry them to your car."

"How many packages are there?" asked Damon.

"We'll be making a couple of trips."

"I'm surprised. Liv hates to shop."

"Can I get you a cup of coffee first? Here, I can make some space," Michael said, turning to the cluttered table. Michael started to move the photos to one side when a group of them fell to the floor. When Damon stooped to help pick them up, Michael noticed the man carried a sidearm clipped to his belt under his suit jacket.

"I'm a police officer ... a detective," Damon explained as he took off his overcoat, carefully folded it in half, and arranged it on the chair next to him. Michael looked at the man more carefully. Steel grey hair and some hard lines on his face placed him in the sixties age bracket, but he had a body of a much younger man, still fit, and toned. Damon Fremont also had an aura of vitality, an energy that filled the room.

"How do you take your coffee?" Michael asked.

"Barefoot."

"Come again?" asked Michael.

"Black, no sugar."

"Would you like a sandwich, pastry?"

"No, thanks," Damon said flashing a quick smile and patting his flat middle.

When Michael returned with a mug of black coffee, he found Damon intently looking at the ads for missing children that Michael had pulled from his backpack when he first arrived. "Are you involved with this organization?" Damon asked.

"They're doing a new campaign. It's been thirty years since photos of abducted children started appearing on milk cartons, and while they had some success with it, they're looking for something new. I'm considering submitting a proposal, but so far my ideas are unimaginative."

"I always thought the ads should also focus on the family of the abducted child," Damon said, "Of course, the number one concern is for the children. But people don't seem to understand what it does to the families when children are taken. They never forget and they never stop looking. A part of their lives is forever suspended. Someone, somewhere knows where that child is. It's just not possible to have a child simply show up out of the blue without a red flag being waved. Time and time again, I've heard relatives, friends, and neighbors say they didn't report it because they didn't want anyone to go to jail when it appeared the child was being provided with a good home. The people who could have, *should have,* reported it. They justify their silence by convincing themselves it's probably best for the child. Who are they to make that determination? Yeah, show an image of the family longing for their child with a strong message which will convince people to report what they know."

While Damon talked, Michael grabbed a pencil and jotted down notes.

"Maybe something like a woman in a rocking chair holding a baby blanket without her baby," Michael brainstormed.

"A baby sock," Damon said. "Just one. Pink. The other one was on the baby when she was grabbed."

Michael looked up abruptly. "Are you talking about an actual case?"

"Yes," Damon said, and then he paused for a long moment before continuing. "Liv's baby was stolen thirty-eight years ago when Liv was twenty-one. I was the detective assigned to the case. I can tell you not a day goes by that Liv doesn't pray and pine for her daughter. One pink sock. It's all Liv has. How wrong is that?"

Michael looked at Damon and saw all the energy drained out of him. He looked grey and tired. *You poor man,* Michael thought. Then he thought, *Poor Liv!* Continuing in the same vein, Michael thought, *that poor child, who never had the opportunity to know these two wonderful people. Poor everyone.*

Chapter Thirty-Two

Meghan Ashley

When Jack pledged to himself that he would find his ex-wife, he meant it. With complete conviction, he believed he would find her quickly.

Katie, he thought, *there's no sense of you trying to hide from me.* He didn't know that Kathleen Louise Dunmore Fox, a.k.a Katie, no longer existed out there in the world. In truth, Penny no longer even thought of herself in those terms. Any legal ties to that name had been severed long ago. Jack would have wasted a lot of time searching for Kathleen Louise if he had put any further effort into it. But for the time being, Jack found his days and nights consumed in ways he hadn't anticipated.

First, the furniture store put on a pre-Christmas blowout sale. They even produced a televised commercial that ran locally. In the last ten seconds of the spot, Jack could be seen helping to move a sofa in the showroom. They even put his name in the credits, his supervisor's idea of treating everyone equally. The ad announced that now was the time to redecorate for the holidays. Jack wouldn't have believed it was possible. People were getting rid of perfectly good furniture and spending thousands of dollars on new, not necessarily better, just different furniture. It bothered Jack. It was as if he was doing work of no value.

Shit, he scolded himself. *What do you want? You're hired for your strong back, nothing more. Besides, this job gives you a ton of overtime and an apartment full of good furniture, customers' last year's rejects.* There was so much to choose from that Jack got quite selective about what he moved into his place. The prize was a replica Hemingway desk with a matching chair. The leather on the seat and back was so luxuriously soft that for days Jack stroked it every time he walked into the room. He had never thought he would ever own anything so fine.

195

I could write at a desk like this, he thought, *anyone could.* And so, Jack began his second unexpected project. He got out a pad of paper and a pen. The idea of using the stolen laptop seemed sacrilegious. Hemingway was Jack's favorite author. While he was in prison Jack read all of Hemingway's books several times. While Jack wrote, he listened to records, another furniture sale windfall. Some guy purchased a monstrosity of an entertainment system, so a record player and boxes of vinyl records were set out for the trash. "If you want that stuff, take it," the customer had said when he saw Jack eyeing it. The records were old and not to Jack's taste which tended to '80s rock and roll. But Jack took the player and records with the intent of selling them. However, he soon grew fond of the music. Ella Fitzgerald, Cole Porter, and Edith Piaf's music filled his apartment. It was reprieve from the tomb-like silence.

The owner of the apartment house, Mr. Glasmire, had been raised in Brooklyn in one of those big tenement buildings where neighbors shared each other's lives through paper-thin walls. He had decided if he ever owned an apartment complex he would make sure it had good sound barriers. "I knew it would be a big selling point, so when I had this place gutted and rebuilt, I considered the soundproofing an investment," Mr. Glasmire had said. Jack had thought he would love it. After all, prison was the ultimate tenement experience, and everyone heard everything, including the guy in the next cell taking a dump. But Jack soon found himself feeling isolated in his apartment; with no sounds it felt like solitary confinement. The records were a welcome relief.

This is probably the stuff Hemingway listened to, Jack thought. As he wrote, Jack imagined himself to be like Ernest Hemingway. They had both lived through hellish experiences: Hemingway through war and Jack through prison. *I'll write about that time,* Jack decided. *I'll write clean and honest prose.* While writing, Jack sipped from a glass tumbler: a splash of tomato juice with hot sauce. He knew Hemingway would have drunk whiskey, but Jack knew he couldn't. *Besides drinking hadn't done Hemingway a bit of good,* Jack reasoned.

The third project involved installing twenty-five ceiling fans in the apartment house. Built in the 1960s, the building had originally been a grade school. It had ceilings so tall, it caused even the most discriminating apartment hunters to gasp, "Oh, it's so open!" But Jack knew your feet felt like ice in the winter when all the heat rose to the "lovely open space" overhead. Mr. Glasmire decided the answer was to have ceiling fans installed in each apartment, one in each of the living rooms and bedrooms.

It was a bitch to do, climbing up and down a platform ladder, measuring, drilling, adapting old electrical boxes, and then struggling to hold the heavy panama-styled paddle fan while trying to connect the wiring at the same time. Jack's first attempt consumed an entire Saturday. Jack fervently hoped that the remaining twenty-four fans went in more easily. He had chosen his own apartment for the first installation so he could cuss when the need arrived. Jack was still cursing at midnight when he finally climbed off the platform ladder, his shoulder muscles burning from overuse. Jack sat down in his Hemingway chair, turned on the fan, and found himself smiling with satisfaction at his work. The fan did help circulate the heat, and Jack liked the ambience.

"Ambience," he said out loud with a snort. "You're getting yourself civilized, Jackie Boy."

In addition to the fan installations, Jack had to keep up with snow removal. Snow had come early, often, and heavy that winter. If it snowed at night, Jack had to get up well before dawn to shovel the walkways before leaving for his furniture job, lest some tottering, old person fell and broke a hip. It was odd living in an apartment complex where everyone was old enough to be his grandparents. Mrs. Jacobs in 17B called him Jackie Dear one time, and the name stuck with the residents. He heard, "Jackie Dear, could you help me with …" more times than he cared to count.

In addition to the sidewalks, Jack also shoveled paths around the playground. It had been installed during the building of the elementary school and showcased the latest in 1960s play designs: swings with wooden seats, a monstrosity of a slide with stairs twenty feet high to get to the top, a merry-go-round, and a wooden blue and white teeter-totter. It was equipment meant to last. The neighbors, who were old enough to have used it as children, said it didn't look much different from the day it was installed. Once when Mr. Glasmire talked about tearing it down and installing park benches, the residents went crazy. There was no way they were going to let their playground be destroyed. It was like Mr. Glasmire had suggested cancelling Christmas. The old folks did make use of the playground. They took walks around it after dinner like it was a Victorian stroll. Sometimes couples held hands and sat motionless on the merry-go-round. All the residents with dogs walked them in the playground. They were supposed to clean up after their pets, but it was difficult for the elderly residents to kneel down, so Jack was the lucky one out there bagging dog poop.

The last unexpected "project" was by far the best. Meghan. Meghan Ashley, a girl whose last name was normally a first name, the first of many surprises to come. They met at the gym. She had the most toned body of any woman Jack had ever met, yet not overly-muscular and freaky from steroids. And she was pint size; Meghan's head came to Jack's shoulder. The first time he held the boxing mitts for her while she punched, he asked how tall she was.

"Same height as Prince."

"Who?" Jack asked.

"You know, Rogers Nelson ... Prince ... Purple Rain."

"I don't know how tall Prince is."

"Well, if you're so interested, look it up," Meghan replied as she threw punches into the mitts with all she had, her dark ponytail flying.

After the class, they drank protein shakes together. The next week they did the same. The third week, Jack walked Meghan to her car.

"This is yours?" Jack had asked. "No shit? A 1970 Mustang Boss!"

"Yeah," Meghan laughed, enjoying his enthusiasm.

"My brother bought it for next to nothing and restored it. It has more bondo than metal. He took a job in China last spring and gave it to me."

"Really? He *gave* it to you?"

"Yeah, he's a good guy. I keep thinking I should take it off the road for the winter. It's a bitch in the snow. My sister has a Toyota 4Runner and loves it for winter driving."

There was a lull in the conversation and they could hear the quiet hiss of snow falling with sleet. "Speaking of which, I should get going before the snow gets any worse," Meghan said.

"Would you like go out?" Jack asked surprising himself more than her. "Dinner ... Friday night?"

Meghan smiled, reached into her purse, tore off part of an envelope, dug further into her bag, found a pen, and wrote her number.

"Yeah," Meghan smiled as she handed him the scrap of paper. "I'd like that."

Jack had what he would have called a shit-eating grin as he put on his motorcycle helmet. But he knew it wasn't good to feel too happy.

Don't get your hopes up, old boy, Jack told himself sternly. *She'll go out once with you for kicks, but she's way out of your league.*

Chapter Thirty-Three

A Pat of Butter

"Are there more worry dolls in the back?" asked Annalise as she stocked the shelves.

"First box on the right," Mayra-Liz called back. They were hurrying to get everything in order before they opened the shop and the hospital employees arrived. They had a lot of regulars who stopped in for coffee and pastries to go.

"The bakery didn't deliver those fudge brownies that went so quickly yesterday, but you should try these chocolate tarts with raspberry filling. Yum!" Penny said. "I'm going to make a fresh pot of coffee. Perhaps I should get another pot of hot chocolate going, but lately it's the coffee that's –"

Penny glanced out the window delighted to see the snow falling when she spotted an elderly woman wearing only a sweat suit and slippers standing on the sidewalk, looking wistfully at the shop's entrance. Penny set down the box of pastries and hurried to the door. When she opened it, a blast of cold air swept into the shop. The temperature had dropped like a rock in the past couple of hours.

"My goodness, it's freezing out. Won't you come in?" Penny called from the door.

"I would my dear, but you'll have to help me up the steps. I seem to have left me cane behind. At least I think I have a cane. Well, if I don't, I should go buy one. However, there seems to be a money shortage at the moment."

Penny hurried down the steps. "Hold on to the railing and I'll wrap my arm around you. Walk over here where it's handicap accessible. There aren't any steps –" Penny's words dropped off as she concentrated on helping the elderly woman.

199

"I've got old legs," the woman informed Penny with a quavering voice once they reached the top. "I don't know how that happened. One moment I was chasing after a house full of children, and the next I can hardly stand up."

"You're as cold as ice!" Penny fussed once they were safely inside.

"It's warm in here. Is that hot chocolate I smell?"

"Please sit here and I'll go get you some." Penny hurried over to the display shelves, grabbed two throws, wrapping one around the woman's shivering shoulders and placing the other over her lap.

The woman pulled the throw tightly around her shoulders, and lifted one of its corners close to her face. "Ain't this beautiful! Violet is me favorite color, and it's so soft."

"Amanda, go get a pair of the new slippers that came in, the kind you can warm up in the microwave. Warm them up, will you? But don't get them too warm."

Penny took Mayra-Liz aside and whispered, "Go in the back and call the Evergreen Nursing Home. The woman is wearing a patient ID band from there."

Penny brought the hot chocolate to the woman. "I don't think it's too hot, but do be careful."

The woman cupped the mug in her hands, raised it to her face and inhaled deeply. She closed her eyes and smiled. "It reminds me of the hot chocolate me mother used to make when I was a girl. We'd come in cold as icicles and me mother would be standing at the stove, grating a block of chocolate into the warm milk."

"That's how we make it, too. Would you like something sweet, a scone or a muffin?"

"Oh, a muffin would be lovely. Blueberry if you have it."

"One blueberry coming right up," Penny said.

"You are very dear ... hmm ... I'm afraid I don't know your name."

"Penny. Penny Morgan."

"I'm Elemona McGinley. Oh fiddle! Why do you suppose I said that? I haven't been Elemona McGinley since I was seventeen. I'm Mrs. Allen."

"I'm very pleased to meet you, Mrs. Allen," Penny said as she served the warmed muffin with a pat of butter on the side. Mrs. Allen's eyes lit up like a child's. For a moment it was easy to see the elderly woman as a young girl sitting in her mother's kitchen anticipating a treat.

"Mrs. Allen, what were you doing wandering around in the cold?" Penny asked as she sat next to her.

"It's simple, my dear, my time is coming soon, and I don't want to be where he can find me." Mrs. Allen leaned in close to Penny and whispered, "He's waiting you know. I see him out in the hallway, waiting for me to draw my last breath."

"Who?"

"Me husband. Oh, I know he'll catch up with me, but I'm not going to make it easy for him."

"He wants to hurt you?"

"He'd kill me if he could. He can't ..." Mrs. Allen leaned in close again and whispered, "because we killed him first."

"He's dead?"

"As a doorknob," Mrs. Allen nodded solemnly as she buttered the muffin.

"Oh Mrs. Allen, he can't hurt you!"

"Here are the slippers," Amanda announced. "All nice and warm."

"I'm going to take your slippers off and put these warmed ones on if that's okay with you," Penny asked Mrs. Allen.

"That sounds nice."

"There you go," Penny announced. "How do they feel?"

"Oh, they're warm and cozy!" Mrs. Allen cooed, "And this blueberry muffin is delicious. How did you know I like my muffin with a pat of butter? I know most folks don't eat them that way. At least that's what my late husband always said. He never liked me putting butter on fancy things that didn't need it, like muffins or pancakes. He thought it was a waste of money and would only make me fat. But I never did get fat." Mrs. Allen looked around and then whispered conspiratorially, "He really didn't know what he was talking about with a lot of things. I know that now."

Warmed by the hot chocolate, muffin, throws, and slippers, Mrs. Allen stopped shivering. "I feel much better now. What a dear child you are. You remind me of my Mary Ellen. She has red hair like yours. I want to rest me head on the table now. Would that be all right?"

"Of course," Penny said. Mrs. Allen made a cradle out of her arms on which she rested her head, and closed her eyes. Seeing the awkwardness of her visitor's neck, Penny asked Mayra-Liz to grab one of the little bean pillows from the back room.

"Do you want it warmed up?" Mayra-Liz asked.

"I don't think so. She's warm now, and I don't want to overheat her."

The poor dear, Penny thought. *I wonder where her family is. Maybe the nursing home will call the daughter that Mrs. Allen mentioned. I hope she lives nearby. Goodness, considering how old Mrs. Allen is, I hope the daughter is still alive.* Penny watched the snow fall. It was coming down hard now and the wind made it look like it was snowing sideways.

Snow wasn't predicted, Penny mused. Glancing at the elderly woman asleep beside her Penny thought, *Well, I suppose most things aren't.*

"Here Penny," said Mayra-Liz as she handed Penny the pillow. "I'm sorry I took so long. I couldn't find them."

"Mrs. Allen, I'm sorry to disturb you, but you're going to get a crick in your neck resting like that. This pillow will make you more comfortable." When Penny moved the old woman's arm, it slipped off the table, and fell limply to her side.

"Is she?" asked Mayra-Liz alarmed.

Penny checked the woman's pulse. "I think so," Penny said with a shaking voice.

Mayra-Liz pulled out her cell phone and punched in 911. She grabbed Amanda's hand, and they escaped to the backroom not wishing to be with a dead body. It felt like an eternity before anyone arrived after the 911 call, and then it felt like everyone did. A silver BMW arrived first. The shop's door flew open, and Dr. Allen rushed in. Penny stood up and stepped aside giving the doctor room to examine the patient.

"I think she may be –" Penny started to say, but gave up trying to converse when she realized Dr. Allen hadn't noticed anyone except the limp-looking woman. He checked the patient's breathing and pulse and then stood next to her, his own arms limp at his side. His normal, confidence-inspiring posture was now slumped. He looked defeated. The blaring ambulance siren could be heard racing down the hill. For the second time in ten minutes, the front door was flung open and slammed shut.

"We need you to stand back, sir," the paramedics said to Dr. Allen as they rushed in. When the paramedics determined that the woman was dead, they called the hospital and reported a D.O.A. They placed Mrs. Allen on the stretcher, and only then did they seem to remember the man who stood observing them.

"Do you know her?" one of them asked.

"She's my mother. I'm Dr. Patrick Allen. I was at the hospital when the nursing home called to say she was missing. I thought they must have gotten her confused with another patient. My mother has been wheelchair bound for months, or at least I thought she was. I don't suppose she could have possibly walked to this shop if she hadn't been walking at least part of the time. I was just getting into my car when the nursing home called back and said she was found here at this shop."

202

"We're sorry for your loss," the paramedic said. "There was nothing to be done. She was gone when we arrived."

"I know," the doctor confirmed. A van with an Evergreen logo pulled into the shop's driveway. The nursing home attendant hurried in and with practiced decorum expressed his sympathies to Dr. Allen. The paramedics wheeled Mrs. Allen out the door of the shop, through the snow, and into the ambulance. As they left, no siren sounded. The emergency and the life was over. Dr. Allen was asked to come to the nursing home by the end of the week to make arrangements for his mother's things. Dr. Allen nodded, but Penny knew the doctor was just giving an automated response. He looked like his mind was a million miles away. Penny guessed the nursing home attendant knew it too because he handed Dr. Allen his business card, and asked him to call when he could. Then, the attendant nodded to Penny and left.

Dr. Allen looked at the table where his mother had sat. A nearly empty mug of hot chocolate and a bit of muffin spread with butter remained. It was his undoing, and he started to quietly weep.

Penny came up to Dr. Allen and held his arm. "I'm so sorry," she told him.

"Penny?" Dr. Allen looked as if he had lost his bearings, and his patients and his private world had somehow merged. He looked around, and it became clear to him. "This is your shop, isn't it?"

"Yes."

"You gave my mother hot chocolate and a muffin."

"She enjoyed it," Penny said simply.

"I'm sure she did. It had butter on it," Dr. Allen said, his voice cracking.

"She's in a better place," Penny said.

"I hope that's true," he said as he turned and walked out of the shop.

Chapter Thirty-Four

Belly Gun

"Not again!" Michael teased as he crossed through the living room with a stack of enlarged photographs in his arms. He had been deciding on the right ones for the upcoming Missing Children conference.

"Hmm?" asked Penny not looking up from her book.

"*Ironweed*. How many times have you read it?"

"I've lost count," Penny replied.

"It's depressing," Michael said.

"It's about redemption, forgiveness, and everlasting love," Penny said with a contented sigh.

"It's about hunger, death, and alcoholism," Michael maintained.

"I'm at the best part," Penny said, hushing him. "Francis is at the door with a turkey."

Penny felt her husband's eyes on her. Looking up, she saw Michael standing stock still. His face had paled.

He looks older, Penny thought. Much older than last year. Penny knew that lately her husband hadn't been sleeping well, but when did he get those dark circles under his eyes?

"Are you all right?" she asked, not sure how to voice her full concern.

"Yes, I'm fine. I'm going out to get some fresh air," Michael said as he walked to the front closet. When he came back, Michael was bundled in a winter coat, hat, scarf, and gloves.

"It's nearly ten o'clock," Penny said. I thought we were going to make an early night of it."

"I'm restless. I need a walk."

"I'll come with you."

"It's freezing out," Michael said flatly.

Penny took heed of Michael's weather report and dressed in warm layers. She was winding a scarf around her neck when she came back into the room, and Michael gave her a small, sad smile. "You look like the kid brother in the *Christmas Story*," he observed.

Penny knew in the old days Michael would have given a hearty laugh. She wrapped her arms around her husband and whispered, "Are we okay?"

"We're better than okay," he said as he squeezed her in return. When they stepped into the front yard, a brilliant full moon on a dark blue velvet sky greeted them.

"I need to get some shots of this," Michael said as he ran back into the house and grabbed his Nikon.

While Michael took photos Penny said, "Every time I see a full moon I imagine Margaret looking down at me. But that's silly. People don't die and go to the moon."

Michael showed Penny an image on the camera, wisps of clouds gliding across the face of the moon. "There's something so comforting about the moon, isn't there?" Penny sighed.

"It looks sinister to me," Michael said darkly.

"Sinister? That doesn't sound like you. Michael, what's going on?"

"What if your ex showed up here? Somehow found your address and just turned up with a turkey under his arm like Francis Phelan did with the family he had left."

"That won't happen!" Penny said too emphatically to be convincing. She took a deep breath and then said more calmly, "My circumstances are different than those in the Ironweed story. Francis's wife didn't divorce him, and she never moved away. With Mr. Bos's help, I not only divorced Ja – my ex, I disappeared. I have remained hidden from him for over seventeen years. Don't you think if he was going to find me, he would have done so by now?"

"There's different technology; it's not as easy to keep the past covered."

"But I told you, Mr. Bos, my attorney, he helped me. Why are you doing this, Michael? I've really struggled not to be worried about *him* and you're making it sound like I should be."

"I don't want to upset you. God knows that's the last thing in the world I want. But we also need to be sensible about this, not stick our heads in the sand. We should have a plan. What if he did show up? He's not a good person like the Francis Phelan character who never raised a hand to his wife, whereas Jack Fox –"

"Don't say his name!" Penny gasped.

"I thought you were over that."

"I just don't like to hear it."

"Okay, what if *he* showed up here, maybe without malice. Once he saw you had remarried, he'd become jealous, possessive. Men like him don't easily give up what they view as *theirs*."

In the moonlight, Penny saw her husband's facial muscles tighten. "Don't Michael," she began to say. "Don't think about it."

"Could you shoot someone if they threatened your life?" Michael proceeded.

Penny pondered the question. "I don't know." She thought a moment longer. "I really don't know," she decided. "And I don't know how I could determine that."

"What if he was threatening me or the girls?"

"Where are you going with this, Michael?"

"I'd like to learn how to shoot your gun."

Penny stared at him with disbelief.

"I know I was against having a gun in the house when we were first married; it was against my philosophies in life," Michael said. "I made peace with it because it was your grandfather's. I grew to regard it not as an instrument of death, but part of your happy childhood memories, shooting apples off a tree with your aunt."

"And now?" Penny asked.

"I should know how to protect myself and my family if the need should arise."

Penny stared at her husband as if he had been replaced by aliens. "I can't wrap my head around this, Michael. This isn't you! You have such strong convictions about gun control –"

"What does he look like?" Michael interrupted.

"I hate this conversation, Michael! I've finally been convinced by everyone including you that I don't have to worry about him. Now my pacifist husband wants to take up arms and have a description of the potential perpetrator!"

Michael ignored her outburst and asked, "Do you have a photograph of him?"

"No!"

"Nothing? Not an image in the yearbook, a snapshot of the senior prom?"

"Nothing, Michael. I got rid of all that stuff."

"Then describe him to me. You know, I could trip over this guy and not know it."

"We're not going to trip over him ..." Penny started to say but seeing Michael's determined jaw said, "All right. If it makes you feel better."

She narrowed her eyes as she gazed up at the moon, remembering. It was to the moon that she spoke. "He's Native American, dark complexion with dark eyes and hair. He sort of looked like Johnny Depp."

"Really?" Michael asked.

Penny nodded.

"I guess that explains why we had to leave the theatre in the middle of watching *Pirates of the Caribbean*."

"It just freaked me out," Penny answered, feeling embarrassed as she looked at the ground.

"Did he wear his hair in a ponytail?"

"No, but before he enlisted he wore it longish. He had a habit of tossing his hair out of his eyes."

"Does he have tattoos?"

"He had the Seabees logo on his right forearm," Penny said as she shivered.

"It's cold. Let's go back in," Michael said as he put his arm around Penny. "I'm sorry to have upset you, but I feel we need to be sensible about this. I think we should buy a revolver. The people at the gun store said your grandfather's pistol is called a belly gun because it won't do much damage, and it's not very accurate unless the target is within arm's length."

"And you think the answer is to get a bigger gun!"

"I don't like the idea of another gun either, but I've known people like him. They're ruthless. They'll do anything to get what they want!"

Penny took off running down the dark road.

"Penny!" Michael called, but Penny kept running. Michael ran after her. When he caught up, she stopped and looked at him with a tear-streaked face.

"I can't ... " Penny sobbed. "I simply can't have this dredged up. Michael, I need to let it go, and I need you to let me, let it go. If you don't, everything will be as it was before."

"Oh Penny," Michael said as he held her close, and she sobbed into his chest. "I'm so sorry. I won't bring it up again."

"Can you really let it go, just like that?"

"I will not mention it to you again," Michael replied with conviction. "We cannot have you upset. I'll keep this to myself. I never should have brought it up."

"But I don't want you to think about it either!" Penny wailed.

"I promise I won't dwell on it. I'll figure out a plan, and then let it go."

"What are you going to do?"

"Keep you safe," Michael replied.

"How?" Penny asked with alarm.

"Do you still trust me, Penny?" Michael asked earnestly.

"Yes, of course I do."

"Okay then. Leave it to me. When we get in the house we'll have some hot chocolate and talk about something else. Let's plan a little trip for Valentine's Day. It'd be good to get away for a couple of days."

"But you're so busy with the conference coming up."

"I can take a few days off. It'd do us both good."

Chapter Thirty-Five

Weaving and Unraveling

Penny looked over at her psychiatrist. He looked as if he hadn't sleep well. His color was off. Of course, Irish folks are known for their pale skin, but Dr. Allen looked grey. Penny felt for him. She knew what it was like to lose a loved one.

Dr. Allen began the session, "The last time we met we talked about how people with Post-Traumatic Stress Disorder, PTSD tend to keep emotionally reliving the trauma. Oftentimes, the memories are disjointed, sporadic and can disrupt sleep. Patients' emotional growth can be hampered. In other words, the trauma makes it difficult for them to move on.

"Productive therapy provides patients with the opportunity to thoroughly analyze the trauma while exploring ways to manage painful memories. With this in mind, your assignment for the past week was to write down a memory from your first marriage while trying to look at it in a different, more mature light."

Penny opened her journal. "I wrote something, but it doesn't have a different, more mature light. I just wrote it as it happened. I have no idea how to comment on it further."

"Can you read it to me?"

"I had spent the entire day polishing the house. Jack liked the house in order, and I didn't want to give him reason to be upset. He came home late ... again. His breath announced whiskey and neglect. He had said he'd be home on time, but I didn't say anything as that would have started a fight. I hadn't begun our marriage censoring my conversation. I don't remember how or when that began. Jack sat at the table waiting for me to serve him dinner. I don't remember how that happened either. We had started out sharing the household responsibilities. On the weekends we had cooked meals together. By the time I was pregnant, I was waiting on him hand and foot, like a geisha. He often didn't have much to say. I remember that night he started talking, and at first I felt encouraged, even though his words were slurred. He told me his pal, Rich was having marital problems; his wife was either overspending or sleeping all day.

"It sounds like she's depressed," I told him.

"Yeah, if she were my wife, I'd depress her all right," Jack snarled.

"What do you mean?"

"I'd show her who's the boss."

"How?"

"Don't be stupid, Katie. You know what I mean." And he showed me his fist.

"You wouldn't hit your wife! That's not how you were brought up. I knew your grandparents my whole life, and I can't believe they had a relationship like that."

"What do you know of my life? You didn't meet me until I was seventeen."

"That's true. Why don't you ever talk about your parents? I have no idea what they were like, what happened to them. Tell me about them."

"You never know when to shut up, do you?" he snarled me at he left the room.

"Jack, you can't talk to me like that," I told him. But he was already gone.

"That's the whole story."

"Interesting," Dr. Allen said while he finished writing down some notes.

"I didn't think so. For me, it was just a painful memory."

"That's because you aren't allowing your more mature insight to look at it."

"I guess that's the problem. I have no insight. If I did, I wouldn't be in this situation."

212

"Let's take it piece by piece. He called you Katie?" asked Dr. Allen with a frown.

"Yes. My given name was Katherine Louise, but my aunt never liked it and called me Penny or Penelope, after the faithful woman in Homer's Odyssey. She only used the endearment when no one else was around. She didn't want others picking it up. It was special to just the two of us."

"Oh yes, I remember you mentioning that now. Getting back to your marriage, relationships don't usually start out abusive. It's little by little that a power shift takes place. Instead of the marriage being equal or nearly so, more and more of the power goes to one person. It's more often the woman who loses equal partner status. It can happen to women who have successful careers, but women who are dependent upon their husband's income can be especially vulnerable."

"I was so unhappy."

"And yet you stayed. I imagine you felt immobile. That happens. It's a byproduct of abuse. I think it's interesting your aunt called you Penelope. If I remember right Penelope was famous for waiting twenty years for her husband to return from war. She was pressed to remarry, so she announced that she would after she finished weaving a shroud for her father-in-law, then every evening she unraveled the progress she made."

"I always thought of Penelope as the faithful wife, a good thing; but you're right; weaving and unraveling a shroud is very passive. She should have stood up for herself. Do you think Margaret thought I was a pushover?"

"I don't know, but what you were doing was in essence weaving and unraveling. You couldn't change Jack's behavior, but you thought you could control it by being the perfect wife – clean house, dinner on the table, offering no argument. Your life wasn't getting any better, but you were trying to keep it from getting any worse ... weaving and unraveling. It sounds like occasionally you stood up for yourself like when you said, 'you can't talk to me that way,' but you had no power in the relationship to change it. What you failed to realize was that he was already abusive. Threatening abuse, no matter how veiled, when there is intent behind it, it is still abuse."

"I wish I had stood up to him in the very beginning. The very first time Jack started disrespecting me I should have been more assertive, and then he would have known –"

"No, Penny," Dr. Allen interrupted. "You need to stop thinking like that. First of all, you can never win with the 'what if' game. Besides, the only thing that can stop a man like that is –"

"Is what?" Penny asked.

Dr. Allen just shook his head.

"Death? Is that what you were going to say?" Penny asked, slightly stunned.

"Professionals in my field believe nearly everyone can be reached with good therapy."

"But you don't believe that?" Penny asked.

"I'm sorry, Penny. I'm not feeling well. Do you mind if we end our session early?"

"That's fine. I understand."

Dr. Allen gave a frown inadvertently signaling that Penny couldn't possibly understand.

"I know your father was abusive. It must be doubly difficult to lose your mother. I'm certain you were very close," Penny said quietly, her tone full of compassion.

Dr. Allen's head shot up at Penny's words.

"She told me," Penny said simply.

"She told you what?" Dr. Allen asked with trepidation, nervously rubbing his head.

"Your mother said her husband was waiting for her to die, so he could get even with her because she killed him. I'm assuming a gentle woman like your mother would not talk of killing her husband unless he was abusive."

"Oh," Dr. Allen said softly.

When it was obvious Dr. Allen had no intention of elaborating, Penny asked tentatively, "She didn't *really* kill him, did she?"

"My mother believed she was morally responsible. I don't normally talk about my personal life with my patients, Penny; however, this situation is different. You were with my mother when she died. You know about part of my life that few people do."

Dr. Allen took a deep breath, took off his glasses, and rubbed his temples. "One by one my four older siblings grew up and moved away. I had a younger brother who died. My mother said my father became more abusive with each child's birth. One evening my father came home stinking drunk for the fifth night in a row. The way it had been going, I think he could have killed us, just beat us until we were dead. The thought must have occurred to my mother because she instructed me to chain lock the door, something we had never done before. In the morning we found he had died in the car."

"How awful! But your mother shouldn't have felt guilty."

Dr. Allen dropped his eyes.

"Oh, but you feel guilty too," Penny said with certainty.

Dr. Allen looked up at Penny and shook his head. "I was just a kid. There was no way I could have stopped him –"

Penny interrupted. "I don't mean that. You feel responsible for even being born, fueling your father's fury and adding to your mother's hardships. I see it in your face."

"How could you have known? I have never expressed those thoughts to anyone."

"I know it's easier to feel responsible, even for awful things than it is to feel like you have no control."

"Who says you don't have insight," Dr. Allen marveled.

Chapter Thirty-Six

In a Single Word – A Glance

Jack couldn't remember the last time he had been on a "date." Sure, he had taken women out or had picked them up, but this felt different. It felt romantic. *Easy Tiger,* he told himself. *You don't even know this girl. Oh yeah ... well, she sure seems like something special,* he told his negative side. He had called her up and suggested an Italian restaurant.

"I'll borrow a car so you don't have to ride on the back of the bike. It's not much fun when it's freezing cold," Jack said.

"There's no need," Meghan replied. "I'm in walking distance from the restaurant. I'll meet you there."

"Sounds like a plan," said Jack. "Actually, I'm in walking distance too, so we could walk each other home."

"Like in 'Wings of the Dove.' Do you know it?" Meghan asked him.

"Oh that I had wings like a dove! For then I would fly away and be at rest," Jack quoted.

"Exactly!" Meghan said delighted. "The line is Biblical, you know, from the 55th Psalm."

"I didn't know," Jack said, enjoying the conversation. It was always fun to discuss good books with a fellow reader.

"In the movie, they messed up when filming the underground stations. Each station on the Piccadilly line had different painted walls and its own tile pattern, so the people who were illiterate could recognize their stops. In the movie, they filmed only one location, but called them different places."

"I've never seen the movie."

"You've never seen it? But you must! After dinner come over to my place, and we'll watch it."

"Okay," Jack said and knowing he had a goofy grin and was glad to be on the phone where she couldn't see him. *How can it be,* he thought,

217

I've talked with this girl for less than ten hours and I'm already half in love?

Meghan had arrived before Jack. She was sitting at the bar in a dark business suit, crisp white shirt, and black high heels. Jack saw her and waved. While he pulled out the bar stool, she said, "Sorry about the outfit. I got tied up at work. I didn't want to be late, so I came directly here."

"I feel like we're going to court," Jack said with a smile.

"Actually," she said a little sheepishly, "I just came from court. I'm an attorney. You can run now if you wish."

Jack sat down.

"What do you do?" Meghan asked, "Besides the gym."

"I move furniture." Jack said while tossing his hair. "I've decided to give it to you straight: no rhymes, no embellishments, no adjectives."

"Ian McEwan's Atonement? You are well read."

"I suppose so, but I wasn't simply quoting. Your turn. Do you have an Atonement quote to fit the occasion?"

"Falling in love could be achieved in a single word – a glance."

Jack pulled Meghan to him and kissed her.

They wakened with arms and legs intertwined at Jack's apartment. The Sunday morning church bells were ringing, calling the faithful. Jack knew it was nine o'clock. He couldn't remember the last time he had slept so late. Meghan stirred in his arms. "Did you sleep okay?" he asked her.

"Uh, huh," she replied still groggy. She sat up and looked at the clock. "I never sleep this late. This is a really comfortable bed. For a moment I thought we were going to be on the floor. I knew about Murphy beds, but I had never seen one before."

"Want some coffee?" Jack asked.

"That would be nice."

"The coffee's in the fridge, filters in the cupboard over the sink, coffee maker is right there."

"Are you kidding?" Meghan asked.

"Yes," Jack answered as he pulled on his jeans. "How about an omelet with toast? I'm a fairly decent cook, and I got some homemade strawberry jam from the farmer's market."

They ate at the mahogany dining room table. The matching high back chairs were upholstered with beige fabric with deep red dragonflies. Meghan asked if he had plans for the day.

218

"Actually, I don't, which is rare. I usually work most days."

"You mean seven days a week?"

Jack nodded as he tossed his hair out of his eyes.

"Man, and I thought I was a workhorse," she said.

"It's just what I need to do."

"Well, since you have this lovely day off, do you want to spend it with me?" Meghan inquired with a smile.

"I can't think of anything nicer," Jack said, smiling back.

While Jack loaded the dishwasher, Meghan looked around his apartment. "Do you know, and I'm not kidding, this is the cleanest, most organized apartment I have ever been in, but beyond that, it's beautifully decorated. Did you hire someone?"

Jack let out a snort. "What you see is what the customers at the furniture store no longer wanted."

"You're kidding!"

"Not kidding," Jack confirmed.

"I'll be embarrassed when you see my apartment. I just cleaned it, but decorating is not my forte."

Meghan walked over to the framed photo that stood on his desk. "A picture of Hemingway?" Meghan asked with surprise.

"It came with the frame," Jack answered with a toss of his hair.

"You said no embellishments," Meghan instructed.

"What can I tell you? I like Hemingway," Jack said as he wiped the counter clean.

"He was so sexist," Meghan said. She picked up a little ceramic figurine from Jack's desk. "A Jack Russell?"

"I guess."

"So what do you want to do today?" Jack asked, as he crossed the room and put his arms around her.

"Do you have a bike? I mean a pedal bike."

"Yes."

"It's warmed up. Let's take a ride to the Great Pond Reservoir. I have often gone passed it; I always think I'll stop someday, but I never have."

"Sure," Jack said as he tossed his hair out of his eyes, "that sounds good. But you know it'll be at least twenty miles round trip, don't you?"

"Yeah, are you not up to it?" she challenged.

"No wonder you're in such great shape," he told her. "We'll stop someplace for lunch."

"Why don't we pack a picnic lunch? I know it's January, but the sun is shining."

"That sounds really nice. Tonight, we'll try that Italian restaurant again. Maybe this time we'll actually stay and eat," Jack said as he nuzzled her neck.

"Don't bet on it," Meghan said as she turned and kissed him.

Chapter Thirty-Seven

The Couples

Penny came downstairs while wrapping her fleece robe around her. Michael hadn't come to bed yet and it was 3:07 a.m. She found him downstairs working at his computer.

"Sweetheart, you can't continue to keep these hours," Penny said.

"You startled me," Michael said.

"You were so engrossed; you didn't even hear me come in. Come to bed. You can work on it in the morning."

"I'm afraid I won't have anything good in the morning either, and the Missing Children conference is in five weeks. I need to have it nailed down soon so I can send photos to the printers and update the website. There's so much to do, and I can't do any of it without knowing the theme, the photos, the text …"

"But the conference already approved your proposal. They liked your general ideas."

"But they were just that … general ideas. I need to complete it, and nothing I've done is good enough. It needs to be a campaign that speaks to people. What if, as a result of this campaign, just one person called the help line and a missing child was found. It would be worth all the hard work. It would be worth everything."

"Your eyes are tired and bloodshot. I don't think you're going to find the answer with no sleep," Penny said reasonably. "Come to bed. We'll brainstorm in the morning. Liv is coming over. We can ask her opinion."

"Don't you think it would be too painful for her?"

"No, I think she'd like to be involved."

Liv Wright and Damon Fremont were also awake. They were drinking warmed Ovaltine, the classic malt flavor, with a splash of whiskey.

221

"I just don't feel right about it, Damon," Liv was saying. "I've grown close to both of them. There's no way Michael was involved in diamond smuggling. He only became a person of interest because of his work in Sierra Leone, and because we know he once met that bastard, Bogdan Sokolov. I wish I could tell them how I came to be Penny's nurse. Today, I'm having coffee *at their home,* for heaven's sake."

"You've been here before. I know it feels like you lead a double life, but that's the job."

Liv sipped her drink while shaking her head. "Ya know, Damon, maybe it's time for me to retire from the Bureau, and just be a regular nurse."

"You do a lot of good. Remember when that kidnapper told you where the child was hidden? Do you think he would have told you if he had known you worked for the FBI?"

"He wasn't convicted," Liv said.

"Yeah, because he wasn't read the Miranda, but the child was saved, and not an hour too soon."

"I wish I could have done both, saved the child and convicted that piece of scum."

"This isn't what's really upsetting you, Liv. I know what today is."

"Do you think anyone got my daughter a birthday present?" Liv asked, as she wiped a tear from her face with the back of her hand.

Chapter Thirty-Eight

Brainstorming

"What a sweet cottage you have here," Liv said as she looked around. "It has such a cozy feel. Not really what I expected with Michael being such a famous photographer and all. I pictured it huge and white with lots of chrome."

Penny laughed. "You've got to know that wouldn't be my style."

"I know, but sometimes we just live with things whether they're our style or not. Take my living room for instance. It's home to *the* ugliest chair that God has ever seen, but Damon loves it ... watches the news every evening in it."

"Love the man ... love his chair," Penny said.

"I wouldn't go that far," Liv said. "I *tolerate* that chair, but just barely."

Penny poured coffee and set out a plate of fudge-filled brownies on the table.

Liv reached for one while saying, "I've got to ask you, Miss Penny, how are you able to stay so slim while having all these delicious treats around you all day."

"I don't know. I seem to be one of those people who has a metabolism that allows for a good amount of calories."

"Well enjoy it while you can, Sister. I was the same until I hit forty. I'll have to spend another thirty minutes on the treadmill for this little morsel."

"Good morning," Michael said as he entered the kitchen. He came over and kissed Penny on the check. "How are you, Liv?"

"I'm just fine."

Michael glanced up at the kitchen clock, "10:20 already! How's the brainstorming? What do you think, Liv?"

"Brainstorming?" asked Liv, before taking another bite of brownie.

"I didn't ask her yet," Penny said. "I thought I'd give her a cup of coffee before putting her to work."

"What's up," asked Liv. "You know I'd be happy to help if I can."

"I'm working on a campaign for missing children."

"Oh that's right. Damon mentioned it."

"Well, my brain feels like a block of ice. I just can't get the flow going," Michael said. "What we need is a dynamic image with a text so moving, it'll inspire people to report what they know about a child who was stolen. I went with this theme because of what Damon said: someone, someplace, knows something, and they have a responsibility to report it even if the child seems to be doing okay. There's the child's family to think of."

Liv stared pensively at the refilled coffee cup Penny had just placed in front of her. "I don't know how creative I am, but I'd be happy to help you brainstorm. You know, my baby girl who is now a grown woman of nearly forty is never far from my thoughts. Holidays and birthdays are always especially difficult. I try hard not to show it for Damon's and our boys' sakes. But I always wonder what she's doin'. Does she decorate a tree? Does she have children of her own? Is she happy? God bless her, is she even alive? Every year that goes by, gives me less hope that I'll ever know these things. Perhaps you could have an image of a tearful woman putting up a Christmas stocking. The caption could say, 'Give her back her child.' And list the reporting number.

Michael chewed on his lip. "No good, huh?" asked Liv.

"It's … hmm … I think too seasonal. Christmas was last month and most people want to put the holidays out of their minds until next fall. We want people to linger at the image, not turn away thinking about their credit card bills from the holidays."

Michael grabbed a notepad and joined the women at the kitchen table. "But what about birthdays? How about different snapshots of a child's birthday party with the child blowing out a candle. The child gets older in each photo representing the passing years. The first one or two could be in focus for when the child was with the family, and the rest blurred representing how the family doesn't know what the child is doing on his or her birthday. The caption could say something like "Make their wish come true. Call 800-123-1234 with information on missing children."

"I don't think it's strong enough. It's not just my *wish* to be with my child. I'm her *mother*. It's my goddamn *right*!" Liv said, her voice angry and rising.

"Whoa," Penny whispered under her breath in surprise. She had never heard Liv come anywhere near swearing before.

"I'm sorry, I didn't mean …." Michael started to say.

"No, I'm sorry. Let's try some more. I'll try to take my emotions out of it."

"We need your emotions, Liv. That's what my ideas were missing."

"We just can't make cussing be part of the logo," Liv said with a sheepish smile.

"Probably so," Michael said returning her smile.

"How about life is an endless search when your child is missing? The photo could be of a woman or man staring at each passerby on the street," Penny said.

"I like it," Liv said. "It's true."

"It's better," Michael replied. "But I feel it's still missing something."

They all continued to stare at the table as they thought. Liv had eaten three brownies in the thought process. "This isn't as easy as it looks," Liv said. "It kind of hurts your brain."

Michael laughed. "Yes, sometimes it does feel that way, but it's wonderful when you find 'it'."

After a long pause Liv said, "You know she isn't hers. The real mother is waiting. Let them reunite."

Michael stopped in the middle of raising his coffee mug for another sip and set it down quickly. He tore the sheet of notepaper half filled with their ideas from the pad and started to write in bold block letters on the fresh sheet THE MOTHER AND CHILD REUNION IS ONLY A PHONE CALL AWAY.

"We could make a video and play it on YouTube. It would be of mothers and daughters, sons and fathers, families being reunited. The organization has tons of footage. They played one for me when I was first hired. It was so emotional, I got teary. I'll ask Paul Simon to get involved and play "Mother and Child Reunion" for the background or at least let us use the song.

"Will he do it?" Liv asked doubtfully.

"It never hurts to ask," Michael called enthusiastically over his shoulder as he was already on his way to his office to place phone calls.

Chapter Thirty-Nine

The Bag Lady

The pace at *Ruth and Naomi* slowed down a bit during late January. However, it was still busy enough to keep Penny, Annalise, Mayra-Liz, and Amanda going all day with the shop, on-line sales, and marketing for Valentine's Day.

Most Mondays, only Mayra-Liz and Annalise worked. Today it was slow enough to give the young women time to set up shelves and display the new merchandise. Mayra-Liz came into the café area with a shipping box full of jewelry when she saw Annalise at the opened door, shooing away a bag lady.

"Go on, get!" Annalise shouted as if the woman were a rabid dog. "We don't want you here. You get going before I call the police."

"Annalise! What are you doing? You know Penny said to never turn anyone away hungry." Mayra-Liz set down the box. "You come right on in here and warm up," Mayra-Liz said to the frozen-looking woman. "Let me get you something to … Mom?"

The woman was dressed in numerous layers of dirty-looking clothes with a ratty brown fur coat as the final crust. The clothing seemed to weigh her down, yet she quickly staggered up the front steps and into the warm shop. The woman's hair was snarled and matted, as if it hadn't seen shampoo or a comb in months. A swipe of dried mucus lay across her face. "Mayra-Liz? Is that you, baby girl?"

The woman set down her numerous bags and held out her arms. Mayra-Liz tentatively embraced the smelly woman. "You have to learn to take my lead on some things," Annalise said to her sister, shaking her head. "Don't sit down," Annalise told her mother. "You're not staying."

Their mother looked to Mayra-Liz. Would she send her away too? "She's our mother, Annalise. We can't just throw her out. Isn't that against what we're doing here?"

"What we're doing here is helping women who help themselves and take care of their families. Do you think the woman before you has done anything to help anyone, even herself?"

"I don't know," said Mayra-Liz. "I was quite young when she left."

"Exactly!" exclaimed Annalise, "when she *left*."

"If I could just have twenty dollars," the mother piped up.

"So you can put it up your arm? No thank you," responded Annalise. "No, thank *you*!"

"Mom, I'm going to walk you over to the City Mission. Annalise and I stayed there for a while. It's clean and safe. They will feed you and give you a place to sleep as long as you stay clean."

"Okay," their mother shrugged as she started to gather up her bags again.

"I'll just get my coat," Mayra-Liz said as she hurried to the back room. Annalise turned her back to them.

A few minutes later, Mayra-Liz returned buttoning up her coat, "I'm ready," she announced with too much enthusiasm for the chore.

"That's a nice coat you have there. Looks warm," said her mother as she stroked the heavy wool.

When Mayra-Liz took account of all the bags her mother had, she offered to drive over in the van. "That's okay," the mother said. "I'm used to hauling these things around."

"At least let me carry some. Mom, this one is leaking."

"Oh, let me have it; that one's special."

"It's alcohol, isn't it? You can't bring that into The Mission," Mayra-Liz said.

"You're wasting your breath," Annalise scolded her sister.

On the walk, her mother murmured, "I do appreciate this, Mayra-Liz."

"It's okay," Mayra-Liz said, suddenly feeling weary.

"You did grow up to be a beauty. I knew you would. Where's your father? Does he live around here, too?"

"Jail. Attempted robbery."

"Really? That doesn't sound like him."

"Well, things got rather desperate. He thought it was his only way to help his family."

"When will he get out?"

"Seventeen months … we hope."

"And Eva? Where is she?" the mother frowned trying to do math in her head. "She must be fifteen?"

"Seventeen," Mayra-Liz corrected while trying to do her best not to judge a women who missed her daughter's age by two years. "She's in school. She goes to … ah … U.C.L.A. We don't see her very often."

"You were never any good at lying, even as a child."

"It would upset Eva to see you like this. She's doing well in school. Promise me you won't come by again until you get yourself straight."

The mother nodded. It was difficult to know if the promise caused her any pain.

"Okay, here we are. There aren't a lot of rules. You need to stay clean and sober. There's a set time for breakfast. They'll assign you work to do within The Mission, and when you're ready, they'll help you to find work in the city."

"Sounds like a lot of rules to me. You know, I think I'll just go in later on. If you could just give me a twenty, it would really help a lot."

Mayra-Liz handed the bags back to her mother. "I'm sorry, Mom. I can't."

Mayra-Liz cried all the way back to the shop.

Chapter Forty

On the Count of Three

Jack was cooking up a storm which normally occupied his complete attention, but today he kept patting his front jeans pocket to reassure himself that the ring was still there. He had been in the breakroom when one of the guys asked if he was interested in purchasing it.

"No," Jack had said automatically.

"It's really nice, only a hundred bucks."

"I don't have any use for it," Jack replied as he started to walk away.

"What about Valentine's Day? Haven't I seen some cutie dropping you off?"

"Let me see it," Jack said. It was a ruby in a gold setting, 'simple, yet elegant' he heard Meghan say in his head. "I'll give you fifty for it."

"Sixty," the man countered.

"Okay," Jack agreed.

On the way home Jack stopped at a jewelry store. If the ring was junk, he'd pawn it off onto someone else. The jeweler assured Jack it was a very nice estate piece and worth at least a thousand. "Do you want it cleaned? It'll really brighten the gold," the jeweler informed Jack.

"How much?" Jack had asked.

"No charge. Just remember to buy your wedding bands here."

Fat chance of that, Jack had thought, but he took the jeweler up on the free cleaning.

Jack prepared chicken cacciatore, rigatoni pasta, and broccoli with red peppers. Meghan claimed she didn't like vegetables. However, Jack felt certain she would if they were cooked properly.

I don't know why I'm so anxious, Jack thought. *It's not like I'm asking her to marry me.* He stood stock-still. What if Meghan thought he was proposing? Somehow he needed to make it clear it was a Valentine present, nothing more and somehow still make it sound romantic. He had not the slightest idea of how to convey that. *Perhaps it would be better if I didn't give it to her,* Jack thought. *I can more than get my money back.*

Meghan arrived late which was no surprise to Jack. He always planned dinner an hour later than the appointed time. She hurried in with snow in her hair and handed Jack a pastry box as she pulled off her black leather boots and coat. "Sorry I'm late … crazy busy day," Meghan said breathlessly.

Jack smiled at Meghan's stock greeting. "You brought dessert? I thought we were forgoing."

"It smells divine in here: chicken … tomatoes … oregano … You made your chicken cacciatore!" she squealed with delight. "Wait a minute. What's that other smell?" she asked suspiciously. "Broccoli?"

"Meghan, something's moving in the pastry box. Did you go to the bakery on Main Street?"

"Open it," she encouraged.

"Are these air holes?" Jack asked holding the box away from him.

"It won't bite you," she said grinning with amusement.

Tentatively, Jack lifted the lid. A grey and white long haired baby kitten with the bluest eyes looked back.

"He's been hanging around the firm. Someone must have just dropped him off. Can you imagine? He's so precious! I thought we'd name him Ernest. I think he even looks a bit like Hemingway."

"That's a stretch," Jack said as he lifted the kitten out of the box and brought him eye level for inspection. The kitten patted Jack's check. "You're a sweet little guy, aren't you? Yeah, we'll call you Ernest."

"So you like him?"

"I like you; he'll grow on me," Jack said as he kissed Meghan and put the cat on the floor. "Let's eat. The vegetables are going to overcook."

Meghan placed the silverware and glasses on the table as Jack arranged the food on the plates making them look like a culinary work of art. "Let me a get picture," Meghan said as she dug her phone out of her handbag.

"You and your pictures," Jack said as he tilted the plate the way Meghan directed for the best angle. Meghan's smile showed she wasn't buying his begrudging attitude. The only matted and framed artwork in Jack's apartment was of the food he had prepared and Meghan photographed. On the wall separating the dining room from the living room, four large photos documented Jack's culinary skills: a plate of lasagna with crisp greens and cranberries with a glass of red wine; a whole roasted chicken with wild rice and baby carrots; a standing rib roast with baked apples and grilled potatoes; and the last one was of a white plate with chocolate cake crumbs on the resting fork, a white cup with Meghan's red lipstick print, and a blue napkin tossed with gustatory satisfaction.

Seated at the table Jack said, "So, tell me about your day."

"You first," Meghan encouraged.

"Not much to tell." Jack took a bite of broccoli while considering if there was anything of interest. "Oh, there was something odd that happened. I delivered this dining room suite: heavy walnut, beautiful wood. I had to heave it around by myself. That kid, Jeff, called in sick again. I bet it's his last call-in. Albert doesn't have a lot of tolerance for that. Anyway, the two guys, the customers, seventy-five if they were a day, were buck naked."

"Alzheimer's?" Meghan asked.

"I wondered that too when the door was answered by a guy, name turned out to be Winston, wearing nothing but a striped blue and white chef's apron. 'Oh, sorry. Sorry,' he had said gesturing to the apron as if that was what caused my eyes to pop. 'I forgot you were coming today, but of course it's Wednesday. Sam, the furniture's here,' he called to someone inside. I hope he has some clothes on, I thought. But no, when I walked into the living room there was Sam seated, grading papers at a desk, naked as a jaybird. 'No, no, no!' he exclaimed while wielding a red pen. As we walked past, Winston patted his roommate's arm who only grunted in reply.

"Once in the dining room Winston said, 'Don't mind Sam. He's grading papers. He finds it painful.' Lowering his voice to a whisper he said, 'because he thinks his students don't learn anything.'"

'Because they don't!' roared Sam in reply.

'He'll be okay after dinner,' Winston said.

'What does he teach?' I asked.

'Freshman English.'

"'What do you do?' "I asked, making conversation as I moved the furniture around."

'Oh,' he said vaguely. 'A bit of this and that. Mostly I keep house, as my mother used to say. After I got out, I found it difficult to find work that didn't involve manual labor. I'm getting a little long in the tooth for that.'

'Out of the military?' I asked."

'No, prison. I was a counterfeiter. A damn good one,' he said with pride."

What Jack didn't tell Meghan, but what he reflected upon now was the rest of the conversation:

'So what were you in for?' Winston had asked.

'Excuse me?' Jack replied, sounding as prim as someone's maiden aunt.

'No need to be embarrassed, I assure you,' Winston said. 'I know the store manager, Albert, hires ex-cons when it feels right. He's a Christian man who believes everyone deserves a second chance.'

'I had no idea,' Jack said astonished. But it made sense to him when he considered the number of ex-cons employed there.

'So, what did you do to be a deviant in society?' Winston questioned again.

'I was at the wrong place at the wrong time.' Jack had replied with the cliché.

Jack looked up quickly, concerned Meghan could be reading his thoughts. It was a stupid idea; but she was really shrewd. He also wondered if it was possible Meghan knew about the furniture store's reputation of hiring ex-cons through her work in the court system. Jack studied her, and saw she was lost in her own thoughts.

Are you kidding me? Jack asked himself. *Do you really think a woman like Meghan would have anything to do with someone with a criminal record if she knew about it?*

"Your turn," Jack said. "Tell me about your day. You're obviously thinking about it."

"I know. You'd think I'd get used to it, but I don't," Meghan said with a sigh.

"Get used to what?"

"The guilty verdict. Watching the realization sink in that they are no longer merely the accused, which in itself had been a horror for them, but now they are the convicted … that involuntary jerk of the arm when the officer touches the prisoner, directing him to come along." Meghan sadly shook her head. "One time, a guy threw up on my shoes. My clients often shake my hand, silently thanking me while looking at the judge. As if by showing good manners the court will recognize its error: this man can't possibly go to prison; he knows societal protocol. 'You'll be okay.' I tell them. They nod, too choked up to speak. Most try not to look at their loved ones, if they have any seated behind them, somehow knowing the pain in their eyes will haunt them. As the prisoners turn to leave, I often see their chins quiver. That's what I'll see at night when I close my eyes … that quivering chin."

They sat there, each with their memories, miles away from each other. It was Jack who broke the silence.

"So you lost one today, huh?" he asked, putting his hand on Meghan's.

"As I stood waiting for the verdict, I visualized the aftereffect of the guilty sentence. It's easier to have a mental dress rehearsal. But he was released."

"You were sure he'd be convicted?"

"Yes, even though he was innocent; but the circumstantial evidence was huge and it was an emotional case. An elderly man who was nearly blind got beaten up, and two witnesses pointed their fingers at my client: a homeless guy with a violent past, and no alibi."

"Why are you thinking about guilty verdicts now? Your guy got off."

"He had the same quivering chin."

"Perhaps he was just relieved to have it behind him."

"I think that's true, but there was something else. He looked as if it wasn't really over. I don't know how to explain it. It was …"

"As if it could happen to him, all over again. That he could continue to keep his nose clean, do what he needed to get by, not be a bother to anybody, and yet somehow some bad shit was just going to spray all over him again anyway."

"Yes! That was how he looked, resigned. As if he had given *himself* a guilty verdict."

"Well, if he's lucky, he'll realize sometimes, something *or someone* wonderful comes along and makes you have faith again."

Meghan put her fork down and smiled up at him. "How do you do it? Pull me out of my slump *and* make me feel romantic in the same breath?"

"Don't be putting your fork down until you finish that broccoli, Missy."

"Missy!"

"I made them special, and you haven't even tried them."

"I told you I don't like broccoli, even when it's dressed up. You might was well stop trying to convert me."

"Isn't that what couples do: help each other explore new horizons?" He got up and turned on the burner under the tea kettle. "Like that for instance," Jack nodded toward the stove. "Here I am having herbal tea after dinner and enjoying it! Guess who I have to thank for that."

"Do you think of us as a couple?" Meghan asked.

"Yeah, I guess I do. Do you?"

"So much so, I'll eat this broccoli."

235

"That's my girl."

"Woman … a grown female is called a woman."

"You sure are that," Jack replied, smiling at her.

A loud crash came from the living room where they found the cat had knocked over a metal waste paper basket onto the hardwood floor. It scared the kitten, causing the fur on his tail to poof up like a bristle brush. Ernest darted under the chair, looking out with his head on his paws. Jack pushed a crumpled piece of paper in front of the cat and Ernest attacked it, and then ran back to the safety of the chair. Jack and Meghan laughed at the cat's antics. "I'll need to get him some cat toys. Say, did you buy cat food?" Jack asked.

Meghan gasped and said, "It didn't occur to me."

"Well, we'd better go out and get him some food and a litter box. Just the way I had planned to spend Valentine's Day," Jack said with a roll of his eyes and then a toss of his hair.

The snow was coming down steadily as they walked to the store. Jack and Meghan held each other's gloved hands.

"What pets did you have as a child? I had a quarter horse. He was beautiful, chestnut brown with white on his face and legs. Rusty. He was such a good jumper and *so* sweet natured."

"Are you crying?" Jack asked in a surprised voice.

"No, it's just … I don't know. Sometimes I really miss him." Meghan cleared her throat. "So tell me about your pets."

"Didn't have any," Jack said looking away and tossing his hair.

Meghan looked up at Jack, her brows furrowed. Jack shrugged his shoulders. "Not everyone did, you know. It's not a prerequisite for childhood."

"Don't you lie to me, Jack Fox," Meghan said. "Why do you do that? I can always tell."

Jack looked at her astonished. "All right," he said. "I had a Jack Russell Terrier. His name was also Jack."

"That wasn't so difficult to say, was it? Why didn't you say so at the start?"

"I don't know," Jack shrugged again. "Maybe it's embarrassing to be named after the family dog."

Meghan studied him. "How did he pass?"

"Old age. Went in his sleep."

"The best way to go," Meghan said philosophically.

"Yup," Jack said as he remembered how the little terrier had actually died. Jack had stayed after school to play some hoops with friends. When

236

he got home his father had a rifle in his hand and was dragging the whimpering dog outside by a leash. The dog had committed the federal offense of being left alone too long and taking a crap in the house. Jack had begged his father not to do it. But begging never did any good with Mack. Jack was sobbing as his father tied the lease to the tree, walked away, and then took aim with the gun. Jack turned his head; he couldn't watch. Jack flinched as he heard the remembered gun shot.

Jack knew Meghan must have seen a trace of sadness in his eyes before he could brush it away. Why else would she ask how the dog had died? He also knew that Meghan saw him flinch, but chose not to comment on it. But Meghan wouldn't forget. Sometime when his guard was down, she would bring it up again. Meghan was good at getting information out of people. It was what she did for a living. He had to be careful or he'd end up telling this woman his whole life story and that wouldn't benefit anyone.

As they visited the pet aisle, Jack willed himself away from the painful memory. *That was in the past,* he told himself. It was a mantra he repeated often. As Meghan and Jack walked to the check out, he said, "You know when I was growing up the grocery store only sold food. Now you can buy nearly everything here."

"Yeah," Meghan said with teasing eyes, "but them were the olden days."

Jack grinned and gave her a playful nudge.

As they walked back Meghan said, "Let's go through the town square. It's so pretty with the snow falling on the evergreens. New England really is the place to be in the winter."

"It's picturesque, but there is something to be said for warmer climates and ice-free roads," Jack countered.

"I wish you drove a car in the winter. I worry about you on that bike."

"Yeah, well maybe someday," Jack said evasively.

The church bells rang for the evening prayer group. "That church is so beautiful with the soft lights glowing inside," Meghan gushed. "It's like a Christmas card. You never said; do you have a religion?"

"Not really. I do believe in God. I *know* there's such a thing as evil. I guess I'm what they call a spiritual, yet non-church going person. Well, that's not true. I go to a church annex at least once a week for A.A. meetings."

"I would like to get married in that church," Meghan blurted out. "That one right there. What do you say? Would you like to marry me?"

Jack was surprised. Stunned in fact. All he could think was, isn't it leap year when women do the asking?

"I know we haven't known each other long," Meghan began. "But it feels right, doesn't it? I've been thinking about it all week, but I almost lost my nerve until you said you thought of us as a couple. But then, I thought perhaps you would prefer to do the asking, and I should wait; but I've never been good about waiting for something I want –"

Jack set the grocery bags down and kissed Meghan deeply, holding her face tenderly in his hands.

"That felt like a yes. Is it?" Meghan asked hopefully.

"That depends," he said.

"On what?"

"I haven't seen the ring."

Meghan laughed and pulled a tattered jewelry box out of her coat pocket. She opened it to reveal a gold signet ring. "It was my Dad's," she told him with pride. He gave it to me when I graduated from law school.

"I got one for you," Jack said as he pulled the ring out of his pocket and held it out to her.

"You planned to propose today, too!" Meghan exclaimed.

"On the count of three," Jack said. "One. Two. Three."

Jack and Meghan both said "yes."

Chapter Forty-One

If Anyone had Looked

If anyone had looked at Drs. Patrick and Judith Allen as they slept, the observer would have thought they looked like sleeping children. The king size bed fit the size of the room, not the occupants. They slept on opposite sides of the expanse under burgundy colored, soft-spun wool blankets. Judith slept with her arms flung wide as if she welcomed the night. Patrick was curled up like a startled woolly-bear. Their dog Molly, who snored and sometimes had terrible gas slept on the far side of the room in a fleece covered dog bed, with a bolster where she rested her head.

If anyone had looked, they would have seen custom-made silk draperies of pink and burgundy peonies. A matching bedcover was draped over the Victorian love seat which had been a beloved possession of Patrick's mother.

If anyone had looked, they would have seen a biography on F.D.R. on the nightstand; Patrick's eyeglasses folded next to it. Judith's table held reading glasses, night cream, a glass of water, a stack of typed papers, and a pen.

If anyone had looked, they would have seen Patrick's facial muscles twitch, and they would have known that all these comforts didn't make for comfortable dreams. If they could have eavesdropped on the good doctor's dream, they would have heard Judith's voice sounding ominous and distant as if she spoke from inside a metal drum: "I love the view. It's just heavenly. A rolling green meadow mingled with wild flowers. However did you find it?"

Patrick replied with a voice which was also muffled, "Just by chance. Does it remind you of someplace?"

"What did you say?" Judith asked.

"What does it remind you of? I think I remember being here before, but I can't place it."

"It looks like England. Oxfordshire area."

"Let's go back to the car. I think it's going to rain."

"I don't remember a cemetery. Are we going back a different way?"

"We didn't go past this. We must be all turned around," Patrick said concerned.

"What kind of graveyard is this?" Judith said, appalled. "There's more mud than grass. It's arranged like a crazy quilt, plots facing every which a way."

"Look at the markers. They're made of slate, not marble," Patrick said. "The names were scratched in, like a child's drawn hopscotch. It's like a derelict trailer park for the dead, complete with that incessantly barking dog."

"Who would choose to bury their loved ones here?" Judith wondered.

"The down and out, those for whom a "fancy" plot would have been an unrealistic extravagance. My father was buried in a similar looking place. It was really nothing more than a cleared field. A cemetery created by a farmer turned entrepreneur. At least my father had a decent marker. It was important to my mother, so all of us kids chipped in."

"Look at the things people left at this grave: a crocheted angel, and a soggy stuffed animal. Oh! It's a child's grave. Do you suppose it was something he had slept with? But why leave the lovey out in the weather? Why didn't they tuck it in next to him?"

"Let's get back," Patrick said with a shudder. "The sky's getting dark."

Judith and Patrick hurried on until they came to an open grave. They stood at the edge of it looking down where they saw a coffin battered and broken as if it had been dropped from the sky. Patrick read the marker: *Thomas P. Allen – Rest in Peace.*

"Run!" Patrick yelled. They ran and ran and ran, but never left the cemetery. Patrick thought of the Econolite motion lamp that had been on their television when he was a child. It looked like a steam train speeding away, but of course it wasn't moving at all.

"I can't go on," Judith finally said as she flopped down trying to catch her breath. Patrick bent over from his waist. He was spent. It felt like his lungs were going to burst, there was a twitch in his side and cramps in his calves. When Patrick straightened up he saw a small child had wandered up to them. He wore sky blue colored pajamas of waffled fabric. The small patch pocket on the chest had crooked topstitching. The feet of the pajamas had a hole worn through revealing a pink toe.

I had pajamas like this, Patrick thought. *Mom had made them.*

"Have you seen my bear?" the child asked while he twirled his ruddy-colored hair with his finger.

Patrick bent down, ready to pat the child's head when Judith yelled, "Don't touch him!" The child gave a quizzical look, then turned and walked away.

"Matthew?" Patrick called and the child looked over his shoulder.

"You'd better get going," the child said. "He's looking for you."

Judith leaped up, grabbed Patrick's hand, and pulled him along with her, running like a marathoner. When they came back to the open grave Judith marched right up to it, placed her toes past the edge, preparing to swan drive.

Patrick grabbed her by the arm and pulled her back. "Are you out of your mind?" he asked.

"It's the only way," she said. She shoved Patrick into the hole and dove in behind him. Patrick screamed as they fell through the air like they were descending from the Empire State Building. When they landed, they were back in their bed.

"You watch from your side," Patrick told his wife, his heart beating out of his chest. "I'll watch from over here. Don't close your eyes for a second." Patrick's pounding heart was slowing, and then it stopped when he realized someone was in the hall. It was his father. The smell alone would have identified him: tobacco and whiskey, with a whiff of gasoline. His father approached, but didn't cross the threshold.

He looked as Patrick remembered. A hand-rolled cigarette was clamped between grim lips. Greasy hair framed his unshaven face. Thomas Patrick Allen wore a mechanic's uniform: dark blue cotton pants and shirt, a grimy red rag lolling from his back pocket. During Thomas's eulogy the priest had extolled the virtues of a working man's attire causing some congregates to think the deceased had only used his hands to earn a living. Those sitting in the front pew, the immediate family, knew better. They bore the emotional and physical scars that Thomas P. Allen had inflicted upon them with those "exalted" working man's hands. And yet, most of the family members would never talk about the abuse with each other, and some would go to their own graves without speaking a word of abuse towards the man who had inflicted so much harm.

Patrick breathed a sigh of relief when he saw his father retreat down the hall. Patrick's eyes felt scratchy, and he rubbed them with the back of his hand. When he opened them Patrick saw his father charging like an angered bull back down the hall towards the bedroom door. *He's going*

241

to force his way across the threshold! Patrick thought. Instinctively, Patrick threw his arm up, protecting his face.

Patrick's flailing awakened Judith. "Patrick?" she asked. "You all right?" When he didn't answer, she turned on her reading light. She saw in the dimness Patrick shaking like a Parkinson patient.

Judith slid across the bed and held him. "Patrick, what is it?" she whispered.

"I will *never* take sleeping pills again. They make you vulnerable and exposed."

"What do you mean?"

"My father was here. I can still smell him."

Judith stared at her husband. Patrick's condition was declining. He had definitely taken a turn for the worse.

Chapter Forty-Two

Who's Your Daddy?

Jack heard a buzzing and looked around for the cause while he moved a table around the foyer for the fourth time as the customer agonized over the perfect placement.

"You know," the customer said, "I do think the original location was the best. Do you mind?"

"Over by the windows?" Jack asked as he heaved the heavy slab.

"Is that your phone?" the customer asked.

So, that was the buzzing. Jack had forgotten he had such a thing attached to his belt. "Yeah, I'll get it later," Jack said as he swallowed a grunt. *Damn, this table is heavy.*

After Jack got back in the truck with a strained back and miserly one dollar tip, he lit a cigarette and looked at his phone. How did he get to his messages again? After much trial and error, he found Meghan's text: Call me! Exciting news!☺ Jack hated smiley faces. He thought they were insincere. Not the user, but the actual face. People were blindly using them in all kinds of messages, not knowing the images were sitting there mocking their non-existent asses off.

I'm sorry she gave me this stupid cell phone, Jack thought. *It has more bells and whistles than everything I've ever owned put together. If I need to make a call, I can do it when I get home. Nothing is so urgent I need to stop everything and call people.* But that was exactly what he did. He found the place for contacts and called Meghan at her office.

"Meghan Ashley," she said with poised and professional voice.

"It's me," Jack said confident that she knew who "me" was.

"Oh, sorry," Meghan breathed into the phone, "Can't talk right now. Call you back?"

"You're coming over after work, right?" Jack asked.

"Yes," Meghan said.

"Then talk to me then. I'm busy too."

"I'm here," Meghan called. "Sorry I'm late. Crazy, busy day! There you are, Ernest Kitty. Does he greet you at the door too?"

"He does. I never thought I'd like a cat, but this guy is really cool. He sleeps right next to my thigh. If I roll over, he just readjusts and settles back down again." Jack kissed Meghan and handed her a Whiskey Daisy, Meghan's drink of choice. When she had learned Jack couldn't drink, Meghan had offered to forego alcohol in his presence for support. "It's not necessary," Jack had said. "It's like a badge of honor for me to have alcohol in the house and not drink it, especially whiskey. A few years ago, hell, a few months ago I couldn't have done it."

Meghan collapsed into the leather club chair and slipped off her boots. "This is exactly what I longed for all day," she said sampling the mixed drink with obvious pleasure.

"I thought *I* was what you longed for," Jack said.

"You're delicious too," Meghan replied with a smile. "How was your day?"

"Exhausting. And yours? You said you have big news."

"I do." She took another sip before continuing. "There's a conference about missing children coming up in Boston. Allen Mayer, our lead attorney was scheduled to present, but he can't go and I've been chosen to take his place! I'll give a workshop on parental rights and help the parents through the legal maze they've found themselves in." Meghan fished the whiskey-soaked cherry out of the glass and bit it.

"Hmm," Jack replied, but his mind had wandered off as he pictured Meghan naked while she pulled the stem off the cherry with her teeth. With an effort, he focused on her words instead of her legs.

"Great opportunity for me and we can make it a romantic weekend getaway! I'll be free after 2:00 on Friday afternoon and after dinner on Saturday. We'll have a gorgeous hotel room. The firm will pay for everything. We'll go out to dinner, walk around Boston, and maybe take in a show. And I won't have to work on Sunday."

"When is this?"

"Next week."

"That's not a lot of notice," Jack observed.

"How much notice do you usually give your work?"

"I don't. I haven't taken time off."

"Ever?"

"Not since I've worked for the furniture store. Once in a while I take a weekend off, but those aren't my scheduled work days. Plus, I need to get more ceiling fans installed. I have to keep up with the apartment responsibilities in order to cover my rent. Lately, I've been otherwise occupied," Jack said with a smile as he seductively stroked Meghan's arm trying to distract her. But Meghan wasn't easily distracted.

"You haven't had a vacation day in over two years?" Meghan asked in an amazed voice.

"I don't get vacation time. I know we've talked about this before," Jack said hurriedly. Surely, there were better things to do than talk about work benefits.

"What about our honeymoon?" Meghan asked.

"I hadn't thought about it. I'll figure something out," The kitchen timer dinged. "Chicken divan and glazed carrots," Jack announced.

"Great! I'm starved," Meghan said.

"Of course, you are," Jack replied in self-righteous tones. "It's eight o'clock and I bet you didn't have time to eat lunch today. They work you too hard."

Between bites Meghan said, "This is scrumptious."

"I'm glad you like it," Jack said smugly. "Even the carrots."

"Where did you learn to cook like this?" Meghan asked.

"No place formal," Jack said vaguely. "Here and there." He dished up the sliced strawberries that had been marinating in orange juice. Jack wasn't about to tell her he had worked in a prison kitchen. It had been a good assignment, much better than working in laundry. One of the inmates assigned to the kitchen had been a chef in a 5-star restaurant before murdering its pastry chef. Jack had thought the cooking skills would help him get a good job when he got out, but finer restaurants wanted resumes with cooking school backgrounds. Greasy spoons weren't as fussy, but they worked the life out of you while paying next to nothing.

Jack admired the dime store crystal dish filled with ripe strawberries with sprigs of fresh mint. *Scrupulous, that's what strawberries and my fiancée are,* Jack thought.

Meghan took a bite, looked up at him with those beautiful blue eyes and said, "This is really good. I like the sweet and tangy taste –"

Jack leaned over and pressed his mouth to hers.

"Wow! Where did that come from?"

"I was just thinking how scrupulous you and strawberries are."

Meghan gave Jack a quizzical look. "Scrupulous?" she asked. "Oh! You mean scrumptious!" Meghan laughed.

Jack gave her a hard look. "Oh, don't take yourself so seriously!" Meghan said. "You're just tired. I get words all twisted around too when I'm exhausted. Say, when are you going to let me read your writing? I see there's another notepad started."

"I'm not ready yet. It's not in novel form. I'm just scribbling down thoughts and ideas. But it'll be a good book when I'm done," he told her defensively.

"Bring your notebook on the trip. You can write in the hotel room while I'm working. That seems rather Hemingway-esque."

"I can't go on Friday. It's too late notice; maybe I'll be able to come on the weekend if I can get someone to cover for me, I already told them I would work, and if I can borrow my friend Rick's car. The bike's been cranky lately."

"That's a lot of ifs."

"That's how it is for me," Jack said as he tossed his hair.

"My offer for a car is still on the table," Meghan said. "We could get one tomorrow. I hate having you ride that bike in the winter. It's dangerous."

"You are not going to lease me a car. You lawyers work hard for your money; you're not going to spend it on me," Jack said as he angrily piled the dishes together, dropping the silverware on top.

"Is this about the word correction?"

"No, it's not about the 'word correction,'" he mocked, parroting Meghan's voice.

Meghan sighed. "I'll help with the dishes. But then I need to get going. The work I've been assigned for the conference is on top of everything else. The only way I can get it done is to do it in the evenings."

"You should just say no to the extra work. They expect too much."

"I'm paid well with sick and vacation time."

"That's a low blow," Jack said, his eyes narrowed.

"I didn't mean it to be. I'm just saying I have a good job with benefits. I don't take it for granted."

"It's still too much of them to ask," Jack maintained.

Meghan sighed again. "I wish you wouldn't do that."

"What?"

"Tell me how to manage my work life. Saying no to an assignment is a sure-fire way to stop advancements. I want to make partner someday. Plus, I want to do this workshop. It's important."

"I'm just looking out for you," Jack said. "You don't seem to realize that they're taking advantage."

Meghan reached for the apron that she kept there and tied it around her waist in quick, angry strokes. "I'm not a little girl. And I don't care to be treated like one," Meghan said as she carried the glasses to the kitchen.

The evening was rapidly deteriorating. In the past, Jack would have allowed his pride to get in the way, but tonight he didn't want the evening to end like this. He had something special with Meghan. How would he ever find that again? Jack came up behind her and untied the apron strings. Meghan turned and gave him an exasperated look as she picked up the apron off the floor.

"I know that was big time childish," Jack said with a boyish *please don't be mad at me* smile. "I used to tease my mom by untying her apron. I haven't thought of her fondly in years, must be the good influence you have on me."

"Have you been angry with her?" Meghan asked placing the glasses in the sink and turning to give him her undivided attention.

Jack swallowed a grin. It worked. It wasn't often that he could get Meghan off track.

"I always thought it was anger, but I suppose it was more hurt. She left when I was young," Jack said truthfully.

"Were you raised by your Dad?"

Shit! Jack snarled in his head. This wasn't the direction he wanted the conversation to go. "I don't want to talk about him," Jack replied in a tone that said he meant business.

"I've told you *everything* about my family."

"Yeah, but your family lived in Mayberry."

"No, we lived on Long Island," Meghan said, confused.

"I didn't mean you *really* lived in Mayberry. Don't you know Andy Griffith? Opie?

"Opie? Rock group?"

"Never mind," Jack said.

"Can you tell me about them?"

"Andy was the town sheriff. Opie was his son, Ron Howard in real life."

"You know what I mean. I really would like to hear about your family."

"Nothing to tell," Jack shrugged.

"Come on," Meghan said. "I just realized I know nothing. I mean literally nothing. How is that possible? I don't even know where you were born." When Jack didn't respond, Meghan held a pretend microphone to her mouth, "We're at the courthouse today with what we

247

call a reluctant witness. However, Jack Fox is getting ready to tell his fiancée just a few basic things about his family. Whenever you're ready, Mr. Fox," Meghan said as she switched the pretend microphone from her face to Jack's.

Jack slapped her hand away. "I said no." His eyes flashed with anger.

Meghan gave Jack a startled stare. She put the apron on the counter, turned, and walked towards the door. Jack caught her around the waist and drew her back.

"I'm sorry," Jack pleaded. "I mean it, I'm really sorry. I shouldn't have reacted like that."

Meghan looked up at Jack with eyes that said, *I don't know you.*

Jack answered the look, "You do know me. That family stuff. It doesn't mean anything. Everything that's happened in the past is gone. It's over. We're starting a new life together."

Meghan didn't say anything.

"Right?" Jack asked.

"I have a lot of work to do. I need to get going. In fact, I'm going to be busy until I leave for the conference. If you can make it, we'll talk then," Meghan said this as she threw on her coat and zipped up her boots. She was halfway out the door when Jack grasped her hand. She allowed it to remain in his, but it just lay there warm and limp like ... *a dead chipmunk,* Jack thought. Looking at his own hand covering hers, he could see the corpse. A little head sticky with blood, the tiny paws curled in surrender. It always shamed Jack when he remembered his tenth summer; the year he was given a BB gun and became a serial killer, shooting every small furry or feathered creature he encountered and hanging their carcasses on the clothes line. Mack had thought it was a hoot. "That'll give The County something to talk about when they come around again trying to decide if I'm a fit parent." Jack dropped Meghan's hand and pushed it away from him as if it was something obscene.

"Fine," Meghan said as she raced out the door.

"Meghan!" Jack called after her. Jack heard her heels rapidly click down the sidewalk. The car door opened and slammed shut.

"Meghan, listen to me!"

But the only reply was the roar of the engine, and the squeal of the tires.

Jack shut the door and leaned against it. "Meghan," he whispered. He allowed his back to slide down the door, and he sat on the floor. Jack pressed his balled fists into his eyes as he rocked back and forth. It was possible Meghan could forgive him for tonight's fiasco, but she would *never* reconcile his history with that of a future husband. Tonight she

248

would decide she had been crazy to not run a background check on her fiancé.

What do I really know about this Jack Fox person, she would think to herself. After his file was read, she'd run for the hills. She wouldn't even give him a chance to explain.

Well, why should she be the exception? Jack thought. *No one else has ever given me the benefit of the doubt.* Jack stood up and marched over to the kitchen cabinet and pulled out the whiskey bottle. He splashed some into a glass and threw the liquor down his throat. It burned and he coughed. Jack poured again, filling the glass this time. Tears came to his eyes. He knew who was to blame for all this: his ex, ex, triple ex-wife. God, he hated her. She ruined him. She destroyed any hope he ever had for happiness. Jack let out a roar as he threw the glass across the room. Ernest skittered into the bathroom to hide.

"Yeah, you'd better hide if you know what's good for ya," Jack shouted after him. *I sound just like my old man,* Jack thought. It startled him. He walked to the whiskey and considered pouring it down the drain. Instead, he picked it up and chugged from the bottle. He was going to get drunk and it was his ex-wife's fault – well, hers and Meghan's. Why couldn't she have just left the past alone?

Chapter Forty-Three

Lavender Soap

"Can't sleep?" Judith asked. She had turned off her light over an hour ago and although she was wearing a sleep mask, Judith correctly sensed Patrick's light had remained on and his restlessness continued.

"Sorry," he replied. "Am I keeping you awake? I'll go downstairs."

"I'll make some chamomile tea, maybe that'll help," she said, her voice worried. Taking in her husband's tense lines around his eyes and mouth she added, "Well, it won't hurt."

"I'll join you," Patrick said. He threw the covers aside as if they had been binding him to the unpleasant task of resting.

Over steaming mugs Judith said, "You can't go on like this. It's been days."

"I know. I just don't know what to do about it." Patrick gnawed at the cuticle of his forefinger. Judith raised a surprised eyebrow. "Oh bloody hell," Patrick exclaimed as he dropped his hand. "I haven't done that since I was a teenager."

"There's a sleep clinic at St. Peters," Judith suggested.

"Yes, and they would spend a great deal of time trying to figure out why I'm not sleeping. We *know* why I'm not sleeping."

"Maybe you could talk with someone about the stress you're experiencing, the loss of your mother –"

"And the reunion with my father? They'll think I've lost my mind."

"Trained professionals aren't there to judge you, Patrick. You know that."

"But we do. All the time. No. I'm not discussing this with anyone else."

"Well then, you'll just have to talk about it with me. Is this the first time you have experienced a dream of this nature?"

"God! Do we really sound like that?"

"Is it?"

"A dream … Is that what we're calling it?

"I don't know. You called it a dream earlier."

"I can't get over the smell! It's still in the room."

"I didn't smell it. Molly didn't notice anything wrong, and dogs have a much better sense of smell than we do."

Patrick's mouth was set in a straight line when he said, "So, you don't believe me."

"Patrick, you're asking me to believe in something I just don't believe in!"

"I thought we were closer than this."

"*This* has nothing to do with our relationship. You make it sound like if I loved you enough, I'd be able to accept supernatural happenings. That's not fair."

Patrick turned in his chair, crossed his legs and arms, and looked away.

"Don't do that!"

"What?"

"Look at you. Your body language is shutting me out."

Patrick turned and faced his wife, but his face had a closed look.

Judith put her hand over her husband's and said, "Parents' deaths often cause us to remember our childhoods, oftentimes in more detail than we have recalled in years. And those memories can trigger our senses, especially scents."

"And scents can trigger memories. Perhaps during the day I caught a combined scent of whiskey, cigarettes, and gasoline and conjured up this image. Yes, that's it. Case closed. Off to dreamland for me."

Judith gave him an even look.

"I don't mean to be sarcastic," Patrick said as he stroked the top of his head.

"You're exhausted. It comes with the territory."

They drank their tea as the kitchen clock ticked away the seconds. "Do you think I could tell if you were having a bad dream?" Judith asked.

"Probably. There would be rapid eye movement seen beneath the lids, sweating, muscles twitching, that sort of thing. You know that."

"Here's what I propose. We go back upstairs. I'll stay awake and monitor your sleep. If it looks like you're in distress, I'll wake you up."

"That can't be the answer. You need to sleep too."

"Just for tonight. I'll sleep later, after you get up."

252

"You think if I have a few hours of quality sleep with nothing bad happening I'll get over my anxiety."

"Let's just work on getting you some sleep tonight."

Judith played soft music to help mask the sound of her typing on the laptop. She had a book deadline, and thought she might as well be productive. As much as Patrick thought it wouldn't happen, he fell almost immediately to sleep. Judith kept glancing over at him, but the most he did was give a contented snore. At one point, Judith felt her head nod. She immediately straightened her spine, took a sip of water, and refocused. Patrick trusted her to keep watch. About three o'clock he got up and stumbled to the bathroom. Their dog shifted in her bed. Then Molly got up and walked over to the love seat. The dog started pacing back and forth.

"What is it, Girl?" Judith asked.

The dog sat down and stared at the loveseat. When Patrick came out of the bathroom he didn't get into bed, but walked over to the love seat and sat down. Judith got up and stood next to him and saw that her husband was sleeping. She hadn't known him to sleepwalk before and attributed this current condition to his high level of anxiety. However, at the moment he didn't appear troubled. In fact, a faint smile played on his lips. Judith chose to let him sleep. She got back into bed but continued to watch her husband closely.

Patrick looked over at his mother. She smiled at him with love. Patrick smiled back. He was her favorite. She never said, but he always knew. "How are you?" he asked. "Gosh, you look wonderful!"

"I'm fit as a fiddle. I needed ya to know."

"But Father! Did he hurt you?"

"Of course not. It was silly of me to have worried about that."

"He came here. He was after me," Patrick told her.

"No, he wasn't, Dear. He can't hurt ya."

"But if you can come here, why can't he?"

She shrugged, "That's just the way it is. Ya need to be listenin' to me, Paddy. I don't know if I can see ya again."

"He was a beast. I hated him."

"Let it be over, son."

Patrick stared at his mother. She was asking the impossible. How could he just let go of all the fear and shame of all those years? He couldn't remember a time when he hadn't lived in the terrifying shadow of his father.

"You can do it," Patrick's mother said. She reached over and took her son's hand. "You'll see."

Suddenly, he realized she was right. It was over. He wasn't sure how he knew, but he had absolutely no doubt. With relief, Patrick wept.

"It's all right. It's all right. I'm here. It's just a dream," Judith said.

Patrick looked up to see Judith standing next to him.

"My mother … It seemed so real," he told Judith. "I dreamt I was talking with her. She told me everything would be okay. I know it was just a dream, but …."

"What?" asked Judith.

"I'm embarrassed to say."

"You can still smell her lavender soap," Judith said.

"Yes," Patrick answered.

"I smell it too," Judith told him.

Chapter Forty-Four

Ex, Ex, Triple Ex-Wife

"Red Rover, Red Rover, we call Jackie Boy over!"

"Ahhhhh," Jack shrieked in terror as he bolted straight up in bed. The motion caused his stomach to allegorically leap up, tear down the hall, and come to a screeching halt in front of the toilet where it contemplated heaving everything received in recent memory. Jack lay still in his bed, willing his digestive juices to quiet down while his brain ricocheted against his skull.

"Pow! Splat!" Jack murmured giving sound effects for his pounding headache.

"Christ on a crutch, get a grip," Jack heard his father's gravel voice, the same voice that had given the playground taunt. That did it. Jack's digestive system exploded.

"Shit," Jack murmured as he wiped the vomit off his mouth with a shaky hand and shook it off onto the pile of puked up dinner and whiskey on his bed.

Ernest got up giving a lazy cat stretch, wandered up to the whiskey infused vomit, sniffed, and contemplated breakfast.

"No! Augh, that's disgusting," Jack said pushing the cat aside.

Jack looked at the clock: seven-thirty. He was supposed to be at work in a half an hour. Jack called in sick trying not to sound hung over. He threw the sheets in the bathtub and wiped up the mattress, lay back down, and slept until the afternoon when Ernest decided he could no longer wait to be fed. He got Jack's attention by walking back and forth across his face.

"Okay, Okay," Jack said as he got to his unsteady feet and fed the cat. "Unbelievable," he said as he looked around his apartment. One of the drapes was pulled off the rod. It appeared he had taken one of the club chairs and bashed it against the wall several times. The chair leg was broken and there were deep gouges in the wall. Slivers of glass coated the kitchen floor.

Jack found a water stain on his Hemingway desk from the whiskey bottle. It disgusted him. He hated to see things marred. Then, he decided it was good to have it there. It would give him a permanent reminder of the consequences of drinking. Jack gave a snort, as if growing up with his old man wasn't reminder enough. He also found a poem on the desk. He had no memory of writing it. As he read it, Jack broke his own rule and once again lit a cigarette in his apartment.

She's Gone

High heeled stride
Mechanical clank
Car door opened
My mind rank.

Domed light
Purse tossed
She's leaving
It's all right
It's just one more loss

Legs swung in
Glimpse of thigh
Door shut
On the intended lie.

Engine turned
Muffled song
Red taillights
And then ... she's gone.

Jack put the notebook down and noticed his hand was shaking. *Christ,* he thought, *that's all I need, get messed up with Lou Gehrig's disease or some shit.* Jack sat in the Hemingway chair smoking and watching his hand twitch when he heard a key in the lock. Jack was striding towards the door when it swung open and Meghan stepped in loaded down with grocery bags.

"Oh! You scared me! What are you doing home?" Meghan said with surprise.

"I took one of those sick days you were talking about," Jack said, looking at her with narrowed eyes.

"Do you have the flu? It smells awful in here."

"Probably," Jack replied. "What are *you* doing?"

"Oh this? I decided to bring some groceries over. I just realized today … that you were … that you've been … doing all this cooking and I … I've never chipped in, let alone cooked a meal."

She's decidedly nervous, Jack thought.

"I've got more groceries in the car. I'll *just* … go … get them."

"And you'll *just* get behind the wheel and drive away, right? You didn't come over here to cook dinner. You brought groceries to make sure things were all square. And you planned to pick up your father's ring and leave your ruby behind. I see you're not wearing it."

Meghan stared at him.

"I know you ran a background check. I get it. I mean who wouldn't." Jack said.

Meghan set the bags down, pulled the ring out of her slacks pocket, and placed it on the counter.

"In my mind I've already said goodbye to you," Jack said. "I didn't know if I'd ever actually see you again. But since you're here could you please do me the one courtesy no one else has given and listen to my side of the story, not that I expect the outcome for us to change."

"Okay," Meghan said. She crossed into the living room, taking in the state of Jack's apartment with a wide-eyed stare. Meghan picked up off the floor the little dog figurine, now with a broken paw, and placed it on Jack's desk. Jack got her father's ring case and handed it to her.

"You never wore it," Meghan said as she put the ring case into her coat pocket.

"It didn't fit," Jack replied.

"Let's start with the first arrest," Jack said as he paced back and forth in front of Meghan as she sat down in the club chair. "That kid on the bike. Yeah, I hit him. He had no reflective gear at all. It was pitch black out. I stopped, but the kid was dead. I pulled him off the road, but I couldn't stick around. I would have been blamed because I had been drinking. I took off, driving fast and went right off the road and into a ravine. I could have been killed. I was not responsible for that kid's death. You know who was responsible for me being on the road that night drunk as a skunk? My ex-wife. My ex, ex, triple ex-wife. You look surprised. You must know about her. I'm sure she's in the report. If she hadn't been such a bitch, been in my face when I was roaring drunk, none of this would have happened. NONE OF IT! What was she

257

thinking, picking a fight when I was in that state? I knew from the age of four to tread carefully around the inebriated. She wasn't a child. She knew better. And there was such a fuss made about that slap. It was nothing. I swear to Christ! It was no harder than the slap I gave your hand. She just wasn't expecting it and toppled over. She was as big as a house. How she carried on that I left her after she fell. Was she kidding? If I had been my old man, she would have been in big trouble. I left because I didn't want things to get any worse. But do I get any credit for having self-control? Nooooo.

"I came back around after my kid was born. I got thinking about it and decided to face up to my responsibilities. I figured we could make a go of it. I would quit drinking, go to A.A. I think I could have convinced her. I had hurt my foot at work and figured I could put the injury to good use. It gave me the excuse to stay overnight, and then I would have fixed her breakfast in the morning, and talked her into dropping the divorce proceedings. But that morning I hear her screaming. I took our child from her, but she was already gone. How she could ever think I would hurt a child, *our* child, is beyond me. It's because of my ex-wife I went to prison. If she had just spoken up for me at the trial …. She ruined my life! If I ever find her –" Jack's eyes went black with fury.

"The baby died?" Meghan gasped.

"Stop it!" Jack shouted, "You know goddamn well she did."

Meghan stood and walked past him.

"Say something!" He yelled at her back.

Meghan turned and faced him. Even in her high heeled boots, she didn't reach his chin. Yet, the straight stiffness of her spine and the set of her jaw made her appear taller. Only the twitch in her cheek revealed her nerves. "I did come over to cook dinner," Meghan said so softly and without emotion it was as if she spoke only to herself. "I thought long and hard about last night and decided *I* had overreacted. It wasn't much of a slap, more like a firm tap. If *you* had been pushing *me*, borderline bullying me to talk about something I didn't want to discuss and then thrust your hand in my face, well, I may well have slapped it away. I decided I had been tired and had behaved poorly."

Jack stared at her in disbelief.

"It's true," Meghan said simply. "The ruby has a broken prong. I was going to ask you to take it back to the jeweler. I assumed it was insured. Obviously, I assumed too much about a lot of things. I didn't run a background check, Jack. That wasn't how I wanted to start our lives together."

Jack continued to stare open-mouthed.

258

"It's always good to let people talk," Meghan said philosophically. "It's astonishing what they'll tell you if they think you already know. So now I know. You hit someone with your car, *killed* him, and left him beside the road to save your own skin. You *hit* your pregnant wife. She fell over. You left her. And it was her fault." Meghan shook her head. "It was also her fault that you were driving drunk. I can still hear your words ringing in my head. It's almost too much to believe, but I must." She turned to leave.

Jack roughly grabbed Meghan's arm. "Don't you think you're the clever little attorney getting me to tell you all that."

"I'm not clever. I wanted to be in love. I wanted you to be someone you aren't. It actually scares me how I had convinced myself that last night was my fault. That's how battered women think. I wonder how far I would have been willing to go. Look at this place, you must have gotten roaring drunk last night. I imagine you think it was my fault because of the argument we had. I see now that's your style. Nothing is ever *your* fault."

Jack's face darkened with anger. With a mocking half smile he moved in close to Meghan's face. "Aren't you *brave?*" Jack said, growling out the words.

"I'm not afraid of you, Jack. I'm just glad I'm not your ex, ex, triple ex-wife. But if I were you, I'd leave her alone. You have enough problems." As Meghan started towards the door Ernest ran up to her. He left a smudged trail of pink paw prints. Meghan picked him up. "What happened?" she asked as she examined his paw.

"He must have stepped on a piece of glass. I dropped one last night."

"Meaning you threw it."

Before Jack could camouflage it, his guilty expression confirmed Meghan's guess. She kept walking with the cat in her arms.

"You can't take him. You gave him to me," Jack said.

"Possession is nine tenths of the law," she replied as she walked out the door.

Chapter Forty-Five

Eva's Journal

One of my birthday presents from Penny was this journal. She suggested I write my thoughts down daily. Penny said it would help me sort out how I feel about things. The journal has remained unopened until now. I'm writing in it because I *really* need to sort out my feelings.

Siena, being a Franciscan college and all, is very big about helping the less fortunate. I don't know for sure, but I imagine very few of the students have had the *acquaintance* of the "less fortunate," as Jane Austen might have said. But you never can tell. People who look at me with the cool phone and laptop Penny and Michael gave me would never guess I had ever lived in a group home.

We had to be on the bus by eight o'clock in the morning. I was running late, so I didn't get to eat breakfast, which made me grouchy. What am I doing? I thought. I could be in my bed at this very moment catching a couple more hours of sleep. But I knew what I was doing. It was personal for me. I was giving back by volunteering at the City Mission. The Mission supported my sisters at a time when they really needed it, gave them a hand up. It's where they met Penny. Besides, I told myself, the project sounds fun. We're to take donated clothes, shoes, purses, and accessories and arrange them in a store-like setting for the people who live there, only the residents won't have to pay for them, which is a good thing because they don't have any money.

When we arrived at The Mission they had donuts, coffee, and cider set out for us. Man, I was delighted to see it. I took two donuts and a cup of coffee.

The Mission administrators told us how pleased they were for our help and led us to the area where the new store would be. I think we were all rather shocked by the size of it. It looked like a gymnasium and there were hundreds, literally hundreds of bags of donated clothing.

There were clothing racks, display equipment, and shelves all in piles. Us kids looked to our professors, waiting for them to tell us how to go about this tremendous project. Sure, there were thirty-two of us, but how were we ever going to get this done by the proposed deadline of three months?

"Don't look at us," one of the professors said. "This is your project. Figure out your work teams and I suggest you come up with a plan of how you want the finished store to look." And with that, they left with The Mission administrators for a tour of the rest of the facilities.

"Okay," announced Eric Huntsby. "We should probably get this show on the road. We've got a lot to do. Let's gather over here by this whiteboard and we'll take twenty to thirty minutes to brainstorm. I'll write down our thoughts."

Before long, we had a plan and arranged ourselves into teams. I was with three other girls who were good friends, but I didn't know them at all; still they welcomed me into the group. Other students sorted the shoes out of the mountain of bags, gave the shoes to us, and my group displayed them by size and color. A lot of the shoes were really nice. But some were really trashed; sneakers with no tread and ripped sides that we had to throw out. Who would donate such things?

A few of The Mission's residents came in and asked if we'd like some help. They were nice women and I was happy they came in. I had the feeling the Siena kids thought only uneducated people from skid row lived at The Mission. I don't think my classmates have any idea how close much of the population is to finding themselves homeless. All it takes is a low income job going away, or a health issue and no nest egg or family support … well … it's a good thing there's a place like the City Mission.

The Franciscan Center had given us bagged lunches, so at noon we all sat down on the floor and ate. The girls in my group were talking about their upcoming dates for the evening. They were going with their boyfriends to a club. It sounded like so much fun and I wondered if I would ever be asked out. I guess it's not like I never go out. I sometimes go to the movies on campus with Edward. But that's with *Edward*. He's nice and all, but it's not like it's a date.

"So what are you doing tonight, Eva?" they asked, bringing me into the conversation.

"We have a shop. It supports women in third world countries so there's always something to do. Mayra-Liz, my sister, is going to pick me up at school. I really should have thought this through and I could have just gone to the shop from here, and saved my sister a trip. But I've

262

got to get my books and stuff to study over the weekend. My sisters said we just got in a new shipment of jewelry, and it's really nice. So, we'll probably spend the evening catching up on family news while we work on the displays."

"That sounds like so much fun!" Heather said. "You're so lucky!"

"I am," I told them, but at that moment I didn't feel that way. I wanted to be like them and go to the club with a real boyfriend tonight.

Around one o'clock we started working again. There was a lot to do and the bus left at 4:00. It was amazing how much we had already gotten done. The shelves and clothing racks were up. We had most of the shoes organized. Because I have experience with displaying jewelry, the girls in my group suggested I show them how to organize the accessories. We were in the process of arranging scarves when this bona fide crazy lady came in. She looked like her hair hadn't seen a comb in months. She had numerous layers of clothing on; the top layer was this ratty fur coat. She looked like she was either on her way in or out and had just stumbled upon us.

The woman wobbled around the room as if all the clothing made her off balanced. What is she doing? I thought. She was going up to the guys and whispering in their ears. One of the guys walked over to us. "Have you seen any of The Mission staff people around?" he asked.

"I think there's some down the hallway next to the office," Nancy said. "What's going on?"

"That woman is asking for twenty dollars for ah … uh… Well, she said she'd do certain services. No credit cards."

"Yuck!" Nancy said in disgust.

"I don't think she's dangerous, but she's drunk. I'm pretty sure The Mission frowns on that."

"They do," I replied. "They all looked at me, obviously wondering how I knew. Shit! I thought. I usually have a better filter.

"Well, I'm going to inform one of The Mission staff people," the guy said. "That woman is really making people feel uncomfortable."

In a moment, one of the staff came in to take the crazy lady out of the room. "I ain't done nothin," the woman said.

"Come on, Maria, let's get you something to eat," the staff member said, firmly steering the woman away from us and out of the room.

"Eva, watch out!" Nancy called out just as a shelf nearly fell on my head. So much for our carpentry work. The crazy lady, Maria, turned and stared at me. "Eva?" she said.

I turned and looked straight into the eyes of my mother.

"Come on, Maria. We've talked about this before. Let's get you a sandwich and a cup of coffee, and then we'll figure out where we go from here," the staff member insisted as she took my mother out of the room.

I looked around. Did anyone else notice that the *crazy woman* recognized me? No, it seemed that they didn't. I kept telling myself to calm down. It doesn't matter, but it does matter. It mattered a whole lot! I don't remember what I did the rest of the day. Displayed purses and necklaces? Maybe, but I couldn't tell you what they looked like. When I climbed onto the bus, I sat next to the window and put my purse in the seat next to me. I didn't want some Chatty Cathy sitting next to me, talking about her upcoming date, or her super boyfriend, or any of the other things "normal people" get to think about. I get to think about my mother, the crazy lady.

I was so deep in thought that I had no idea what was going on when a shriek went through the bus. "Oh-h-h!" they all said in unison and then again, "Oh-h-h!" like they were watching ice skating during the Olympics and the performer kept falling down while trying for a triple toe lutz.

"What's happening," I asked.

Eric Huntsby turned in his seat in front of me and said, "It's a deer."

I looked out the window and saw a deer had been hit by a car. From the earlier sounds in the bus, it was probably hit by one car and then hit by another. It lay at the side of the road, its legs jerking. One of the professors stood up and announced he was calling the police, and the highway patrol would come and put it out of its misery.

This flood of emotion that I couldn't keep inside broke through, and I sobbed. I mean, really, *really* sobbed. And to make matters worse, the whole bus was silent except for my crying. I was so embarrassed I wanted to die, and that made me cry all the harder. Eric Huntsby got out of his seat, moved my purse over, sat down, and put his arm around me. I cried into his chest.

"It's okay; it's okay," he kept murmuring into my hair. After a bit, he reached into his pocket and handed me a crisp, white handkerchief. Why is it that cool guys just know to carry handkerchiefs? If I ever get married, it'll be second nature for my husband to carry a handkerchief. I have just decided that!

So, anyway we get to Siena and Eric took my hand. HE TOOK MY HAND! LACED HIS FINGERS IN MINE!

"Can I walk you to your dorm?" he asked.

"Sure," I said. We walked in silence, my feet not touching the ground. The only thing that kept me tethered and prevented me from floating through the atmosphere from pure joy was the feel of his hand in mine.

When we got to my dorm he said, "Would you like to go out with me next weekend?"

Somehow I managed to be calm and said, "I'd like that … very much." I scribbled down my number and gave it to him.

He gave me a quick kiss on the cheek and said, "I'll text you."

I know I should be really distressed over Mom and part of me is. But a bigger part is over the moon. Eric Huntsby, the coolest guy at Siena, if not in the world (!) is going to take me out.

Chapter Forty-Six

A Scottish Holiday

"What happened?" Patrick asked when he walked into Judith's office. It occupied the second floor of the house's turret, a large room, ideal for Judith to spread out research material while writing her books. The room's castle-like structure with its narrow windows, high ceiling, and stone walls made it difficult to heat, just like her childhood Scottish home. The space heater's purr warmed both Judith's feet and her nostalgia. It was because of this room that they purchased the house.

All of Judith's books, journals, and notes were neatly stacked in piles on the window seat and the large circular table was bare. Patrick couldn't remember when the room didn't look busy, as if it could take on the job of writing a book on its own. Without the clutter, the room looked bored. Judith handed him a manila folder containing flyers of fun-filled tourist destinations. Patrick looked at one that featured Scotland. "Are you taking a trip back home?" he asked.

"No, *we're* taking a trip," she said with determination. "I received an extension on the book. I want us to go to Scotland and breathe the fresh, crisp air... hike, relax, and rest. Of course we don't have to go to Scotland. We could maybe go to some tropical island. I have some flyers on those too."

"But you'd prefer to go to Scotland."

"Who wouldn't?" Judith said.

"If we go to Scotland, I suppose you'll want to stay with your aunt."

"Not a chance. I'll devote one day to visiting her while you golf or something. But we won't be staying in her dreary, barn of a house."

"She'd be disappointed," Patrick pointed out. "She loves to play the host."

Judith shrugged. "My husband comes first on this trip. There's fly-fishing too," she said showing him a printed web page. "You always said you wanted to try that again. Don't you have fond memories of trout fishing with an Uncle Marvin?"

"Martin," Patrick replied.

"We could do the tour of Edinburgh castle. We always say we're going to do it, but we never do. I haven't been there since I was twelve on a school field trip. We should really play the tourist, see Mary King's Close and go on a haunted underground tour."

Patrick raised an eyebrow.

"You're right; we'll skip the haunted tour," Judith said. "I emailed my cousin, Addie, and she suggested a B&B called Amar Agua. She said they have *the* loveliest rooms and serve the most exceptional breakfasts. She said they treat you like royalty. It's on Kilmaurs Street, walking distance to Arthur's Seat, that place we went hiking last time. Such beautiful views. Do you remember? It was possible to stand in one spot and see in the distance the ocean, the castle, and those beautiful rolling hills."

"Do you know when you talk about Scotland, your accent thickens? I love the way you pronounce your Rs," Patrick said.

Judith frowned at him.

"I wasn't avoiding your question. Of course, I remember. I just don't know if I can get away any time soon. I have my patients. When would you like to go?" Patrick asked.

"As soon as possible. In March," Judith answered.

"Next month?" Patrick asked, stroking the top of his head.

"I'd go tomorrow if we could arrange it, but I don't think that's feasible."

Patrick grimaced, "Is this because you're concerned about my state of mind?"

"If you're asking if I think you're crazy? No, I don't. Not even a little. But I *am* concerned about your stress level. Look at your cuticles. You're still gnawing at them. And I'm worried about how exhausted we both are. I saw my reflection in a store mirror yesterday, and I didn't recognize myself. Who is that haggard, middle-aged woman with bags under her eyes? I thought. She needs a haircut, and some general sprucing up. A person isn't meant to work twelve hour work days, six days a week. We need a holiday. If we stay here, the hospital will be calling you, and I'll end up writing just a wee bit on the book, which we both know will morph into marathon writing sessions. I know we're sleeping better, but we also need some down time. It's time we practice what we preach to others and take better care of ourselves."

268

"I love you," Patrick said. "And you don't look like a haggard, middle-aged woman with bags under her eyes."

"Humph," Judith replied, "you either love me beyond reason or you're too tired to see clearly. Promise we'll go in March."

"Okay," Patrick replied. "I promise."

Chapter Forty-Seven

Time to go

Jack waited on his motorcycle a block away from Meghan's apartment. It gave him a good view for when she drove out of her cul-de-sac. He didn't have to wait long to see her black Mustang leave which was nice since it was damp and cold waiting out in the open air. A small dog carrier Jack had stolen from his neighbor's back porch was strapped on the back of his bike. It was one of those cream-colored, molded plastic things, and it stuck out like a sore thumb. Jack was relieved Meghan didn't see him. She would have known exactly what he was up to.

He waited for fifteen minutes, time enough for her to return if she had forgotten or needed to check on something. Jack undid the bungee cords and as nonchalantly as possible walked to Meghan's apartment carrying the monstrosity. He wished he had purchased one of those collapsible fabric carriers.

If any of the neighbors know of our history, then I couldn't be more conspicuous if I carried a bomb with a sputtering fuse, Jack thought. Holding his breath, Jack put the key Meghan had given him weeks ago into her lock. Jack knew he was going in one way or the other. He preferred to do it with the key, instead of breaking and entering. The key didn't turn.

Shit! Well, here we go, Jack thought as he got out the tools of the trade and flipped the lock. Easy as pie. Jack was again struck by the lack of personality Meghan's apartment had: white, blank walls and basic furniture purchased during her college days. The only thing in her dining room was her helmet and bicycle that leaned against the wall. She spent no time making this place a home. Her office at work conveyed more warmth. He set the carrier down on the kitchen table as he read a note Meghan had obviously left for her neighbor.

Gail, thanks for being here on Saturday at 10:00 for the locksmith. I changed the locks myself, but he's going to put in more substantial ones. He should give you two sets of keys. I just watered the African violets, so you don't need to, besides I don't think they're going to make it. I appreciate your offer to look in on Ernest, but I've taken him with me. If you need me, I'm at the Boston Marriott Long Wharf, room 556. You can always call my cell phone but it'll be off part of the time during the presentation. Sorry to give yet another reminder, but do not let <u>anyone</u> other than the locksmith into my apartment for <u>any</u> reason. Forgive me for being a little nuts about this. Thanks again. See you Sunday. Meghan

Damn! She took my cat to Boston, Jack thought. *Now I need to make a stupid ass road trip.* Jack looked around the apartment; he could really use some cash. He went to her bedroom. What a mess! Clothes were piled all over the bed, suits mostly, and silk shirts to go with them. It looked like she had a difficult time choosing what to pack.

She shouldn't have worried, Jack thought. *She looks great in everything.*

He picked up a raspberry pink shirt. Jack could clearly picture her in it, her dark hair sweeping her shoulders, her firm breasts. He gathered the fabric up to his face and inhaled. The scent took him back to when she had wrapped her arms around his neck, pulled him close, and danced with him in his driveway. They had said their goodnights earlier; Jack had shut the door and was drinking a glass of water in the kitchen when he heard her knock. "You've got to come out and see this moon!" she had said. They stood there for a long time, looking up at the heavens. "Aren't you glad you didn't miss it?" Meghan had said to him. "Yes," he had replied and looking at her said, "So glad." That's when she pulled him into a slow dance and sang, "Close your eyes and I'll kiss you," an old Beatles tune. Those were the only lyrics she knew, so she had hummed the rest of the song to him, her head resting on his chest. That had happened less than two weeks ago. It felt like a lifetime. With a clenched jaw, Jack jerked open the drawer of her bedside table. No cash, just some face cream, tissues, and a pair of reading glasses. Jack wondered if she had another pair or if she needed them.

What you going to do, Jackie Boy, take them to her? He slammed the drawer shut in a temper. Then, he stood still with his heart racing concerned someone might have heard the noise in a supposedly empty apartment.

I need to be more careful. What the hell is wrong with me? I should just go. He peeked out the front and side windows getting ready to open the door when he noticed the refrigerator. He knew a number of people who kept cash in the butter compartment. When Jack looked, he found no cash; in fact there wasn't much of anything: energy drinks, yogurt, a takeout container of Chinese food, and a dozen eggs past their expiration date.

Yeah, she is going to miss me feeding her, Jack thought. He pulled open the vegetable drawer and found a fresh bag of baby carrots.

So, my girl has started to eat vegetables on her own. A lump formed in his throat.

Time to go, he thought. *Time to go.*

Chapter Forty-Eight

Such a Trifle

Penny pulled up to the dorm and saw Eva and Edward outside drinking coffee. Penny was certain that Edward had gotten up early, rushed out to get the caffeinated beverages so he could spend a few moments with Eva while waiting for Penny to arrive. When Penny first noticed Edward hanging around Eva all the time, Penny got a little concerned. But as she got to know him, she realized he was a sweet boy and respectful of Eva.

Eva put her book bag and laptop carrier on the back seat, pulled open the front door and threw herself into Penny's arms.

"Whoa, you okay?" asked Penny. "What's wrong?"

"Nothing," said Eva. "I'm just really happy to see you. I've missed you."

"I've missed you too," Penny said. "I want to hear everything about your date – start to finish."

"Oh, it was the best time ever!" Eva said as she snapped her seatbelt closed.

As Penny started to pull out, Eva gave a distracted wave to Edward, and Penny saw his crestfallen look. "He really likes you, you know," Penny said.

"Do you really think so? How do you know?"

"From the look on his face. Edward really cares about you."

"Oh, I thought you meant Eric. So, we went to Jack's Oyster House."

"Jack's Oyster House? Really? That place is so expensive."

"It's really elegant. I was glad I wore a dress and not jeans. I had really debated about that."

"He's a college student and he can afford to go to Jack's?"

"That doesn't seem to be an issue for Eric Huntsby. He drives a Porsche. I felt like a movie star riding it in."

"Huntsby? You mean *the* Huntsbys who are huge donors to area museums, libraries, hospitals, and the like?"

"His grandfather," Eva said. "He's a real philanthropist, like you and Michael."

"Honey, Michael and I like to do our part, but we are hardly in the same league as Mr. Huntsby. He's closer to the Bill and Melinda Gates level of wealth."

"Eric said sometime he's going to introduce me to him, his grandfather, not Bill Gates, although I suppose he probably could."

Penny nodded.

"You seem concerned," Eva said. "Is it because his family has money? I can't imagine you feeling the same way if I dated someone who didn't have money. Isn't that, in its own way, discrimination?"

"I don't imagine the Huntsbys often feel slighted."

"That's not fair," Eva said. "You haven't even met them."

"What did you eat?" Penny asked trying for a neutral topic.

"He ordered for us. He had a steak and lobster and I had a salad."

"He ordered you a salad?"

"It was a beautiful salad. It had tomatoes, and cucumbers, salad greens, grilled chicken, with dressing on the side. Eric said you should always order salad dressing that way. If you don't, there are too many calories and it negates eating healthy."

"And for dessert? I went there with the Capital District Professional Women's organization and had the best cheesecake in my life!"

"Oh Eric said we should skip dessert, we didn't need it."

"Is he heavy?" Penny asked.

"No," Eva replied.

Once they arrived at the shop, Eva couldn't stop talking about Eric and his opinions about everything from politics to movies. They heard, "Eric thinks … Eric says … so much they started listening with only one ear. However, when Eva said she was going to have blonde highlights put in her hair like Amanda, Annalise could no longer keep quiet. "Highlights in brown hair like Amanda's make it look sun kissed, blonde highlights in jet black hair like ours looks cheap. Why would you want to do that?"

"Eric's sister gets highlights done in New York and Eric said the next time she goes, I can go with her and have my hair done. And I'm going to grow my hair long."

"Because Eric wants your hair long?" Annalise asked.

276

"No, *I* want to grow it long. He just happens to like long hair too. And for your information, I'm going to have my hair dyed brown and then have blonde highlights put in. So, I won't look cheap!"

"It'll be really expensive to have your hair done in the city," Mayra-Liz said.

"How much?" asked Eva.

"Probably $250, maybe more."

"It doesn't matter," Eva said. "Eric's going to pay for it."

"Oh no, he's not!" Annalise said. "What's next? Is he going to buy your clothes?"

Eva had a guilty look cross her face. "Eva Louise, has that boy bought you clothes?" Annalise asked.

"Just a dress," Eva said. "For the next time we go out."

Annalise gave an exasperated sigh.

"It wasn't like that, Annalise. He just helped me pick out a dress that makes me look slimmer."

They all looked at her with shocked expressions.

"Why can't you just be happy for me?" Eva said as she burst into tears. As she ran out of the room, she knocked over a chair.

Annalise walked over and picked it up while calling after her sister, "Because you *aren't* happy! What happened to Edward? He likes you for who you are."

At the threshold of the room, Eva turned and shouted at her sister, "Maybe I want to be better than I am!"

"It's fine to improve, as long as you're doing it for yourself and not for some *boy*."

Eva stormed back into the room in a temper, looked at Jen and then Annalise, and pointed her finger at Annalise. But before Eva could speak Annalise held up her hand and said, "Don't. Don't say something hurtful. You'll only regret it."

Although Eva was really angry, she also knew her sister was right. Eva lowered her hand, turned on her heels, walked out of the room, and went to the storage area where she cried.

Oh Eva, she wrote to herself in Jane Austen style in her journal, *this is no occasion for crying so much about such a trifle. But it didn't feel like a trifle*, it felt like nothing in her world was right.

Chapter Forty-Nine

Lost and Found

Other than the two day vacation spent in Vermont when Michael and Penny celebrated Valentine's Day, Michael had worked exclusively on the conference for missing children for weeks. There were so many details to work out. But he had spoken with the attorney, Meghan Ashley who was leading the workshop and Michael was impressed with her skill and passion.

Michael had been up before daybreak going over his lists and packing up the car. Penny had remained in bed. He was concerned for her. As the conference approached, she became more quiet, subdued even. She kept reassuring him she was fine, but her face had lost its color.

Michael knew it didn't take a psychiatrist to figure out his obsession with the conference. Since he couldn't reunite Penny with her child, Michael would work to reunite *someone* with theirs. But a photographer could only do so much. Michael wanted to wipe Penny's past away, wash away her sorrows. Yes! Be her savior. *How arrogant,* Michael scoffed. Then he eased up on himself. It wasn't like he thought he was divine, he just wanted to move heaven and earth to make his wife happy and it frustrated him that he really couldn't do anything about her painful memories except wait until they faded.

I need to be careful about how I proceed. Even with the best of intentions, it wouldn't be the first time I made a bad situation worse, Michael thought. *Dr. Allen said Penny was recovering nicely and patience was the key. But why was she still in bed? Normally Penny was excited about my photographic exhibitions and was up early, raring to go. Ah yes, but this isn't quite the same thing, is it? Penny's going to a conference where hundreds of people still had hope of being reunited with their child. Penny had no hope, unless she believed it would happen in an afterlife.*

Michael looked at his watch. *Eight o'clock. Mayra-Liz will be over in an hour. I'd better wake up Penny now so she has time to shower and eat,* Michael thought.

"Penny?" Michael whispered. Her auburn hair was fanned over her pillow. Her mouth was slightly open as she breathed deeply.

"Hmm?" Penny replied.

"It's eight o'clock. I thought you'd want me to awaken you."

"Oh gosh! Yes, I need to get going." Penny stretched, sat up, and swung her legs over to the side of the bed in one motion.

"Ohh!" Penny said as she held onto her forehead.

"You're getting up too quickly," Michael said. "Just sit for a bit. You have time. Are you feeling okay? You went quite white."

"Headache," Penny said. "And I got a bit dizzy."

"Were you able to get an earlier appointment with the cardiologist?"

"Yes, it's on March 20th."

"Only a week earlier?"

"Two. It was the earliest appointment I could get."

"Chronic headaches can be caused by heart disease," Michael said. Penny stared at him.

"I read about it on WebMD," he said with a shrug.

"But those people usually have high blood pressure. My pressure is actually low. I read WebMD too," she smiled at her admission.

"I'll just feel better after you talk with him."

"Her. Dr. *Janet* Jackson."

"Really, Janet Jackson. I bet she gets a lot of comments on her name."

"I bet she does too. Actually, the picture of her on the website looks a bit like the singer. I need to get going," Penny said interrupting herself. "I'll feel better after I've had a shower."

Mayra-Liz arrived while Penny was eating dry toast. "Well, there's the breakfast of champions," Mayra-Liz said. "You okay?"

"Yeah, my headache is making my stomach queasy, is all."

"Is all? I hate feeling nauseous. Anything I can do for you?"

"Yeah, don't say the word … *nauseous,*" Penny whispered it. "Just hearing it makes me feel more…"

"Nauseous? Oh, sorry!" Mayra-Liz said. "I'll get out of your hair and help Michael pack up the car. He has a crazy idea all that stuff is going to fit in the trunk."

By ten thirty, a half hour past the time Michael had planned to leave, all the equipment, luggage, posters, and handout materials had been moved from the front porch, to the car trunk, rearranged several times and finally hauled into the van. Mayra-Liz said it could have made a nice skit for a sitcom.

"You mean one of those shows that portrays how stupid men are?" Michael asked as he struggled with the last piece of luggage.

"All you need is an abundant supply of duct tape," Mayra-Liz said teasing him.

Penny stumbled out, shielding her eyes against the sun.

"Photophobia?" Michael asked with sympathy.

Penny nodded.

"Poor Penny," Mayra-Liz said. "I have some aspirin."

"No, I'm at my limit," Penny replied.

"You know, I never understood why they call it photo … phobia. You aren't *afraid* of the sun," Mayra-Liz said.

"At the moment I'm feeling pretty shy of it," Penny replied.

"Perhaps you should stay," Michael said. "I can't imagine a three and a half hour ride is going to do you any good."

"I can stay with you if you need someone," Mayra-Liz said.

"No, I'll be fine," Penny said. "Let's get going. You know, I have a good feeling about this conference. I think someone's going to be found."

Chapter Fifty

Lucky Bastard

A steady drizzle turned to sleet and Jack decided he would have to pull into the next diner, get off his bike and warm up or risk catching pneumonia. No sooner had the decision been made when Jack's bike started coughing as if it too was coming down with something. He eased it off the road and pulled out his cell phone praying Meghan hadn't cancelled the service. He asked this "app thing" for the nearest motorcycle repair shop and a map appeared showing one .47 miles away, and it had good reviews. Instantly Jack became a believer in technology. It really was God-sent: a miracle! However, after an hour of pushing the bike in freezing rain, he was swearing to a point of incoherence: son of mouse; horse mother; flowerin' shit. Cars flew past him, showering him with grey highway water. At first he yelled, but as time went on, it got so it wasn't worth the effort to tell those "sons of b-b-b *bitches*" what he thought of them. When he finally arrived at the repair shop he found it open, but empty. *Jesus,* he thought. *I can't push this bike any further.* He sat down on a bench and pulled his wet jacket off. It didn't help; he was wet to the skin.

"I'm shivering like a motherless h-h-hamster," he said out loud.

"Then sit next to the goddamn furnace, you idiot." Jack heard someone say.

"Who's here?" Jack called out half wondering if he was hallucinating.

A mechanic's floor creeper rolled out from under a car. "Just the frigging mechanic," said the man. "Who the hell are you?"

Jack stood up and with shaking legs walked over to introduce himself. He was halfway across the room when the mechanic exclaimed, "I'll be damned. It's Jack Fox."

Jack remembered the man from prison – Larry Parry. What a name. What a guy. He was the second person Jack had ever known that didn't give a shit about anyone, absolutely no one. Not that the guys he had been locked up with were the "generosity of spirit" kind of folks, but this guy was absolutely stone cold.

Well, Jack thought, *I'm quickly getting to that place myself.*

"How you getting on?" Larry asked as he shook Jack's hand, sizing him up.

"All right," Jack replied as he shivered. "You? You're a long ways from OPP."

"Shut the *fuck up.* What's wrong with you?" Larry hissed as he looked around. "They know that I served time, but they don't know that it was anyplace as hard core as that."

"It doesn't look like there's anyone else here," Jack said. "Besides you think they'd know what OPP means?"

"They got the Internet, don't they?"

"Sorry," Jack mumbled as he continued to shiver.

"No harm done, I guess," Larry said as he continued to scan the garage for potential eavesdroppers before he looked back at Jack. "It's just that it's a bitch, ya know. Nobody wants to pay shit for guys like us. They know they can screw us over and there ain't nothin' we can do about it. I wouldn't want to lose my place here. They don't pay what I'm worth, but the owner turns a blind eye to my little side business."

"What's that?" Jack said, his teeth chattering.

"You'd better get out of those clothes before you get sick. There's an extra set of uniforms in the back. Put your socks and shoes next to the furnace."

Jack was grateful to get into dry clothes; yet he was surprised Larry made the offer. Simple kindness wasn't in him. Jack was further surprised when he walked back into the garage and Larry handed him a mug of hot coffee. Larry sat down in one of the two lawn chairs he had pulled up in front of the furnace. The mechanic shook out a cigarette, lit it, and as he inhaled deeply gave Jack an appraising look. It was obvious Larry had settled upon some decision when he nudged a chair in Jack's direction with his foot and said, have a seat. Larry got up and went behind the furnace and retrieved an old tool chest. He looked like he was bringing a present out from behind the Christmas tree.

"Look at this," Larry said. It sure didn't look like anything special; a beat up grey metal box, the corners chipped and rusty, but Larry's eyes took on a gleam when he lifted the top tray and exposed an assortment of bags filled with pills and powders. "I can get most anything you'd like."

"No thanks," Jack said holding a hand up.

Larry nodded approvingly, "So you haven't changed. We used to call you the professor because of all your reading and clean living."

"Then why show me?" Jack asked, suspicious of what *Crazy Larry* might have in mind.

"Cause I've got a business proposition for ya. I need someone who ain't a druggie. I need you to go to Boston and pick up a shipment of … *stuff* and hand over some money. Your bike's got problems; I can fix it while you drive my truck there and back." Larry took a long deep drag on the cigarette, and appraised Jack through the grey cloud of smoke. "It's that simple," Larry said with a shrug.

Jack warmed his hands around the coffee mug as he stared at Larry. He didn't trust the man. "Why don't you go yourself," Jack asked.

"Because I can't. I have other commitments," making himself sound like a businessman. "Look, it's perfectly safe. I know the guy you'll meet."

Jack felt as if he was out of options. He needed his bike to get back and forth to work and had no money to pay for repairs. Besides, Boston was where he wanted to go anyway. "Okay," Jack replied. "When do I leave?"

"Tomorrow, early. You need to be back here by two in the afternoon."

"I need a hundred dollars up front. I'm the one taking the risk," Jack said.

"Fifty," Larry replied. "I guess I don't need to tell ya how serious it would be if you got creative."

"You don't need to explain," Jack said. "And I'm sure I don't need to elucidate that my bike needs to be in good working order when I return."

"Elucidate? Elucidate! Hell no, you don't need to *elucidate*," Larry said mocking Jack.

Jack pulled out of the garage not in Larry's new "sagebrush pearl" colored Dodge Ram, but in an old green battered Ford that had been purchased for parts. The truck still ran, but it had a rough sounding engine and shocks that probably needed to be replaced a decade ago. Jack didn't care as long as it got him to Boston and back. Jack was feeling pretty good. He'd go to Boston in the morning with fifty dollars in his pocket, have the repairs on his bike done, and come back with his cat. *I am one lucky bastard,* Jack thought.

The next morning, Jack didn't feel like a lucky anything. His head was stuffy and his body ached from a fever. As miserable as he felt, Jack knew there was no possibility of putting off the job.

285

The radio in the truck didn't work, so there was nothing to cover up the rattles and squeaks it made. As Jack drove, he entertained himself by planning Ernest's rescue, but Jack had a difficult time keeping his mind on the strategy. It was so simple, it was boring. Jack had taken pains to dress well. After he walked away from the truck, he wanted to look like he stayed at the fancy hotel. Jack dressed in black: jeans, cowboy boots, button down shirt, and a western sports jacket. He completed the persona with a black cowboy hat he hadn't worn in years. But its worn edges made it look like hat and owner were rarely separated. If he needed to, Jack could pull the wide brim of the hat down and shade his face using it as a casual disguise, with his dark hair tucked inside. The final touch was a western bolo tie, the choice of wealthy, southern men who don't give a hoot about current fashion.

Okay, he thought, *I walk down the corridor and see some not quite pretty housekeeper. I'll give her a little tip of my hat, an interested smile, and go past. Her eyes will follow me. At room 556 I'll reach into my pants pockets, then my shirt pockets while making a face that conveys, I can't believe I left my key behind. I'll turn to her, 'Sorry to bother you ma'am, could you help me out here?' I can sound like a good ol' boy when I put my mind to it. The maid will probably make some noise about me needing to go to the front desk. 'Sure, sure,' I'll tell her. 'I understand. I wouldn't want to get a pretty little lady like you into trouble,' smiling at her mouth. 'It's just I've got this here international conference call comin' in five minutes and I sure would hate to miss it. Them Japanese are so crazy about punctuality, I could lose the deal if I don't pick it up on the first ring. You'd be doin' me a huge favor.' If she asked about his cell phone he'd say his battery died and he forgot to bring his charger. 'I'm havin' one heck of a trip, I'm tellin' ya. I'd be happy to show you my driver's license so you know I'm who I say I am.' Then he'd look at his watch again.*

Jack knew, chances were he'd be let in. Women always wanted to help. Jack glanced at himself in the rear view mirror and smiled. *Yep, many a time that smile had worked wonders,* he thought, *no reason to think it won't work again.*

Okay, so where was I? Jack asked himself. *Oh yeah, I get in the room, put Ernest into the carrier and ...* Without hope, Jack glanced over at the passenger side of the truck.

"Son of a bitch!" Jack yelled. "I tell you Jackie Boy you've got shit for brains! Where the hell did you leave the carrier?" Jack quickly backtracked in his mind until he remembered: "Meghan's apartment!" He glanced at his watch. He didn't have enough time to turn around and get back before the locksmith arrived. As soon as Meghan saw the carrier she would know he had been in her apartment. The only saving grace was that he had worn his motorcycle gloves all the while he had been in there. There was no way she could prove he had left it. It wasn't even his carrier.

"Yeah," Jack said reconsidering. "Let her know I was there. Put a little fear of Jack into her, maybe it'll draw some of the cockiness out of her."

Jack drove first to the hotel. If there were any problems he didn't want contraband in the car. He parked in the back next to the kitchen. People would assume anyone driving a heap like this worked there.

Jack was eating a breakfast burrito thing that he had purchased from a drive-through place. It tasted like sawdust thanks to his cold. At least he hoped that was the reason. Three black cats with white spots were lingering at the kitchen back door. A kitchen worker came out to have a smoke and the cats darted towards him. The largest cat tried to affectionately rub against the worker's leg, but the man pushed the cat away with his foot. Then he tried to shoo the other two away, but the cats just moved a few yards away and yowled at the man. Jack couldn't hear them, but saw their mouths opening and closing. Jack smiled at this. He had never before realized how cool cats were. Obviously, they weren't feral. What happened that they were now alone? Jack wondered. The kitchen worker picked up a bunch of rocks and hurled them at the cats, hitting one soundly. The cat walked away shaking his head as if he had gotten water in his ears from swimming. The worker took aim at another cat.

"Hey, what the hell are you doing?" Jack yelled, as he bounded out of the truck.

"We can't have these cats around. It's a problem with the health inspector."

"Better than rats," Jack said.

"We don't have any rats," the kitchen worker replied.

"All right, mice. I'm sure you've got some of those, all restaurants do."

"Look, what business is this of yours? You want them cats? Take them."

Jack saw the deal, if he didn't take the cats, they were in for the same treatment as the cat who was now scratching his ear with his back paw, not knowing what else to do with what must be a terrible ringing inside his head.

Jack grabbed his burrito and waved it at the cats, broadcasting the greasy meat scent. The cats came rushing over, meowing the entire way to this new food source. It didn't take much to coax them into the truck. Since the kitchen worker was now between Jack and the back door, Jack drove the truck around to the front. There he saw Meghan with two women; one had exotic black hair down to her waist. The other had auburn hair like his first wife. Jack pulled into a parking space down a ways so he wouldn't be noticed, but close enough that it still gave him a good view of Meghan. He wasn't worried about Meghan seeing him. She wouldn't associate him with the truck. However, Jack hadn't taken into consideration the cats. They were now freely walking back and forth across the dashboard bawling for more food. He had given them all he had. It caught the eye of the young woman with the exotic hair who smiled and pointed at the truck. The other women looked too, including Meghan. Jack pulled his cowboy hat down and with great restraint slowly pulled out of the parking lot. With a willed nonchalant glance in the rear view mirror, Jack's eyes locked with the woman with the auburn hair.

"That was close," he told his new feline friends. "We'll have to get Ernest another time. Don't piss on the seat, Larry will skin you alive."

The cat loudly meowed a reply.

"I'm not kidding," Jack told him.

Chapter Fifty-One

Engagement Rings

It was one of those bitter-winter days that felt like spring would never arrive. Winter boots, coats, and fur-lined accessories were required articles of clothing for stepping outside. The purple knitted hat that Amanda thought was so cute when she purchased it in November, now got on her nerves every time she pulled it down over her ears. On Jay Street, the air snapped with cold. A bookstore and a craft shop up the street were closed because their water pipes froze; however, the lights in the *Ruth and Naomi* shop were on. The windows were steamed from freshly baked goods and hot beverages. Many, who normally drove past the shop on their way to work, now pulled in for something sweet to ease the winter doldrums.

"How we doing with the hot chocolate?" Mayra-Liz called.

"No more than ten cups," Amanda answered. "I keep trying to get back to make another pot but –" The bell over the front door cling-a-linged, announcing another customer. This woman knew exactly what she wanted: three hot chocolates; a coffee with cream, no sugar; and four ham and cheese croissants. "And I'm in a bit of a hurry," the customer informed Amanda.

"I'll get the hot chocolate going," Mayra-Liz said. "You aren't going to make it into the back room anytime soon. I can wait on restocking the jewelry. Where's Penny? We need some tables wiped down."

"She went to the bank. We're short of ones."

"How is that possible? Didn't we start with a full cash drawer?"

"No, Michael didn't bring it in."

Mayra-Liz frowned, but made no comment other than to say. "I've got to get the hot chocolate going."

The door chimes announced another arrival. It was Michael. He looked like an advertisement for sleep aids, the before picture.

"Hey, Michael," Mayra-Liz said.

Michael nodded and poured himself a cup of coffee. Not long ago, Michael would have looked around the shop, grabbed an apron and towel and started busing tables. Today, he sat down and stared out the window. The bells over the front door chimed once again. Mayra-Liz looked up to see Annalise and Jen entering, stomping snow off their boots, unwinding their scarves, and pulling off gloves.

"Can't stay away, even on your day off?" Mayra-Liz asked. "Good thing, because tables 3, 5, and 6 need to be cleared. I'm going to get some hot choco –"

"Ta-da!" Annalise and Jen said as they held out their ring-adorned hands. "It's official!"

"Oh my goodness!" Mayra-Liz squealed. "You're getting married?"

"We are!" Jen replied. Mayra-Liz hugged her sister, and then Jen, and then her sister again.

"I'm so happy for you!" Amanda cooed.

The nurses seated at table four broke out in applause. The commotion was enough to bring Michael out of his reverie. "What's going on?" he asked as he walked up to the young women. Annalise and Jen again proudly held out their hands.

Michael's mouth formed a hard straight line as if he was zipping it shut. "Congratulations," he mumbled. "Well, I have to get going."

Michael was almost to the door when Annalise stopped him. "Michael, what is it?" she asked softly. "I know you like Jen. Why are you acting like this?"

"I can't believe you need to ask. Did you really think I'd be excited over the purchase of diamonds? *Children* are often the miners, sent down narrow shafts. They are beaten and starved. But why am I telling you that? You *know* that! Did you at least receive a certificate stating the gems were retrieved legally? It doesn't matter. There are so many ways around it." Michael stood there shaking his head, looking at the floor as if he couldn't bear to look at the young woman he often claimed to love like a daughter.

Annalise waited him out. When Michael looked up, Annalise said softly, "They aren't *diamonds*, Michael. We bought these at PeopleCare. We wouldn't buy our engagement rings some place that didn't represent who we are. How could you think –"

Annalise didn't complete her thought because Michael pulled her into his arms, crushing her to his chest. "Forgive me. Please, please forgive me," he whispered into her hair. "Of course, you wouldn't …." Michael released Annalise, went to Jen and bear hugged her too. "I'm sorry," he again repeated to the couple. "I'm very happy for you. I have to go. There's something I must do."

The bells jingled twice as he opened and closed the door behind. The girls stood dazed as they looked at each other. *What in the world is going on with Michael,* their faces said.

Michael hurried to his car, got in, and quietly closed the door. He leaned his head back and took a deep breath. Michael pulled his phone and a business card out of his jacket pocket and called the FBI.

Chapter Fifty-Two

The Fighters

Jack handed the package to Larry who put it unopened into his tool chest. "You need to look at it and confirm it's all there. I don't want any accusations down the road," Jack said.

"Too many people in here," Larry said. "Go to the third shed in the back. I'll meet you there. But I'm sure it's all here. My Boston friend wouldn't get creative; he's not smart enough to think outside of the box. You wouldn't short me because you're too smart."

"I don't want there to be any question," Jack said, remaining firm.

"Okay, I'll see you out there in five, with the rest of what I owe you."

Jack was pacing by the time Larry arrived, not in five minutes, but twenty.

"Calm down," Larry said. "I know my reputation, but I'm not going to hurt someone I can use." Larry opened the package, replenished his supplies in the toolbox and said, "Yep, it's all there. Next Saturday I need you to go in the afternoon."

"I'm not doing it again," Jack said.

"What? You got something against making easy money? You prefer to haul furniture around?"

Jack stared at him with surprise.

"I saw the commercial," Larry explained.

"And you recognized me from it?" Jack asked.

"Your name is on the credits, you dope. I figure making deliveries for me is a step up."

"Running drugs? Nope, can't do it. No offense," Jack said to Larry.

Larry shrugged. As he started to put the top tray in place, Jack stopped him. "What's that?" he asked.

Larry gave a lazy, half grin as they looked down among the wrenches and screwdrivers to the chrome plated revolver partially wrapped in an oily, red hand rag. "That my friend is a snub nose .357 Magnum." Larry picked it up and handed the revolver to Jack. "Pretty, ain't she?"

"Is it clean?" Jack asked.

"Virginal," Larry replied.

"How much?"

"Who said it's for sale? Besides I don't think you have the money."

"I can get the money. How much?" Jack asked again.

"What you going to do, rob a bank? If you rob a bank, you'll need a gun. You have what they call one of them revolving dilemmas."

"I'm not robbing a bank, and I'm not entirely without resources."

"You could have fooled me."

"Look, do you want to sell the gun or not?" Jack asked.

"A grand," Larry said.

"I'd pay half that at a gun store."

"Yeah, but a gun store won't sell to you."

"So, you're taking advantage," Jack said.

Disinterested in Jack's righteous indignation, Larry scratched his arm as he looked at his nonexistent watch. "Look, I've got to get back to work. Do you want the gun or don't ya?"

"I want it," Jack said handing the gun back to Larry. "I'll bring you the money by next Saturday."

"I won't hold it for you. Somebody else comes through with cash on the barrelhead, it's theirs."

"How many people try to buy a revolver off you out here in suburbia?"

"You'd be surprised," Larry replied.

A few days later, Jack returned to his apartment after a trip to the pawn shop. Jack was greeted at the door by three cats starved for attention, even though he had only been gone for a few hours. Jack sat down on the floor so they could better rub their heads over his body. Sugar Ray Leonard had a particularly loud purr. Muhammad Ali was a fastidious groomer. When he was done, Muhammad groomed Sugar Ray who only did a cursory job at best. Mike Tyson was a dirty fighter. The other cats would be sleeping and he would pounce on them. Of course, he was just playing, but Jack knew if Mike ever got into a scrap he'd come out the winner. He wouldn't be above taking someone's ear off.

"How are my boys, huh? You guys miss me? Yeah, yeah, you missed me all right. How about some moist food to go with that dry, crunchy stuff? Yeah, yeah," Jack said as he got up and walked to the kitchen. "Who wants ..." Jack read the can. "Salmon pâté? Oh everyone! Okay,

okay. There's enough for everybody. Slow down. You'll get an ulcer eating like that and Uncle Jack doesn't have the resources to pay vet bills. Keep it in mind."

"Somehow the place feels empty with the watch gone," he said to the cats. "I don't know why. I hardly took it out, but I never thought I'd sell it. I can still remember the day my grandfather gave it to me – a railroad pocket watch in a gold hunting scene case that had been his father's. I thought that I would get a grand for that alone, but the guy could smell desperation and gave me $500, only half as much as it was worth. He gave me $500 for the ruby ring, also a rip off. I had planned just to sell my grandma's pearls, but the appraiser didn't want to buy them, said they weren't worth more than twenty dollars. They're not even pearls, just some kind of glass. Jack sighed as he again pictured his grandfather proudly giving him the watch. Jack wiped his watery eyes on the back of his sleeve.

Enough of that, he told himself. *The watch wasn't any help to me. But with the gun I can get me a big slice of payback-pie, if I'm ever lucky enough to find my ex-wife. I'm tired of playing the putz.* "Yes, I am. Yes, I am," he cooed to the cats.

Chapter Fifty-Three

Dayo's Man

"Don't forget to call me as soon as you get there," Penny told Mayra-Liz and Eva as they sat at the kitchen table drinking coffee. "You have the GPS so it'll take you right to their door. Don't try a different route. And don't go anyplace else. It's not a great neighborhood. Just pay them, load the scarves into the van, and leave. Okay?"

"Sure, Penny," Mayra-Liz said absently as she wrapped her hands around her coffee mug for warmth.

"I wish I could go with you," Penny said wistfully. "Maybe I still can. Perhaps this headache will let up if I just go for a car ride."

"Penny, you have a migraine. If you come with us, it'll only get worse," Mayra-Liz said. "When do you see the doctor?"

"March twentieth."

"So, next week. I hope she can discover why you're getting all these headaches and make them go away."

"That would certainly be nice," Penny sighed. "I hate having you girls go alone. If only Michael didn't have that photo shoot in Philly today, he could have gone with you. You have the Triple A card for the van, right?"

Mayra-Liz nodded.

Penny also nodded, and took another sip of her coffee. "Are you sure you don't want some eggs? It would take no time at all to fix them."

"Thanks, but it's too early," Eva said, and Mayra-Liz agreed.

"You both have your cell phones, right? And they're fully charged? Mayra-Liz, we've got to get you a better phone. Yours is always breaking up."

"We'll be fine," Eva said. "I don't know why you're so worried. It's not like Mayra-Liz and I haven't driven twice as far on buying trips. You're acting like you're sending us off to war."

"I know, and I'm sorry. You're grown women, able to take care of yourselves," Penny said, but a worried frown remained on her face. "I just have such a bad feeling –"

"I don't know why we're buying from them," Eva interrupted. "Our storage unit is full. You and Mayra-Liz are going to South America in a few weeks to buy more. It's not like we need more merchandise, especially from people we don't know anything about."

"These women wrote to us saying they are in need and sent a sample scarf. They met the criteria: quality products, hand-crafted by women who are trying to improve their lives."

"But we can't help everyone, can we?" Eva reflected.

"We do what we can, where, and when we can," Mayra-Liz responded with the mantra she had heard from Penny and Michael more times than she could count. "And right now, we're going to help Penny by leaving."

"Now? You don't have to go for another 45 minutes," Penny protested.

"I know, but if we leave you can lie down, perhaps get some sleep. If you can't fall asleep, try listening to one of the old time movies that you like. Casablanca, you love that one, right?"

"I do."

"All right, we'll see you later. Don't fret. You can't be giving up one worry to just take on more. It's not good for … I don't know, your blood pressure or something," Mayra-Liz said.

In spite of Penny's fears, the drive east was uneventful. Eva chatted excitedly about her classes while Mayra-Liz drove.

"Do they give you enough time to get all that homework done?" Mayra-Liz asked.

"Yeah, it's doable, but it's important to balance your time. It'd be easy to spend the evenings watching T.V. on the huge screen in the dorm lobby. But what would be the point of that? Are you thinking about going back to school?"

"I don't know. Sometimes I think about doing something entirely different."

"I thought you loved working at the shop," Eva countered.

"I do! But don't you ever think about living someplace else? Meeting an entirely different culture? Doing something that you never before thought was possible?"

"I got an A on my Philosophy paper. I never thought that was going to happen."

You have reached your destination, intoned the GPS. Mayra-Liz pulled off to the side of the road.

"Do you really think this is the place?" Eva asked as she stared out of the car window at the little bungalow situated on a tiny plot on a side of a hill.

"It's the address they gave us," Mayra-Liz said equally skeptical.

"It's just so —"

"Purple," Mayra-Liz completed the sentence.

"It wouldn't be so bad if it was just one shade, but why so many?"

"They're struggling. They probably just made do with the various paint cans they came across. I like their sign: "Only God Knows Better. Palmists: Baako and Dayo," Mayra-Liz read.

"Didn't they say in their letter that their names are Leila and Sofia?"

Mayra-Liz nodded. "Perhaps they think Baako and Dayo sound more mysterious."

"We could have our fortunes told while we're here," Eva mused.

"Not on bet, we're going to complete this transaction and get out."

"So this place gives you the creeps too?"

"Let's just get this over with," Mayra-Liz said with a sigh as she turned off the engine, undid her seatbelt, grabbed her purse, and opened the car door with determined purpose.

Most of the snow had melted, and they climbed the hill following the path of beaten down weeds. A handwritten sign on the door invited customers to ring the bell and walk in. The heavy front door creaked and groaned on its hinges as if it were a stage prop. Heavy, faded ruby-colored tapestries with gold embroidery covered the windows blocking the winter sunlight. Red flickering candles of various shapes and sizes created deep and undulating shadows. A large round table covered with the same fabric as the drapes dominated the room. When the door clanked shut behind them, Eva jumped. "It's okay," Mayra-Liz whispered to comfort her sister, only to then let out a shriek. A rooster, his chest puffed out with red and black shiny feathers, his red comb bobbing, strutted back to the side of the room. He crowed and preened in front of a flock of chickens, protecting his harem. Stacked against the wall was a row of open cages where the hens roosted.

"They're so cute," Eva cooed.

"He attacked me!" Mayra-Liz said as she pulled up her pant leg looking for a mark. "He bit me!"

Eva looked too. "No blood," the younger sister shrugged.

"It still hurts," Mayra-Liz said peevishly, rubbing her ankle.

"What is that *smell*?" Eva whispered, fanning her hand in front of her nose.

"The barnyard smell is from them," Mayra-Liz said with a nod towards the poultry. "That heavy musky smell is marijuana. They must be growers."

The sisters heard a commotion in the back room. Someone said in a loud stage whisper, "Get moving. Someone's out there!"

Eva drew her sister close and whispered, "I don't think it's legal to keep barn yard animals in your place of business, even the cute kind."

Mayra-Liz whispered back, "I don't think these are women who worry about legalities."

A large, ebony-colored woman sashayed silently into the room. She wore a billowy dress made from the same bolt of fabric as the draperies and tablecloth. A matching turban was piled on her head. It created a strange juxtaposition as if part of the room was moving. She said in a deep, eerie, dramatic stage voice contrived from the movies of the 1940s, "I am Sister Baako. I know the future. I communicate with the past. How can I help you?"

"Shouldn't she know?" Eva whispered to her sister.

Mayra-Liz gave Eva a nudge. "We're from *Ruth and Naomi*. We came to pick up an order of scarves. I know we're early." Not seeing any recognition on Sister Baako's face, Mayra-Liz added, "Perhaps we have the wrong place?"

"Oh no, you've got the right place all right," Baako said in her *civilian* voice, suddenly hinting more of a Jersey than Jamaican childhood. "Dayo, they're here for the scarves!" Baako unwound the turban, revealing hair that looked like the coveted witch's broom of Oz, a dry and scraggly bush.

I wonder if a good haircut and a deep conditioner would help, Mayra-Liz absently wondered. *Of course conditioners can be expensive. Maybe I should tell her about ....*

"*You've* got nice hair," Baako said giving a contemptuous sneer showing uneven and stained teeth.

Color crept into Mayra-Liz's cheeks as she realized how easily her thoughts were read. "I ... I sometimes make my own conditioner with mayonnaise, egg yolks –"

"Dayo!" Baako bellowed again.

"I'm coming, I'm coming," Dayo hollered back. "Keep your big girl panties on and don't wet yourself." Dayo lumbered into the room causing the floorboards to groan and sending what could have been mistaken for low level seismic shock waves under their feet. She was by

300

far the largest woman in both height and girth Eva and Mayra-Liz had ever seen. Dayo carried a large shipping carton, but in her arms it looked more like a shoe box. Both girls stared silently for a full five seconds until Mayra-Liz found her voice and asked, "Do you need help?"

"Does it look like I need help?" Dayo demanded with raised, bushy eyebrows.

"No," Eva replied in a small voice, taking the safer bet.

"The answer is yes. There's another two boxes in the back."

"Okay," Mayra-Liz and Eva answered in unison.

The room had floor to ceiling windows covered with cardboard. Grow lights hung from the ceiling. Tables with empty potting trays were situated underneath. Potting soil had been spilled on the tables and floor. It looked like they had just moved "merchandise" in a hurry. A loom was set up and half a dozen skeins of yarn were in a basket next to it. Mayra-Liz was surprised that they didn't have more yarn lying around. Weavers she knew couldn't stop themselves from buying in bulk when they came across a good buy. *Perhaps these women don't have the resources to do that,* Mayra-Liz thought. Across the room, Mayra-Liz saw that a large screen television was on, muted, and tuned into a soap opera.

"I like watching the shows while doing my weaving," Dayo said. Eva looked up at Dayo and saw the woman had a wall eye over which she had no control. It just randomly rolled around in the eye socket, focusing on nothing. Eva stared at the woman with her mouth open. To distract her sister, Mayra-Liz walked to the loom and picked up a completed scarf that was folded next to it. *We're here to help these women, not judge them,* Mayra-Liz scolded herself, trying to get back on track of their mission.

"It's beautiful," Mayra-Liz said as she examined the soft garment. "I don't know how you can make such a complicated pattern on a hand loom."

"Well, it ain't easy. I've got this bad eye, don't ya know. And you all are getting these scarves at bargain-basement prices. We normally get lots more."

"How much do you normally charge?" Mayra-Liz asked.

"Seventy-five each," Dayo boasted.

"As nice as they are, I don't know if we can sell them for that price," Mayra-Liz said as she put the scarf back. "I don't want you to lose money by selling to us. There must be some misunderstanding. Our shop exists to help women in need. If you have a better outlet, then you should sell to them."

"Have you gone and lost your mind?" Baako cried out as she entered the room. "You know we have never gotten more than –"

"Shhh!" demanded Dayo, while vigorously waving an enormous hand and arm at Baako to shush her. "My commercial's on."

All conversation stopped while they watched a muted ad for furniture. When it ended, Dayo sighed and said, "That's him, *my man*! Sexy Jack."

"He is *not* your man. When we went down to the furniture store pretending to buy a chair, he didn't even look at you. You and that crazy imagination of yours … and you know darn good and well, we can't sell those scarves for forty dollars, let alone whatever number you were spouting! Lord Almighty, we only paid ten for them."

"You don't make them yourselves?" Mayra-Liz questioned.

"Yes, yes, we do! She means they *costs* us ten dollars in *material*," Dayo said, casting an evil eye at her sister. "And when you consider our time and talent –"

"I would love to see you weave. I've always been fascinated with the process," Mayra-Liz said as she gestured towards the loom.

"I don't like nobody watching me," whined Dayo. "It makes me nervous."

"Well, we'll just go out and call our employer and see how she wants us to proceed," said Mayra-Liz. *Go!* Mayra-Liz's eyes said to Eva and they hurried out of the palm reading, chicken raising, marijuana growing shop as fast as they could.

Driving down the road, Mayra-Liz said, "Well, that totally freaked me out."

"Oh yeah. Those women were *super* freaky."

"I meant the commercial. Didn't you notice?"

"Notice what?" asked Eva while she stared out the window.

"That guy. *Dayo's man*. He had jet black hair that he tossed out of his dark eyes."

"So?"

"His name is Jack Fox. It was listed on the credits. Furniture mover: Jack Fox. That was Penny's husband's name. And he fit the description Michael gave us. Remember, he said if we saw anyone lurking around that looked like that to let him know right away."

"Mayra-Liz, You know how many men named Jack Fox could fit that description?"

"And he had a tattoo on his arm," Mayra-Liz said. "I couldn't tell what it was of, but he definitely had one."

"So what do you want to do?" Eva sighed. "I have a midterm to study for."

"Nothing, I guess, other than to tell Michael privately. We don't want to upset Penny."

"I don't want to upset Michael either," Eva said. "He hasn't been himself since this whole thing came to light. Remember how he reacted to Annalise and Jen's engagement rings? What was *that* about? Chances are this furniture mover isn't *the* Jack, so why don't we take a ride down to the furniture store, check it out and know for sure it's not him, and then we don't have to say anything or upset anyone."

"What if it's him? What would we do?" Mayra-Liz asked, concern coating her words.

"Nothing. He doesn't know us. We'll just look around the furniture store like we're customers. Then we'll leave. If we need to, we'll tell Michael; he'll know what to do."

"How could we possibly know for sure it's him?" Mayra-Liz said. "I hate to borrow trouble."

"If he has a Seabees tattoo, I think we can feel pretty certain. But he won't have one. I mean, what are the chances of finding the guy because *Dayo* has a crush on him! Gees, what a day! I can't wait to get back to Siena."

Chapter Fifty-Four

Rich Bastard

Jack was working inside the furniture store and would be for the next nine months. It was, in its own way, serving time for driving under the influence.

It's so stupid, Jack thought. *Maybe some people can't handle drinking the amount I had, but I have a better capacity. The only reason I was pulled over was because the bike's taillight was out. God, I hate working inside the store. Showing stupid people, like this couple, dozens of stupid couches, like I care whether they get a plaid or a solid colored one to go inside their stupid trailer where their stupid brats will trash it.*

Jack felt the manager's eyes on him from across the showroom. The man looked like his name: Albert. Jack wondered what combination created this effect. Did his parents have an innate sense of how their child would look at age forty? Or did the name have so much influence it caused Albert's body to appear sloth-like, as if his muscles had never picked up anything heavier than a pound. Did the naming of Albert cause his skin to look like a champignon mushroom, all white and bumpy? Jack shook himself out of his reverie. He owed the man ... big time. It was time to pay up. Jack tossed his hair, squared his shoulders, and tried to have an interested expression as he said, "You know, since you have children – four you said? A plaid couch will hide the dirt better. The fabric is treated, but if your kids are like mine ..." It was the first suggestion he had given the couple. They looked startled as if they had forgotten he was there.

"Oh, you have kids too?" the woman asked smiling.

"Three," Jack said thinking of his cats. "They're a handful, but I don't know what I'd do without them."

"Okay," the husband said. "Let's go with the plaid. It makes sense."

Jack smiled and nodded at them before he glanced over at Albert who gave Jack a discreet nod in return.

Jack had thought he was totally screwed when he first got arrested. The police impounded his bike. There was a fee to get it back, court costs, fines …. Yeah, they really raked old Jack over. He couldn't imagine who he could call that would lend a hand. Jack thought of Larry who would probably buy back the gun. Of course, Larry would smell desperation and give pennies on the dollar and Jack needed a whole lot more than pennies. Finally, Jack called his boss, Albert. Jack knew it would probably result in simply getting himself fired. Who needs a driver who can't drive? But Albert came down and bailed him out. Driving Jack home, Albert had said, "You'll have to pay me back twenty-five dollars each week. That was a loan, not a gift. I'll put you on sales. I know you don't have a way to get to work, so you can ride with me. It'll mean longer days for you. The plus side is you'll get paid a little over-time which will make it easier for you to pay me back."

"That's fine," Jack replied meekly. "I really appreciate it."

"I know you do," Albert said sternly. "But you listen carefully, Jack. You're on probation with me. Part of the probation is you keep going to your meetings and stay sober, *stone-cold sober*. I know it's hard. I've been there, and I also know it's the only way. You were given your first chance when I hired you. I think you know what I mean by that. I have a responsibility to the store owner who isn't always impressed with my hiring philosophies. You mess up again and you and I will have to part company."

"I understand," Jack said as the car stopped in front of his apartment. "I really am surprised you've done all that you have. I've gotta ask; why did you do it?"

"Because that's what Jesus would have done," Albert had replied simply. Jack got out of the car and stared at it while it went down the street, until it turned left, and was out of sight.

"What Jesus would have done," Jack mumbled to himself as he looked over at Albert working the cash register. *If there were more guys like him, there'd be fewer guys like me, feeling screwed and angry.*

The day was dragging on forever. Jack promised himself he would never again complain about hauling furniture around. No one of interest ever came into the store. They were all fat and ugly, and you had to spend way more time with them.

Hold the phone, he thought. *Who* is *that*? A beautiful woman with dark wavy hair that hung to her waist walked into the showroom with someone who looked like her kid sister. Jack started to make a beeline over to them, leaving the woman he had been helping. But Nate got to the young women first.

Of course, he would, Jack thought. He quickly looked back at the customer he had just abandoned. She had a confused look on her face. He could feel Albert's eyes on him. Jack quickly snatched up a ring of fabric swatches. "Here it is," he said to the customer. "I was thinking this color might be nice." The woman smiled and took the fabric sample from Jack considering it.

As discreetly as possible, Jack kept his eye on the dark haired beauty, and he saw she was keeping her eye on him. Jack gave her a slow smile and immediately the woman dropped her eyes. Man, she was beautiful. He had seen her someplace before. Where was it? She had been outside. Jack remembered a breeze had blown her hair, and she brushed it out of her face.

The young women were walking closer to him. The younger one was taking pictures with her phone. Nate was practically tap dancing in his efforts to impress, but they paid him no attention. In fact, they didn't even seem to look at the furniture. The phone seemed to be pointed at Jack.

Okay, this is getting weird, Jack thought. *Where do I know her from?* All of a sudden it came to him. She had been the one talking to Meghan at the hotel in Boston. Now Jack understood; Meghan had sent the dark haired beauty in to meet him. The women's scheme was to get Jack to fall in love with the dark haired beauty who would then drop him, breaking his heart.

Gees! He thought. *Don't they have anything better to do with their time? How high school!* Jack was going to put a stop to it right now. He strolled down the aisle with purpose. He saw the dark haired beauty's eyes widen. She grabbed her companion's arm, and the two hurried through the furniture store and out the door. Jack followed them as far as the door. The women jumped into a van with the logo *Ruth and Naomi* on its side and took off.

"What was all that about?" asked Albert, who had walked up next to Jack.

"Damned if I know," Jack replied.

That night Jack googled, "Ruth and Naomi" on the laptop. He could no longer do searches on his phone. It was dead. Obviously, Meghan had it cut off. The first few sites that came up were Biblical in nature. There were also websites that suggested Ruth and Naomi were gay, and thus proving God sanctioned same-sex relationships.

Jack rolled his eyes. *Whatever floats your boat,* he thought. Jack didn't believe Meghan was a part of some gay women's organization. There were several outreach programs. Jack could picture Meghan being involved in those, giving free legal advice. Jack wanted to know the dark haired woman's name. When he called Meghan he wanted to say, don't send your friend "Jane," or whatever her name was, into the store again. Jack wanted to make Meghan's jaw drop. *Let her know that for all her fancy education, she isn't as smart as me.*

There were lots of websites to go through. He found one about a shop that was not far from Albany. *Didn't Meghan go to Albany sometimes for work?* He tried to remember as he scanned the site. The shop sold crafts made by women in need. *Well, that sounded just like Meghan's bailiwick,* Jack thought. He read the owners' names were Penny and Michael Morgan. That didn't mean anything to him. He googled Penny Morgan and saw several references where she received community service awards, but no photos. He googled Michael Morgan and received dozens of hits. The man was some big deal in the photography world. *The shop was probably a tax write-off,* Jack decided. He saw a photograph of Michael Morgan receiving an award and thought, *handsome, rich bastard.* Jack scrolled down and came upon a second photograph; this one had his wife standing next to him. Jack stared at the photograph. She looked like … Sure, the picture was out of focus and it had been a long time since he had seen her, but could it be? Jack read the caption. "Michael and Penny Morgan accepting the award." Jack's eyes blurred as he re-read the name: Penny. He remembered once he had heard Katie's aunt call her Penelope. "Why can't it wait, Penelope? Give it a year!" Penny from Penelope, it fit. Jack stared again at the picture. Without a doubt, it was her! Jack's eyes shifted over to Michael and said, "That rich bastard is fucking my wife."

Chapter Fifty-Five

The Lace

"Hello, Penny?"

"Hey, Liv. How are you?"

"I'm goo-o-o-d," Liv replied with a singing voice. "And you?"

"I'm okay. So, what have you been –"

Liv gave a giggle.

"Liv, I hope you'll forgive me for saying this, but you sound like you're stoned."

Liv giggled again.

"You aren't helping your case," Penny said.

"Oh Penny, the most wonderful thing has happened. At least I think it has. I tried to call Damon, but he's in Brooklyn and his phone is switched off. I'm just bursting at the seams."

"Liv, what's going on?"

"I just got a phone call. I have imagined this day for most of my life! The woman said her name is Eliza Johnson, and she thinks she could be my daughter."

"Did she say why she thinks this?" Penny asked with restraint in her voice.

"Eliza said she had been raised by a single parent. The mother recently died and last week when Eliza was cleaning out her mother's house, she found baby clothes including one pink sock and newspaper clippings inside an old chest. The articles were about a missing baby – *my* missing baby!" Liv exclaimed. "Eliza asked her aunt over for tea. Eliza put the teacup and the articles on the table and asked bluntly, "This is about me, isn't it?" Her aunt cried and said, 'I was never sure what the right thing was for me to do. In the end, I did nothing because my sister loved you and took good care of you. I couldn't face sending her to jail.'"

"Oh Liv! It sounds very encouraging –"

"I know," Liv interrupted. "I'm trying to keep my nerves steady. I don't want to be devastated if it isn't her. When I think of all the investigations that turned up nothing!"

"Are you going to meet her?"

"Yes, today at two."

"Today!"

"Yes, and I was wondering if you could come over. I need someone with me in case it's her. Or in case it isn't her. Can you come?"

Penny pulled the ice pack off her forehead. She eased aside her cat that had been sleeping on her lap, sat up, and said, "Of course, I'll be there. I'll come over now if you'd like, so you don't have to wait for her alone."

"I must confess that's exactly what I hoped you would say."

"How do I look?" asked Liv when Penny arrived.

"You look lovely."

"I look like I'm on my way to church, don't I? How is it that what I have in the line of clothing is stuff I go to work in, worship in, or clean and run my errands in. I should have a pair of dressy slacks and a nice sweater set on hand. How can I not have something like that in my wardrobe? Do you think the pearls are too much? You're frowning at them."

"They look nice. By dressing up, you're showing her this is an important meeting for you."

"I wonder what she'll wear," Liv said. "What do you think she'll wear?"

"I have no idea. It doesn't matter what she wears."

"I know, but if I'm too dressed up I don't want her to feel uncomfortable."

"I imagine it's going to feel a little uncomfortable no matter what."

"I baked cookies … chocolate chips with walnuts. But what do I know? Maybe she has a nut allergy. A lot of folks do these days. Did you hear a car?"

Penny and Liv went to the window and saw a late model car pull into the driveway.

"She's early," Liv said. "That's one of my traits. She has a nice vehicle. That could mean she's not destitute and doing a scam or it could mean she's very successful at scamming."

Penny gave a surprised look.

"I got thinking about it. The video Michael made went viral and on it I talked about my one pink baby sock. Now thousands of people know about it. Michael asked to take a picture of it, but I said no. It's too … personal, you know? You have to remember, Penny, nurses can get rather hardened. We see so much of the seedy side. I'm going about this wrong. I see that now. I should have waited until I got the results of the background check."

"You mean one of those internet reports?"

"No, a police background check."

"How could you possibly get that run? You haven't even been able to get through to Damon," Penny asked.

Liv bit her lip and said, "That's a story for another time."

"But you actually had a police background check ordered on her? That doesn't feel right, on so many levels."

"I know, I know," Liv muttered. "But what are the chances that it's really her? It sounds like one of those 'true life' stories that can't possibly be true. You know, those 'we were separated as twins but had coffee in the same café and found each other' stories."

"But sometimes those things do happen. I'm not saying it's her, but life is different now with the Internet than what it was even five years ago. Remember how folks were able to learn what was going on with their loved ones in Japan during the tsunami through other people's Facebook accounts. It's a different world."

The car engine turned off, but the woman continued to sit in her car. Liv and Penny watched the woman look into a compact, fuss with her hair and put lipstick on. She put a scarf around her neck, took it back off, and then, put it back on.

"I think she's as nervous as you," Penny observed.

The car door opened and the woman stepped out. "Let's stand back or she'll see us watching her!" Liv said as nervous as a cat in front of strangers.

"Looks like she dressed up," Penny said, "if that beautiful trench coat and high heels are any indicator of what she's wearing underneath."

"She has slim legs like the Wright side of the family," Liv said.

"She looks like a librarian. The type that takes off her glasses, unpins her hair, and turns into a goddess."

"She's a professor," Liv said with pride. Then with a mumble said, "at least that's what she *says* she is."

311

"Do you realize your emotions are all over the place? In one breath, she's your daughter and the next, she's a conniver. You're simultaneously euphoric and suspicious."

Liv nodded, "I'm a mess. That is true."

The doorbell rang, Liv took a deep breath, and hurried to answer it. "Hello. You must be Eliza. Please come in. This is my friend, Penny."

"Hello, Mrs. Wright. Penny. It's nice to meet you," Eliza said. She had a smoky voice, the kind that turns men's heads. She didn't look like a conniver, more like someone who could confidently chair a committee.

"You have a nice home," Eliza said as she glanced around, and then frowned when she saw the large tattered chair.

"That's my husband, Damon's chair," Liv said.

"Ah yes, our men and their chairs.

"May I take your coat?" Liv asked.

Liv and Penny exchanged a look when they saw Eliza wore a beautiful plum-colored silk dress with a tied fabric belt that accentuated her slim waist. Around her neck, she wore a string of pearls, a church going outfit.

Everyone sat down and Eliza said, "Funny, my husband has a chair similar to that. We got new furniture last year, but Dillon said his chair had to stay."

"You're married," Liv said.

"Yes, and I have two daughters: twelve and ten. I have photos." Eliza reached into her purse, pulled out her wallet, and brought it over to show Liv, and then Penny.

"They are beautiful little girls," Liv said. "Daughters. If you turn out to be … that would mean I'm a grandmother. I had always hoped …"

Eliza looked at the framed photo on the mantle. "Are those –"

"Yes, my boys," Liv said as she took the photo down. Eliza stood up to take it. "This is Martin, Mathew, and Merrill," Liv said, pointing to each in turn as she named them.

"They're handsome men," Eliza said, her voice quavering slightly. "I'm sorry. I promised myself I wouldn't get emotional. I never had siblings." She handed the photo back to Liv who carefully placed it back on the mantle. Eliza looked at Liv with sympathy. "If it turns out you're my mother, I don't mean to make it sound as if I didn't miss you, but I didn't know to miss you. I thought I knew who my mother was, but I have always longed for an older brother … and a father."

"Your father …" Liv started to say and then needed to clear her throat from emotion. "He didn't know about the pregnancy. He was married. I knew he would never leave his family. He was a medical doctor; I was an R.N. I was twenty-one years old, not a kid. I knew better than to get mixed up with a married man. When I told my parents the difficult spot I was in, they took charge. They sent me from Georgia to New York State to be near an aunt. They expected me to give my baby up for adoption, and no one would be the wiser, except hopefully me. But, I couldn't let my baby go. She was mine. I loved her so much."

Liv saw Eliza scrutinizing her.

"You have earlobes like mine," Eliza said. "One is a little bigger than the other."

Liv nodded. "Do you," she started to ask, but found her voice was again thin with emotion. She tried again, "Do you have a little mole on your left palm?"

Eliza held out her hand to Liv. "She does!" Liv said to Penny. "Just like when she was a baby." Turning back to Eliza, Liv asked in a trembling voice, "Did you bring the sock?"

Eliza reached into her purse and held out a pink baby sock with variegated green and yellow crocheted lace around the edge. It was a beginner's effort. Several stitches had been dropped, and the ones that remained varied in gauge.

Liv took the sock, held it in her hand, and then rubbed it on her cheek as tears dropped. Liv reached into her skirt pocket and brought out its mate. "I crocheted the lace the week I decided I couldn't bear to give you up. The next week you were gone. I never gave up looking for you. I always missed you. And I always loved you."

Eliza took her mother into her arms. "I can't wait for you to meet your granddaughters," she whispered.

Chapter Fifty-Six

The Celebration

"Remember," Mayra-Liz said to Eva, "we need to be calm when we tell Penny."

"The guy chased after us!" Eva exclaimed.

"I know," Mayra-Liz replied. "We'll tell her in such a way that it doesn't sound alarming. Don't forget her psychiatrist is in England someplace. Geez, it must be nice. I could certainly use a get-away."

The girls found Penny and Michael sitting on the front porch drinking wine as if it was a summer day, only they were bundled up in winter coats, white and red scarves wrapped around their necks. They were both smiling broadly as the girls came onto the porch. "Here," Penny said as she stood up. "I brought sparkling cider and glasses out for you." Penny poured the non-alcoholic drink and handed the glasses to the girls. "We have exciting news!"

Penny started to raise her glass when she took in the look on the girls' faces. "What is it?" Penny asked as she set the glass down. "What happened?"

Mayra-Liz went first. "We went to a furniture store in Braintree, Massachusetts because we saw a commercial and one of the workers looked like …."

The girls looked at each other. How to say this gently?

"Your first husband," Eva said.

Mayra-Liz gave Eva a nudge. "Well, how else are we going to say it?" Eva asked defensively.

"I took a few pictures of him. We weren't very close, there wasn't good light, and the images are blurry," Eva said as she dug her phone out of her bag. "What do you think?" Eva asked as she held the phone out to Penny.

Penny sat down hard into the chair as if unplugged. "I can't believe you did that. I asked you to not go anyplace other than to pick up the scarves and come back. That wasn't exactly the best section of Boston you were in."

"But Braintree was nice," Eva said.

"Look, I don't mean to treat you like children. Obviously you aren't. But you promised me you'd go there and back, and no place else. You broke your promise. You trailed someone who looked like my ex-husband and took pictures! I have no words ...." Penny said as she stared out into the yard, shaking her head, ignoring the offered cell phone. Michael took it. He deleted the images of the furniture worker, and handed the phone back to Eva.

"I'm sorry, girls," he said. "I never should have told you to keep an eye out for him. I should have known your caring nature would cause you to be overly protective. But the thing is, we don't need to worry about Jack Fox anymore."

"Is he dead?" whispered Eva.

"No, and I'm sure the man you saw was indeed Jack Fox."

Penny gasped. "How do you know that?"

"I hired a private investigator." When Michael saw Penny's eyes widened, he quickly replied, "Don't worry, he's the best P.I. on the East Coast, if not the country. I'm certain Jack Fox had no idea. The report detailed that Jack Fox has a job working for the furniture store. He also works under the table for his rent."

"How could he know that?" Mayra-Liz asked.

Michael shrugged. "The report also stated Jack hasn't had a run in with the law since he was released. He's engaged to a woman who is an attorney. The investigator said Jack seemed content, happy even. Obviously, he has moved on."

"When did you find all this out?" Penny asked.

"I hired him over a month ago. He had finished the investigation a couple of weeks ago but was called out of the country. He just got in touch yesterday."

"You didn't tell me," Penny said.

"You had a searing headache last night so I was going to tell you today, but I wanted us to just enjoy Liv's news first. Penny, you said you trusted me to handle this. Hiring the detective was the best way. Now that you know that your ex has moved on, living a calm and decent life, I think you're going to be much more relaxed, and the headaches will stop."

The girls scrutinized Penny for a reaction. Seeing it, Penny said, "Of course, I'm pleased. It's the best news possible!"

"There's something else we should tell you," Eva began. Mayra-Liz gave her a warning look to leave it alone. "I don't *want* to tell them, but Penny and Michael should know. He made eye contact with Mayra-Liz making us nervous, so we hurried out and got into the van. He followed us to the parking lot. He stood in the doorway. His eyes looked cold and angry. I know the investigator said Jack is happy and content, but we thought he looked *scary*."

"So he knows the name of our shop," Penny said gesturing at the van.

"I forgot about that!" Eva gasped.

Penny got up and started walking to the front door.

"*Scary* is probably too strong of a word. I think he was just annoyed, is all. Maybe he had hoped that we would buy something and was disappointed by the lack of a sale. What's the celebration about?" Mayra-Liz asked trying to change the subject.

"Liv found her daughter," Penny said flatly as the screen door closed behind her.

"Penny," Michael called as he jumped up and followed her into the house. "Penny," he repeated, "Don't let this upset you. It's nothing. You were right. He's not going to come looking for you. He's moved on."

"I hope you're right."

"*You're* the one who told me that we had nothing to worry about."

"But I never really *believed* that!" Penny exclaimed. "It's what I tell myself to get through the day. In my heart, I know he'll never stop blaming me. That's just who he is."

"Penny –" Michael started to say.

"I need to lie down. I have a splitting headache."

With shaking legs, Penny went up the stairs to her bedroom and shut the door. Leaning on it, she silently wept. With dogged steps she went to her desk drawer, got out her gun and bullets, and put them in her purse.

I didn't want it to come to this, Penny thought.

Come to what? She asked herself. *You make it sound like a showdown.*

The thought stopped Penny dead in her tracks. She got out the ammunition and breaking Margaret's rule, loaded the gun.

Chapter Fifty-Seven

What Ya Gonna Do?

"Quit it," Jack murmured to Muhammad Ali as the cat put his wet nose in Jack's ear. Sugar Ray was walking across Jack's chest. Only Mike Tyson slept quietly at his feet. "Come on, boys. Knock it off." Somewhere just outside of Jack's foggy state he heard a car horn. Jack rolled over and put the pillow on his head when the doorbell rang. Jack threw the pillow down and looked at the alarm clock: 8:35! "Shit," Jack exclaimed.

Jack stepped into his jeans as he walked to the door. Bare-foot and bare-chested, Jack opened it. "Sorry, Albert, just give me a minute and I'll be right out," Jack said with a thick voice, his hair hanging in his face.

"Jack," Albert said.

"Yeah," Jack replied.

"Look at me, son."

Jack looked up.

"You are in no shape to come to work today," Albert said evenly.

"No, no," Jack started to say. "I'll be fine –"

"As I told you before, I've been there. You can't fool me. It smells like a brewery in here. You're hungover. You and I had a deal. I'll stop by tonight, and we'll talk."

The cats were rubbing against Albert's legs and meowing. "I think your cats are hungry," Albert told Jack. "That's what happens when you drink. You aren't responsible to anyone, including yourself." Albert walked out the door and closed it quietly behind him.

"Shit!" Jack whispered. He went into the kitchen and got a can of cat food, the cats trailing his every move, meowing the Hallelujah chorus. As Jack walked over for the plates, Sugar Ray wound his way between Jack's feet causing him to trip and bang his head onto the refrigerator.

319

Jack drew his foot back to kick the cat across the room and stopped himself just in time. "Ah Jesus!" Jack said as he sat down onto the floor. "Everything has turned to shit." He put his head to his knees and cried. The cats came to him, climbing over and around him. "It's okay, boys. It'll be okay," Jack sobbed. Finally, Jack pulled himself together and fed the cats. He walked over to his Hemingway desk to get his cigarettes. As he lit one up, he noticed his notebook. Sometime in the night Jack had written, "Katherine Louise, Katie, Penelope, Penny" over and over until her names filled the page with blue ink. Jack threw the paper into the waste paper basket. A blue ink smear stained the desk. *She's to blame for all of this,* Jack thought. *If she hadn't abandoned me like my mother, I wouldn't have gone to prison. After you serve time, it's never over. It's never done. It's never all right.*

"Well, what are you going to do about it Jackie Boy? You know where she lives." He pulled opened the drawer and got out the revolver, spun the cylinder while repeatedly saying, "What ya gonna do? What ya gonna do?"

Chapter Fifty-Eight

Crazy or Desperate

"Penny," Mayra-Liz whispered. "This is probably nothing, and I don't want to upset you, but I'm down the street in the van. There's a guy on a motorcycle who slowed down in front of our shop, went down the street, only to turn around and go past our shop again. He could be the guy from the furniture store. Should I call the police?"

"Is he wearing a helmet?"

"Yes, with a face shield."

"Then, how could you possibly know it's him?"

"I said it *could* be."

"My head is pounding," Penny said wearily. "I don't know what to say except it sounds a little crazy to call the police because someone slowed down in front of our shop. Mayra-Liz? Mayra-Liz? Can you hear me?" *We need to get that girl a better phone,* Penny thought.

"I'm sorry. Just coffee for you?" Penny forced a smile for the customer in front of her, a nurse who daily braved the winter weather, and walked from the hospital to the shop for a cup of java and some solitude. "You know, you're getting to be my best customer."

"I just can't seem to get through my shift anymore without some fresh air and this excellent coffee," she said as she raised the cup in a salute. "It was a great idea to sell these mugs with discounted refills. I love the design of the two women picking up firewood."

"They're gathering wheat," Penny couldn't help explaining.

"Gathering wheat? You mean like gathering wool?"

"No. It's not a *saying*." Penny tried to steady her voice to keep out any tones of amazement. But what Penny thought was how could any educated, professional woman not know of this story? No matter one's religious beliefs, it seemed a shame that in some circles, Biblical stories

321

were becoming obsolete. If only from a literary perspective, it seemed like an incredible loss. "The women, Ruth and Naomi actually gathered wheat from fields because they were poor. They took care of each other. That's why we gave the shop its name, because we help women in need."

"*O-kay*," the nurse said looking annoyed. "I just come in here because the coffee's good." *Not to be given a sermon* was not said, but was clearly written on the nurse's face.

With a sigh, Penny handed the nurse her change. "We appreciate you coming in." The nurse pocketed the change, pulled her knitted cap over her head, and picked up her umbrella. "It looks miserable out there today," Penny said brightly. It was silly to lose a good customer.

"Yes, it's been a steady mix of rain and sleet. I almost didn't venture out," the nurse reported.

"It'd be an awful day to ride a motorcycle," Penny said absently.

"A motorcycle?" the nurse said. "You'd have to be either crazy or desperate!"

Penny's mind froze and her body took over. She was like a dog that had been kicked and sensed it was about to happen again. *He's here.* Suddenly, Penny knew it. She had no doubt.

"We're closing," Penny announced to the room. "You all have to leave."

"What's wrong?" asked the nurse. But Penny didn't reply. She went to the back door and locked it. When Penny came to the front she was amazed to find that no one had moved. "You'll all have to go *now*." She held the front door open and the customers begrudgingly complied. Penny needed to lock down the shop, and she couldn't very well lock her customers in with her. As the last customer filed out, Penny locked the door. She got her grandfather's pistol out of her handbag and put it in her pocket; her butcher apron covered the bulge.

Penny was shaking all over. Being resolute didn't mean she wasn't afraid. The most dangerous dogs are those shaking with fear. She tried to call Mayra-Liz to warn her to stay away from the shop, but the call went to voicemail. Penny then called 911.

"911. What is your emergency?" Penny was astonished to find herself in the nightmarish situation of fright rendering her mute.

"State your emergency," the operator said more loudly.

Penny tried again to speak, but produced no sound other than a squeak.

"You'll need to speak clearly and directly into the phone," Penny heard the operator say. Penny heard a crash that sounded like it came

322

from outside of her back door. Penny ran to the solid steel door and listened, but heard only her own rapid breathing.

Where was Mayra-Liz? she thought.

"Send police to *Ruth and Naomi* at 95 Jay Street –" Penny heard the lock turn, and then the door flew open. Mayra-Liz called out "Penny!"

Sagging with relief, Penny answered, "Mayra-Liz, you scared me to – "

"Death?" Jack finished for her. He held a gun on Mayra-Liz and then pointed it at Penny. "Put the phone down."

Penny placed it face down on the table. "Stand away from the table." Jack picked up the phone. He gave Penny a snide smile. With a flourish, he pressed the off button. "Getting clever, aren't you? Both of you move to the front." Mayra-Liz looked like a cat that had been pulled out of a shaken sack: her hair disheveled and her eyes wild with rage and fright. Penny and Mayra-Liz grabbed hold of each other, hugging each other close. Penny whispered, "The police are coming."

"I *hate* him," Mayra-Liz whispered back with gritted teeth.

"No talking and pull down the shades," Jack commanded.

As the women worked the cords with stiff and unresponsive fingers, Jack sauntered around the shop. "Nice place you have here. Nice little scam. A good tax write-off for your wealthy husband."

"It's *not* a scam," Mayra-Liz spat out the words.

"Don't," Penny whispered hoarsely.

"Yeah," Jack mocked. "Don't aggravate the crazy. That's what you think I am, don't you, Katie. Someone who could kill his own child."

Penny continued to look away from him as if Jack hadn't spoken.

"Not going to answer? Oh that's right, you aren't Katie anymore. You're *Penny*. Well that fits; it's about what you're worth."

Mayra-Liz turned, her eyes blazing. Penny discreetly put her finger to her lips, giving Mayra-Liz the silent message to stay calm and quiet. Penny then rubbed her forehead. The gesture wasn't lost on Jack. He knew under his ex-wife's calm façade, she was a bundle of frayed nerves. Studying her, Jack realized that there were few changes in Katie's appearance. Her skin was still smooth, eyes bright, that beautiful auburn mane. Jack's eyes softened.

"Katie," Jack said with a break in his voice, "There were times when I got inside your head. I heard your thoughts. Did you know?"

Penny nodded.

"It's because we're *one,* you and me. We're meant to be –"

"No!" Penny choked out the word with a shudder.

"Penny has a good life," Mayra-Liz said. "If you care about her, you'll leave her alone."

Jack swung the gun back at Mayra-Liz. She gasped as she looked at the weapon, but still asked softly, "Haven't you put her through enough?"

"What *I* have put *her* through?" Jack said incredulously. "What a joke! It's because of her that I went to prison! Have you even *seen* the inside of a cell?"

Mayra-Liz looked away. "Look at me when I'm talking to you!" Jack stormed up to her and grabbed a handful of her dark hair, yanking it hard. "You think you're so special with all that hair." Mayra-Liz winched in pain. Jack's glazed eyes almost seemed to glow red like an intoxicated demon.

"You're drunk," Penny blurted out.

"You're drunk. Jack, you're drunk. If I had a nickel for every time I heard that from you," he said in an affected, whiny voice. "It's because of *you* that the drinking began. It's because of *you* that the drinking started up again. You're right. We could never make a go of it. But this one … she wants me. You should have seen the way she looked at me in the store." He gave a much harder yank to Mayra-Liz's hair causing her head to jerk back. Then, Jack clamped his mouth on hers.

Mayra-Liz pulled her face away. "Get away from me," she hissed.

Jack released her hair, took a step back, sneering at her with contempt. He turned away as if he had nothing more to do with her. Then, Jack narrowed his eyes as if he had come to a decision, and slapped Mayra-Liz hard across the face.

Penny had planned to bide her time. Hopefully, the police would be here soon and take over. All that changed with the slap, Mayra-Liz's cry of pain, and Jack's smug, satisfied look. The situation had changed from verbal to physical. What would Jack do next? The words, *we're all done with that game* rang through Penny's head as she gripped the gun and charged at Jack with an outstretched arm like a soldier at Gettysburg rushing across the expanse of mortal danger. She didn't hear the pop of the gun shot, only a rustling in her ears like that of dried autumn leaves. With fuzzy, darkened vision Penny saw a look of consternation and surprise on Jack's face as he dropped his gun and clutched his upper arm. Mayra-Liz tore away from him. With the swiftness of a ball-boy at a tennis tournament, Mayra-Liz ducked low, grabbed Jack's gun off the floor, and ran to the other side of the room.

"It's not real! It's not real! It's a toy. Look, it's a toy gun!" That, more than anything, sent Mayra-Liz into a state of hysterics.

"Mayra-Liz, stop!" Penny commanded. "Call 911 again. Tell them the situation and get an ambulance, and make sure the police are coming."

Mayra-Liz ran to the back of the shop. Penny could hear her sobbing as she went. Jack was leaning to his left, his arm hanging down, pulled in tightly against his side. His right hand was clamped tightly over the spot where his leather jacket was torn and blood was oozing out. "Your grandfather's gun. I had forgotten about it."

"Sit down," Penny ordered. "The police will be here soon." As he settled down into a chair, she threw a dish towel at him. "Use that to staunch the bleeding."

"I didn't come here to hurt you, just give you a scare," Jack said. "You deserved a good one after all you've put me through. I did consider killing you, I won't lie. Because you killed all the chance I ever had for a decent life. I even bought a gun, but I knew I could never use it, and left it behind." Jack stood up.

"Sit down." Penny gestured to the chair with the gun that shook in her trembling hand.

Jack looked at her, gauging her response. He made a decision and bolted for the front door. He unlocked the door and yanked it open with his good hand, leaving smeared blood on the latch, and lurched through the opening, banging his injured arm against the frame, leaving another bloody smudge. The door slammed behind him, and he was gone.

Penny stepped to the door and threw the deadbolt. She walked back to a table, set the pistol down, and sat heavily into the chair.

"What? What's happening?" Mayra-Liz called, running into the room, the phone in her hand.

"He left," Penny said.

"You just let him go?"

"The alternative was to shoot him in the back. He knew I couldn't do that."

Mayra-Liz stared at Penny. "But he came to *kill* you. He could have killed both of us. He's a monster …. He –" Mayra-Liz started to sob.

Penny went to her precious darling and wrapped her arms around her, stroking Mayra-Liz's hair while she continued to weep.

"Here, sit down. It's over. It's all over," Penny said when Mayra-Liz remained inconsolable.

"The back door! I didn't lock the back door. He could come back in!" Mayra-Liz screeched as she ran again to the back of the shop.

Even though the police and ambulance sirens were at the moment the most welcomed sound in the world, it still caused Penny's nerves to jump. On shaky limbs, she walked to a front window and raised the shade to see an approaching motorcycle. Jack's hair was flattened back by the wind stream, his mouth set like a grinning jack-o-lantern. He had twisted the bike's throttle to full-stop with his right hand, making the engine scream, but his left arm was tucked in tight against his body. He'd obviously somehow managed to work the clutch with his left hand at least once, but he'd need both arms and hands to wrestle the bike around. The bike flashed past.

"He'll break his neck," Penny whispered.

Chapter Fifty-Nine

Things to Know

In a church courtyard where Jack had attended A.A. meetings, Albert Stein gave a eulogy. A half a dozen people stood outside around a table gazing at a handmade, wooden box that held Jack Fox's ashes. Penny felt her throat tighten, but she remained dry-eyed. Most of the snow had melted. It was the last day of March, with a lamb's exit, the first day of the year to reach fifty degrees.

Albert compared drinking to the darkness of winter nights and a sober life to that of a sunny, spring day. After a few more such metaphors, the eulogy took a turn and Albert started talking about three cats that now made their home in the furniture store. They had been strays rescued by the departed, only to find themselves again in need of a home. "It is like that for us, too," Albert preached. "We never know what the next day will bring, and we need to trust in the Lord to provide." Albert didn't mention the deceased's name until the very end.

"Rest in peace, Jack Fox," Albert said reverently, his Bible clutched in his hands. "Rest in peace."

All eyes remained on the wooden box until one by one the attendees silently turned and walked away. Penny was almost to her car when a young woman stopped her. "Excuse me, but we've met before. I'm Meghan Ashley."

"Oh yes," Penny said. "I remember, from the conference on missing children."

They politely shook hands, and then Penny turned wordlessly to continue the walk to her car. Meghan fell in step. "How did you know him?" Meghan asked, nodding her head towards the church.

"Oh, hmm."

"I'm sorry; perhaps it was impolite to ask."

"No, it's fine. We were married, a long time ago."

"I wondered, but I thought his wife's name was Katie."

"It was. I am. I mean, I was Katie. I changed my name to Penny later on."

"Because of him?" Meghan asked bluntly.

"Yes," Penny said simply.

"Look, there are some things you should know. Do you have time for some coffee?"

"Some other time, okay? I think attending the funeral was enough for one day. I don't think I can handle hearing anything more right now."

"When Jack was drunk, he did run into that boy who was on his bicycle," Meghan blurted out.

Penny stopped, closed her eyes, and nodded. She had often wondered, and now she knew. Penny started walking, picking up the pace as she hurried to her car as if she wanted as much distance as possible between Jack and the memories around him. She unlocked the door and gave Meghan a polite nod goodbye.

"Look, I'm not some kind of crazy," Meghan said. "There really are some things you should hear. I think it could make a difference to you."

Penny sighed. "I'm sure you're a very nice person, Meghan. I don't want to appear rude, but I never should have come here today. It was a mistake. And there is *nothing* you can tell me about Jack Fox that I'd want to hear."

"I know what happened to your baby," Meghan said softly.

Penny swayed on her feet, reached her hand out to hold the door handle to steady herself. "Are you all right?" Meghan asked as she grabbed Penny's arm to support her. "Come on. Forget the coffee; I'm buying you a drink."

The tavern owner, Logan, knew Meghan, and gave her a friendly wave when they walked in. The women sat at a booth in the front window that looked onto the town's main street. Meghan ordered two Bloody Marys and launched into the tale of Jack's unwitting disclosure of his past when he thought their relationship was over. With a blank face, Penny listened to the story.

Logan set two tall glasses of tomato juice with vodka on the table. "Sorry," he said, "I don't have any celery stalks. Not many people request Bloody Marys anymore."

"It's fine," Meghan replied, not taking her eyes off Penny.

Once Logan left them, Penny said, "How can you possibly believe anything that Jack Fox said?"

"He had no reason to lie and he certainly didn't put himself in a good light. Jack told me he was involved in the hit and run; he hit you and left

328

you where you laid; but Jack was also adamant that he had nothing to do with the death of your child. Also, Albert asked me to help him clean out Jack's apartment and retrieve the cats. I was listed as Jack's emergency contact at the furniture store where he worked, so Albert told me to take whatever I wanted. We didn't know of any family or friends to contact. I only took two things, one was Jack's manuscript. I intend to periodically read it over and remind myself of the bad judgment I had. I really thought I was good at reading people."

"His manuscript?" Penny asked, furrowing her brow.

"Yes, Jack was very fond of Ernest Hemingway and wanted to write like him. Jack had at least a half a dozen notebooks that were mostly about his own life. He wrote a great deal about his innocence regarding the death of his child. I hope that gives you some comfort."

Penny's gaze was far away, staring into the past when she replied, "I guess it's true; Jack didn't have anything to do with Nicola's death. It does help to know my daughter died in peace. Of course, that means Jack went to prison for a crime he didn't commit." Penny's eyes returned to her tomato juice and vodka sitting on the Formica table top. She picked it up and took a chug as if it would fortify her. "What was the other thing?"

"What other thing?" Meghan asked.

"The other thing you took from Jack's apartment? Don't answer if it's too personal."

Meghan reached into her large bag and pulled out the silver music box. The last time Penny had seen it, she had thrown it into the walled room in their first apartment's basement.

Penny caught her breath; but Meghan didn't notice. "It's really quite valuable. I had it appraised and the jeweler said it's a real ruby. And see how it has that hint of blue, that's what makes it more desirable. It's a shame that it's so damaged. Look at these entwined hearts; one of them was scratched out," Meghan said as she held it out for Penny to inspect.

"Put it away!" Penny nearly screeched.

Meghan quickly put the music box out of sight. "I'm sorry. I didn't think. Had that been a gift to you? Do you want it?"

"No," Penny whispered, as perspiration dotted her forehead. "And if anything bad starts happening to you, get rid of that box right away."

"You mean something worse than Jack Fox? He probably bought it for me, and then scratched out a heart when I left him. I believe he was capable of destroying something valuable while in a temper. Jack wrote about terrible things he had done with seemingly felt no remorse. It was always someone else's fault. It scares the life out of me to know I let a person like him into my life. I even asked him to marry me!" Meghan shook her head and took a swig of her own drink. "He did have a horrible childhood, brutal really, and part of me … Well, it's impossible not to feel pity for some of the stuff he went through."

Penny wiped a tear, the first she had shed all day. "He wasn't born under the heavenly moon,"

"What?" asked Meghan.

"It was something my aunt used to say. The gist is people who were not loved and nurtured as children miss out on something vital in life. Those who were loved are so fortunate, it's as if they were born under the heavenly moon; they never feel alone for very long. I always felt that Jack was very much alone. When I was young, all I wanted was to heal him. As it turns out, it would have been better for him if he had never met me."

"Please don't tell me that you feel any kind of responsibility for what happened to Jack," Meghan said.

"I should probably get going," Penny said, but she made no effort to leave. She stared out the window while Meghan looked at Penny. It was obvious the lawyer had something more to say but was debating about how to say it. Finally Meghan asked, "Have you seen the video of the man holding up a pawn shop and getting beat up by the grandmotherly attendant a couple of weeks ago? They showed it on the Today Show."

"I heard about it. Eva mentioned it to me, said it was funny."

Meghan pulled out her phone and found the YouTube video. She started it, turned up the volume and handed the phone to Penny. A surveillance camera showed a would-be robber wearing a cowboy hat low on his head and a bandana over his nose and mouth like a Western outlaw. He brandished a gun, demanding money and his grandfather's railroad watch. The clerk didn't hesitate; she grabbed a baseball bat from under the counter and knocked the gun out of the man's hand with one swift downward blow. With her mouth set in an angry, determined line, the grandmother kept on swinging, turning the tables on the would-be thief, cowing him backwards, his arms flailing in an attempt to fend off the blows. In the last moments of the encounter, the robber's bandana fell from his face, as he turned to run out the door, his face was revealed to the camera.

"Oh, dear God," Penny said.

"It's Jack, isn't it?" Meghan asked.

"Yes. When was it filmed?"

"The day he died."

"So he didn't leave his gun at home. He lost it," Penny mused as she handed the phone back.

"I think it was a fortunate thing for you that the store clerk was so feisty," Meghan said. "I have something you should read." She pulled a notebook out of her large purse. Penny felt her heart flutter with anxiety when he recognized Jack's handwriting.

"Are you all right? You've gone even paler." But she didn't wait for Penny to answer as she flipped through the pages. "Here it is," Meghan said as she started to read out loud, "She ruined my life that ex, ex, triple ex, wife. Katie gets a nice life and I get shit. Am I going to just let her get away with it? No! Jackie Boy says no! Let's see how smug Katie feels when she's wearing my grandmother's pearls around her broken neck."

Penny held her hands to her mouth, her eyes closed while her whole body started trembling.

"He was coming to kill you! You should know that, I mean really *know* that. Yes, he had a miserable childhood. That is true. But the very thing he would have wanted was for you to feel guilty and responsible for his unhappy, shitty life. But let me tell you, sister, once we become grownups, we have choices. True, some have more opportunities than others, but that doesn't take away the fact that we are all responsible for our own actions."

At the end of her rant, Meghan looked closely at Penny, "You *really* don't look well. I'm sorry; maybe it was the attorney in me, trying to make my case. After all you've been through; I thought you had a right to know the whole picture of Jack Fox, so you can put it behind you."

"I'm not feeling well," Penny said. "It's my heart .... It's going to burst."

Chapter Sixty

Theme Wedding

"Ohhhh!" Eliza said as she and Liv stood at the edge of Penny and Michael's back lawn. It was a beautiful October evening. The setting sun made the changing autumn leaves glow.

"It's always looked beautiful back here, but now it looks like one of those elegant, old-world wedding venues," Liv said. "Look, there's Penny. Doesn't she look lovely?" Mom and daughter watched Penny interact with the caterers while a light breeze caused Penny's delicate dress to flutter about her ankles showing her dyed-to-match-the-dress, strappy shoes.

"That moss green color suits her perfectly," Eliza said, "Wherever did she find that dress? It's so elegant!"

"It was her Aunt Margaret's gown. I told her she was going to be chilly wearing it, even with the wrap, but I was wrong. What a beautiful evening! I've known times when it's snowed in October. I love how Marya-Liz pinned up Penny's hair with just those few wisps of escaped curls. She looks just like a movie star."

"Is she doing okay, now?" Eliza asked. "What a trauma she had, shooting that insane man who came into her shop when he threatened Mayra-Liz. Did they ever find out anything more about him? The news reports made it sound so random. First, the guy tried to hold up a pawn shop, then he drives his motorcycle in sleet and freezing rain, and ends up at Penny's shop. How crazy is that?"

"Pretty crazy," Liv agreed, not letting on that she knew the back story.

"Then, Penny had that heart episode," Eliza said.

"Panic attack. It doesn't really involve the heart; it just makes the patient feel like it does. But yes, it was awful, no getting around it. The only good thing to come from it was Penny stopped having migraine headaches."

"Really! Why do the doctors think that happened?"

"No idea," Liv replied with a shrug.

"I heard Dr. Allen moved to Scotland."

"Yes, Edinburgh. His wife is from there. I think it'll be nice for them. A whole new start."

"Did they need a new start?"

"Oh, it's just nice to have new beginnings, don't you think? Just look at that white birch arbor covered with teacup roses," Liv said changing the subject, "Looks like it's been there for generations. Jen built it last week. The girls installed all the fairy lights that are along the path, in the arbor, and around the gazebo."

"Shall we take a seat? We have our choice since we're early. By the look of the number of chairs, they're planning on what, a hundred guests?" Eliza said.

"Eighty-five. Let's walk over to the tent first; I want to see how the caterers are doing. In honor of the girls' first date, the cake is supposed to have some kind of moon and Adirondack Mountains theme. I wonder how they're pulling that off."

The two women walked with the same purposeful stride to where a crew of workers was draping tables with silver, organza tablecloths. Florists were arranging the centerpieces of fall colored roses, while others set the tables with china and silver.

"It looks like a bunch of bees buzzing at a single branch," Liv observed.

"It smells divine! I'm having chicken Marsala. You?"

"The beef tenderloin. I went to a sampling with Penny and the girls. These caterers are out of this world, such great cooks and the meal presentations are nothing short of artistic."

"The cake's over here," Eliza said. The women walked to the front of the tent where the cake table was set up with twinkling lights. A five layered cake with swirling white frosting held a cake-topper with a shimmery, crescent moon on which two miniature brides sat: one dark and one blond, holding hands.

"It's so beautiful!" Eliza said. As the tears spilled over, she reached into her purse for a tissue. "I tell you the last couple of months, I seem to get teary at the drop of a hat."

"You've been through a lot; losing a parent is always difficult, and your situation is so … complicated."

Around them, guests had begun to fill up the rows of chairs. "I meant to tell you how much I like your dress. The gloves match it perfectly," Eliza said trying to lighten her own mood as they found their seats and

334

sat down. "What a brilliant full moon. You know, I've never been to an outdoor, evening wedding before."

"Won't be much longer now," Liv said when the musicians started to play. "I think the string quartet was a good compromise. Jen wanted a jazz band and Annalise wanted a harpist. I haven't seen the girls arrive yet. Only fifteen minutes to go. I know both really wanted to be on time."

There's the van," Eliza announced. The van's doors opened, they stepped out, and there stood the girls in their gorgeous gowns.

"Oh, don't they look beautiful!" Liv gushed.

"Mayra-Liz cut her hair!" Eliza gasped.

"Just to her shoulders so she could more easily pin it up when she's in uniform. Didn't I tell you she joined the Navy? She's going to a Mass Communications Specialist. She's going to be stationed in Japan. We're all so proud of her."

"You didn't tell me. Well, that's a big change. Is Eva still enjoying Siena? She looks really happy."

"Eva's doing well. She decided on a Sociology major with a Criminal Justice minor. That's her date over there – Edward."

"Do you like him?" Eliza asked.

"He's a dear boy," Liv said.

As they watched, the wedding party organized at the edge of the lawn. The musicians started playing Pachelbel's "Canon in D." Another compromise, Jen had wanted to start with a country and western song, "God Gave Me You." Liv saw Penny look up at Michael, smile, and take his arm. Michael cut a handsome figure in his evening jacket. He returned Penny's smile. Michael looked up and across the expanse of the yard. The smile vanished from his face, and clouded with dark concern.

"Something's wrong," Liv whispered. She followed Michael's gaze and saw a guest walking purposefully towards the house, his eyes locked on Michael. The man suddenly increased his speed, almost running up the path.

"What is he doing?" Eliza asked.

Liv ignored Eliza's question as she studied the hurrying man for a moment longer. "He has a gun!" Liv shouted. "Get down! Get down!" As Liv pushed her firstborn to the ground, Michael shoved Penny backwards and they both fell to the ground as a shot rang out. At the sound of gunfire, several guests screamed. The woman seated in front of Liv shrieked and crouched down.

"What are you doing?" her husband asked. "It's just one of those theme weddings."

When the man charged at Michael, Liv quickly opened her purse, reached in with her gloved right hand and produced a black pistol as deftly as a magician might pull a white rabbit out of his hat. "FBI. Drop your weapon," Liv shouted. But the shooter was already running past the bridal party toward the driveway.

"Call 911," Liv ordered as she stepped over Eliza, who was staring, wide-eyed at her mother. "Get an ambulance, call the police, tell them '11-99'," Liv continued as she started to sprint after the gunman.

"What does that mean?" Eliza called.

"Officer needs assistance," Liv shouted over her shoulder.

"Liv, what are you doing?" Eliza yelled at her mother's quickly departing back. "Leave it for the police!"

But Liv didn't look back.

Chapter Sixty-One

The Pearl

"Emergency waiting rooms are *the* most depressing places," Penny said.

"Nurses have a theory about that," Liv said. "Many of us feel that all the stagnation, sickness, and sorrow that occurs in here just never leaves. Some nurses claim that they have seen auras, sort of a haze of emotions."

They drank the bitter coffee from the machine, grimacing with each sip. Penny looked at her watch again. "It feels as if time has stopped, doesn't it?"

Liv looked at her own watch. "I don't imagine that it'll be much longer."

Penny heaved a sigh and stared at the floor.

"You might as well talk about it," Liv said. "Get it off your chest. Besides if you're talking about *that*, it'll keep your mind off Michael's surgery."

"I don't know how I feel," Penny said as she distractedly brushed her hair out of her face. What had been a gorgeous hairdo now had the pins freed as Penny had worried her fingers through her locks for hours. Her hair looked as if it had had a fright.

"I'm just trying to wrap my head around it …. Michael was a *diamond smuggler?*" Penny shook her head. "I can't seem to absorb it."

"Well, as I said earlier, he thought he was doing right. Every criminal I ever met has told me they were innocent. Michael was different. He acknowledged what he did wasn't legal, but he did what he believed was moral. Michael thought the profits would go to the actual miners, those poor people, some of them children, who were worked nearly to death. The diamonds were to be sold directly to distributors in Russia, avoiding the Sierra Leone corrupt government, and large profits would go to the people of Sierra Leone, enough money to build a clinic. As it turned out, the miners saw none of the money. Then, they suffered terribly at the hands of the RUF when they found out about the plot. The Russian distributors made huge profits which had been their plan all along.

"As soon as Michael realized it was a high-level scam, he got out. But he paid a lot of money to those monsters for the privilege of letting him go. I can't tell you the link we found connecting Michael to the diamond racket, but it wasn't strong enough to convict him, and he knew it. We had called Michael in for questioning a few days before your overdose, and he sailed right through the interrogation. In fact, when Michael left, most of us wondered if we were wrong about the connection. That goes to show the power of his convictions; he had entered into this thing with the purest of intentions."

"I don't understand it," Penny said. "After he was in the clear and no one was bothering him, not the bad guys, not the good guys, by that I mean *you guys,* he went in and told you everything he knew, and said he would help apprehend the smugglers. Why would he do that? For him it was over."

"Michael never said why. He's a man of few words, as you know. I've thought a lot about it, and I think Michael came to us because of Jack Fox."

"Jack?"

"I think Michael just got tired of people being taken advantage of. Here was his sweet wife who would do anything in the world for anyone, and she had been terrorized by her ex-husband. There wasn't anything Michael could do about Jack, but those diamond thieves, your husband is going to hang them out to dry."

"It'll help then, the evidence he provided?"

"Most definitely," Liv said with a smile.

"Will Michael face any charges?"

"No, that was part of the agreement."

Liv and Penny sat in silence again, staring at the green wall in front of them.

"I appreciate you bringing me clothes," Penny said. "It was a welcomed relief getting out of that dress with Michael's blood all over it. I could lose my mind when I think of it. Michael bleeding and lying unconscious on top of me."

"Your backyard looked beautiful," Liv said, changing the subject. "It's too bad about the wedding. It would have been lovely. You know, I bet there's a guy out there who's still claiming the gun fire was just a part of a themed wedding."

"It's all part of the show," Penny said with an ironic half-smile. "I felt so badly for the girls. It would have been a beautiful wedding."

338

"I'm surprised they aren't here waiting with you."

"Oh, they followed me here in the van. They were a sight in the ER, I can tell you: two beautiful bridesmaids in amber-colored silk and two gorgeous brides in white organza. I begged them to go home. I love my girls, you know I do, but they were killing me with their "what if" talk. 'What if the bullet had been inches to the right? It would have gone right through Michael's heart. What if there had been a second assassin?' The girls didn't mean any harm, but I thought my head was going to explode. I finally convinced them to go home. As it is, they call every fifteen minutes. But, I'm happy you're here," Penny said as she took Liv's hand.

"I'm glad you feel that way. I was afraid that maybe you wouldn't want to see me again once everything came to light."

"I trust you, Liv. I don't believe you'd do anything to hurt me. Besides, if you hadn't been there, that man might have killed –"

Liv squeezed Penny's hand.

"You done with your coffee?" Penny asked. "I'm going to throw mine out. I'm done punishing myself with it."

When Penny walked back from the garbage can, she said, "So explain this to me again. You're an FBI agent. Does that mean you have a law degree?"

"A degree in Criminal Justice and there were exams for getting into the Bureau. I started the program part-time and worked full-time after my baby was stolen; I needed to keep my mind busy. Plus, I wanted to catch some bad guys."

"But you gave me medicine. Don't you have to be a nurse or a doctor to do that?"

"I am a nurse, an RN. It comes in handy. It's really quite amazing what people will tell a woman in a white uniform."

"But what about HIPPA or whatever it is that says you can't talk about patient information?"

"I would never divulge someone's medical information."

"But you use what patients tell you in confidence against them in a court of law?"

"Nothing can be used until after they've been read their Miranda Rights. But information I have gained as a nurse has helped solve cases. Most of the time, I have no moral conflict about what I do."

"So you just happened to be working the night shift when I was brought into the hospital?" Penny probed.

"We had a wire on Michael's cell phone and heard the 911 call."

"But I thought you believed him when he was released from questioning."

"*Most* of us believed him; my supervisor had some concerns. So, we thought we'd listen in for a few days, see if it took us anyplace. After people have been questioned, they'll often make contact with their associates. But all we heard from Michael's conversations were his concern about you, the girls, the shop, the poor, the hungry. He's a good man – your Michael."

"I know," Penny said as she started to cry.

Liv's cell phone rang. "Wright," Liv said as a way of a greeting. She listened for a while and ended the call with, "Good work."

Liv turned to Penny. "Well, they got the guy."

"The guy who shot Michael?"

Liv nodded.

"Who is he?"

Liv frowned, "The news will be all over this, but it's nothing that –"

"You should talk about, I understand." Penny shook her head. "Who would think I'd ever say such a thing, 'the guy who shot Michael.' But it's obvious it happened because Michael will testify against those diamond smugglers. When did Michael get started in this mess?"

"In the spring of 2001. It was a desperate time in Sierra Leone. I'm sure Michael has talked about it; over 50,000 were killed during their civil war. Those that lived survived in a level of poverty that's difficult to imagine."

"Yes, we went to Sierra Leone last year and bought items for the shop. I've been to many underdeveloped countries, but Sierra Leone was by far the most disturbing."

"Mrs. Morgan?" asked a doctor, dressed in scrubs.

"Yes," said Penny as she jumped up and hurried to the physician.

"Your husband's out of surgery. The reconstruction went smoothly, but he's lost a lot of blood. We gave him three pints and will keep him in recovery until he is stable."

"Can I see him?" Penny asked.

"It'd be better if you waited until morning. He's sleeping now. Looks like you need some rest, too. We'll call if there's any change. Michael's not completely out of the woods, but it's very possible he'll make a full recovery."

"Come on, Penny, I'll drive you home. And I'm staying the night with you, what's left of it. No argument."

"Our clock stopped," Penny observed as she stepped into her living room. "Michael said it stopped when I was in the hospital, but it had started again."

Liv walked through the house, room by room with her gun poised, looking into closets while Penny dropped to the couch, fatigue taking over.

"What are you doing?" Penny called.

"Just playing it safe. We made arrangements with the Schenectady Police department for a patrol car to make rounds in the neighborhood. We don't expect any more trouble tonight, but we're going to keep an eye out," Liv said as she climbed the stairs to Penny and Michael's bedroom. "Did you notice the man sitting outside of the waiting room? He's one of ours."

"Good God," Penny mumbled from downstairs.

"Oh, that's too bad," Liv said.

"What is it?" Penny sighed as she heaved herself off the couch and started to climb the stairs.

"Looks like you broke a strand of pearls," Liv said. With her search of the house complete, she placed her gun on the bed. She started to gather up the loose pearls. "Do you know how many there should be?"

Penny ran up the last couple of steps, and swung into the room, her eyes wide with fear as she looked at the pearls scattered across her bed. As if it waited for her to appear, one pearl dropped off the bed and rolled across the room, stopping precisely at Penny's feet.

"Jack?" Penny whispered as she took a step back.

"What's wrong," Liv asked.

"These look like Jack's grandmother's pearls. How did they get in here? Do you think Jack's spirit has somehow –" Penny started to asked, her voice emotionally rising until it became like a taut thread that broke.

"Now, don't go down that road, Miss Penny. You had a house full of people here today. In all likelihood, one of the wedding guests –"

Penny raised her foot and slammed the heel of her shoe down on the pearl, grinding it into powder.

"Are you okay?" Liv asked.

"I think so. It felt good to crush that pearl. Liv, I'm so tired of being scared. I know the police have my home under surveillance, looking out for Russian mafia or some such thing, and my husband is lying in a hospital bed, but still –"

"Little things like that," Liv said with a wry smile.

"Yeah, I know it's been a big deal. It's been a horrific day, that's for sure. But you know, it always seems to be something. I'm just so tired of being afraid."

"As Dr. Allen said, it's a difficult way to live your life," said Liv as she put the pearls down on the bed and picked up her gun.

"It is," Penny agreed. "I'm going to have a glass of Avala. It's a lovely, non-alcoholic drink that Michael is helping the Kenyans to manufacture. You want one?" Penny squared her shoulders and walked towards the stairs. "We can take our drinks out in the gazebo and enjoy the night air."

"You're not afraid something is going to *get you* in the night air like your old Pennsylvanian neighbors thought?" Liv said to lighten the mood as she put her arm around Penny's shoulders.

"I'm tired of being afraid," Penny repeated.

As Penny and Liv left the room another pearl dropped from the bed and rolled across the floor towards the stairs.

Made in the USA
Columbia, SC
06 April 2018